For CAROLINE

V.V. Andrews

I enjoy x

# Rhythm of Echoes

## by

# J J Andrews

 Bloomington, IN  Milton Keynes, UK

authorHOUSE®

AuthorHouse™
1663 Liberty Drive, Suite 200
Bloomington, IN 47403
www.authorhouse.com
Phone: 1-800-839-8640

AuthorHouse™ UK Ltd.
500 Avebury Boulevard
Central Milton Keynes, MK9 2BE
www.authorhouse.co.uk
Phone: 08001974150

First published by AuthorHouse 2/29/2008

ISBN: 978-1-4259-9879-0 (sc)
ISBN: 978-1-4259-9880-6 (hc)

Printed in the United States of America
Bloomington, Indiana

This book is printed on acid-free paper.

*I dedicate this book to my sister Kath.*
*The girl with short blonde hair and cheeky smile.*

# Chapter One

*Flora* Ballardine wished for a rainbow of colours.

Red as rich as a ruby or as vivid as a paper poppy, yellow crisp and bright, green so dazzling it hurt the eyes, a dark velvet indigo, spectacular orange, sparkling violet, midnight blue.

Or virginal white; hands clasped to her breasts with blushing cheeks and innocent eyes cast down to her feet. She knew her cheeks wouldn't be a problem, as for the eyes…

Any other colour than brown!

The dress hung limp and dreary on the wardrobe door, and it looked at least 10 years out of date, the kind of style they wore in the forties.

"Burnt gold." Elizabeth Montgomery stroked the thick material, her hand caressing a precious possession.

It still looked brown to Flora. "You shouldn't have Aunt Elizabeth. You've already paid for my train fare; I thought that was my birthday present."

Elizabeth gave a small shrug and hurried out of the room. "And who said it was your birthday present?"

Flora looked at the dress; apprehension scuttling up her spine and tickling the back of her neck. She sat on the bed and pulled off her heavy boots and thick woollen socks. A late snowfall the night before said the winter hadn't quite left Scotland, feeling the fool as she clumped out of King's Cross to a warm spring day in London.

"I did promise Lady Derman I would wait until she arrived but I must tell you now Flora."

She looked up to see her aunt smiling at her at the doorway, and another shrug. Flora waited.

Elizabeth took a deep breath. "Your actual birthday present is a night out with an escort. And your escort is to be no other than Lady Derman's grandson Freddie."

"Freddie!" shrieked Flora.

"You did not think I would allow you to spend your birthday night sitting around your boring old aunt's flat did you?" scolded Elizabeth. "That is what the dress is for. Mind, you only have it for tonight Flora. It has to be returned after Cinderella has been to the ball."

This did not console Flora, at all.

"And while you are sitting with the tea ladies Flora would you please hold your knees together?" A nod from Elizabeth at the offending items.

Flora looked down. She'd pulled her skirt up to take off her boots and socks, her bare knees pointing in opposite directions.

"And your hair Flora, would you like me to dress it for you?" Elizabeth patted the bun at the back of her head. "A bun would be perfect." She walked over to Flora and stood above her with fingers pinched against thumbs, a surgeon about to operate.

Flora put a hand on the top of her head. "No Aunt Elizabeth, I don't want a bun."

"But Flora your hair is so…" the word looked for, "untidy."

"Ach, it will be fine when I've brushed it," huffed Flora, and waited for the next criticism.

"And your cheeks." Elizabeth patted one of her own pale cheeks. "You should tone them down a little Flora."

"I will," snapped Flora, not at all surprised concerning the red cheek situation. Her luggage consisted of a small white cotton duffle bag with narrow blue stripes; she picked it up off the bed and rummaged inside it until she found her brush and face powder. "Aunt Elizabeth…" Another rummage for her lipstick. "It was really very good of you to arrange this night out but…"

Elizabeth cupped Flora's cheeks in her hands.

She looked up to her aunt's smiling face.

"Indulge me Flora. I know I have taken liberties. But I was so happy when you finally agreed to visit. "

Flora couldn't quite remember the time 'I might visit' changed to 'I will visit'.

"And it was the least I could do; arrange something special for your twenty first birthday. You will remember tonight for the rest of your life Flora. I promise."

The doorbell rang.

"Ah!" exclaimed Elizabeth. "The tea ladies. I will leave you to prepare yourself." She left the room, turned to Flora with the sweetest of sweet smiles and closed the door.

Tea ladies! Flora flopped back on the bed thinking a hundred years must have vanished while she was on the train. Time travelling back to March 20th 1858, and if she opened the bedroom door she'd see the 'tea ladies' in their long Victorian dresses and large hats. All sat with their knees together of course.

She heard a twitter of voices, jumped up with the hairbrush and stood in front of the wardrobe mirror. Aunt Elizabeth always said they both had the Montgomery women's hair and eyes, hair as black as a tarry sky, eyes brown moons waiting to cast a spell on the right man.

Flora laughed at herself in the mirror and brushed her hair away from her face and down her back. It reached as far as her shoulder blades, and despite being very thick and heavy tended to have the habit of rising from her head with the threat of floating away. The brush pointed at the mirror. "Stay!"

Her hair obeyed her command, for the moment.

Elizabeth's happy voice at the door. "Are you ready Flora? The tea ladies are dying to meet you."

Flora answered the death knell with an overloud, "Coming Aunt Elizabeth."

As instructed a thick covering of face powder, for the face of a Geisha to grimace back at her. Fingertips used to rub away the excess powder, extra care with her cheeks because they took little encouragement to blaze forth like a beacon. A slash of bright red lipstick, a pull at her clothes, her woollen jumper and skirt showing more than a few winters' wear. Another rummage inside her bag, for her shoes, Flora's birthday present to herself, dark cream, 4 inch heels, a pattern of perforations over the front. Head down to push her feet into them, and of course her hair decided to go off in a different direction. She flattened it down with a hand and went to meet the 'tea ladies'.

Lady Derman, Flora decided, would be wearing a gigantic hat with a brim-full of birds and grapes and a huge ostrich feather sticking up in the air. She imagined it wafting up and down while the genteel lady nodded at the idiot who couldn't think of a thing to stop her grandson taking her out for a blind date, and wearing that dress.

# Chapter Two

*Lady* Derman didn't have a hat on. If it wasn't for her skirt and blue silk blouse with a round brooch of sparkling stones pinned above her extremely generous breasts she might have been a little man, stubble as well. She also had a baritone voice to put any mature male voice to shame.

"We all know young men like to kick their heels and have their flings before they find a suitable girl." Her booming voice filled the room. "But it is time he settled down Elizabeth, he will be thirty next year."

'Tea' consisted of a few tiny sandwiches and cakes. Flora, who'd been manoeuvred to sit beside Lady Derman at the table, hadn't eaten since breakfast at home, her ration of two sandwiches and a cake gone in a bite and a swallow. She eyed the last cake on the plate, the finger of sponge with an almond on top daring the greedy one to pick it up.

Lady Derman, who ate with her mouth open, turned with legs wide enough to encompass a horse to plonk her cup and saucer onto the table, and gave Flora an excellent view of her blue silk knickers. Flora tucked her feet under her chair and glued her knees together. The discarded cup with a semicircle of lipstick, crusted remains of sandwich and cake stuck to the rim. A drop of tea dribbled down, Flora decided against the cake.

"My Daphne refused to wear a thing unless I bought it from the very best of the French fashion houses. You should have seen her when she was presented at court; my Daphne was the best dressed debutante there."

This was the dress culprit who had grey sausage roll curls balanced on the top of her head, and the greedy one. She picked up the cake, almond and sponge in front of thin lips as she looked at Flora. "What a shame you missing the last of the presentations by two days. And of course you need the adequate funds to do the season and you are rather old to be brought out now my dear. I had my Daphne married off long before her twenty first birthday. Have you tried the dress? My Daphne used to very slim. She could have been a model."

Flora hoped Daphne had ballooned to the size of an elephant. The frumpiest and most out of date of her cast off dresses must have been chosen with great care by her horrible mother.

"Do not let those thick clothes fool you Bernice," said Elizabeth, "Flora has a very attractive figure."

Flora could have reached over and hugged her.

"My Freddie has the pick of the debs."

Lady Derman's deep voice dominated the conversation again, and the topic the famous Freddie. Again!

"He has cost me a fortune. My Freddie can wheedle anything out of me." The stubbly chin quivered, an invisible feather tickling away beneath it. "I told him. If I am going to buy this car for you, you have to carry out a favour for me and entertain the neice of a very good friend of mine. And he did not utter one word of protest, he simply walked away. My Freddie will do anything for me."

This left for her audience to consider, and if Flora thought she was

worth the price of a new car her high value was soon discarded.

"It isn't even a new car," droned on Lady Derman. "I bought him a new car a year ago. Goodness knows what happened to that." The white head shook at the puzzlement of it all.

Flora under scrutiny again, her bare legs noted with startled glances when she first entered the room. This time Lady Derman's little eyes looked at her face.

"You never know my dear; my Freddie might take a fancy to you."

This was more of a statement of the impossible rather than a complement. The shrill titters from sausage rolls stretching on into that long afternoon.

At last it was over, the 'tea ladies' on their way to the door.

Flora opened it for them, anything to get them away as soon as possible.

A pat on her cheek from the squat figure of Lady Derman as she strutted past.

"You have a sweet accent my dear but a little less of the rouge."

Flora slammed the door shut after her and kicked it.

"Temper Flora," chided Elizabeth who was at the table clearing away after the tea.

"Aunt Elizabeth…" Flora hovered around her. "About tonight…"

Elizabeth stacked plates and saucers. "Yes, it is quite a coup Flora, you and Lady Derman's grandson."

"Yes…But…"

Elizabeth turned to Flora with the plates and saucers. "I think you should take a nice long soak in a hot bath. If you go now it should give us ample time to prepare you for your big night out."

"But Aunt Elizabeth…"

Elizabeth laughed and shrugged her shoulders. "You should have seen Bernice's face when I told her Flora." She motioned to the bathroom with the plates and saucers. "Go."

Flora looked at her aunt's happy face, and went for her bath.

The long hot soak, borrowed stockings, her aunt insisted. Powder and lipstick, hair brushed into submission. It couldn't be put off any longer; Flora stepped into the dress.

"Breathe in Flora," instructed Elizabeth as she struggled with the zip.

Flora plumper than the 'could have been a model'. If she had a proper meal inside her all of her problems would be over, the zip wouldn't have made it.

Unfortunately it did, Elizabeth stood with a hand to her chest heaving for breath while Flora looked at herself in the mirror. Flared skirt to her calves, tight nipped in waist, a wide low collar that swept across her shoulder blades and over the tops of her arms to finish off with a dramatic plunge down her front.

Her high heels transformed the dress; lifting the skirt into a soft arc around her legs. A shiny thread in the material caught the light, a touch of sparkly gold.

"You look…" started Elizabeth.

"Like my mother?"

"Would you like to talk about her?"

"No."

The answer Elizabeth expected, her sister Beatrice not for discussion. Flora thought the gifts of money Elizabeth gave her occasionally came from her aunt. She wouldn't accept them if she knew they came from her mother. Beatrice paid for Flora's train fare to London, her birthday present for her daughter, and the money she sent just about covered it. The value of the two sisters' inheritances from their grandparents diminishing as the years went by until they were left little room for extras, and Beatrice Ballardine had more reason to be short of money than Elizabeth.

"I'm so bare." Flora put a hand to her front. The tight dress and plunging neckline created a cleavage that rose and fell as she breathed. She turned and scowled at Elizabeth. "You must think you are my best aunt in the whole wide world to get away with doing this to me."

"Your only aunt you mean," laughed Elizabeth.

Flora smiled down at her aunt. She towered over the smaller woman. Her high heels pushed her up to almost 6 foot and the thick material of the dress increased her feeling of largeness.

"Aunt Elizabeth how tall would you say Lady Derman is?"

"Oh, I would say around five foot."

Flora opened her eyes wide in mock alarm and pushed a finger between her breasts. "If this Freddie's the same height as his grandmother it means his nose will be right here." She put her hands on her hips and glared down to Elizabeth. "Well if this Freddie whatever his name is thinks he's going to spend all night with his nose between my bosoms he's sadly mistaken."

"Stop it Flora!" exclaimed Elizabeth. "You know his name is Freddie Thompson- Smythe." She started to straighten the bedcovers, which didn't need straightening. "Freddie is due to inherit his grandmother's fortune. He will be a very rich young man one day."

Flora sighed and looked up to the ceiling and thought how Robert used to protect her from devious aunts. She saw where pieces of plaster had fallen away from the ornate rose around the light, her aunt's flat the same as Clairgowan House, threadbare carpets, old furniture and faded curtains.

Elizabeth plumped up the pillows, which didn't need plumping. "And how are things at Clairgowan House?"

"Auld Mungo?" Flora shrugged, a laugh. "I asked him this morning if he knew what today was. He said of course he knew. It was the day I was off gallivanting to see you and who was going to cook for him. Not a word about my birthday. And of course I had to prepare all his meals so he won't starve to death while I'm away."

"Your father is quite capable of caring for himself Flora." Elizabeth hurried out of the room. "I almost forgot." Returning moments later with a silky cream material folded on outstretched palms.

Elizabeth carried the offering over to Flora. "There!" She loosened the material and held it up with a triumphal sweep.

It was a silk shawl with an extravagantly long fringe and embroidered with flowers so rich and thick they glittered like jewels.

Flora lifted her hair while her aunt draped the shawl over her shoulders. It shone out against the dowdy dress; nothing could be as beautiful. She hugged her aunt, her eyes moist at the hours of love put into the shawl.

"Happy birthday my Flora," whispered Elizabeth.

Flora saw her check her watch. "He's late?"

"A little." Elizabeth plucked at the shawl.

Flora vowed to kill this Freddie if he let her aunt down. Anger and relief rolled backwards and forwards as the minutes ticked by.

"Freddie's grandmother may have a title Flora." Elizabeth gave more plucks at the shawl. "I remember my grandfather telling me once he had a cousin twice removed who had a title. So the Montgomery's are just as good, if not better. It is Freddie who is the lucky one tonight."

Flora noticed her aunt didn't say the Ballardine's were just as good, and she didn't need to be told it was Freddie who was the lucky one.

Her shoulders jumped at the sound of the doorbell, and the giantess went to meet the dwarf.

## Chapter Three

Flora stepped forward as her aunt opened the entrance door to the flats, and looked into eyes the purest of light blue.

"Freddie?" enquired Elizabeth.

A nod her reply.

Freddie Thompson - Smythe immaculate in an evening suit and black patent shoes, handkerchief a meticulous fold of white, black bow tie in perfect alignment with his collar, pin tuck shirt a dazzle of white. Fair creamed back hair, a fresh complexion with the start of jowls perhaps but nothing to worry about. Taller than Flora, thank goodness, wide shoulders, a little stocky and the closed mouth spread in a nervous smile.

Flora returned the smile and raised her eyebrows to say, 'I feel the same.'

"And this this is my niece Flora," said Elizabeth who turned to Flora with a face so bright and vibrant she might have been the one about to spend the evening with an escort.

The blue eyes moved to Flora's cleavage, followed by a quick glance to her aunt to check she hadn't noticed and a look at Flora's face to check she had. All of this with the same spread of the mouth, which she realised had been nothing more than lips clamped together. She saw a smile because she wanted to see a smile.

Flora looked down to the shawl, put a hand under the material and covered her breasts with it. Then she leant down to receive a kiss on her cheek from her aunt and stepped outside.

"Now you two young people have a wonderful evening," sang out Elizabeth.

Flora heard the door close behind her with a quiet snap. A taxi waited in the dark by the pavement, she started to negotiate her way down the flight of steps to it with face down to her high heels.

Freddie hurried past her. "Come on for Christ's sake, get a move on."

Flora looked up to see him jump into the taxi, a fog from the idling engine swirling around the large black cab. She did consider turning to go back to the flat, after she screamed down to the taxi that Freddie could get a move on without her, but the thought of her aunt's devastated face stopped her. So Flora continued her careful progress down the steps, held her head up high and walked to the black hole of the taxi door.

"Hello."

Flora welcomed by a high pitched voice. The door slammed shut behind her, the taxi already moving away as she stepped past Freddie and sat beside a girl with short blonde hair.

"Kath… Kath Stevens," said the girl. She turned to the man beside her who had a quiff combed into his dark sleeked back hair. "And this is Reg…"

He lit a cigarette and leant over to Flora. "Reg Purvis."

"Flora Ballardine," responded Flora.

Kath tried to look at Flora's shawl in the dark of the taxi. "Ooh, that's lovely Flora. I'll take a proper look at it when we get to the

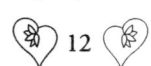 12

dancehall."

A foursome! Flora could have hugged the girl, but she was the one to get the hug. "It's my birthday present from my aunt," she told Kath.

"It's your birthday!" exclaimed Kath. She put her arms around Flora and kissed her on the cheek.

The happy scene did not help Freddie's mood. With his blue eyes and boyish looks it used to be easy to squeeze anything he asked for out of his grandmother, but time was changing his appearance and it made him more and more the slave to his grandmother's capricious demands for 'favours'. Freddie couldn't speak at the indignity of this latest 'favour', to entertain a coarse country girl from Scotland for the evening because of all things it was her birthday. He had to walk away from his grandmother to stop himself from putting his hands around her thick fat neck and throttling her.

One big fear dominated Freddie's life, that his grandmother might live long enough to celebrate one of her birthdays, her next one! He'd often pass his time by ruminating over the different strategies he could use to prevent this happening. Such as the accidental bump into her on a flight of stairs, and it would have to be at the top of course so he could watch her short fat body bounce all the way to the bottom. Or the accidental trip over his foot strategy, and of course a hard object would be waiting in the right place to smash into her skull.

Another fear dominated Freddie's life and it was almost as important as the first, and that was not keeping up with the crowd he moved around in, or even worse being the focus of their derision. He had to have the car or he'd look the fool after boasting about it for weeks. It was considered 'de rigueur' to own a sports car, even more 'de rigueur' to own something rare. The car fitted into both categories, an updated Javelin-Jupiter, highly prized in his circles. Then the panic of being seen with this girl. Reg and his tart took care of that, Freddie conveniently latching on to their plans to go to a dancehall. No one he knew went near the dead end place, and it would be cheap.

Freddie might have lost his boyish looks but it didn't mean he'd lost the childish tantrums that went along with them. Someone had to pay for that night, and who better than the birthday girl?

"No bagpipes?" he asked.

Flora turned her back to him.

"I thought everyone from the wild and woolly north didn't go anywhere without them." Freddie ended this with a well practised snigger.

Kath pulled at Flora's arm. "Ignore him Flora."

She did, but this made Freddie more determined to provoke her.

"I'll tell you something now darlin'. If you think I'm going to be seen with some tart wearing something out of the ark you are sadly mistaken."

Flora swung around to him. "Then I'd better go. I'm sure your grandmother will be delighted to know the night lasted less than five minutes."

"Do what you want darlin'," responded Freddie who gave a well practised shrug of indifference this time.

"That is exactly what I will do," said Flora leaning over to the taxi driver. "Will you stop the taxi?" She decided she'd wander around for a while and return to her aunt's flat full of smiles and stories about her wonderful evening.

The driver turned his head. "You want to stop here love?"

"Well, go on then," goaded Freddie as the taxi slowed to a stop. "Either stay or go." He opened his mouth to bluster on but the worry of Flora actually going closed it. His grandmother and her money controlled every moment of his life; to disobey her meant a life of penury, or even worse. Employment!

Kath pulled at Flora's arm again. "Come on, stay Flora."

Reg didn't seem interested; he was staring out of the window smoking his cigarette.

"Is anyone getting out or not?" shouted the driver.

"He's trying to upset you Flora and spoil your birthday." Kath gave a cheeky smile at Freddie and pulled a face at him. "Well you aren't going to win curdle face, so there."

Flora couldn't help but smile at Kath. "Sorry." She leant forward to the driver. "I'm not getting out."

## Chapter Four

Freddie sulked in the corner of the taxi until they reached the dancehall.

The faded old building welcoming once they were inside. A glitter ball splintered a myriad of colours over couples waltzing on the crowded dance floor. At the far end a large stage with a drummer and two guitarists in suits and ties. They looked lost in the space meant for rows of bandsmen, one of the guitarists emulating the honeyed tones of Perry Como, singing 'Magic Moments' into the microphone with his guitar swung over his back.

Flora and Kath left Freddie and Reg at the bar, linked arms and walked down several steps to the dance floor. Most of the dancers were dressed the same as Kath and Reg, the girls in flat shoes and flared skirts with wide belts, the boys in casual jackets, narrow ties and drainpipe trousers. Flora saw a few dresses, but none of them as formal as her dress. They found a table at the corner of the stage. Flora let Kath have a look at her shawl, folded over the back of her chair and sat in the shadows so she wouldn't feel so conspicuous.

Kath checked Reg and Freddie were still at the bar and leant over the table to Flora until their noses almost touched.

"Don't say a word to Reg. I share a flat with three other girls and we play this game. One of us has to pick someone up and take him back to the flat and the other three have to think of something to frighten him off. We all put money into the pot and the best one wins the money." Kath put her head back and laughed. "It's a scream. The last time one of the girls sat knitting, the other had the ironing board out and I borrowed a neighbour's baby. It cried so loud he couldn't get out quick enough, so I won. I can't wait to see what the other three have ready."

Flora and Kath laughed at each other's face until Reg arrived with three drinks in his hands. He put them onto the table, a glass of beer for himself, a small glass with a clear drink for Kath and an orange drink in a tall glass for Flora. She tasted it, a flat orangeade.

"That's all Freddie would pay for," said Reg. "He said he's going to stay at the bar." He sat at the table and took a drink of his beer, lit a cigarette and looked up to the bar jigging a knee.

"You would think you were babysitting him," said Kath. "Go and look after the miserable sod if you want to."

"Yea, I think I will." Reg picked up his glass and made way back to the bar with his cigarette hanging from his lips.

Kath nodded after him. "He's done nothing but toady after Freddie all night. Freddie's buying this car. But I don't think that's why they met at the pub." She shrugged. "Anyway this car was supposed to be delivered tomorrow but as soon as the lord and master found out it was coming up tonight he insisted he saw it right away. Reg rang the mechanic at the garage in Birmingham to tell him to bring it here. It's his own business the way Reg talks."

This surprised Flora, Reg looked more like a spiv than someone who owned his own business, and she didn't say who was actually buying this car.

'Magic Moments' ended; the floor almost emptied, leaving a few couples waiting for the next dance.

Kath leant over the table to Flora again. "I'd been sitting in the pub for ages before Reg turned up. If you don't bring anyone back to the flat you have to treat the other girls to a night out. I was starting to get desperate." She sat back and clicked her fingers in the air. "He might own his own business but I prefer them with a bit more zing than Reg."

The band crashed into the quiet, the beat of 'At the Hop' filling the hall.

Kath jumped up. "Come on Flora Ballardine," she shouted. "I'm not going to let you hide away on your birthday."

Flora dragged onto the floor. She stopped thinking about how she was dressed and jumped around to the beat of the music with Kath, the two of them laughing and spinning under each other's arms. The stalwarts who insisted on holding onto each other jostled and pushed until they separated and joined in with the exuberant rock and roll dancing.

The trio on the stage pulled the dancers into their world of frantic beat. One guitarist impersonated a gyrating Elvis Presley; the other gave a cheeky looking Tommy Steele performance followed by the two of them together to become the more sedate Everly Brothers.

Flora danced with Kath for most of the night. They didn't see any more of Freddie, but Reg came down to the dance floor a few times to dance with Kath when Flora would sit at the table until he returned to the bar. She was asked up to dance, once, by one of the Teddy boys who were hanging around the edge of the dance floor. The skinny youth had a quiff that defied gravity and quite a few inches shorter than Flora despite his high crepe shoes. His red draped jacket with its velvet collar outshone all of the other dancers around them, and he soon disappeared when the music stopped. Flora had the feeling he danced with her for a bet but she was enjoying herself too much to care.

It was the time of the night when the dance floor was full of bodies reacting to the ever increasing beat of the music. Reg pushed his way down from the bar to dance with Kath again. The two of them small and agile, Flora sat at the table laughing and clapping at them bouncing around the floor. Her dress had become a tight woollen corset in the heat of the dance floor, and she was hot and thirsty. The flat orange soon gone with so sign of another drink. She tried to cool herself down by lifting her hair from the back of her neck and arching her back.

Reg pushed his way through the dancers to return to the bar. Kath pulled a face at his back and waved Flora over to her.

Freddie saw the little scene, the tart posing for him with her head back. He started drinking as soon as the pubs opened and had downed quite a few at the dancehall, along with a couple of purple hearts he bought off Reg.

Freddie decided he needed to get into the drug scene. He couldn't think of an easier way of supplementing his grandmother's dribbles of money to him, but the people he knew wouldn't look at him; they took his other car a few months back because of his debts. He met Reg while visiting the garage to view the car. Reg followed him out, scurrying down the street after him with a few purple hearts in box to see if he could sell him a couple and said he could introduce Freddie to some people he knew. They met at the pub to arrange a meet the next day at a club at the other side of London, where Freddie wasn't known. Reg thought he was going to be paid for his troubles. Freddie sniggered at that one. The money he extorted from his grandmother for the night would give him a good start, and he'd turn up in the car to show these people they were dealing with a person with some substance about him.

Freddie's mood zoomed up with the mix of alcohol and amphetamines, and along with this his view of Flora started to change. Though she wasn't his type, Freddie preferred his tarts willowy with plenty of make up. Flora's cleavage started to dominate his euphoric mind, those white, living, breathing mounds waiting for him. He saw her surprise when she first saw him. Most probably she couldn't believe her luck. And the Madonna like pose, the modest look down before she covered herself with the shawl.

He saw a couple emerge from the dark at the side of the stage, the tart straightening the back of her skirt as they walked past Flora. Freddie decided he'd have to enquire into the Madonna look; he left the bar and staggered down the steps to the dance floor.

Kath spinning under Flora's arm at the corner of the stage, sparkling splinters of light to the front, blackness behind.

Flora's turn to spin, but she couldn't keep hold of Kath's small hand. She watched Kath disappear amongst the heaving mass of dancers.

A sweaty hand grabbed hold of Flora's wrist. Dizziness, lack of balance with her high heels stopped any control.

Freddie pulled her to him and marched her backwards. Flora's heels skidded on the floor, she held onto Freddie so she wouldn't fall.

She did fall, because Freddie pushed her. Expecting the jarring thud of landing on the floor she fell onto something soft, thick mounds of old stage curtains. A heavy weight crashed down onto her and forced the air out of her lungs. Freddie!

They were no more than a few feet from the dancers, the splinters of light, the whoops, the screams, above them the noise and pounding vibrations of the band.

Flora struggled to breathe against Freddie's heavy weight, she couldn't, and she didn't know if she needed to breathe in or out. She twisted her face away from wet lips; strong hands pushed her shoulders down. Freddie's voice shouted in her ear. "Come on darlin', I'll give you a birthday treat." An arm across her throat pinned her down, a hand pushed down the front of her dress. Her arms lashed out, a hand under the skirt of her dress, she heaved herself sideways, Freddie pulled her back. A hand under her skirt again but Freddie was having problems with the thick material. Another heave away from him with arms lashing out, her elbow cracked hard against something, Freddie shouted out. Flora rolled away, her shoes slipping on the floor while she tried to stand.

She stood heaving for breath, air rasping in her lungs.

The band crashed to a stop, Kath pushed her way through the crowd. "I lost you there," she gasped.

"Have you seen Freddie?" Reg pushed his way through the crowd and walked up to them looking around him.

Flora hoped she left him dead under the stage. She hadn't, because Freddie materialized with a blotch under one of his eyes and a face saying he thought the same about her.

"Well!" He glared at Reg. "Am I going to see this car tonight or not?"

"That's why I was looking for you," whined Reg. "He should be here any minute now. I told him to bring the car to the side door."

"Oh great!" shouted Kath. "Come on Flora we'll take a look at this car." She plonked the shawl over Flora's shoulders, grabbed a hand and dragged her along behind her.

Flora didn't have the strength to stop her. She stumbled out of the dancehall behind Kath to the darkness of a narrow road lit by a soft glow above the doorway. Still heaving for breath when Kath left her to peer down the road with Freddie and Reg.

Flora propped herself against the door, pulled the shawl around

her and crossed her arms. She was shivering, but she didn't feel cold.

Freddie turned to snarl at Reg. "I thought you said he would be here."

He turned his head again to the sound of voices as three youths in tight jeans and leather jackets emerged from out of the dark. They jeered at Freddie and Reg and whistled and leered at Flora and Kath.

Flora saw Reg put a hand into his jacket pocket, take something out and put it behind him. Two powerful headlights cut through the dark, the youths swung around to the light, three statues caught in the glare. The approaching roar of a car shocked them out of their trance. They ran, the approaching white light sweeping them up road.

Reg put his hand back into his pocket.

# *Chapter Five*

The car stopped in front of Flora. It was small and chunky with the back dipping down to the road, a light coloured hood, and the body of the car darker, turquoise. Lights cut, engine silenced, a small door opened.

John Mason unravelled himself out of the car. At 6 ft 4 he had to concertina himself into the sporting jobs and reverse the process to get out.

He looked around him. Thompson - Smythe with Reg close behind him and being his usual obsequious self if he thought some money might be coming his way.   A girl with short blonde hair, another girl in a muted spotlight from above a door, face a pale oval surrounded by a dark cloud of hair.

Flora saw the driver look over to her. A beard cropped close to the skin, hair not the usual fashion, short, brushed back, almost a crew cut. In an evening suit the same as Freddie, but taller and much slimmer, and he didn't have the look of a mechanic working for Reg.

"Put the hood down," ordered Freddie. "I'll have a run in it with the hood down."

The night seemed pleasant enough in the shelter of the narrow

road but John knew how cold it would be driving open topped. He tolerated fools like Thompson - Smythe who demanded to see the car in the middle of the night, because a sale was a sale, more money in the bank, and it wouldn't be for ever.

He nodded at Reg to put the hood down and hoped the cold would freeze the blotches on Thompson - Smythe's face.

John stepped away from the car and stood facing the girl against the door. Eyes deep pools in the white of her face, and she was panting, lips and cheeks sucking air in and blowing it out.

Kath helped Reg unclip the hood. "Will you run me to my flat? It's only a few minutes from here."

"Yes," replied John looking at the eyes.

Kath looked at Reg, she asked him the question.

"Where's the keys?" shouted Freddie.

"I have them," said John. He couldn't stop looking at the eyes. "You can have a test run tomorrow, in the daylight." It was obvious Thompson - Smythe had been drinking all night; John wasn't about to allow him damage the car and put the sale in jeopardy.

The driver's hair looked dark at first, but once he stepped nearer the light Flora could see the colour, red, very red. A narrow nose and face, eyes black orbs under the brows.

"Come on Flora," shouted Kath. "Get in, it'll be a laugh."

Flora had no intention of going anywhere near the car and Freddie. She pushed herself from the door to walk away, but she felt dizzy and had to put a hand out to balance herself. A warm hand took it and led her to the car. Flora stopped heaving for breath, and she followed the hand because she couldn't think of anything else to do.

The hood down, Freddie sat behind the wheel with Kath and Reg beside him. Flora hesitated at the open car door; the one bench seat looked full and she didn't want the warm hand to leave her.

"Come on Flora." Kath sat on Reg's lap. "Squeeze in."

Flora sat beside Kath and Reg. The hand left her to close the door and lock it.

"Why should I have these in my car?" whined Freddie. "They could have caught a taxi."

John pushed in beside him to get behind the wheel. Freddie gave a rough push at Reg and Kath, which in turn flattened Flora sideways across the door.

"It isn't your car until you've paid for it," said John. He looked around Freddie to Kath. "And your place had better be a few minutes away."

"It is, I promise," lied Kath.

"You might as well drop me off at a club while you are at it," said Freddie.

John shook his head at himself for agreeing to have them all in the car. It was the girl at the far end of the seat, she'd distracted him, and she had to be with Thompson - Smythe. He wondered why that bothered him.

Flora's shawl slipped off her shoulders. All she could do in her confined space was hold it above her head to straighten it before she tried to wrap it around her shoulders again. A roar from the car, headlights on, the car moved forward, turned a corner and gathered speed. The cold wind took her breath with it and snatched the shawl out of one of her hands, the shawl a fluttering banner above her head as the car roared down the road.

Kath's 'few' minutes turned out to be a lot more. She shouted directions to the driver until she told him to stop, scrambling over Flora out of the car without waiting for the door to be unlocked. Reg followed her out, and battered and squashed Flora all over again.

Kath leant down to Flora and gave her a kiss. "Happy birthday

Flora." She winked and turned to Reg. "Would you like to come up to my flat Reg?"

"Yea, that'll be great," replied Reg agog at his good fortune.

Kath walked away with Reg, put a hand up in the air and gave the victory sign.

Flora bit her bottom lip and turned away.

Her body shook with the cold. She wrapped the shawl around herself and wished she could be warm, the night be over and anywhere but next to Freddie.

The driver got out of the car and went to the hood. He didn't look very pleased at the length of time it took to get to Kath's.

"I want the hood to stay down," snapped Freddie.

Flora saw the bearded face look over to her for a moment before looking down at Freddie.

"Get out."

Freddie cringed at the face above him, slid under the wheel and jumped out of the car.

The driver walked around the car to Flora's door. A thump of fear in her chest, he was putting them out, leaving her alone with Freddie. He unlocked the door, air rasping in her lungs as he hauled her out of the car and pulled the back of the seat forward to search for something. Flora stepped away from the car desperately trying to remember the direction Kath and Reg went. She put her head down to steady herself, ready to run.

Soft warmth fell around her shoulders. A blanket pulled over her front, Flora led back to the car and sat on the seat, the blanket wrapped around her and the door closed.

The bearded face looked over to Freddie. "Why should she freeze because you feel the need to act the fool?"

Freddie jumped back into the car without a word.

Flora sank down until her nose was just above the blanket and enjoyed the ride in the car despite being sat next to Freddie, but it wasn't for long, the car soon stopping at the entrance of a nightclub. She sat up to look at the bright lights and people while the driver got out of the car at the pavement.

"I'll see you tomorrow," said Freddie jumping out after him.

John shook his head at Thompson - Smythe hurrying into the club and leaving him to see to the girl. He walked around the car to open the door for her. Flora the other girl called her, the name suited her.

Flora pushed herself down on the seat and pulled the blanket tight around her. "I'm not going in."

The road was very busy, a horn blared at John who had to jump out of the way when a car almost collided with him. He had enough, striding over to the entrance of the nightclub to look for Thompson - Smythe.

"I've told you," shouted Flora over to him, "I'm not going in."

John walked back, sat inside the car, slammed the door shut and sat sideways to Flora, one hand on the steering wheel, the other along the back of the seat.

She saw he had long slim hands, the fingers pink, well scrubbed. "If you think I'm having anything more to do with that…" Flora looked for a suitable insult.

John shook his head. "Your argument with your boyfriend has nothing to do with me."

"He's not my boyfriend," argued Flora.

Why did that please him?

A couple stopped to look at the car, and the couple in it, a man joined them. Flora knew how odd they looked, the driver in an evening suit and her head stuck out of the blanket, and her burning face said how red her cheeks would be.

The bearded face turned towards the people and back to her with eyes jewelled under the bright lights, flashes of green beneath the brows. Flora wished it was him stood at the door at the beginning of the night.

"OK." John nodded his head. "He's not your boyfriend."

Flora ignored the placatory gesture because she decided it was a patronizing nod to shut her up.

"That's what I've just told you," she shouted over the inches separating them. "My aunt arranged a night out with him for my birthday without telling me. I just met him a few hours ago." Flora took a deep breath. "And do you know something I don't care what you think." She shook her head shrieking. "I don't care what anyone thinks."

John tried to say something.

"I suppose I'm spoiling your night by expecting you to help me," screamed Flora. "I suppose a good night for you would be to pick a girl up and dump her in the morning. Go on your way and think how clever you are."

John stopped trying to say something, and winced inside at her accurate accusation. His plans for the night were supposed to start hours before with a good session at the clubs and followed, hopefully, by a decent hotel with a girl. A girl he wouldn't see again. He'd been up since the early hours working on the car so he could bring it up that night instead of the following day. The work on the car took longer than he expected, Thompson - Smythe's demand to see the car took more time away along with providing a chauffeuring service for Reg and his girl. John had worked non stop to finish the car by the completion date; it was supposed to be his first night off in months.

"It's all self self self with some people. Ignorant and selfish and with no consideration of other people and their feelings." Flora in full flow, and starting to feel a lot, lot better. A hand struggled out of the blanket. "And all I've eaten since this morning was a couple of tiny wee sandwiches." Finger and thumb demonstrated their small size. "And one wee cake." A catch in her voice, self pity a threat to her anger.

John tried not to smile at this, and more fascinated by the large brown eyes. The cheeks now full of colour, flame red, her soft Scottish accent wonderful to hear, even if it was loud and accusing. He almost put a hand to the wild mass of hair, thick and black around her face, but he had a suspicion it might be bitten by the white teeth under the rapidly moving red lips.

Flora saw the half smile and decided she was being laughed at. "Ach, I'll not be bothering you any longer. You can get on with your night of passion with whoever takes your fancy." She scrabbled at the door handle. "There's no need to worry about me, I can take care of myself."

By the time John sorted the passion bit out Flora had the door open and in the act of jumping out of the car, with the blanket still wrapped around her because she wasn't going anywhere without her comfort and warmth. He saw a car hurtle towards her and lunged forward to grab the blanket. To miss by an inch, lying across the seat with gritted teeth waiting to hear the crunch of a car against a body or the door. Neither happened, what he did hear was a scream, a blaring car horn and the door close with a click.

Flora ran to the pavement, hitched up the blanket and tried to ignore the odd looks as people walked past her. Three men staggered towards her full of the inebriated cheer of a good night out, and ready for any kind of entertainment.

Flora Ballardine stood in Soho wrapped in a blanket an ideal candidate, in more ways than one.

"I see you've been waiting for us darling," shouted out one

comedian.

"That's service for you, blanket at the ready," shouted the second comedian.

"How much?" asked the third who decided to get straight down to business and not waste time.

A huddle to decide who was first before they turned to see the subject of their complex conversation had vanished. One of the comedians nodded to a gap in the buildings.

The alleyway was very dark, very smelly and full of rubbish. Flora gave a shriek; sure she felt something scuttle over her foot. It took her ages to slip and slither her way to the other end, and it started to rain. She sniffed, stood in the dark and wet at the end of the alleyway feeling very forlorn. Heart thumping at what might be waiting for her she poked her head out, peered down a quiet road and saw the car a few yards away with the hood up. The driver stood beside it brushing the wet from his head and shoulders. He turned and saw her.

Flora looked the other way to pretend she hadn't seen him, and to stop herself from running up to him and flinging her arms around his neck. Head back again to see him stride up to her, face tight, lips a thin compressed line. Her arm gripped and marched to the car, no twisting out of that hold.

"If you'd stopped shouting and screaming for a second I'd have told you I'll take you to where you want to go." Words to his front, lips tight shut again.

Flora stuck her nose in the air. "I can look after myself thank you."

His lips opened to expel breath through clenched teeth.

Flora checked to see if the blanket might be trailing on the ground. "You should have seen the state of that place. I'm sure there's a rat or something running around in there. There's really no need for you to be worried about me you know." She couldn't stop jabbering on. "It was really disgusting in there; you would think people would take better care than that. I'd have found my own way…" She closed her mouth at the car, waited for the door to be opened and sighed down to the seat, and it stopped raining.

John didn't think it was worth mentioning that he ran over to the pavement to see her go down the alleyway, and he had to square up to the trio to stop them following her. Surprised they accepted his story she was drunk and his girlfriend, laughing on their way. He couldn't see her, jumping in the car and racing around to the other side to find her. The rain, he had put the hood up to protect the inside of the car. His night and its promises vanishing along with this girl down the alleyway and he still had to find a hotel.

Part of the blanket trailed out of the car. The driver picked up and tucked it around Flora's legs. The red hair inches from her face, warm breath on her skin as the bearded face turned to her. It lifted away, the door shut and locked. She felt safe and warm while she watched the driver walk around the car, open the door, squeeze himself in behind the wheel and close the door.

The two of them shapes in the dark.

A sigh beside Flora. "Where would you like to go?"

"Clairgowan."

The word with all her longing hung between them.

"And in what country would Clairgowan be?"

"Scotland," replied Flora feeling as pathetic as she sounded

"I'm sorry, but this chauffeuring service is restricted to this area. Can you think of somewhere a little nearer?"

Silence while he waited for her answer.

"Kensington," said Flora, and thought how wonderful it would be if he did drive her home. All that way with the blanket wrapped around her and him sat by her side, though her bottom was starting to feel a bit damp.

They sat in the quiet and dark for a few moments before the dark profile turned to Flora.

"You are supposed to say 'Home James' when you give the chauffeur instructions."

"Home James," sighed Flora feeling pathetic again.

She couldn't find Aunt Elizabeth's road, the driver the one who spotted the name plate high up on a wall.

Seconds later and they stopped outside her aunt's flat. Flora waited for her door to be unlocked and hoped the driver would do the same as outside the dancehall, hold her hand. The door opened, a flush of pleasure at the slim fingers, wrist, white cuff out of a dark sleeve. She took the hand and followed it up the steps.

It left her the moment they reached the door. What else could she do? She opened the door, and remembered the blanket. It didn't want to leave her shoulders; a sharp tug and it did, for it to fall out of her hands. Two faces almost collided as they tried to catch it, a brush of the beard against Flora's skin, silky hair on her cheek. Neither of them caught it, the blanket a lump on the wet ground. The driver scooped it up and walked down the steps without a word. He opened the car door and threw the blanket inside.

"Thank you James," shouted out Flora.

The bearded face up to her, a grin, teeth white and straight. "It's John... John Mason."

He disappeared inside the car, the roar of the engine. The car drew away and took with it the shape inside.

Flora closed the door behind her and leant against it holding her bare arms, and looked down at herself. The shawl! She must have taken it off with the blanket.

# *Chapter Six*

*A* soft white haze veiled the sky, the sun a tenuous lemon disc above the vague shapes of the mountains. Saturated soil expelled its peaty load with such force it edged the road with small gurgling fountains and golden laced froths. A murmuring crowd of thin ripples hurried away over the hard surface, all with one intent, to find the lowest point in the glen.

Flora put her purse and bag of shopping into one hand so she could touch her cheek and looked over to the other side of the road and the people in a field. Wellingtons trudged through sodden grass, a sparkling cascade poured from a sagging marquee, wooden stages and stalls checked and hammered at. A storm threw down enough rain the night before to launch Noah on his travels, but Clairgowan wouldn't allow anything as insignificant as that to stop the 'Gathering'.

Clairgowan held its gathering in May, one of the first in Scotland. People from the old Ballardine Estate, the villages throughout the glen and beyond would meet at the village. Some to compete in the games, others to judge, most to watch the events and gather together with old friends to catch up with the latest news.

A small woman in Wellingtons rushed out of the shop behind Flora with arms through the handles of two large baskets of scones, her wrap around pinny and hair white with flour. The warm moist air inside Mrs Stewart's shop so heavy with the wonderful mix of flour, butter and eggs Flora sure she could have taken a bite out of it.

Mrs Stewart splashed her way over to the field with her face to Flora. "I expect we will not be seeing you until long after the opening Flora Ballardine."

Flora took her fingers from her cheek and shook her head. "I'm sure the laird can cope without me Mrs Stewart. And I doubt if I will be coming at all; you can row a boat in that field today."

Mrs Stewart stopped at the other side at of the road to check her baskets. "Ach, it will soon dry out. Bob Brown put good drainage in that field for the gathering. And the sun will be burning everyone's backs before the end of the day, you wait and see." She smiled over to Flora. "Come to the gathering Flora, you shouldn't be hiding yourself away."

Flora hated that, the sympathetic looks, the real reason why she didn't intend to be seen at the gathering.

Mrs Stewart hurried away determined to set up her stall before Mrs Brown. The two women competed with each other to see who sold out of scones first, not that it mattered because neither of them would have a crumb left at the end of the day.

Flora smiled when she saw Mrs Brown hurry out the farmhouse and run down to the field with her baskets of scones. The farmhouse overlooked the village and built on the spot where a crofter's tumbledown home used to stand, a high pillared entrance and ornate stone walls a declaration of its owner's wealth.

Flora walked past the red telephone box outside the post office and up to Andy McManus who was stood on a ladder repairing sagging bunting above The Glen Hotel. He leant back to examine his work before making a quick descent down the ladder so he'd be in time to meet Flora.

She nodded, put her shopping down and opened her purse. "Do we owe you anything Andy?"

Andy scratched the top of his head. It was covered with a thick thatch of grey hair, the same as his father, and most probably his grandfather and great grandfather. They all owned the hotel before him and Andy's 10 year old son Alex would inherit it from his father one day, and most probably the same head of hair.

"You know I wouldn't run after the laird Flora." Andy continued with his head scratching. "But he didn't have any money on him when I delivered that last bottle of whisky for him. He said he would settle with me later. I expect he forgot."

"I expect he did Andy," answered Flora. Not a word from her father while he sat in front of her drinking the whisky. Pleased she didn't use all of her money at the shop she emptied the remaining loose change into her hand and offered it over to Andy. "Will that be enough?"

Andy stopped his scratching to receive the money. He gave it a quick check and pushed it into his trouser pocket. "That should cover it Flora."

It was bound to be a few shillings short; Flora could have kissed Andy for being so considerate, the start of a giggle at his reaction if she did.

Andy scratched his head again. "I only said it to stop any awkwardness if the laird asked for another bottle Flora." The awkwardness over Andy stopped his scratching and lifted the ladder from the wall. "I cannot recall the last time I saw you in the bar Flora. You should tell the laird to bring you down some night."

"And all the mountains would crash into the glen if I walked into the bar alone," muttered Flora walking away. She hadn't been inside The Glen Hotel since the last gathering and remembered how she giggled into Robert Brown's face while they stood nose to nose in the crush at the bar. Robert waited until the following day to tell her he was leaving. The day he left for America.

Robert said he was going to do the same as his father. Bob Brown was the son of a poor crofter when he left for America to find his fortune. He returned to Clairgowan 20 years later a wealthy man and delighted to find his childhood sweetheart hadn't married. Robert didn't say if finding his own fortune might mean a 20 year wait for Flora.

She shouted and screamed at Robert and chased him out of the house. Then ran up to her room to lie on her bed, but not to cry. Flora lay on her back and stretched her arms out in anticipation of her new life without Robert, which turned out to be no life at all. No more evenings with him at the bar at The Glen Hotel, or meals in town, or trips out with him in his father's car. Shocked at a local dance to find at 20 years old she was the oldest girl there without a partner, and every boy without a partner a young teenager, most of them still at school. Flora caught the early bus home.

Her one night out since then spent with the loathsome Freddie Thompson - Smythe. She returned home the following morning. Sat on the train gazing out of the window with fingers to her cheek all the way to Scotland.

Flora walked past a line of houses and crossed over the road to a high stone wall in front of a kirk and graves, and a stone commemorating her brother Alasdair. Fingers to her cheek again as she looked up an incline to a screen of pine trees, the feel of silky hair as fresh as the moment it happened.

The road ended at a pair of high gates in a gap in the trees, Clairgowan Village at the furthermost point in the glen. Behind the gates stood Clairgowan House hidden in a circle of trees. Bob Brown owned all the land in the village up to the trees, beyond that mountains and wilderness.

Flora carried her shopping through the wrought-iron gates with large daisy like flowers, they always stood open. Tall ornate chimneys towered above grey tiles and grey stone walls, the tops of other chimneys from one of the two wings at the back of the house. A dried up three tiered fountain with daisy like bowls stood in a circle of gravel at the front of the house, no water ever fell from the bowls in Flora's memory. She ignored the large carved door set in the grey stone, two large plain windows at one side, two at the other, all twinned with one above. Their watch of blank eyes following her to the side of the house.

A red post office van raced around the corner and past Flora with a scatter of gravel, the postman in a hurry to return for the gathering.

She ran down the side of the house and through a door, in time to see her father throw a letter on the fire.

"What was that?" she shouted.

"None of your concern," retorted Mungo Ballardine.

A stranger would presume it was grandfather and granddaughter stood glaring at each other. Mungo Ballardine stood tall and straight, but his lined face and grey thinning hair told of his 70 years.

"It is my concern if it's a bill," shouted Flora.

"You do not speak to your father in that way." Mungo sat on a winged, high backed leather chair so old and worn it might be red or black. It stood with its back to the outside door and at the side of a black fire range with a vast grate full of burning logs. Flames roared up the chimney, the side of the range stacked with more logs waiting for the fire.

The kitchen with a high cream washed ceiling, flag stoned floor, wooden cupboards and a pot sink with dripping tap by the outside door. Flora dumped her bag of shopping onto a long wooden table in the centre of the room, and almost knocked the oil lamp over.

Mungo put his head around his chair, pale grey eyes to Flora. "And I sincerely hope you are not attending the gathering dressed in that attire."

Flora looked down to her old cotton skirt and gypsy blouse with its frayed elastic threads. "I'm not going."

"The lady of the house should accompany the laird to the gathering and to the kirk," lectured Mungo. "And in a modest dress with your shoulders covered. And the correct shoes with heels and stockings covering your legs. And you should be wearing a sensible hat with your hair dressed up, not tied back the way you have it with a tail down your back."

"I've told you," snapped Flora, "I'm not going. And I'm not the lady of the house I'm your daughter." She pushed the shopping into the cupboards and clashed the doors shut. "And you could have said something about owing Andy for the whisky."

Mungo crossed his legs and turned to the fire. "I forgot all about it." A quick turn of his head to Flora. "If you had held your tongue Robert would not be in America and we would not be in this situation."

Flora flopped down on a soft low chair opposite her father, the brocade as faded and worn as the leather chair. She put a hand to her brow at the year long arguments and accusations.

Mungo looked down to his old trousers and waistcoat. "I had better prepare myself before Bob Brown comes to collect me." He looked at Flora. "Will you be attending the party at the farmhouse?"

"No!" exclaimed Flora. "I've told you, I'm not going to the gathering. And I'm not sitting up all night with a bunch of old men…" She shut her mouth to stop herself.

No merriment and highland flings at Bob Brown's parties, even though they were night long affairs. The year before sat in the next room with Robert. Flora snorting and giggling while her father, Bob Brown and their cohorts dissected and analysed every detail of the day's events. Robert insisted she leave early, silent while he walked her home. Flora ran from him at the gates certain he was about to ask her to marry him.

Mungo jumped up. "I have had nothing but your temper since you went off to London. If you had deigned to return earlier and not dawdled up from the village you could have made me tea. And if you had behaved yourself we would be having the party here at Clairgowan House." He strode over to a door at the far end of the kitchen and opened it. "It should be the laird hosting these events." And before he slammed the door behind him. "If he could afford to do so."

Flora ran outside to the trees and wandered around them until she heard the sound of Bob Brown's car leave. She returned to the house and lay on her bed for a few hours to pass the time and sat by the fire for another few hours. Something to eat to pass more time, her plate clashed onto the table and plodding off to the gathering with her skirt flapping at the top of her Wellingtons. Right at the moment the sun decided burn the mist away, and as Mrs Stewart predicted, burn everyone's backs.

Her feet poaching in their rubber prison by the time she arrived at the field. Wellingtons kicked off and hidden behind a stall, feet blissful and free on the cool damp grass.

The activities and competitions had ended and people were starting to leave, but the food stalls were still busy and The Glen Hotel, the drinkers who couldn't get inside stood in groups on the road. Flora was pleased she decided to go; all she saw were friendly hails and smiles, no sign of the dreaded sympathetic looks. She walked past the marquee where her father would be ensconced with his faithful followers. He'd be there in all of his finery, kilted in the Ballardine colours of red, green and gold, the opening and judging at the gathering the last vestige of his role as the laird.

The field was the last piece of land owned by her father, the thousands of acres which used to belong to the laird of Clairgowan sold to Bob Brown and many others to pay off his debts. Clairgowan House the last remnant of the once great Ballardine Estate not to be sold and the part Bob Brown coveted the most.

Mungo Ballardine and Bob Brown imagined they found the perfect solution to their problems, the marriage of Flora and Robert. The land around the village would be returned to the ownership of the Ballardine family, and the Brown family would own the jewel of the Ballardine Estate, the laird's residence, Clairgowan House.

Flora grew up with the perfect solution. She often questioned if that was love, the security of who she was going to marry. It started to go wrong the year before Robert left. He'd criticise her clothes and tell her to get her hair cut, and he refused to take her into town once because of her 'clown' cheeks.

Flora wandered up to the edge of the field and sat on the sloping bank, for the damp to seep right through to her skin. She pulled her skirt up, moved over to a dryer piece of grass and rearranged her clothes while watching the people below. Then she pulled her blouse off her shoulders, lifted her ponytail, lay back and closed her eyes.

Someone started the pipes with a high pitched moan, followed by the slow strangled sigh of someone who decided to do something else. Shouts and laughter, a glass smashed on the road, a fiddle, silky hair on her cheek…

# *Chapter Seven*

*The* golden globe hesitated above snow covered peaks before starting its slow descent behind them. Fingers of blue shadows felt their way down into the glen and touched the narrow winding road, and the white car racing along it.

A black leather jacket lay on the seat beside the driver, inside one of the pockets Flora's shawl.

John finally found himself a hotel in London, and after a lonely night tidied the car for the sale. About to throw the dirty blanket away when the shawl fell from it, catching it this time before it fell to the ground. He put it to his face, a smile at those large eyes, flaming cheeks, wild hair and that temper. Another smile, at himself, when he put the shawl into his bag.

The promised test run an unnecessary procedure, John knew Thompson - Smythe would buy the car. It went well until Thompson - Smythe started to guffaw on about the bruise under his eye and the fight the girl put up at the dancehall. John almost added another bruise under the other eye, but he thought of something much more satisfying. Thompson - Smythe hadn't bothered to query the cost of the car. John quoted such a ridiculous amount of money he thought he'd refuse to buy it. Another buyer would have to be found if he did and John needed the space in the garage. A smile to the back of the head when the fool leant down to fill the cheque out.

Reg appeared and jumped into the car. He didn't seem very pleased and looked though he spent the night on park bench.

John knew there could only be one reason why Thompson - Smythe would have anything to do with Reg who knew better than to bring his devious transactions near the garage. As long as he continued to do that John had no interest in what they were getting up to. He watched them drive off hoping Reg would feed Thompson - Smythe enough junk to kill him, and he saw Thompson - Smythe hadn't signed the cheque.

John, his bag and the shawl made their way to Birmingham, back to the garage, back to the slog.

John followed his father by owning his own small business; but any resemblance ended there. His father was in the building trade, more a jobbing builder. John's early childhood idyllic, a loved and protected only child living in a comfortable home. He'd often secrete himself in his father's truck while he worked his way around the Shropshire plains. John couldn't quite remember the exact time his perfect view of life disintegrated, he might have been 7 or 8 years old, but the occasion would stay with him with the clarity of the day it happened.

With the burning impotence of a young child John saw a red faced pompous customer harangue his father over some miniscule grievance over his work. He watched his father scurry around to correct the insignificant complaint, even wringing his hands at one point when the customer threatened not to pay him.

John complained to his mother, for her to dismiss it and tell him they wouldn't have food for the next week if his father wasn't paid.

He saw this happen to his father again and again, year after year more determined this wouldn't happen to him.

John viewed his small business as a tool that would take him to a world far removed from his father's life of servitude. It wasn't to be used as a way of existing so he'd have enough money for a home or to eat. Every hour he worked, every pound he put into the bank took John Mason nearer to the day when he would powerful enough not to be indebted or ingratiating to anyone. Another determination was in tandem with this, just as important, nothing and no one would divert him from this path.

That was why he pushed the shawl out of sight in the back of the wardrobe, but not before he put it to his face again.

Edinburgh! The logic of checking the pin prick on the map, which he looked up more than once, several times in fact. And the times he almost threw the shawl away, if he found it, or looked for it.

The elegant SS100 white Jaguar turned heads with its gleaming chrome, huge headlamps and sweeping wings. It was more of a repair job than an update or a restoration, and the buyer lived in Edinburgh which led to the rationale of John making up for his lost break in London, and the matter of a small detour...

His usual breaks a night out in town, pick up a girl, a couple of hours at her place, or if necessary a hotel. Keep her away from the garage to prevent complications, back to work the next day and forget her.

John laughed at vast empty glen and the girl living so far away.

He stopped to put the hood down in that glorious evening, stepping out of the car to an invigorating breeze from the mountains. Or did he feel that way because he'd almost reached the pinprick on the map? John left the hood up; it meant he'd arrive all the sooner.

Another laugh at the outskirts of the crowded village, at the futility of finding the girl amongst the hundreds of people.

He didn't have the width he needed to make a full circle on the narrow road, he'd have to reverse onto the grass.

John turned his head.

# Chapter Eight

*An* old coach wheezed and coughed its way past John with faces at the windows to the car. Several vans and cars followed its black oily wake, a horse and cart, a truck, a couple of horse riders trotted by, the village was starting to empty.

John waited for several minutes while the slow exodus continued. He eased the car forward and manoeuvred around people on the road while watching for the flame red cheeks at the windows of the houses, or the black head of hair in a field with people and stalls. A group of children started to trot alongside him, he accelerated away from them and stopped the car beside a high stone wall, well away from the activity and harm.

He needed a drink and something to eat, but the hotel looked too crowded to try for anything there. Head up to look for the black head of hair as he walked over to the field.

A cup of tea bought off one stall and a scone from another. It was the last one, John sure the small woman almost jumped up and kissed him.

"I see Flora decided to come after all," said the woman to someone behind him.

John followed her eyes to the far end of the field, to someone lying alone on the grass. How many Flora's lived in Clairgowan?

"Ach! Look at that the waste of that." Mrs Stewart shook her head at the untouched scone and full cup of tea left on the stall.

The low sun a slanting spotlight, Flora's blouse pulled tight across her breasts, nipples dark circles under the thin material. Bare feet, ankles crossed, skirt a second skin on her hips, a smudge of dark where it rested in the hollow at the top of her legs.

No wild hair that day, a smooth black cap on her head, a curl of tail behind it. Face pristine, white skin, round cheeks with a blush of pink, not the fiery red of that night. Her closed eyes gave her a peaceful air. Lips still, or was that a smile? John remembered to breathe.

He was stood below the slope, the heat of the sun on his neck, his long shadow over her face.

Lips pressed together, small dimples in the pink of her cheeks. "Ach, couldn't you find another place to cast your shadow?"

The eyes opened, those wonderful eyes, but instead of recognition they narrowed, creases spread up to her brow. John was so intent on finding her he forgot he was the focus of her anger in London, disappointed it might happen again.

A brilliant halo of sun dazzled Flora, a black shape of a head in the centre. She sat up, the black shape moved; a frisson of sparks up her spine, heat suffused her cheeks.

Light casual trousers, a belt, white shirt, the top buttons unfastened so she could see a jumble of ginger hairs. Sleeves rolled up above the elbows, muscular arms, the same coloured hairs, this time an ordered brush in the same direction. Beard and hair golden strands in the light, lips open, uncertain if they should smile.

Flora put a hand out to his arm as he turned and crouched down to sit beside her. Yes! Her fingers touched warm live flesh, other sparks, this time throughout her body.

"Don't!" she exclaimed, "unless you want to walk across the field with two wet patches for the entire world to see."

John stopped his attempt to sit and stayed by her on his hunkers. "What about you?"

Flora knelt and pulled down the back of her skirt. "Ach, these wee pockets have their uses." She pulled her damp knickers out of the pocket of her skirt, a smile, lower lip behind her teeth, a direct look into his eyes.

John laughed, his head back.

Flora saw a line under his beard.

They walked across the field to the road, a silent compliance they would go together.

"How did you find me?"

"A look at the map. I didn't expect to find you."

"So you came all this way not expecting to find me."

"I'm delivering a car to Edinburgh. I decided to take the roundabout route."

"A three hundred mile roundabout route!"

Flora enjoyed his smile. He looked less severe than that night, no angles and shadows on his face, his eyes with a need as strong as hers.

They were at the road; John took Flora's hand to lead her to the car.

"Do you always walk around bare foot?"

"When I'm in a hurry to get away I do."

They both laughed. Their happiness encapsulated them, distancing them from the people around them.

Flora put her eyebrows up at the car, and it was surrounded by children. She laughed at them and clapped her hands. "Get away with ye."

The children laughed back, but they did as they were told and ran off down the road.

John sat inside the car and opened the passenger door. Flora picked up a black leather jacket off the seat, sat beside him and closed the door.

John nodded at the jacket. "Your scarf thing's in there."

Flora unfolded the jacket, pulled the shawl out a pocket and made a sweet smile to John. "All this way just to return it to little Flora."

Faces inches apart, a small smile from John as his face neared Flora's. Both heads turning together to the shouts of the children running back to the car.

The car started with a roar. "Where are we going?" shouted John.

Flora laughed and pointed up to the trees. "Why home James of course."

She must have pulled a small white card out of the jacket pocket with the shawl, picking it up to see 'MASON'S GARAGE' in bold black letters. It confirmed what she had thought all along, that Reg wasn't the owner of the business. The actual owner beside her and trying hard not to run over the future generation of the glen.

Flora put the card back into the jacket and put it behind her seat along with the shawl.

"Is it far?" asked John.

Flora tried to look very serious, lips pursed, brow creased. "Miles and miles, but I'm sure your flash car can manage."

A boy ran after the car because he knew it didn't have far to go. It accelerated away from him; leaving him stood panting with his hands on his knees and laughing at the screech of brakes when the road ran out.

"Here!" exclaimed John ducking his head to look at the house.

He drove the car through the gates, circled the fountain and stopped in front of the large door.

"Yes," laughed Flora, "and it's not as grand as it looks."

Their kiss long and hard after their weeks of waiting. At last they separated, John's face to Flora again, he exclaimed, his head jerking back at the small nip on his bottom lip. Flora laughed, jumped out of the car and ran on the balls of her feet on the gravel to the side of the house.

John jumped out of the car sucking his lip, about to go after Flora he hesitated and turned to check the children hadn't followed them.

"Ach! Can't you can think of something better to do?" Her face at the corner, those wonderful eyes, a smile and she was gone.

John tried not to run, no sign of Flora at the side of the house. He found the open door and walked into another age of oil lamps and times past.

"Tea?" asked Flora throwing a log into the huge grate. She put a hand on the handle of a large black kettle at the side of the fire. Flames roared up the chimney while she stood with eyes wide waiting for his answer.

John laughed, pulled Flora to him and kissed her with a hand around her waist. His other hand found the back of a leg, the indentation at the back of a knee and the soft cool skin inside her thighs. They moved together as they kissed until Flora had her back pressed against the table. She pulled at John's shirt, hands on his skin, legs opening as he pushed himself against her.

Her face moved away to whisper something.

John followed her lips not wanting to lose their sweet contact, her lips moved against his, whispers again, lips to his ear.

"Not here, not here John."

Flora pushed John away, a hand in his. She looked back at him, a smile, eyes wide, a door, stairs, skirt soft against her shape above him, doors, a room, a bed, a rumpled gold cover glossy with sunlight. Flora knelt on the bed with a hand at the band in her hair; the blackness released and bouncing into freedom. John knelt on the bed with her and pulled her blouse up and over her head. Full breasts and dark pink nipples emerged; her smiling face to him, cheeks red and eyes looking into his very soul. She lay back and arched her back while he slipped off her skirt, the black fuzz startling against the milky white of her skin. John put his face to it, relished it, breathed it in, tasted it.

John's hands to his belt, Flora stopped him and pushed him down to the bed. She undressed him, shirt buttons unfastened and pulled from his arms, chest and belly hairs nibbled. John reached for her, Flora pushed him down. Shoes and stockings slipped from his feet, belt unfastened, trousers undone, eased down his legs and off. Pants pulled from his erection, her nose in the dark ginger hairs, testicles kissed and fondled.

"Wait!" A quiet command as John rolled away to his trousers on the floor. He rolled back with a condom in his hand.

Flora's cheeks dimpled. "I see you were expecting more than tea." She took the condom from him; John lay back as she rolled it on and kissed the tip. Flora straddled over his body while she guided him into her.

They were drawn to each other in London, the passing weeks generating a passion neither experienced before.

The brilliant sun cut an oblique shaft of light through the window before it departed from the day. Tiny pendants floated down to the bed while they dozed with arms and legs entwined. They woke, kissed, and enjoyed each other's bodies again.

John's head lifted off the pillow with a start. It was dark with no more than a silvery light between the open curtains, the silence as black as the shadows in the room. He was covered with the warmth of the bedclothes, the space next to him empty, he explored it with a hand, it was still warm. Flora's white shape floated through the open door with a light ting of glass on glass. Her face to John to give him a soft kiss on his lips, he tasted whisky. She knelt on the bed with a bottle and glasses in her hands.

"Do you usually run around the house in the middle of the night with no clothes on?" asked John sitting up. He took the glasses from Flora; she took the top off the bottle, gurgles, the aroma of whisky.

"If I have to put the logs on the fire and shut the outside door to stop wee four legged creatures coming in I do," giggled Flora as she put the bottle onto a bedside table, the bed bouncing as she pulled her legs from under her. She took her glass and saw John look at the open door. "There's no need to worry, no one will wander in."

"It's a big house, but it seems so empty." John cuddled Flora's cool body into him and drank back the whisky. "Do you work here?"

Flora drank her whisky. "I suppose you could say that seeing as we are in the servants' quarters."

"How many servants are there?" asked John.

Flora considered this. "Just the one."

"It seems a large place for one servant," said John. "Do many people live here?"

"Two," replied Flora picking up the bottle, "the auld laird Mungo Ballardine and his daughter."

John nodded. "And you are the daughter."

A kiss from Flora. "And that's for being so clever."

They drank more whisky.

"And where would the laird be?" asked John.

"Where he should be," laughed Flora, "not here."

John laughed, both happy, the whisky helped. Flora nipped at John's stomach; it made him jump and laugh. Flora screeched at John's tickles. Both tried to outdo the other and exhausted each other with laughing, kissing, holding, caressing and gently loving each other before they slipped into a deep relaxed sleep.

A mouth fresh with mint found John's lips. He turned his face from the pillow and returned Flora's quick kisses. Her scent sweet and desirable, cheeks red, wet hair brushed down her back, wearing a cotton blouse and jeans. John pulled her onto the bed and looked down to her face in the bright morning light.

Flora kissed the bridge of his nose. "Do you know you have a bump on your nose?"

John pretended to snarl. "I do not have a bump on my nose."

"And you have a scar from here to here."

Soft kisses on the line below his left ear, they followed it to under his jaw and along to the point of his chin.

"Is that why you have a beard?"

Large brown eyes waited for an answer.

"People see the scar not the person."

John surprised himself, not lifting his head away. The ones physically close enough would remark about it, the girls. If they didn't he knew they were thinking about it, some embarrassed, some pretending they hadn't seen it. Not that it mattered because they wouldn't see him again.

"I think you are a very nice person," said Flora.

"You don't know me."

There it was in the small space between them. After a night of highs, of supreme emotions were they going to know each other? To consider this another surprise for John.

"Did you see a man in the field with a gun?" Flora's solemn face looked up to John. "That was my father; he's notorious for his temper. If he finds you here goodness knows what would happen."

Her eyes were so wide John didn't know if she was joking or not. She slipped away from under him.

"You might have time for a drink of tea before he chases you." A smile before she left the room.

John couldn't remember seeing anyone in the field with a gun, but the thoughts of red faced Scotsman chasing him with a one a good enough impetus to move, and fast. He looked around him as he pulled his clothes on, old wooden furniture, a fireplace set and ready to light. A quick glance out of the window to see the car, fountain and gates.

He tried to find the bathroom, Flora's room at the end of a dim passage. The door opposite led to a man's room with the same kind of old furniture, trousers thrown onto an unmade bed. John more than pleased to see no sign of the occupant. Another room at the top of the stairs looked more feminine with a flowery quilt on the bed; the room opposite, next to Flora's a jumble of furniture, dusty. Flora appeared behind him, led him down the stairs and to the first door in a corridor lit up by two windows. It was a bathroom with a huge cast iron bath where Flora must have bathed occupying most of the room, her sweet smell in the damp air.

"The man with the gun seems to be taking his time." John sat at the kitchen table with his back to the roaring fire enjoying bacon, eggs and toast and the promised tea.

Flora smiled over the table; she was sat with her chin on a hand watching him eat. "He'll be recovering from yesterday along with everyone else. If you go now no one will need to know you were here all night."

John nodded, drained the last of his tea and checked his watch, and grimaced at time. It wasn't even 6 o'clock, but he should have been back at the garage by then, and the car was due to be delivered the day before. He thought an hour or two, if he did find Flora, deliver the car and head straight back to Birmingham on the next available train. Why it hadn't worked out like that easy to understand. Flora looked fresh and lovely with her drying hair fluffing up around her shining face, her red cheeks inviting him to put a hand over the table and touch them.

Flora stood, walked around the table, took John's hand and led him away from the roaring fire.

They walked hand in hand to the car, the trees whispering around them in the early morning air.

John put his arms around Flora, his tactics for his usual speedy departures forgotten.

She put her face to his shirt, her warm moist breath reaching through to his skin. "The man with the gun."

True or not, she wanted him to go, and he had to go. John about to get into the car when he remembered the shawl. He reached behind the seat for it and handed it to Flora, the circle started in London complete. She took it and walked away without a word and around the corner of the house before he started the car.

# Chapter Nine

*Elizabeth* Montgomery put her head back against the seat, closed her eyes and listened to the train roar its way north. Sixty years old and there she was on another of her solitary pilgrimages to Clairgowan.

Elizabeth was a 14 year old girl when she first met her half cousin Mungo Ballardine the handsome young laird of Clairgowan, and fell in love with that wonderful smile.

Not that her sister knew of it, the beautiful tempestuous Beatrice whose dazzling light always outshone her younger plainer sister.

Elizabeth sighed and wept in private while she watched Mungo chase and marry Beatrice two years later. Mungo left his new bride to fight in the war to end all wars and Elizabeth moved into Clairgowan House as a companion to Beatrice. They were the days of servants and the house full of laughter. It didn't last long with the two sisters puzzled at why they had to pay for food and bills. But you don't discuss such mundane issues with a hero fresh home from the war, or ask him why the servants had to go one by one, or why he had to sell off half of the great Ballardine Estate. Poor Beatrice begged Elizabeth to stay with her while she struggled to cope with such a large house and a husband who fumbled and bumbled his way through more losses.

Mungo became increasingly dependant on the two sisters' inheritances from their grandparents to prop up the estate, but Elizabeth's love for him still remained true. At last Beatrice gave birth to her longed for baby Alasdair, and it was then when Elizabeth realised Mungo knew of her infatuation, how he fostered it with his smile. Elizabeth left Beatrice with hopes for a better future with her new baby and fled to London desperate to find a new life, and a new love. The new life easy in the high-spirited London of the twenties, a new love impossible because of Mungo Ballardine's tenacious hold over her.

Time cut Elizabeth free from her obsession, to leave her with the narrow life of a middle aged spinster. Her friends dispersing to live their new lives of children and grandchildren until she was forced to depend on the 'tea ladies' to occupy her empty days.

It was Beatrice and Alasdair who first drew Elizabeth back to Clairgowan, with the added attraction of Mungo, but that all changed along with the passing years and heartbreaks. Now she visited Clairgowan to break up her dull life and to see Flora. Fiery, exuberant Flora, the same as Beatrice before Mungo changed her into a fretful, bitter woman. Elizabeth hoped Flora would escape the confines of Clairgowan House when Robert left. She often tried to tease her away herself, but no, Flora was still there, the last one to be held in her father's grasp, Mungo and his helpless air demanding loyalty and support.

The juddering train and screeching wheels told Elizabeth she had arrived. She opened her eyes to see Flora laughing and waving through the steam and smoke. Hair pulled back in a pony tail, sandals, blouse, the tight jeans young people insisted on wearing, Elizabeth's heart lifting at the beautiful woman she had become.

"Aunt Elizabeth!"

Flora ran up to Elizabeth and gave her a tight hug as she stepped from the carriage. She picked up the suitcase and linked arms with

Elizabeth while they walked along the platform, hissing steam around their legs as the train huffed and puffed its way past them out of the station.

"I see you put a special order in for our wonderful Scottish sunshine," said Elizabeth.

"Of course," replied Flora, "the very best for my very best aunt."

"Your only aunt," laughed Elizabeth.

The old joke laughed at as they walked to the bus stop outside the station.

Flora put the suitcase onto the ground and peered down the road. "Ach! The bus is always late."

An over-bright smile flashed at Elizabeth, a sure sign something was wrong. That was why she confined her visits to a week at a time, the never ending problems of Clairgowan House always chasing her away to her small safe world.

Flora full of her usual chit chat while the bus trundled its way out of town and through the glen. The last stop at the stone wall in the village where the road widened a little and where the bus would make half a dozen manoeuvres before making its slow journey back to town. Flora strode up the incline with the suitcase and left Elizabeth to follow at a slower pace.

Flora waited for Elizabeth at the gates, face solemn. "We have to go to Inverness to see Mr Boyle the solicitor." She looked at the ground, a shrug. "Well, father has to see him, but you know how he is, conveniently ignoring it."

They walked past the fountain.

"Would Mr.Brown take your father in his car?" asked Elizabeth. "He might agree to go if he did."

The suitcase plonked onto the gravel. "It's going to be humiliating enough without having an audience," retorted Flora. "We know it will be bad news."

Elizabeth pleased at the spark of anger, a reminder of how Beatrice used to be.

"Will you try to persuade him to go Aunt Elizabeth?" asked Flora. "You're the only one he listens to."

Elizabeth gave an exaggerated sigh. "Of course I will Flora." Her words put a smile on Flora's face, the reason why she agreed.

Flora picked up the suitcase. "And you wouldn't believe it; auld Mungo's had a bath. I hope you feel honoured. He usually reserves a bath for very special occasions or attending the kirk." Mungo tidying himself for Elizabeth's visits another old joke. "And a shave." Eyebrows up at Elizabeth as Flora walked away. "If I didn't know better Aunt Elizabeth I'd say there's something going on between you two."

Elizabeth thought of the time when those words would have gladdened her heart. She followed Flora around the corner and into the kitchen.

Mungo rose from his chair and smiled at Elizabeth.

Elizabeth became wise to that smile many years before, how it could beguile you into being a devoted follower. Not that it stopped her experiencing pleasure at first sight of the smile, the feeling always transient, reality not far behind.

"And what have you brought for me this time Elizabeth?"

The customary 'me' with Mungo, no greetings or enquiries asked of Elizabeth.

She returned the smile. "An embroidered tablecloth Mungo."

Flora carried the suitcase to the door at the far end of the kitchen. "Oh, that's lovely Aunt Elizabeth, thank you."

"Make tea for your aunt," snapped Mungo, the smile gone as he sat back down to his chair.

Flora shook her head. "I will when I've taken Aunt Elizabeth's

suitcase to her room." Poking her tongue out before she went through the door.

"That girl is cheekier everyday," muttered Mungo.

Elizabeth sat on Flora's chair. "Flora is a young woman now Mungo, not a girl.

"If she had behaved..." started Mungo.

"Stop it Mungo!" exclaimed Elizabeth. "You have had your say concerning Robert and Flora for over a year now."

Mungo shook his head at the fire.

"Flora tells me you have to see Mr Boyle the solicitor," said Elizabeth.

"It has nothing to do with her," muttered Mungo to the fire. "She snatched the letter out of my hand and read it before I could stop her."

The years poor Beatrice had to do that.

"And when is this appointment for?" asked Elizabeth.

Mungo spoke to the fire. "Friday. A week today."

The day Elizabeth was due to return to London, which Mungo would know. He turned his face away from the fire to smile at her.

"I will go if you go with me Elizabeth."

Elizabeth shook her head. "No Mungo. It is Flora who should go with you. But I will stay until Sunday if you agree to go."

Mungo smiled at the fire.

# Chapter Ten

*The* week soon went by, Elizabeth stood at the door on Friday morning to watch father and daughter leave. A pony tail down Flora's back, and despite Mungo's protests wearing flat sandals and dressed in a cotton skirt and blouse. Her father dressed in his best tweed suit, looking distinguished and in control, how the laird should be. Mungo could always give an impression of competence and determination if needed, and fool everyone not close to him.

It was going to be a long day for them with the bus ride to town, the train to Inverness and the journey to Mr Boyle's office, all to be repeated again on their return to Clairgowan.

Elizabeth picked up her embroidery, sat on Flora's chair and prepared herself for the long wait. She stopped her sewing when her fingers started to ache and found a duster for something to do. Stood with it in her hand at the kitchen door at bottom of the stairs looking down the threadbare carpet to the end of the corridor to the large door leading to the main house, the door Mungo locked the day Beatrice left.

Two smaller door stood at the side of the corridor facing the two windows. The first led to the bathroom, the second to a small room which had been turned into a study. Elizabeth opened the study door and smiled at the dusty room, Flora mustn't have been in there for days.

Elizabeth busied herself around the room, dusting glass fronted cupboards full of books, the chairs by the fireplace and small tables. A large old desk stood in front of a window, she sat on the leather chair behind it and picked up Alasdair's photograph. His eyes looked directly at the camera, uniform, peaked cap, his wide smile showing the world the bright future ahead of him. A stranger might say the photograph was a younger version of Mungo, but there was so much more in that smiling face. Alasdair had the verve of the Montgomery's, dynamic, clever, reliable, the opposite of his father. Beatrice saw Alasdair as the saviour of the Ballardine Estate, but it wasn't to be. Another war and another hero, and destiny decided Clairgowan House was due no more than one hero to live within its walls. Flora arrived so late in Beatrice's life her worn out mother saw her as another burden to carry. Poor little Flora left to grieve alone for the death of her much-loved brother.

Beatrice left her husband and daughter two years later, she couldn't cope with her loss and the hopes Alasdair took with him. The first Elizabeth knew of this a letter from Beatrice to say she intended to live in France, where her son's body lay. She also enclosed a sum of money and asked Elizabeth to give it to Flora, a practise she was to continue over the years. Elizabeth dashed to Clairgowan to find a 9 year old girl responsible for the care of Clairgowan House and her father.

Elizabeth wiped her tears off the glass and put the photograph back down to the desk. She finished her dusting, returned to the kitchen and prepared a stew. Then she put it into the oven and waited for father and daughter to return.

They arrived late in the afternoon. Mungo was fit and spry for his age, but he looked exhausted as he slumped down to his chair.

"Trailing me all of that way," he grumbled. "When the man could have sent a letter."

"And we all know where your letters finish off Mungo," said Elizabeth sitting on Flora's chair.

"Mr Boyle says father owes two thousand pounds," said Flora. "That's why he needed to see him." She breathed in the aroma from the oven and smiled at Elizabeth for preparing the meal. Her face over to Mungo as she spread one of Elizabeth's embroidered tablecloths over the table. "You did say two thousand pounds didn't you father?"

"I can speak for myself girl," retorted Mungo. "Two thousand, four thousand. What difference does it make?" He looked at Elizabeth. "Mr Boyle said I will lose the house if I do not put money in every now and again. But I cannot put money in if I have none. And he said it might be best if Flora found somewhere to live, but I told him I need her here to cook and clean for me."

"I suppose it's nice to be needed even if it is to cook and clean," remarked Flora as she arranged knives and forks over the table.

Elizabeth shook her head at Flora to stop her and leant over to Mungo. "What about Mr Brown? He has always helped you out in the past Mungo."

Mungo turned to the fire. "Bob Brown has already loaned me over one thousand pounds."

Elizabeth and Flora looked at each other.

"And he says his wife has forbid him to give me more." Mungo shook his head at the fire. "What kind of man is that?" A quick look at Elizabeth. "I would fight them if Alasdair was here Elizabeth. I would fight them to the death to save the house for Alasdair."

Flora turned from a cupboard with a handful of plates and clashed them down to the table. "Thank you for that father," she shouted. "I suppose I'm not worth fighting for."

"Your father did not mean that Flora," said Elizabeth looking at Mungo for confirmation.

Mungo turned his face to the fire.

"Oh yes he did Aunt Elizabeth," shouted Flora. "I always knew he'd rather it was Alasdair here instead of me."

Eyes grey flints of anger as Mungo looked over to Flora. "And what use are you to me?" he shouted. "All you do is get yourself a bad reputation. The village is full of tittle-tattle over you bringing strange men to the house." He nodded at Flora's open mouth. "Yes I have known all along."

"I have not brought strange men to the house," shouted Flora. "I brought one friend."

"Alasdair would not have brought disgrace to the Ballardine name," shouted Mungo. "And he would see to me which is more than you have done."

"What do you mean?" asked Flora shaking her head.

"Robert," bellowed Mungo. "If you had married Robert and not sent him packing I would not be in this situation."

"I did not send Robert packing," screamed Flora. "He went of his own accord."

"There!" Mungo looked at Elizabeth. "What man would put up with that temper?"

"And I'll tell you now I'm pleased Robert went," screamed Flora, cheeks flaming, ponytail shook from side to side. "I'm pleased." She ran out of the room and up the stairs.

Mungo rose from his chair.

Elizabeth looked up to him thinking he was going after Flora.

The smile down to her face. "That should teach her not to bring men here. Would you care to join me for a dram Elizabeth?"

"No, I would not care to join you Mungo," replied Elizabeth

hurrying over to the door. "Flora has stood by you for all of these years and this is the way you thank her. And she is not a bad person because she brings someone to the house that is not of your choosing and therefore of no benefit to you. One day you will be alone. And when you are you can look back at this moment and know why."

She found Flora lying on her bed looking up the ceiling, her face white except for two pink spots at the top of her cheeks. Elizabeth sat by her and took her hand.

"I'm good enough to cook and clean for him but I'm not good enough to fight for." Flora's chest heaved with the effort of speaking. "He wouldn't even allow me to go into Mr Boyle's office with him." She turned her face to Elizabeth. "He blames me for everything Aunt Elizabeth. I think he even blames me for mother leaving."

"I am sure that is not true Flora," replied Elizabeth. "Your father is tired, that is why he spoke as he did. And I cannot see him losing Clairgowan House for the sake of two thousand pounds. He will find a way out of it; he always has in the past." She rubbed Flora's hand. "But I do think you should take Mr Boyle's advice and find somewhere to live. You know you are always welcome to stay with me in my little flat in London."

The thoughts of sitting with the 'tea ladies' pressed Flora down to the bed. "No." She shook her head and tried to smile at her aunt. "You needn't worry Aunt Elizabeth. I'll be fine."

Elizabeth kissed Flora on the brow and returned to the kitchen to find Mungo sat by the fire with a glass of whisky in his hand.

He lifted the glass up to Elizabeth. "Are we going to eat your special stew Elizabeth, or are we going to leave it to dry out in the oven?"

# Chapter Eleven

*Flora* lifted her aunt's suitcase into the carriage.

Elizabeth hadn't seen her until it was time to leave for her train. Mungo his usual self when Elizabeth walked down to the kirk with him that morning, complaining at how Flora always refused to go with him.

"Remember Flora, I would love to have you with me in London."

"I know, thank you Aunt Elizabeth."

"And this friend of yours?"

Flora shook her head.

Elizabeth didn't want to pry. She pressed money into Flora's hand and kissed her on the cheek.

"You shouldn't Aunt Elizabeth, you can't afford it."

Elizabeth didn't say the money wasn't from her. She stepped into the carriage and turned to Flora. "It will pay for your fare if you do decide to join me."

Doors slammed shut as the guard made his way to the rear of the carriages. A shrill whistle to start the train on its slow progress out of the station.

Flora waved at her aunt at the window until she was out of sight,

folded her arms and walked to the bus stop looking down to her feet. 'I would fight them to the death to save the house for Alasdair' her reward for walking way from John. She didn't dare look back, because if she had she would have jumped into the car and left with him. Just a few weeks before and her life was so certain, she was so sure she had no choice but to stay.

Her arms still folded while Flora leant against the bus stop and prepared herself for a long wait, the bus service always sporadic on a Sunday. John returning to Clairgowan to see her was all she could hope for. She kicked at nothing in particular on the ground. And why should she have to wait for him?

Flora looked at the money in her hand. She had a little hidden in her room, away from her father who would always find something to spend it on. It meant she could go to John, if she knew where to find him.

She looked over the road to the Seed Merchant's office where she used to work. Flora's first and only step into the world of employment, and a life separate from her father and Robert.

Robert laughed and said she wouldn't last long. Her father said it was demeaning for the laird's daughter to find work as an office junior and she had plenty to occupy herself with at Clairgowan House. He meant she wouldn't be there to cook his meals, not that he objected to the occasional treats her tiny wages brought into the house.

She soon caught on with the paperwork and even considered taking typing lessons, and Robert was right she didn't last long. The winter took care of that, a month into her new job and the first heavy snowfall blocked the road through the glen. It took several days to clear it, and it happened again and again until she was taken aside and told she would have to take lodgings in town during the week if she wanted to retain her position. Flora couldn't leave her father alone for so long so of course she slammed her way out shouting they could keep their job, and stopped any hopes of her returning in the future. Her father made no comment as to why she stopped working. Robert laughed and said he told her so.

Flora loved her job; she was often complemented on her friendly approach to the customers, especially on the switchboard, and her good memory. If a file couldn't be found the call would go up; 'Ask Flora!'

Flora's head snapped up. The card! She was so excited at seeing John she couldn't remember if she read it before pushing it back into his jacket. Birmingham! Kath said that at the dancehall. Or did she read it on the card?

The bus eventually arrived, a pensive Flora at the window. She closed her eyes to concentrate and the card could have been in her hand by the time she jumped off the bus at Clairgowan. Except for the telephone number, her memory not up to that. It didn't matter because it was going to be a surprise.

Flora laughed and ran up to the house; she could imagine John's face…

# Chapter Twelve

*Flora* took special care with her father's breakfast that Monday morning. Toast, bacon and eggs they way he liked them and put into the oven to stay warm. As soon as she heard the water running from the range, which meant he was out of bed and in the bathroom, the teapot filled and put onto the table along with the food. A quick look at her note, her third attempt, finishing off with, 'YOU WILL HAVE TO FIND SOMEONE BETTER THAN ME TO COOK AND CLEAN FOR YOU. SOMEONE WORTH FIGHTING FOR'. She put the note onto the table, put the sugar basin on the top of it, picked up her cotton duffle bag and ran out of the house.

She broke her journey at Inverness to find something special to wear for John, and to match her mood. Wandering around the shops until she chose a sleeveless white cotton dress printed with large blocks of bright and pale lemon. It had a deep square neckline, a wide belt to match and a skirt so full it flounced up around her legs. Her cream high heels and a white Alice band in her loose hair the perfect finish to her summery look.

Flora decided her new life would mean new everything else. She boarded the train to resume her journey to Birmingham and put her cotton duffle bag onto the seat beside her. It contained her purse, a few essentials and the clothing she wore when she left her old life at Clairgowan.

She knew she looked good, her buoyancy helped by the looks from a young man in the carriage. It became a bit of a game. Flora would look over to him, he'd turn his head and stare at the window with the tips of his ears flushing to a strawberry pink and Flora would stare at her window and try not to giggle.

Birmingham! Hurrying out of the sooty Victorian station eager to start her new life, meet new people, make new friends, find work. They were all out there in front of her, John the best, the first part of her new life.

Her steps faltered a little as she walked into the busy city and hectic traffic. She didn't have enough money for a taxi, and everyone seemed to be leaving the city at the same time. Flora pushed her way through the crowds to a bus, feeling a foreigner in a foreign land with the different languages, skins and clothing around her. The conductor shook his head at the name of the street she needed, perspiration on her brow as she battled her way through the throng to another bus, and another. A nod at last, the crowded bus drew away with Flora hanging onto the strap and constantly checking with the conductor so she wouldn't miss her stop. He called out the name of the street; she jumped off the bus and returned the broad smile on his dark face.

The bus roared off down the main road, Flora turned full circle.

She was stood at the bottom of a long line of shops. At the other side of the street houses, brick walls, windows, doors, no sign of a garage, and she realised why the city was emptying when she saw most of the shops were closed. Flora walked past the shops and berated herself for spending so much time in Inverness, and money. She saw cards in a newsagent's window advertising rooms to let; if the garage was closed she'd have to find somewhere to stay. The prices made her grimace, twisting her bag in her hands and studying the cards as though one would magically change to a lower price. Several stipulated, 'NO BLACKS. NO IRISH.' Flora wondered if being Scottish would be a problem. She turned away from the window to see a car come out of a gap in the buildings opposite her, crossing over to it to find it led to a narrow cobbled street and a terrace of old Victorian houses. They towered up behind high brick walls and gates painted in different colours.

Flora walked past the gates; she had to watch her high heels because they kept slipping between the cobbles and had to jump back when a pushchair was almost wheeled into her.

"Soo sorry."

A smile as an apology from a young woman with small gold rings through the side of her nose and a red coloured mark on her brow. She was dressed in a sea green sari with the silk pulled over her head, her pale skin covered in large dark freckles. A baby was in the pushchair, two small boys holding onto the sides, one a little older than the other, the children darker than the woman.

"Mason's garage?" asked Flora.

"Soo sorry." The young woman smiled again.

"You've come the wrong way down. There's some garages down there," said the older boy in perfect English. The accent with a twang Flora heard on the bus, a nasal emphasis when he said 'wrong'.

He pointed to behind her; she'd turned left instead of right.

A couple of houses past the gap and the street changed to rows of small workshops facing each other. Some of the occupants were pulling the shutters down, wolf whistles at Flora and shouts of, "This way love." It stopped her looking inside the open shutters for John. She walked up to a man in a turban loading tins of paint into a van. He had a thick bushy beard with the widest moustache Flora had ever seen.

"Mason's garage?" she asked him.

A flashing smile amongst the hair before the turbaned head turned to look up to a white board with 'MASON'S GARAGE' on it in bold black letters, the same as the card. The board was situated above three shutters, the first shutter half way down, the third closed, the middle one pushed all the way to the top.

Flora swallowed hard, held her bag behind her to do something with her hands and walked through the middle shutter.

All she could see was equipment and cars, then movement as someone walked out of the dark at the back of the garage. It was Reg, the supposed to be owner of the business. His first reaction at seeing Flora a very unpleasant smirk, followed by open mouthed recognition and a look over to a car behind the half open shutter. The car had the bonnet open with a light inside and someone in overalls and heavy boots beside it with his head deep inside the car. John!

Flora could have stood there until eternity that moment so wonderful.

Reg went over to the car.

Flora noticed he walked all the way to the other side so John wouldn't see her.

Reg looked down at John. "I'm off now."

Flora saw the head come up, the red hair.

John looked up to Reg and pushed himself away from the car. He leant down to pick up an oily piece of cloth when a flash of bright colour caught his eye. Lifting his head to see Flora stood with her feet together and hands behind her back and giving him a wide smile.

It wasn't the smart man in an evening suit in London, or the casually dressed man at Clairgowan. Flora knew this was the real John, face with the sheen of hard work, grubby, the smell of oil as he walked up to her wiping his hands on the cloth. Not sure if he was about to smile or ask a question.

She opted for the question. "A card fell out of your jacket."

"I'm going now," said Reg hurrying over.

"You've already told me that," said John. He looked at Flora while he took a wallet from under the back of his overalls and gave Reg a pound note out of it.

Reg pushed the note into his jacket pocket and walked out to the street. "I'll see you tomorrow John."

Reg hadn't spoken a word to Flora, and neither had John.

He walked over to the car he'd been working on while pushing the wallet back under his overalls and looked down to the engine.

Flora swallowed hard.

John turned as though he suddenly remembered she was there. He nodded at her dress. "Not the best thing to be wearing in a garage."

Flora took her bag from behind her and lifted it in the air, her smile a bit of an effort. "I can always change."

John looked up some wooden steps against the wall behind him. No rail, chunks of wood scuffed away, a small platform at the front of a door. "It's not very good up there," he warned.

"Ach, it can't be all that bad," responded Flora. She pulled her dress to her and manoeuvred her way past a grimy sink and a chair pushed against a table at the bottom of the steps. The table covered with a clutter of papers, an electric kettle covered in oily fingerprints, dirty mugs and spoons and a telephone. A hand on the wall to help her walk up the uneven wood.

"I'll be around thirty minutes," said John.

Flora dismissed with his head down to the car.

She opened the door to a small narrow room with a wooden floor and a bare electric bulb hanging off centre. Behind the door a narrow bed against a grubby wall, pillows, a sheet and blanket half on the floor. A dirty window faced the door at the other end of the room, curtains of indeterminate colour drooping from an overstretched wire. Under the window a sink full of dirty crockery and cutlery, and under the sink a rubbish bin with more food wrappings on the floor than in it. Flora held her dress from the sink and looked out of window to see the shops. At the side of the window a gas water heater and a wall cupboard. A tall cupboard stood against the wall, it was a wardrobe with John's clothes inside. Flora ran a hand over them, several suits, they looked expensive, well tailored, one the evening suit he wore that night in London. Several pairs of trousers, light and dark, lots of jeans and the black leather jacket he had with him at Clairgowan. A line of shirts on hangers, all white, other clothing on the shelves, a neat row of plain ties on a hanger, shoes placed side by side at the bottom. A door beside the wardrobe led to a shower, sink, toilet, another water heater, towels over a rail, a clutter of soaps and toiletries on a shelf under a mirror. Then a wooden table pushed against the wall, more a desk and covered in papers, invoices, receipts, letters, a chair pushed sideways to it. A grey filing cabinet underneath it on the floor, locked, and full circle to the door she came in.

Flora picked up the bedclothes and saw a small rumpled up rug on the floor. She straightened it with her foot; for it to bounce back to the shape she started with.

She tidied the bed, took her dress off, put it on a spare hanger and hung it beside John's clothes, high heels placed next to his shoes. Her cardigan, jeans, blouse and flat shoes taken out of her bag and put on. Then she sat on the chair to wait, pulling her cardigan tight around her.

A car started and stopped below her in the garage, the telephone rang and stopped at John's voice. Another man's voice, the car again, the car moving away, the screech of metal and a loud clash, another screech and another loud clash. The long silence made Flora think John had left the garage; she looked out of the window, no one in sight. She turned to face the door at the sound of footsteps on the wooden steps. John's 30 minutes had turned out to be more than an hour.

He opened the door, overalls off, white vest, jeans, a wide belt with a buckle, shoes instead of the heavy boots.

"I had to finish the car. I said he could pick it up tonight." John walked over to Flora and put his hands at either side of her on the sink. "And you are certainly a surprise."

Flora looked up to his eyes, the green less intense, they looked tired, and the straight line of his mouth didn't say it was a nice surprise.

John pushed himself way from the sink. "I must have a shower." He stripped off; he looked lean and muscular, and went to the shower room, the sounds of the heater and running water.

Flora joined him a few seconds later; John turned to her the water coursing down his face and body. He pulled her to him and kissed her, the passion they had at Clairgowan had finally returned.

Their bodies warm and damp from the shower while they dozed on the bed in each other's arms.

John kissed Flora on the brow, jumped off the bed and pulled his clothes on. "Come on then." He grabbed a shirt from the wardrobe. "Are you going to lie there and starve?"

"Where are we going?" Flora followed John down the steps buttoning her blouse.

"To the best place to get food around here, the fish and chip shop." John led Flora to a door at the back of the garage and a small carpeted office; it was bare except for a desk and chair. Another door opened to the street. They ran over to the other side hand in hand, as two lovers would. Returning with their warm parcels and eating the greasy food out of the paper while they sat on the bed.

John took Flora's paper from her, scrunched it up with his and threw the papers over to the bin under the sink, and missed. He lay Flora down to the bed with him and cuddled her into him. She had her back to the wall and would have been more comfortable in the small space with her clothes and shoes off and under the bedclothes, but she snuggled into John happy and content just to be there.

John pulled her to him. "It's getting late. I'll get the car out and drop you off."

Her long deep breaths didn't help, Flora sure she could feel the bed vibrate like a drum along with her beating heart. Long deep breaths again before she pushed John away, stood and stepped on him to get off the bed.

"That hurt," he shouted.

"Good!" shouted Flora. "And you can stay right there because I wouldn't let you drop me off anywhere." She clashed the wardrobe door open so hard she almost took it off its hinges.

John jumped off the bed. "You didn't expect to stay did you?"

"No," screamed Flora. "Of course I didn't expect to stay. Why would I think a silly thing like that?" She couldn't find her dress and shoes, grabbing at anything in front of her and throwing shirts, jeans, suits and ties over her shoulder.

"Stop that," shouted John trying to catch them. "You'll dirty everything."

"Good," screamed Flora. She hadn't brushed her hair since the shower and she'd lost her Alice band. Cheeks blazing, hair falling over her face as she turned and flung John's shoes at him.

He ducked out of the way of the missiles, grabbed hold of Flora, turned her to him and held her still with his hands on her shoulders. "You can see you can't stay here Flora. I'll take you to the station so you can go back home. I'll wait with you until there's a train."

The day had swung Flora from supreme heights to devastating lows, and it left her feeling sick and exhausted. It was a struggle but she succeeded in lifting John's hands with her shoulders. "No. I'm not going back home. I'll find somewhere to stay and look for a job tomorrow." Flora didn't know if she had the strength to open the door and go down the steps.

She sat on the bed while John gathered up his clothes and shoes. "I'm sorry if I hurt you."

"I'll survive," said John. He put the clothes and shoes back into the wardrobe, checked everything and turned to Flora to see her lying on the bed fast asleep.

John wrapped the bedcovers around her and lay beside to her with a hand under his head. He watched the evening light change to the glow of the street lamps and saw a spectre glide across the ceiling and down a wall. The car passed beneath the window a second later, on its way to create other ghosts in other rooms.

John looked at Flora and gently brushed her hair away from her peaceful face. The other girl had dark hair, more of a brown than the black of Flora's, a neighbour's daughter, little more than a child. How she used to flirt with him and how he used to laugh at her antics.

They were kind people, her parents, the neighbours; they gave John an old three wheeler Morgan left to decay and rot away in their barn. He spent most of his time in that barn, to get away from the pity, and the inquisitive ones who came to see the severity of the red puckered slash. John saw how eyes were always drawn to the scar, in moments of madness he imagined people were talking to the scar.

The girl called into the barn to watch him working on the Morgan, for a few minutes, he didn't see her again.

It took John two years to restore the Morgan. During that time he had plastic surgery and grew a beard to hide the line the scar had become, walking out of that barn for the last time with his future fixed in his mind.

John worked long and hard to reach the next step towards that future and hadn't allowed anything or anyone to distract him, until then. But he hadn't met the beautiful distraction of Flora before, and he was the one responsible for her lying beside him because he started it all by going to Scotland to find her.

He must have slept. It was shortly after midsummer, opening his eyes to the early false dawn casting a grey light on the glow of the street lamps.

John missed the true dawn; because he was down in the garage working on the cars he intended to finish before Flora disturbed him.

# Chapter Thirteen

*Flora* sat on the edge of the bed and grimaced down at her crumpled clothes. The bed tidied and rug straightened, which bounced back to its original state. Hair brushed, toilet, teeth and face washed and hair brushed again. Doing anything rather than think of the tedious incidentals of having little money and nowhere to go.

A hand in the wall cupboard for something to eat, to find it contained the dust on her fingertips. She rinsed out the least dirty mug in the sink to realise there wasn't anything to make a drink with or even a kettle. Flora clashed the mug down, threw the door back and stamped down the steps.

The shutters closed, the lights on. John with his head down to a car at the far end of the garage.

"It's disgusting in that room," shouted Flora walking up to him. "And I couldn't find anything to eat or drink."

John pushed himself up from the car. "If I knew you were coming I might have tidied up."

Flora hesitated; she hadn't expected such an amiable response.

John looked at his watch, his hands covered in oil. "It's seven o'clock. The baker's sell a mean bacon sandwich and they should be

83

open by now." He nodded down to the car. "I'm finished here. If you go and buy a few for our breakfast I'll make a drink while you're out."

Flora's stomach told her how long it was since the fish and chips, but she couldn't spare the money to buy sandwiches for herself never mind John.

"Newly baked buns fresh from the oven," tormented John. "And they sell sausage sandwiches."

Flora swallowed the saliva in her mouth. "I'm not hungry," she lied, and knew she said it a little bit too loud.

"I am," said John. "And I'll pay for them."

Pride took second place to hunger and it meant Flora wouldn't have to leave the garage so soon, which meant more time with John. "I suppose I could go for you." She tried to sound reluctant.

"I'll have to get at my wallet." John looked for a cloth to wipe his hands on.

"I'll get it." Flora unfastened the top of his overalls before John could stop her and reached around him to get to the back pocket of his jeans. Taking great care her cheek touched the warmth of his vest and not the buckle on his belt. Cursing the injustice of the wad of notes in the wallet she took out two 10 shilling notes.

"I must be buying a lot of sandwiches," said John.

"I'll buy some cleaning stuff. I'll clean the place up in exchange for me staying the night," said Flora, a little bit of pride still there. Aware of a deep breath on her cheek while returning the wallet to the back pocket.

John smiled into Flora's face as she fastened up the overalls. "You needn't have undone them there's an opening at the side."

"Ach, and get oil all over me," laughed Flora. She rushed over to the office door. "How many shall I buy?"

"As many as we can eat," said John walking over to the sink to wash his hands. "Pull the latch back on the door or you won't be able to get back in." And shouting at Flora's back as she disappeared through the door. "You'll find the baker's next to the chip shop."

John smiled at Flora playing games. She hadn't brought much with her in the way of clothes and it was obvious she didn't have enough money to pay for the sandwiches. He washed his hands and pushed up a screeching shutter, the fresh air and bright sunshine of the new day flooding into the garage. About to fill the kettle he looked up the door at top of the steps thinking of the one girl who'd been in that room before Flora.

She returned with the post off the office floor and two paper bags of sandwiches.

Two steaming mugs stood waiting on the table.

"I'm going to be eating a lot," remarked John. He sat on the steps, took the letters from Flora and threw them onto the clutter of papers on the table.

"I realised how hungry I was when I was in the baker's." Flora sat on the chair by the table and peered into the bags. "Bacon or sausage? I bought three of each."

"Bacon," said John. "The sausage has a habit of shooting out of the bun."

Flora gave John his bag. The two of them took a bite out of their sandwiches at the same time, both trying not to laugh with their mouths full when the sausage tried to escape out of Flora's bun.

She swallowed down her mouthful. "The other shops aren't open yet. I'll have to buy the cleaning stuff later."

"See Jagroop next door," said John when he finished his sandwich. "He should have some."

"The man with the turban," nodded Flora. She picked up a mug, black tea and no sign of milk and sugar. Screwing her face up as she sipped at the scalding liquid, it tasted wonderful.

"You'll have to keep your eyes open for Jagroop," said John, a hand in his bag for another sandwich. "He's a busy man. He owns his own chain of shops so he's in and out all day. He uses next door as storage."

"What are the other places used for?" asked Flora. She started on her second sandwich, more care with her first bite this time.

"Another couple of garages," said John. "I specialise in engines and restorations. And anything else to earn a penny, joinery, storage, machine shops, builders, decorators, metal work, a bike repair shop."

"So I should be able to find a job," said Flora. Not having enough money to stay anywhere to be worried about later.

The tea soon gone. Flora filled the kettle and switched it on. She couldn't eat her third sandwich, holding up her bag to see if John wanted it.

He shook his head as he took a bite out of the last of his sandwiches.

Flora scrunched up the top of the paper bag and put it at the back of the table to take with her later. She found a packet of tea bags and fussed around making the tea so she wouldn't have to think of later, and it was another way of spending more time with John.

The telephone rang just as she put fresh mugs of tea onto the table.

John grabbed for his mug to wash down the contents of his bulging cheeks.

Flora picked up the telephone. "Mason's garage." Her response bright and welcoming, a few seconds silence while she listened. "Of course." She held the telephone away from her mouth and looked at John. "It's Hilda the midwife, she says her car sounds poorly and would you take a look at it."

John nodded and took a drink of tea.

"Yes, when would…" said Flora back to the telephone, and with a look at John. "Tomorrow morning at seven before you start your rounds."

Another nod from John along with another drink of tea.

"Yes, that will be fine Hilda. Goodbye." Flora put the telephone down, grimaced at the oil on her hands and wiped them on the least dirty towel at the sink. She found a diary and pen amongst the clutter on the table and entered Hilda's name. "Would you like me to tidy these?" She picked up some of the papers and arranged them into a neat pile.

It surprised John at how capable Flora looked and how well she dealt with the telephone call. "You can put them on the desk upstairs. I'll have to sit down one night and get them all up to date."

The telephone again, Flora answered it. John finished his sandwich and tea and stood beside her while she checked an entry in the diary with him and had a little chat with the caller. He understood why they would like to talk to the friendly voice.

"I'll sort some of the paperwork if you want me to," said Flora to the table, more time with John. "I'm not very experienced, but I can always ask if I'm stuck."

Updating his paperwork meant John sitting up all night, several nights in fact.

"Where is everything, your books and ledgers?" Flora at the papers and the telephone again, she looked in control, not at the least anxious with the constant interruptions.

"In the cabinet up in the room," said John, "It's locked." Taking the keys out of his jeans pocket before Flora had the chance to.

She laughed, took them out of his hand and ran up the steps. Out of the door a few minutes later with books and the mountain of work off the desk balanced in front of her.

The noise and bustle of the start of the day, the telephone, cars picked up and delivered. John found he could get through his work a lot quicker with Flora answering the telephone and the car owners going to her to pay their bills, a pleasant change from the constant interruptions.

The paperwork was hopelessly out of date; all Flora could hope to do was arrange it into some kind of order. She took her cardigan off and put it on the back of the chair and sat sideways to the table so she could call over to John with her queries, and to be honest with herself so she could look at him while he worked.

John enjoyed listening to Flora's voice on the telephone, a look over once to see a white area of exposed skin at the top of her jeans while she stood and leant over to the back of the table. He saw her check outside several times until she disappeared for a few minutes, returning with a cardboard box her face dimpled with vexation.

"I kept calling him Mr Jagroop. I didn't see the name board said Singh until I came out."

"Jagroop would be too polite to say anything," said John enjoying her smile.

He walked over to the kettle later to make himself a drink and saw Flora had cleaned everything up, the kettle, telephone, clean mugs and spoons lined up on the table, even the grubby sink with its years of encrusted dirt and oil. John made the two of them a drink of tea and sat on the steps while they sipped at their mugs, an enjoyable and unused to interlude in his usual working day.

Reg wandered in well after 11. He ignored Flora and walked over to John who was working on a car. "No word about the MG?"

John didn't reply or lift his head.

Reg waited for several minutes then he put his face down to the

back of John's head. "I called in to tell you I've got something on. So I won't be in later on and I'll be away for a few days."

Still no reply from John.

Reg shrugged his shoulders and walked over to table.

He reached over Flora and picked up the paper bag before she could stop him. "Thought that's what it was." Reg took the sandwich out of the bag. "Might as well have it, didn't have time for breakfast."

Flora watched her food for the rest of the day disappear in three bites.

Reg rubbed his mouth with the paper bag, threw it to the floor and walked out of the garage.

Flora stood up so quick the chair almost toppled over, and it wasn't to run after Reg and scream at him. It was because she knew she had to stop her silly games and acknowledge the fact that she had to leave. She looked down at the table to prepare herself to go up the steps, pick up her belongings and go. A hard swallow at the lump in her throat, it wouldn't move.

"I've tidied everything as best I can John." She heard her voice waver and turned to see him walking up to her.

Both mouths open to speak at the same time.

Flora spoke first. "John, I'm …"

John nodded at the table. "Flora, how long will it take you to sort that lot out?"

Flora thought about it. "A few days, it might take a week. I know what's needed, but I haven't had that much experience so it will take me a little longer. But…"

"What about you staying until you have?" asked John. "I'll pay you the going rate. You can look around for a job and somewhere to live while you're here."

Flora looked at the work on the table. "I suppose I could."

# *Chapter Fourteen*

*Flora* continued with her work, answered the telephone, called over to John with her queries and took the money from the customers. All of the normal day to day activities associated with working in the garage with John, and it all belonged to her, well… for a few days.

Twelve thirty, John slammed down the bonnet of a car, went to sink and started to scrub his hands.

"These all need a reply," said Flora to quite a few letters. She picked up that morning's post. "Shall I open these?"

John nodded and looked over Flora's shoulder to read them while drying his hands. "Can you type?"

"I did think of taking lessons once."

Smiling faces looked at each other.

"Who usually does your typing?" asked Flora.

"A solicitor's secretary used to stay back in the office and do them in her own time," replied John. Until she realised their one off night was just that and she told John the many painful things he could do with his letters.

He shrugged his overalls off and hung them by the sink. "I'm going out." A nod over to the cars he'd been working while kicking his boots off and pushing his feet into his shoes. "They'll be in for those." Scribbling the charges in the dairy. "Tell the next lot to pick them up at five. And if anyone wants a job doing today that's not booked in tell them to park out in the street and they can pick it up after seven."

Flora watched him run up the steps in his vest and jeans, and run back down a minute later with a shirt and his leather jacket on and a large brown envelope. She looked in it while checking the contents of the cabinet, it was stuffed with money.

"Where's today's takings?" asked John.

Flora had put them in a tin box full of loose change she found in a drawer in the table, she took it out and opened it.

"I usually put the notes straight into my wallet," said John. "But while you are here you might as well keep on using the box and take the notes up to the cabinet at the end of the day." He took the notes out of the box and a few more out of the envelope and counted out 20 pounds in one pound and 10 shilling notes onto the table. "I'm off to the bank now; it isn't far so I shouldn't be long." A nod down to the money on the table. "And that's your wages for the week."

"That's more than the going rate and you know it," said Flora. "And you are supposed to pay me at the end of the week."

John had an idea she would react like that. "I'm sorry Flora." He shook his head and frowned at her. "Crumpled jeans and a grubby blouse don't quite fit into my corporate image."

Flora looked down at the splodges of oil on her blouse. She must have splashed it while cleaning the sink.

"So half for your wages," continued John. "And the other half for clothes. And seeing as I'm the boss I'm the one who decides the amount you get paid and when." The money and clothing problems solved.

Flora picked up the money, looked at it and put it into a pocket in her jeans.

"Right!" said John. He opened the office door and turned to Flora. "A George Gibson might ring. He has an MG he wants me to restore. If he wants it collecting tomorrow contact Sunny to check he can pick it up. His number's in the front of the diary."

Flora engrossed with her work at the table.

John hesitated at the door. "You will remember?"

Flora looked up with a patient smile. "If a George Gibson telephones about an MG, and he wants it collecting tomorrow I have to check with Sunny." She opened the diary. "On…"

John closed the door behind him quite happy with his 20 pounds worth. It meant he could leave the garage and not lose work and the pain of his paperwork taken care of and the comfort of Flora in his bed…

The cars duly collected and delivered while Flora plodded her way through her work. She saw the substantial amount of money coming into the garage, and the work John must be doing to achieve it. The telephone rang.

"Mason's Garage." Her well practised response quite polished by then.

"The MG, I would be obliged if the pick up would take place tomorrow at two." The deep voice sounded cultured.

"And to whom am I speaking to?" asked Flora, even though she had a good idea who it was.

"George Gibson. And to whom am I speaking to?"

"Mr Mason's personal secretary," replied Flora smiling at her self promotion. Sure she heard a chuckle.

"John must be doing well to afford a personal secretary," responded Gibson.

"I really cannot see how that concerns you Mr Gibson," replied Flora.

A definite chuckle from Gibson now. "I agree my dear, but you are so busy being a personal secretary you have not confirmed my request concerning the car."

"Ach, of course the car will be picked up," snapped Flora.

"At two?"

"Of course," shouted Flora.

"Excellent!" exclaimed Gibson. "We have finally arrived at the point we started with. Goodbye my dear I will leave everything in your able Caledonian hands."

Flora slammed the telephone down, stuck her tongue out at it and realised she should have checked with Sunny first. In despair while the telephone rang and rang, a voice at last. "Sunny?"

"Yes, it is Sunny." An accent, he wasn't English.

"This is Mason's garage, a Mr Gibson called regarding his MG…"

"Oh, yes. When?"

"Tomorrow at two," replied Flora.

"Tomorrow at two," repeated Sunny, and that seemed to be the end of the conversation.

Flora put the telephone down. She was starting to feel hungry and wished all the burning coals in the world would fall down on Reg's head for eating her sandwich, and John seemed to be taking a long time visiting a bank that wasn't far.

He rushed through the office door an hour later and ran up the steps, back down a minute later minus his coat and his shirt. "Get yourself a break Flora."

"Are you sure?" she asked.

"I told you I'm the boss. Go out and do some shopping. Spend some of your wages." John pulled his overalls on, threw his shoes down and pushed his feet into his boots.

"I'll buy some food," said Flora. "Aren't you hungry?"

John winced, he forgot about Flora needing something to eat. "I'll have something when I'm finished."

"You'll be ages yet," complained Flora. "No wonder you're skinny."

"I am not skinny." John put his brow to Flora's with an imitation snarl. The light kiss on her lips a natural progression.

Flora gathered her work together to take up to the room. "Mr Gibson rang and I contacted Sunny. He's picking the car up tomorrow at two. There's another three cars parked outside in the street, and there's a late booking for after six."

"How did I cope without you?" asked John already at a car.

"Very well by the looks of it," replied Flora looking down to the pile of paperwork.

"Oh, by the way."

Flora halfway up the steps, she held onto the books and papers and turned to look down to John.

"There's a present for you in the office," said John. He saw her indecision to continue up the steps or go down to the office.

Flora decided to continue up the steps, running down them a few seconds later and over to the office. "I said I thought about taking lessons on how to type," she wailed running back into the garage. "Not that I could type." Secretly expecting to see something nice, flowers or chocolates, a small sign of welcome for her. Not a large grey typewriter sat on the desk.

"I'm sure you can cope with the intricacies of a typewriter," said John.

Flora glared at him and walked up the steps.

She tidied the room before herself, picking up the rubbish off the floor and running down the steps for Mr Singh's box. Hot water and bubbles bringing a shine to everything in the sink and the wall cupboard. Her grubby and crumpled clothes thrown into the bottom of the wardrobe, face washed before she put on her dress and high heels. Hair brushed down her back and Alice band retrieved from a puddle in the shower. All the time planning what she might buy, calculating what she could spend in the little clothes shop she saw the day before...

John looked up at the sound of the high heels on the wooden steps and saw Flora descending them with face down to her feet, purse in one hand, the other with fingers to the wall. Her concentration gave her a vulnerable air; her dress amongst the oil and grime a beautiful fragile butterfly fluttering down to him.

He put his head back down to the car as she walked up to him. "Whenever you need money for food take it out of the tin box. Spend half your wages on clothes and keep ten pounds back for when you leave." His throat raw at the harshness of his voice.

Flora stood beside him until he lifted his head.

"Yes boss." Face shiny, cheeks red, large brown eyes looking into his. Her hair swayed with the skirt of her dress as she walked over to the table. A quick turn as though to catch him watching her. "I could always stay; let you get on while I take the calls."

"No need, it always quietens down in the afternoon."

Flora took a pound in change out of the tin box, put it into her purse and went out of the garage through the office door.

John pushed himself away from the car and cursed himself for telling Flora she could stay, pacing around the garage and cursing himself for going to Scotland and starting all of it. He finally got back down to work when he convinced himself she wouldn't return; after all she had plenty of money to keep her going for a while, but he still listened for the office door, waited for the flash of colour to catch his eye.

Flora returned over an hour later, face flushed, bags in both hands.

John breathed in her freshness.

"We've plenty of food now." Flora tottered up the steps with her load, and reappeared several minutes later. Stood at the top of the steps with her Alice band off, dressed in a black pencil skirt, white blouse with short sleeves and low heeled black shoes.

"Do you like my new work uniform?"

John looked up to her.

The clinging skirt gave Flora an elegant air; she looked sophisticated rather than workmanlike. She looked down at herself at his hesitation.

He had to say something. "You look very efficient."

Flora smiled, returned the room, brought out her papers and books and took them down to the table.

"I bought a jumper and trousers, and another two the same as this." She picked at the blouse and put her head down to her work. "I've ten pounds left for when I leave."

It was after 8, John working on the last car while the owner waited. The middle aged man grateful for the kind act of a drink of tea at the end of his working day. Suited, tie loose while he stood beside the table and looked down at Flora, her large brown eyes lulling him into a dream world of hope where the past 20 years of his life could be wished away. Until she turned her head and looked at the other man there. Her soft profile and her smile telling him it was just that, a dream.

John wiped his hands, slammed down the bonnet of the car and walked over to the table to see the man lift his eyebrows to him along with a slight incline of his head down to Flora. The indication of ownership surprised John, and the good feeling that went along with it.

The rush to shut up the garage, the screeching shutters clashed down.

Flora ran up the steps with the notes out of the tin box, put them on the desk  and returned down to the garage to wait for John. He'd taken his boots and overalls off, watching the muscles move on his shoulders as he stood at the sink scrubbing his hands, a scatter of freckles, the skin with a different paleness to hers. He turned to her wiping his hands, eyes deep and black under his brows.

"Tired?" asked Flora.

John nodded. "Have you eaten?"

"No," answered Flora walking up the steps in front of him. "I decided to wait so I'll be as skinny as you."

John hoped Flora would never be skinny, she looked perfect the way she was to him.

Plates of cold chicken and salad stood on the side of the clean and tidy sink, along with a mountain of bread and butter.

"I need a shower," said John ramming a slice into his mouth.

"So do I," said Flora.

The taste of bread on John's lips creamy and sweet.

# Chapter Fifteen

*Serene* in her midwife's uniform, felt hat set at a debonair angle, Hilda Timms stood beside John while he checked the engine of her pale blue Morris Minor.

"Everything seems fine to me Hilda."

Hilda, almost as broad as she was tall, did not look very pleased with this.

"But she doesn't sound right to me John."

Flora walked through the office door with her paper bags of breakfast sandwiches.

"What do you think of her?" Hilda asked her.

John started the engine.

Flora looked up, creased her brow and pursed her lips in the hope it gave her the appearance of an experienced listener. "Something sounds sore to me."

"There I told you!" said Hilda to John.

John put his head down to the engine so Hilda wouldn't see him smile. He gave the engine a tweak here and there and started it again.

Flora listened with the same expression, a nod this time. "That sounds a lot better."

Hilda quite happy with Flora's diagnosis. John shook his head at her purse and slammed the bonnet down. Hilda rubbed at the paintwork with a duster and checking for finger marks before she eased her bulk into the car.

She stuck her head out of the window to John and Flora. "You two young people give me a call anytime you need me."

John, who'd taken a bite out of his sandwich, coughed and choked. Flora laughed and watched the car's sedate progress down the street. A low grumble from the exhaust as though complaining at the indignity of bumping its way over the cobbles.

The morning busy, the same as the day before. One of the car owners waited while John worked on his car; he stood so close to Flora she put a hand to the top of her blouse.

"You are a new addition," he remarked.

"It's only temporary," said Flora. "Until I have John's paperwork up to date."

"And how long will that take?" he asked.

"A few more days," replied Flora. A card put in front of her. She glanced at it and saw, 'WALLACE and TINDALE Chartered Accountants'.

"I'm the Tindale. Roger Tindale. My secretary's leaving at the end of the week and I haven't had the time to advertise for anyone else. If John's fool enough to let you go why not give it a try?"

Flora looked up to him, a pleasant smile, in his thirties, smartly dressed.

She shook her head. "I don't think I'm up to working in an accountant's office Mr Tindale, and as a secretary."

"Roger, call me Roger. I could train you. My wife said she would help." He shrugged. "But she has her hands full with the children. Give me a call if you are interested, my office isn't far from here."

Flora gave the card a closer look at the mention of the nearness of his office.

John walked up to them and stood beside Flora until Roger Tindale drove away. "Was he bothering you?"

Flora shook her head. John hadn't seen the card; she put her hand over it. "Do you mind if I take a break this afternoon?"

"No, take a break every afternoon," said John. He filled the kettle. "The tea bags are running low you can buy some while you are out shopping."

Flora didn't say she bought tea bags the day before and they were in the wall cupboard, and she wasn't going out to go shopping. She waited until after two, until it looked as though John intended to work on without a break.

"I shouldn't be long," she shouted, going through the office door with the card in her purse.

The first person she asked gave her directions, Roger Tindale's office in the opposite direction, at the back of the garage. Flora turned the corner at another small cut at the top of the workshops and found the address in less than two minutes.

She returned to the shopping street. The shops were closed because it was Wednesday, but a little café was still open. Lemonade and a cake to see her through until later that night; she only bought two sausage sandwiches that morning. The clothes shop window perused, happy to see the red dress she saw the day before still there. A look in the newsagent's window to check the rooms to let. Some of the cards advertised jobs, but they were all part time. Flora needed more than the few hours work they offered to pay for lodgings and food. She walked through the office door to find John guiding in a large truck as it reversed into the far side of the garage. It had the wreck of a car on the back of it which Flora presumed must be the MG. A small Indian man jumped out of the cab as soon as the truck stopped. He wore baggy trousers, a collarless shirt and a waistcoat fastened over an extremely rotund tummy. His thick black shiny hair fell to a natural parting in the middle, his moustache the barest touch of a line on his upper lip, and he had a smile from ear to ear, it had to be Sunny.

The car winched down to the floor, all of the wheels rusted, one buckled, little sign of the tyres. Patches of red on the surviving bits of the frame, no top and the inside of the car looked as though some animal had made a very comfortable home inside it, along with its family.

Sunny worked on the car without a falter in his smile. He cleared away all of the rubbish and threw it into the back of the truck along with the seating and remains of the body work. A wave before he drove the truck away, leaving behind a lopped sided skeleton of a car and a rusted block of what used to be an engine.

The shutters closed well after 8. Flora ran over to the fish and chip shop for supper which they ate down in the garage. John at the rusted engine of the MG while still swallowing his food.

Flora sat at the table for a while watching him. A clutter of old machinery and equipment lay around her along with discarded bits of car engines. It was tidier at the far side of the garage where the wreck of the MG stood. Long benches, new and old car parts hung neatly on the wall, newer equipment. She wandered over to the darkness at the side of the office. A sturdy old black car stood in the shadows. Behind it, at the back of the garage, rusty old steel cupboards with a pair of overalls hung on one of the doors.

John came up behind her and nodded at the car; he didn't have his overalls on. "I see you've found Minx the Magnificent."

Flora smiled at him.

"That's what it says on the badge," laughed John. "Well… Near enough. Someone didn't pick it up; most probably they couldn't afford the bill. It's over twenty years old and still going strong. It's still a crank start and it isn't as flashy or as quick as the sporty jobs but the old work horse gets me around."

He stood behind Flora and put his arms around her waist. She leant against him and put her hands on his bare arms.

"I'll take you to Patrick Malloy's bar tomorrow night," said John. "Paddy's gone missing. I'll have to search him out to start work on the MG. If you think I've been busy the last few days you haven't seen anything yet."

"Then it's just as well I'm here to help you," said Flora.

Her head down at John's silence.

"Come on." John pulled her to him. "The shower and bed's calling."

# Chapter Sixteen

*John* finished his bacon sandwiches, drained his mug and looked over to the stack of letters waiting for a reply. "I see there's little progress with the typing."

"I thought I might make a start this afternoon," said Flora.

The big problem being the grey shiny monster sitting on the desk, Flora sure it gave a malicious grin every time she went into the office. She read John's scribbled replies, again, and shuffled them into a different order, again. John looked into her face, she returned his look. "Your beard's thicker," she observed, "and your hair's starting to get curly."

John enjoyed the feel of her fingers in his hair.

The afternoon galloped towards Flora, and the dreaded typing, for her to be granted a last minute reprieve.

"I'm going out." John went to the sink to wash his hands. "Do you want me to pull the shutters down while you are typing in the office?"

Flora checked her watch; yes, it was precisely a minute to midday. "No." She put her head down to her work. "I'll wait until you get back."

"I thought you might say that," grinned John.

He left through the office door, no word at how long he'd be and where he was going. Returning less than an hour later and sticking his face in front of Flora, his beard and head cropped.

"You've had your curls cut off," she protested.

"Good," replied John. "That was the intention."

Their lips inches apart, and drawn together for the long gentle kiss. Flora saw John's eyes study her as he took his face away.

"I'll take my break now to do some shopping." She couldn't think of a more excellent reason to put off the typing.

Flora did her shopping and saw the clothes shop still had the red dress in the window. She went inside to try it on, which was silly because she didn't have enough money to buy it, but it did put the typing a little further away and the dress was a perfect fit. Flora asked if they needed a shop assistant, they didn't. Her prevarications continued with a visit to the café, a wander up and down the shops, twice. A good half hour debating which flowers to buy to brighten up the office, and of course another few minutes spent choosing a small vase to put the flowers into.

She chose freesias. Their wonderful scent filled the office, not that it helped with her typing.

"Eejit!" she screamed hands in her hair.

John put his head through the door, his overalls off. "Is that you or the typewriter?"

"Both!" shouted Flora pushing a drawer shut; it contained all of her mistakes, which consisted of all of her typing so far.

"I thought I'd get something to eat before we went to the bar," said John. "You did say all of those pies were for me?"

"I didn't say anything of the sort and you know it," snapped Flora.

Her cheeks blazing as she jumped up and marched past John. He followed her through the garage, up the steps and right behind her when she saw the pies on the side of the sink. They fell onto the bed laughing in each other's face.

Flora took her dress out of the wardrobe and put it in front of herself. The shower and bed a distant memory, or it seemed that way to John as he lay on the bed watching her.

"Are you sure my dress wouldn't do for the bar?" she asked.

"No, it's not that kind of place, you need something more casual," replied John pleased she'd covered herself. Watching Flora run around in just her pants not an easy thing to do.

Flora put the dress back and searched for her flat shoes in the bottom of the wardrobe; John groaned and pulled her back to the bed.

They rushed out after 9, John pulling on his leather jacket while he closed the office door behind them.

"Is it far?" asked Flora.

"Around the corner where every local should be," said John guiding her over the street and to the top of the shops.

He looked sideways at Flora as they hurried along. Apart from her wonderful shape in red trousers and a black jumper she looked no more than 15 with her shiny face, scarlet cheeks and hair pulled back in a pony tail.

It was not the quiet Thursday night at the bar John expected, pushing the door open to a crush of bodies and a thick fog of smoke. He let go of the door and turned to go. "I think I'll leave it for tonight…"

Flora darted past him and in the bar before the door closed. "They might be looking for a barmaid," she shouted back to him.

Whereas a path seemed to miraculously appear for Flora John had to heave his way in after her, eventually catching up with her at the bar where she was stood with her back to it laughing at him. He put his hands on the rail, shook his head down to her and looked up to see the landlord Patrick Malloy at the other side of the bar do exactly the same thing to the back of the pony tail.

Patrick indicated over to John.

John pressed his lips together and leant over Flora to hear Patrick confirm he'd been right to be uneasy over her looking so young.

Flora leant back, face inches from John's.

"I never took you for a cradle snatcher John," shouted Patrick over the noise.

Flora opened her mouth and wriggled around to face her accuser. "I'll have you know I'm twenty one," she shouted.

"Now is that so?" replied Patrick, a trace of an Irish accent. Fair thinning hair, thick set, round face pink and perspiring from the heat of the bar.

"Yes it is so," retorted Flora. "And I was thinking of asking if you were looking for a barmaid, but I'll not be bothering now." She looked down at John's hand on her arm.

"I think I'll go now Patrick," shouted John. "I only came in to find Eamon Goggin."

"Eamon, I haven't seen him since last week," shouted Patrick. "I'll let him know you are looking for him if I see him John. Anyway you stay for a drink; they're on their way out now to finish the birthday party at the house." Patrick smiled the smile of a man who had a prosperous night as he checked the number of crates being carried out of the bar. The holders of the chinking crates imitating the Pied Piper as the crush of bodies and noise followed them out.

"Caitlin will take care of you John," said Patrick. No need to shout once the bar had almost emptied, and set on continuing his good night by encouraging John to spend his money.

A fair skinned hand placed a pint of beer in front of John. Flora looked into pale almond eyes, a fringe; dark blonde hair resting on slender shoulders. Caitlin smiled at her, but before the smile a flicker of the eyes to above Flora's head, to John's face.

Patrick poured out a glass of fizzy lemonade and plonked it in front of Flora. "First of all I do not need a barmaid young lady, and secondly that is the strongest drink you'll be having in this place seeing as you look at the most sixteen." He looked at John. "And that will be on the house John seeing as I had to turn down the young lady's job application." Patrick's expansive act the result of enjoying the best night in the bar for weeks.

Flora snatched up the lemonade and leant over the bar with it to Patrick but John picked up his glass and pulled her away by her arm before she could say anything. He marched her over to a table, sat her on a chair with her back to the bar, sat beside her and downed half his drink in one go.

Flora glared at him. "I hope you are enjoying that."

"Of course I'm not," said John wiping his mouth and shaking his head.

It didn't take him long to finish his drink and with a look at Flora's untouched lemonade returned to the bar with his empty glass.

For all of her bluster Flora was disappointed over the barmaid job. It would have been ideal working so close to the garage, with the added bonus of seeing John some nights. She wasn't very confident about her abilities as a secretary or working for Roger Tindale, but his offer was the only option she had left and his office wasn't far from the garage, and John.

She looked around her. The bar had almost emptied; half a dozen people at the most, a scatter of plain wooden tables with chairs haphazard around them. Patrick the landlord talking to a man at the end of the bar, which meant… Flora twisted around on her chair to see John, leather jacket tight across his shoulders as he leant over the bar to Caitlin. She gave a quick look over to Flora, mouth moving while she held up a small slim cigar. John nodded and took the cigar. Caitlin's head down to strike a match, her face lit up with the flare of light, John's head towards Caitlin and the match. Flora excluded from their intimacy along with the rest of the world, she turned away.

That's why John didn't want her to stay. He brought her to the bar so people wouldn't know about him and Caitlin and to show her she didn't stand a chance with him. Would Caitlin tell him to kick her out? How long would Caitlin tolerate her staying with John?

Flora drowning as she spun down into the dark clutches of jealousy. She jumped at John's presence behind her. He sat beside her, bringing with him the aroma of his cigar.

Caitlin arrived seconds later with a pint of beer. She put it on the table in front of John, smiled at Flora and sat at the table beside her. "Daddy enjoys playing his games I'm afraid. We all have to put up with it." Her accent nothing like her father's, more resembling the boy who gave Flora directions to the garage.

Flora thought under different circumstances she could have liked Caitlin. Her smile revealed slightly protruding front teeth which gave her face an attractive fairylike look, and she was so slim it made Flora feel large and clumsy, but yes she could have liked her.

Caitlin put a hand on her stomach, Flora noticed the wedding ring.

"I've just found out I'm pregnant so daddy might need a barmaid in a few months time." Caitlin laughed and leant over to Flora. "Danny and I have told him not to put a banner behind the bar with the news just yet."

Flora felt such a fool.

Caitlin stood up to go. "I'll try to persuade him to give you something a little stronger the next time you're in the bar Flora. "

She must have asked John her name.

"Flora's leaving in a few days," said John. "So you won't be seeing her again."

"She might," retorted Flora. "If I find work around here." She shrugged her shoulders. "Anyway, I think I might have found a job."

John about to take a drink of his beer, the glass hesitating at his mouth. "Where?"

"At an accountant's office," replied Flora. "Mr Tindale says he's looking for a secretary."

"Roger Tindale!" exclaimed John. "I asked if he was bothering you because he's the biggest lecher around here." He slammed his glass down and jumped up while stubbing his cigar out. "Come on, we're leaving."

"So soon?" asked Caitlin stepping back.

"It looks like it Caitlin," said Flora hurrying after John.

John seemed to have a problem unlocking and opening the office door. He waited for Flora to go inside, slammed the door shut and stood with his back to it. "I'm getting the car out. I'm taking you back to Scotland."

"Then you'll have to tie me up and put me in the boot," said Flora with her back to the garage door.

Faces challenged each other over the top of the typewriter.

"Roger Tindale's notorious around here," shouted John. "He's the talk of the place. He's looking for a secretary because he promises them the world and drops them as soon as he's got what he wants from them."

"And you don't," shouted Flora.

John hesitated, took a deep breath. "I do not make promises I have

no intention of keeping Flora."

"No," said Flora, her voice quiet. "You are very, very careful about that part John."

John pushed his way past Flora, eyes dark, mouth a grim line.

She watched him stride through to the garage and up the steps and followed him a few moments later to find him in the bed with his head turned away from the door.

Flora took her trousers and jumper off and opened the wardrobe door to put them inside. John pulled her to the bed with his hands on her waist and loved her with an intensity she didn't know existed.

She lay awake for hours, waiting for John to ask her to stay.

# *Chapter Seventeen*

*Flora* checked John couldn't hear her before she made her telephone call. She put the receiver down and turned on her chair to him. "Would you mind if I took my break at two?"

He was working on a car at the far end of the garage next to the MG. A grunt her reply, he hadn't spoken all morning.

She smudged her last clean blouse and the day was too hot to wear her jumper with her skirt so Flora changed into her lemon dress, leaving her Alice band off and shaking her head to loosen her hair to help her stay cool.

John looked up from the car at the sound of her high heels on the wooden steps and watched Flora as she stood at one of the open shutters. She looked down to check herself, hair falling over a shoulder. A hesitant turn to him while she flicked it back with her purse in her hand. Cheeks a quiet pink because of her makeup, half open lips generous and red, she looked beautiful. He waited for her to say something, but she turned her back to him, put her face to the cobbles and walked out to the street.

He didn't know why, but John had the need to rush out to the street when he heard the wolf whistles. No sign of the culprits, or Flora.

She returned an hour later, to the accompaniment of more wolf whistles, and walked up the steps with a box under her arm. "I've bought some soap powder from Mr Singh to do some washing. Do you want any doing?"

"No, Sunny's wife does the washing," said John. "I'll show you tomorrow. You throw everything into the bed sheets and take them to her. She'll bring it back later in the day all clean and ironed. And she usually brings some curry with her."

Flora stood at the top of the steps thinking about it, the box under her arm, skirt flounced up around her legs.

"You have had curry before?" asked John.

"No, it's just I don't know if I like the idea of someone else washing my knickers," replied Flora.

John turned his head away to smile.

"It's not funny," she shouted.

"I'll give her some extra money to wash your knickers," said John.

"Right," said Flora, still thinking about it and happy John seemed in a better mood. "I'll get on with the typing instead." She knew she'd rather be washing instead of fighting with the typewriter, and thinking of other things.

She decided to keep her dress on because of the heat and filled the vase with fresh water in the hope it would keep the wilting freesias alive for another day. The office was hot and airless, the one window high up on the wall above the outside door and it was a solid sheet of glass. Flora opened the door a little to let in a cooling breeze.

She decided to be less frenetic with her typing and tried the slower two fingered approach, and it worked. Congratulating herself while she read her third completed letter without a mistake she looked up to see a well tanned middle aged man walk through the open door.

"Ah!" Teeth white against the tan. "I simply had to come and meet the wonderful accent."

Flora recognised the voice of George Gibson the MG man.

Gibson sat himself sideways on the desk and smiled down to her. "I said to myself, George you will have to meet the Scottish voice and see if she is as beautiful as she sounds. And I am pleased to say you are."

Flora's upturned face looked up to his gaze. Sun bleached hair, a well tailored light suit, a gold chain at the waistcoat. Hands grasped on a knee, a ring on his little finger which might have been a large ruby, sparkling stones set in gold cufflinks.

"I'm pleased you are pleased Mr Gibson," she retorted. "But I'm not here for your entertainment." Flora gave him her best glare. "Some people have work to do, and I would prefer to do it without being disturbed. And it would have been polite for you to have knocked or rang the bell before you entered."

Flora enjoyed the last part, she picked up a sheet of paper with a flourish and threaded it into the typewriter, a prayer it went in straight, it did.

Gibson gave an exaggerated wince and put his face down to Flora. "Let me give you some advice my dear. The correct way for a personal secretary to behave is to assist her employer and not be disagreeable to his customers."

Flora felt her cheeks flame up. "If you had the good manners to tell me why you are here I could assist my employer," she snapped, and immediately wished she hadn't.

"And flashing eyes too," chuckled Gibson jumping off the desk. "The man will be in here I presume." His game with Flora over he walked over to the garage door.

Flora jumped up and opened the door before he could get to it. "I'll let Mr Mason know you are here." She opened her mouth to call out to John for Gibson to sweep past her into the garage.

"Just the man," he announced striding over to John with hand outstretched.

John turned from a car he was working on and took Gibson's hand. Flora slammed the door shut praying his hands were thick with oil.

Gibson walked over to the remains of the MG. "Started already I see."

"I'll take the engine out tonight, it will need a total rebuild," said John following him. "The whole car in fact."

"I thought it would," said Gibson. "It used to belong to my uncle; the old duffer bought the TA when they first released them. He must have given it a good prang and simply walked away from it. It must have been sitting in that overgrown ditch for twenty years before we found it. Gloria my wife decided it would make a wonderful twenty first birthday present for our son Sebastian. Would it be possible to restore it by September the fourteenth?"

"It will cost you," said John.

"Doesn't it always," said Gibson with a small smile. "But Gloria shall have her wish whatever the cost." He looked at the cars waiting in the garage. "You look busy."

"Busy enough," answered John.

"Have you thought of expansion?" asked Gibson ever the business man.

"No," replied John. "Another year and I should have the capital to move on."

"Better than kissing the bankers' feet, I had exactly the same attitude when I started out," said Gibson. "And stopping you won't help the pennies roll in. I'm dashing between here and the south of France at the moment. My wife seems to think no one but me can be trusted to deal with the car."

Gibson walked away, stopped and turned to John with a forefinger to his lips. "Your personal secretary, the pink cheeked beauty. The personal will be that I presume." He smiled at John's look of studied thought. "I thought as much lucky devil. She reminds me of my wife in her younger days, full of spark and gusto. I visualised her sitting in the open topped car with that hair blowing in the wind. I couldn't think of a more perfect complement to Sebastian's birthday present." Gibson continued his walk towards the office. "A fanciful thought old man, no hard feelings. I shall return in five weeks to reassure my wife, let her know how things are getting along." He opened the office door and pretended to check inside. "I'd better keep my hands away so they won't be bit." A chuckle as he closed the door behind him.

John hurried over to the office to see if Flora might be causing any trouble.

She'd kept her head down to the typewriter while Gibson swept past her  determined he wasn't going to make more fun of her, turning her head to John at the sound of the door opening behind her.

"He thinks he's Mr Clever."

"You can think what you want about yourself when you have as much money as he does," said John. He turned to go back into to the garage.

"I went for an interview with Mr Tindale this afternoon."

John waited at the door.

Flora looked down to the typewriter and fiddled with the keys. "He's offered me a post as his secretary. I'm to start on Monday morning."

"After what I told you about him," exploded John.

"I'm almost up to date with the paperwork, and it shouldn't take me long to do the letters," said Flora. "I had to find a job somewhere

John."

She knew she shouldn't have worn her dress the moment she walked into Roger Tindale's office. His hands up and down her bare arms while he sat her in front of his desk and aware of his eyes looking down her front as he leant over her. No sign of the secretary, or photographs of his wife and children. Monday seemed so far away then, her confidence she could deal with him seeping away by the minute.

Flora turned at the silence thinking John had left, he was still there looking at her. "I need a reference," she rushed on. "Mr Tindale said his partner will insist on it. He said I can take it with me on Monday."

"And I expect you want me to give you this reference," laughed John. He looked up pretending to think. "And how long shall I say you've been working here? Four days? Or should I break that down to hours or minutes so it will sound better?"

The door swung shut behind him before Flora could reply.

She sat with her hands to her face, and restarted her typing.

She stopped as soon as she started to make mistakes again, went up to the room to prepare food for their supper and returned to the garage to sit at the table.

The shutters pulled down at 8. Flora watched John winch the rusted engine out of the carcass of the MG and place it on a stand. Nothing said between them since they discussed the reference.

Flora returned to the room well after 11, the food untouched on the side of the sink. She lay on the bed listening to John work below in the garage. Asleep by the time he finally joined her in the bed.

# Chapter Eighteen

*The* flushing toilet woke Flora, water running at the sink in the shower room. She lay and watched John dress, it was dark because of the clouds, it looked like rain.

John looked over his shoulder at her.

"If you wrap all the dirty washing in the bed sheets I'll show you where to take it."

Flora left looking at the door.

Little said at breakfast, Flora tied the corners of the sheets together later that morning to make a kind of giant pudding. The street quiet with most of the shutters down when she leant towards John with it in her hands as he pointed down to the cut, Sunny's house three streets behind the garage. The day was cool because of the clouds, but Flora started to feel very warm in her jumper and skirt by the time she carried her awkward bundle past more terraces of old Victorian houses. Thankful to reach the gate John described she opened it and walked up the narrow yard.

A smiling Indian woman in a sari met her at the door.

"Is this the right place to bring the washing? Is this Sunny's house?" asked Flora.

"You could say." The smile widened. "Everyone will insist on nicknames. It is Sanjeev; I am his wife Neelam Kamwar." She took the bundle from Flora and ushered her into the house and over to a chair. "Sanjeev said John has a flower with him with cheeks as bright as the red Frangipani."

Flora laughed. "My name might be Flora, but I wouldn't say I looked like a flower Mrs Kamwar."

A protesting finger held up. "Neelam, you must call me Neelam."

Neelam made a pot of tea, the two women laughing and chatting together over their cups

"I will return the washing this evening. Do you want curry?" asked Neelam as Flora stood to leave. She smiled at her hesitation. "I will make it mild for you."

Flora left the house right at the moment the threatened rain finally happened. She ran up to the garage to see John's old car stood in the street with the engine running. John sat at the table drinking tea, his leather jacket on ready to go out.

He clashed his mug down and jumped up. "You took your time. I need to chase up some parts for the MG and some of the suppliers close early on a Saturday. See to it that the bookings finish at four from now on. There's a car due in this afternoon. Don't accept anymore, tell them I'm busy."

No enquiry regarding Flora's plans for that afternoon, such as finding somewhere to live.

"Any more orders?" she mocked.

"You are the personal secretary," shouted John rushing out. "And your orders are going to be a lot more personal than that in the future." He jumped into the car, slammed the door shut and drove away.

Flora soon completed the paperwork; it hadn't taken her as long as she thought it would. Cars collected and the one due in delivered. She couldn't go the office to do the typing and leave the garage unattended so she sat at the table watching the rain bounce off the cobbles while she waited for John.

"Well, well, well, and look who is still here."

It was Reg; he stood in front of Flora and ran a comb through his wet hair to bring back his quiff. His eyes looked glazed, as though he'd been drinking. A smile as he looked around him and saw John wasn't there. He put his comb into the breast pocket of his jacket and pushed past Flora to get to the steps.

Flora jumped up in front of him; she didn't want Reg near to where she slept. "Where are you going?" she demanded.

"To use the bog, what do you think you stupid bitch?"

Flora gave a hard swallow, Reg was smaller than her, but she knew he'd be far stronger.

"A few days and you think you own the place."

His face inches from Flora's; he didn't smell as though he'd been drinking.

"Well I'll tell you something now bitch. I'll still be here when you are long gone."

Reg turned away, much to Flora's relief, and walked over to the MG to take a look at it before disappearing into the dark at the back of the garage. He emerged minutes later, lit a cigarette and stood at the open shutter smoking it until the rain stopped, flicking it out to the cobbles and walking away without further acknowledgement to her.

John arrived back at the garage an hour later and unpacked the boot of the car, lining up boxes and shiny new car parts on a bench by the MG.

Flora stood at the open shutter looking out to the street. "Neelam said she'll bring some curry tonight and Reg called in." She saw John's busyness, his disinterest in her and decided not to mention Reg's behaviour towards her.

John checked the contents of a box, a look up to see Flora, black hair, skirt and jumper a silhouette against the light. He moved the box along the bench, another look up, she'd gone, turning his head to see the office door close.

John didn't start on the last car until the owner called in to collect it. He sat on Flora's chair to wait, John wondering why he bothered with such a small job; it was hardly worth getting his hands dirty for the small amount of money it would bring in.

He heard the office door close followed by the slow clicks of the typewriter, a smile at Flora's perseverance.

Flora worked on until the door opened behind her.

"Neelam's here with the curry." John looked at the back of Flora's head; her hair blacker against the jumper. "You'll enjoy it," he said to her lack of response.

Flora stood and followed John into the garage.

Neelam uncovered the plates on the table and looked over to Flora. "Now where have the frangipani gone?" She frowned and put a gentle hand on Flora's white face. "Eat your curry; it will put the flowers back into your cheeks."

A young boy of 9 or 10 stood behind Neelam with the clean washing in his arms.

Flora took it from him; lustrous dark eyes looked up to her before the black shiny head bowed down.

"Madhar is always so shy around the ladies," said Neelam smiling at him.

Flora took the clean washing up to the room and picked up knives and forks for the curry. She saw John give Neelam some money, two faces up to her as she walked down the steps. Most probably John had told Neelam she was leaving.

"You eat it before it is cold," said Neelam. She put a hand on Madhar's shoulder, draped the sari over her head and led him outside with a slow graceful walk.

John filled two mugs with cold water, put them onto the table and sat on the steps with a plate of curry and a fork.

Flora put her face over her plate and breathed in its aroma. "It smells wonderful." She tasted the curry. "It's lovely, it's sweet and…" A grab for a mug of water.

"Hot?" laughed John. "And this is one of Neelam's milder curries." His face over his plate as shovelled forkfuls into his mouth.

"I've found a room," said Flora.

John guided the fork into his mouth and swallowed. "When do you move in?"

"Tomorrow."

John looked at Flora; Neelam mentioned her white face, as though she was his responsibility. "What's this room like?" he asked, and questioned why he needed to know.

Flora shrugged. "It's a room."

"Anything must be better than up those steps," joked John.

No response from Flora, she pushed her plate away.

"Too hot?" asked John, and without waiting for a reply. "Wait until you've tasted one of her really hot curries." He puffed his cheeks out, and realising the meaning of his words slammed his plate onto the table and walked to the far end of the garage. "You can see how it is," he shouted. "How I live. It wouldn't be fair on you Flora. I didn't ask you to come. You shouldn't have expected to stay. It's better I get on with my life and you with yours."

"That is exactly what I am doing," shouted Flora. She ran over to the office and swung the door back. "And you needn't worry. I'll have everything finished by tomorrow. Before I go and get on with my life."

She sat in front of the typewriter and thought of the rooms she looked at, the dirty ones, a family of six living next to one with a screaming baby, the ogling landlords. Relieved to find a clean, quiet room. The landlady reciting a long list of rules; no male visitors repeated more than once, Flora almost asked if she permitted breathing. A bed, a chair, a cupboard, a brick wall so close to the window she could almost put a hand out and touch it. No light would ever penetrate into that room, no sunlight allowed to warm it. She thought of Clairgowan, a wash of longing for the space, the light, the freshness. Her father! A flash of concern for him and the threat of him losing Clairgowan House. Overriding all of this her love for John, Roger Tindale's office and the room as near as she could be to the garage, John's nearness her comfort.

It took Flora until 9 that night to complete the letters. She put them into a drawer for John to sign the next day.

He worked at dismantling the rusted engine of the MG while Flora checked the paperwork to ensure it was all correct. She took it all up to the room along with the notes out of the tin box, everything put onto the table ready to be locked away in the cabinet.

The day had exhausted her, undressing as soon as she put the washing away and the clean clothes onto the bed. Asleep the moment she lay down and covered herself, dreaming John lay beside her in the small space without touching her skin.

He must have taken great care not to waken her when he rose the next morning.

# *Chapter Nineteen*

*It* was two o'clock in the afternoon; Flora had been sitting at the table waiting for her reference since early that morning. The shutters down, no cars in and out, the telephone quiet. She'd put on her jeans and blouse, the clothes she wore when she left Clairgowan less than a week before to start her new life with John. Her other clothes packed in the bags from the clothes shop and her cotton duffle bag, ready for her to pick up and go. Apart from the odd drink of tea John hadn't stopped working on the engine of the MG since she walked down the steps, the sandwiches she prepared for breakfast winged pieces of bread sticking up from the plate.

"Are you enjoying this?" Flora threw her chair under the table and walked over to John. "You know I'm waiting for the reference. You could at least give it to me."

John straightened up to look at her face. "What I could do is take you to the station so you can catch a train back to Scotland."

Flora laughed and nodded her head. "Ah, so that's it. Flora has to sit waiting for John to come to see her when it suits him."

John shook his head. "No Flora that is not it. I had no intentions of going back to see you."

"Right." Flora swallowed this down. "Then give me the reference and you'll be rid of me."

John leant down to the engine again. "No."

"Why?" cried Flora.

"Because I'm not letting Roger Tindale loose on you, that's why."

"That's up to me. Not you or anyone else," shouted Flora. She leant down to John's ear, emphasising each word as she said it. "Give me the reference."

John continued to work on the engine.

"Give me the reference," screamed Flora shaking her head, hair flying from side to side. "Give it to me."

John gripped the side of the engine and looked down to it. "Put anything you want. Make up your own reference. I'll sign whatever you say."

"Thank you," shouted Flora walking away. "I'll do just that."

"Don't forget to put something about sleeping with the boss." John looked over the garage to Flora, his eyes dark.

"That's not fair and you know it," shouted Flora. She slammed into the office and sat in front of the typewriter.

John crashed through the door after her and prowled around the desk. "We need more chairs," he muttered, crashing back out and returning with Flora's chair. He threw it down and sat astride it, facing her with his hands across the back.

"I shouldn't have said that."

Flora's head down to the typewriter as she threaded a sheet of paper into it.

John leant over to her. "You're not going to cry, are you?"

"I don't cry," said Flora. She gave John a steady look. "Do you?"

John ignored her question. "Why did you come here Flora? What did you expect of me?"

Flora put her head down to the typewriter and tapped on the keys. "Because father might lose Clairgowan House." A pain in her chest at the thought of him walking out of the house for the last time. "He owes a lot of money, and if he doesn't pay off his debts he'll be out. So I decided it was time to live my own life." Flora put her hands on her lap and flashed a smile at John. "So I thought why not Birmingham?"

"It must be a fair bit for a place that size," said John.

"Two thousand pounds," said Flora.

She saw John's face relax at the safety of their talk. To answer his second question and say she expected him to love her as she did him to be left for another time, if there was another time.

"I expect your father will be putting up a bit of a fight up to let it go for that amount," said John.

Flora dismissed this with a shake of her head and swallowed hard. Another pain in her chest at her father saying he would fight for the house if it was Alasdair. She tapped at the keys again. "All of the paperwork's up to date now." A nod down to a drawer. "And the letters, you can sign them when I've finished this."

She continued with her typing. "I hope I'm not wasting my time with this."

"It depends on what you are saying," said John.

"I'm not that far on," said Flora. She changed lines. "I'm only as far as, to whom it may concern."

John pressed his lips together to stop a smile. "Shall I tell you what to say?"

"As long it's not about sleeping with the boss," said Flora.

"What you can say," said John. "Is that Miss Flora Ballardine has conscientiously applied herself to all aspects of clerical work in this garage."

Flora hunched herself over the keys. "You'll have to go slower."

John left the chair and stood behind Flora, his lips at her ear. "Or you could say. Miss Ballardine's old boss should have appreciated her coming to stay. And he would like to offer her a permanent post."

Flora rested her fingers on the keys and looked at them. "Why?"

"You aren't going to make this easy for me are you Flora Ballardine?"

"No."

John thought about it. "Because I enjoy listening your voice while I'm working. I enjoy knowing you'll be there sat on the chair when I look up. I enjoy the two of us being here alone." The startling realisation of the truth of his words as they left John's mouth, and a jolt at how his well practised avoidance from any closeness almost worked with Flora, how he almost lost her because of it. John wasn't sure if it was love, but he knew Flora brought with her a light so full of colour and warmth he'd feel a physical pain if she left. He also realised he'd have been drawn back to Scotland again and again, to seek the light she switched on in London.

"I don't know if I'm going to accept this offer of a permanent post," said Flora turning her face to him with a smile that said she would.

"Is there any way I can persuade you?" asked John. He kissed her.

Flora thought about it, and kissed him back. "You've persuaded me. I've decided to accept your offer."

"Good," said John. "Now can I get back to work please?"

"If you insist," said Flora opening a drawer. "You might as well sign these while you are here." She took the typewritten letters out, arranged them over the desk and sat back to look at them. "And not one mistake. I've even typed the addresses on the envelopes."

John hesitated; he didn't want to spoil it for Flora. "The copies. You have filed them away?"

Flora pursed her lips while she thought about it.

"The carbon paper," said John. "Remember. You use it to make the copies."

They laughed in each other's face.

John decided work would have to wait. He pulled Flora up from the chair and took her up to the room.

They luxuriated in the knowledge that the future held many more wonderful moments. Their movements slow and deliberate as they undressed each other and lay on the bed, bodies enjoyed until they lay sated and relaxed in the afternoon light.

Two heads lifted off the pillows at the sound of someone hammering on a shutter.

"Ignore it. It'll be Reg looking for his usual handout," said John. He pulled Flora's head down to his chest and put his face to her hair. It wouldn't leave him, her asking if he cried echoing in his mind.

Would the looks of pity be more of sympathy if he needed crutches, or wore a sling? His face contorted with the wound.

Did the blame belong to the person who decided to buy the pony as a plaything for some child? Or was it the person who didn't close the field gate correctly? Or the rain, or slippery road, or his National Service because it delayed him going to university? Or his mother because she needed to go shopping that day? Or himself when he squeezed into the small cab because of the rain instead of sitting in the back of the truck? Or because the three of them decided at that precise moment to shift around? Or his father who turned his face away from the road to make a joke about it? Or the pony who trotted out of the field to nibble at some titbit at the other side of the road?

A jarring thud the start of the convulsive change, the skid, the spinning truck. His face, the pain and blood, the screams of the pony and the silence beside him.

The great unveiling, his changed face under public scrutiny at his parents' funeral, the last time he cried.

John eased himself out of the bed. He accepted this other drastic change, the end of his solitude, even anticipated it with relish. But Flora couldn't change the fixed goal in his life, no one could.

Flora gave him a sleepy smile. "Back to work?"

John returned her smile and pulled his clothes on.

Flora sat up at the sound of voices and singing.

"That will be the two sisters Esme and Shirley," said John. "They use next door to hold chapel services. They can get quite lively." He kissed Flora on the brow and left her listening at the wall.

Flora smiled as the sweet voices rose and fell in happy abandon. She waited until it was quiet, dressed and put her clothes back into the wardrobe. Then she walked down the steps and over to the office, sat at the typewriter and started to type the letters again.

## Chapter Twenty

*Flora* telephoned Roger Tindale early Monday morning, who didn't seem surprised she was staying on at the garage. She decided not to contact the landlady, imagining her reciting rule 333 which said she'd have to live in that awful room whether she wanted to or not.

That afternoon another look at the red dress in the shop window. After all she did have her wages to spend, and the promise of the same every week.

"It would suit you."

Flora turned to see Caitlin smiling at her.

"Well, are you going to buy it?" she asked.

Flora laughed. "Yes, I think I will."

Caitlin accompanied Flora into the shop while she bought the dress, followed by a drink of tea together in the café.

"Are you going to take that job with Roger Tindale?" asked Caitlin.

"No," replied Flora. "John decided to keep me on at the garage."

"I thought he might after his reaction at the bar," smiled Caitlin. She told Flora all about her husband Danny who worked at Longbridge and their plans to rent a council house because of the baby.

"We live above the bar with daddy," said Caitlin. "It will break his heart me leaving. So Danny and I are not going to tell him until we've been allocated a house. But daddy's just found out he won't be losing the bar because of the new motorway so I think he'll cope a little better when I do leave." She leant over to Flora with a serious expression. "I have something really important to ask you Flora. Will you promise to meet me tomorrow so we can look for shoes to match your dress?"

Both still laughing while they left the café.

A battered old van drew up outside the garage later that afternoon. A small, wiry man with a tatty trilby hat rammed down on his head got out and walked over to Flora at the table. His hat, clothes and boots covered in a white dust.

"Well, would you be looking at that?" He stood and looked at Flora with fists on his hips.

John was sat on the steps drinking tea, his face to his mug ignoring the blatant scrutiny of Flora.

"Now didn't I always tell you to go and get yourself a good Irish colleen John, and didn't you go and listen to old Paddy at last."

Paddy spoke with a strong Irish accent, his voice high pitched, melodic.

"Where have you been you old reprobate? Over to Ireland to impregnate your wife again I bet," said John to his mug.

"Never you mind getting off the subject. What I want to know is where this rosy cheeked colleen might be from." Paddy held his chin with a dirty hand as though in deep thought and gazed intently at Flora who started to giggle. He clicked his fingers in the air. "County Cork! That is where you are from." He pointed a finger at Flora his face screwed up in a smile. "Now tell me I'm right."

"Way off Paddy," laughed John putting his empty mug onto the table.

"I wouldn't mind a one of those," said Paddy eyeing the mug, "I'm parched after a day on the buildings."

"Ach, it'll be nae bother," said Flora up to the kettle. A grin at Paddy's surprised face.

"Well, would you believe it!" Paddy pulled his hat off and with a theatrical swoop pretended to throw it to the floor. "Ah bejayzus I was sure with that skin and black hair you could only be an Irish colleen. But never mind about that." He pointed at Flora's legs with his hat. "With legs like that she'll be giving you lots of lovely babies John."

"I'm sure Flora will be delighted to hear that Paddy," laughed John.

Paddy rammed his hat back onto his head and followed John over to the MG. "And I have been home. And seeing as we are expecting another addition to the family in a few months not to impregnate the wife as you so nicely put it." He walked around the remains of the MG. "So, this is it. I'll take the wheels tonight." A nudge at the buckled wheel with a toe of a boot. "I think this one might be past redemption. But I'll see if the lads can perform their magic on it. And I'll be thinking you might be having trouble with the chassis, it's had a good bump this car. I'll be back tomorrow night to strip it right down and give it a good look."

Flora took a mug of tea over to Paddy.

"Now are you sure you have no Irish blood in your veins?" he asked with his screwed up smile.

"No," she laughed.

Flora's light hearted mood stopped at Reg's appearance. She couldn't stop a smile at his surprised look at her, he obviously didn't expect her to be there.

He hovered around John. "I came yesterday but you must have been out."

John didn't reply.

"You timed that right," said Paddy to Reg. "You can give me a hand to get these wheels off then I can be away for my tea."

Reg didn't look over keen, but he walked to the dark at the back of the garage and returned wearing a pair of overalls.

The wheels put into the back of Paddy's van within an hour. "I'll be seeing you tomorrow night my beautiful Irish colleen," he said holding his hat in the air as a farewell. He walked away and sat in his van singing 'When Irish eyes are smiling' in a beautiful tenor voice. His hat waving out of the window and still singing as the van drove off.

Reg hung around the garage for another hour. Flora noticed he didn't seem to do much in particular and there wasn't any sign of his previous belligerent behaviour on Saturday. He went to the back of the garage to take his overalls off and hovered around John until he gave him a pound note out of his wallet, Reg pushing it into his pocket and hurrying out to the street

Paddy arrived on Tuesday evening with his non stop talk and singing, and so began a routine that would continue until the end of July. No breaks or time off for John who'd be up early every morning to work on the engine of the MG until he opened the garage, and back at the car the moment the shutters went down. Paddy worked at the chassis until it reached his high standards, finishing off with a black metal frame resembling a wide ladder. Then he worked on the remainder of the car with John. The benches more crowded with lines of new and reconditioned car parts as the weeks went by. Sunny called occasionally to check on the progress of the car and to bring in parts of the body work. Reg came in most nights when he'd go straight to the back of the garage for his overalls. His contribution to the industry around him to fetch and carry, when asked.

The little clothing shop saw a lot of Flora; she had to spend her wages on something. She'd meet with Caitlin sometimes and go into town with her during the afternoons, laughing together while they looked at furniture for Caitlin's new house. Flora's weekly meetings with Neelam to deliver the washing evolved into a quiet and valued friendship while they chatted over tea. The clean washing always accompanied with Neelam's wonderful curries and Madhar's shy eyes. Esme and Shirley, who held the chapel services next door to the garage, said hello to Flora one day at the office door. As twins they wore long brown coats and matching felt hats, their black shiny hair in a tight roll at the nape of their necks. They told Flora they were from the best island in the Caribbean, Saint Kitts; she told them how she enjoyed their lovely singing on a Sunday. Flora would often chat with the shopkeepers and Mr Singh, and always the wolf whistles as she'd walk past the workshops. Until John followed her out one day with an extremely large spanner. Everyone took it as the joke he intended, or presumed he intended. The wolf whistles replaced by waves and hails of, 'Flora'. An acceptance she was a part of that energetic place, one of the workers.

The mornings and evenings the most wonderful part; Flora would open her eyes to the start of another day with John and sit with him while he worked on until late at night, the closed shutters locking them into their own small world.

"Don't you get sick of sitting there?" asked John one night.

"No," replied Flora.

John returned her smile.

He found Flora sitting at the table writing a letter one night.

"I'm writing to Aunt Elizabeth."

John made them tea and sat on the steps with his mug. "And the man with the gun?"

Flora addressed an envelope, folded her letter and put it inside. "Aunt Elizabeth will tell father anything he needs to know." Her happy words to her aunt flowed from the pen; to do the same to her father seemed disloyal. She licked the envelope and stuck it down. "She'll miss Clairgowan House if father loses it, she's always visiting. I don't know what the big attraction is."

"Will your father still be at the house?" asked John.

"Yes, he'll hang on and pretend it isn't going to happen." Flora didn't want to discuss her father, or think of him. "And your family?" she asked.

"My parents died in an accident when I got this." John lifted the mug to his face. "I have an aunt and uncle and cousins but they conveniently disappeared after the funeral." John looked at his mug while he thought about that time. "I sold my father's business and my home to fund this place." He gave a grim smile. "I almost lost it all the first year until I found out I had to undercut all the other garages and work twice as hard to make a profit. Reg turned up a few months after I started here."

"Old friends?" asked Flora.

John puffed his cheeks out. "Not really, most probably he decided it was payback time and came running as soon as he found out it was me. I met him while we were doing our National Service in the army. I thought it was rough being a carrot top at school, but the army..." He winced and shook his head. "That and being a six foot four beanpole seemed to make me a handy target for the sergeant. Reg seemed to be well in with him because he always knew where you could find anything and get it for you. I expect he thieved most of it." John shrugged. "Anyway the sergeant thought we were friends so I hung around Reg for protection. And to give Reg credit he went along with it. He's the same now, thieving and other things. He thinks he's smart by getting by without a job but he's always showing up here when he's short of money."

"Alasdair my brother died in the war," said Flora. "Aunt Elizabeth said my mother couldn't cope with his loss. So…" She gave an over bright laugh. "At nine years old Flora Ballardine was told it was her responsibility to care for her father." Flora looked over John's shoulder and saw her mother's face while she told her this, minutes before she left Clairgowan House.

John put his mug down, took Flora's hand and led her up the steps.

# Chapter Twentyone

*It* was Friday August 1st; the day George Gibson was due to inspect the car, which consisted of the bare chassis and hundreds of car parts on the benches.

Flora walked into the welcome shade of the garage, sat on her chair and lifted up her ponytail to cool down, her 'work uniform' now sandals and cotton skirts and flowery blouses.

"No shopping?" asked John. He shrugged his overalls off, changed into his shoes and went to the sink to wash his hands.

"We don't need any," said Flora "And I took the washing to Neelam this morning so it will be curry for supper." She scratched at the table with a fingernail. "Caitlin's expecting to hear about a house soon so we went into town to look at curtains. I saw some nice ones for the room but I didn't have the measurements."

"No!" John shook his head. "Stop trying to make this place into a home Flora. It's somewhere I have to get out of not be comfortable in."

Flora noticed the 'I', and sighed at another rejection to any of her suggestions to brighten up the room.

John nodded at a car. "I'm taking that out for a test run."

139

Flora jumped off her chair. "But Mr Gibson's due in," she cried. "He'll make even more fun of me if I'm here alone."

"Oh I'm sure my personal secretary can cope with him for a few minutes," smiled John. He gave Flora a quick kiss, jumped into the car in his vest and jeans and drove out of the garage.

The office doorbell rang a few minutes later. A deep breath before Flora opened the door. It had to be George Gibson of course, his skin a deeper brown against a cream linen suit. He stepped back in mock fear before making great play of easing himself past Flora while gazing into her eyes. A chuckle at her reddening cheeks.

"The man will be here I presume."

Gibson through the door and into the garage before Flora could say otherwise.

"Ah!" He stood in the empty garage and turned to Flora as she followed him in.

"John shouldn't be long," said Flora willing for it to be true.

"Then I shall have to make do with his personal secretary," said Gibson. He pushed his jacket back to put his hands into his trousers pockets and walked over to the benches, face down to the parts as he circled around them.

"All set for the components to be fitted," said Flora in the hope she sounded knowledgeable.

Gibson lifted his head to smile at her. "I am sure Mrs Gibson will be delighted to hear that my dear."

"Would you like a drink of tea Mr Gibson?" asked Flora. Anything to pass the time until John returned

"That would be wonderful my dear," he replied.

Gibson paced around the garage while Flora made the tea, and wincing more than once at the nearness of his suit to the dirty machinery.

He took the mug from her hand and looked into it. "No lemon?"

Flora laughed.

"Ah!" Gibson motioned to her with the mug. "A smile at last." He put the mug into his left hand and extended his right hand out to Flora. "I would say introductions are in order."

"Flora Ballardine." She took the hand.

Gibson pressed Flora's hand to his lips, an eyebrow up as her name registered. "The Ballardine Estate!" he exclaimed releasing her hand. "I shoot near there. You wouldn't be any relation to Mungo Ballardine?"

"My father," replied Flora.

Gibson raised his hand up to the garage. "Then what on earth are you doing in this place?"

Two heads turned to the car as John drove into the garage.

Flora's smile the answer to Gibson's question. He nodded, put the mug onto the table and strode over to John as he got out of the car.

"Miss Ballardine informs me that you are all set for the components to be fitted."

Flora screwed her face up behind Gibson's back and shrugged at John.

John tried not to smile at her. "Yes, everything's on schedule."

Flora escaped to her chair and left John and Gibson at the benches discussing the car.

"I will return two weeks before the delivery date," said Gibson on his way to the office door. A nod and a polite, "Miss Ballardine," to Flora.

She went over to John. "Do you think you'll have it completed in time?"

He nodded. "We should make it; the upholstery's coming along nicely. There's a hold up with the buckled wheel, but they haven't let me down before. We'll start the assembly on Monday. I've given everyone the weekend off. It will give me Sunday to myself to work on the engine." John put his arms around Flora and pulled her to him. "Apart from a few jobs tomorrow we'll have most of the day to ourselves, and seeing as Gibson has agreed to my price for the car we might go somewhere special to celebrate."

"Where?" asked Flora. Apart from the night at the bar they hadn't been out anywhere.

John rocked her in his arms and looked up while he pretended to think about it.

Flora saw the scar under his beard, a surprise reminder of something she forgot, she wondered if he ever did.

John put his face down to her. "I think we deserve a meal in town. Then you can show me what you look like in some of those new clothes that seem to be taking up most of the space in the wardrobe. I haven't seen you in that red frock yet."

"It's a dress," argued Flora.

"I hope you two young people are not quarrelling." Neelam walked in with the plates of curry and put them onto the table. She turned to Madhar who was stood outside in the street with the washing in his arms. "Come Madhar."

The boy walked up to Flora with his face down to the washing.

The two women smiled at each other; they both knew Madhar had a crush on Flora.

"Thank you Madhar." Flora took the washing, dashed upstairs with it, put it away and remade the bed in 30 seconds flat and ran back down with the forks in her hand.

"Enjoy your curry," said Neelam as she led Madhar away. "I have made it extra hot today."

"We will, thank you Neelam," said Flora already at the table with her fork poised over a plate.

Gallons of water later and still gasping from the heat of the curry John pulled the shutters down as soon as the garage emptied of cars so they could take to the bed to recover.

Flora tried hard not to burp into his face while she fidgeted in the heat.

"You're not going to settle, are you woman?"

"I'm hot and thirsty," complained Flora.

"We'll soon sort the hot bit out."

John pulled his clothes off, and Flora's and dragged her to the shower. She put her arms around his waist as he reached for the controls, shrieking at the cold pin pricks of water. It soon chased them back to the bed, crashing down to it with arms around each other.

John lifted his head to look at Flora, water dripping off his beard onto her face. She looked into his eyes, and saw for the first time some semblance of her love for him.

"Come on." John jumped off the bed and grabbed a towel. "We'll go to the bar and quench our thirst there."

They arrived to see Caitlin busy serving drinks, which meant...

Patrick put John's beer in front of him and smiled at Flora. She put a lot of careful thought into that moment, hair brushed down her back, make up, high heels with her cotton skirt and blouse.

"And don't you be thinking you can fool me with the powder and lipstick young lady." Patrick poured out another fizzy lemonade and plonked it in front of her. "You look at the most seventeen now, so it's still the lemonade you'll be getting from me."

Flora looked at John for support to see him laugh and pick up his beer. "You're not much use," she snorted.

They found a table, Caitlin joined them a few minutes later and smiled at Flora's lemonade. "I see Daddy's still playing his games." She called over to Patrick. "Give Flora a proper drink daddy."

Patrick ignored Caitlin and continued to discuss his future grandchild with anyone who didn't have the sense to move away.

"Go on, give her a Babycham daddy," persisted Caitlin.

"We have none of those namby-pamby drinks in here Caitlin," retorted Patrick.

"We do," replied Caitlin. "I brought them in especially for Flora; they're under the bar in front of you."

Patrick's head ducked down to look and bobbed back up again. Down again at Caitlin's directions and up again with one eye wider than the other, starting to resemble a Cyclops when at last he plonked the offending item onto the bar.

"And the glass and cherries daddy."

Patrick found them and banged them down beside the small bottle.

"I would go for it now Flora if I were you," said Caitlin. "Before he thinks it's beneath him to serve such a namby-pamby drink."

Flora jumped up. "I will," she laughed, "anything's better than a lemonade."

Patrick pushed the small champagne glass over the bar to Flora, along with the unopened bottle. Flora giggled and pushed them back. Patrick gave an exaggerated sigh, took the top off the bottle and poured out the sparkling drink.

The little scene looked at by an audience of two, John and Caitlin.

"Danny and I should have our own house soon," said Caitlin.

John drained the last of his beer. "Yes I know, Flora told me."

"Building a nest for my baby." Caitlin smiled while still looking at Flora. "Wanting everything to be perfect."

"I'm sure it will be," said John looking at Flora. "I wouldn't want to spoil it for you Caitlin."

They watched Flora and Patrick argue over the cherries. Patrick stabbed one with a cocktail stick and with his mouth twisted in disgust plopped it into the drink.

Flora walked back to them with eyes on the bobbing cherry. "Ach, now you two wouldn't be hatching a plot would you?" She sat at the table and watched the bubbles fizz up as she stirred the Babycham with the cherry.

"What plot?" asked Caitlin with a quick look to John.

"Why, who is going to be after my cherry," laughed Flora.

She picked up the stick and put the cherry in front of Caitlin, and about to comment on her unsmiling face when John leant over and snapped at it with his teeth, the cherry gone, Flora open mouthed at the empty stick.

John stood with his glass and mumbled something about another drink while he tried to swallow the cherry.

"Caitlin," shouted Patrick motioning to her to help him at the bar.

Caitlin hurried over, served John his drink and held up a cigar.

John took it and leant forward to the match.

"Thank you," whispered Caitlin who had one more item to cross off her list before she could burrow down into her now safe world. The last which should have been the first, her father cried with joy at the news of the baby, and he'd cry again at the news she was leaving.

John turned from the bar with his cigar and beer, Caitlin called him back.

Flora looked up to see John stood above her with his cigar clenched in his teeth, a pint of beer in one hand and a cherry on a stick in the other.

One more Babycham, a couple of cigars and more than a few

pints later, "You're drunk," laughed Flora pulling John away from an approaching car as they crossed over the street.

"Of course I'm not," said John dropping the keys at the door.

Flora picked them up and unlocked the door. The taste of beer and cigars on John's kisses as they stumbled through the office and into the garage with arms around each other.

"That's where the real money's coming from." He waved a hand over to the MG. "That's what's getting us out of here, and right on time."

Flora enjoyed the 'us' part of his drunken talk, John hadn't spoken of her being a part of his future before. "Where to?" she asked.

"To begger and bitter things," said John his foot missing the bottom step. He pulled Flora up to the door and put his brow to hers while he thought about it. "Or I should say bigger and better things." He dragged Flora into the room with him. "That's what the great scheme's all about. Now there's a team of two in the great scheme of Mason."

John pulled his clothes off and crashed down to the bed, and asleep by the time Flora joined him. She kissed his brow, covered them both and snuggled into him.

## Chapter Twenty Two

"*Still* a hangover?" asked Flora.

John pulled the shutters down and pulled her off her chair. "What hangover?" he growled.

Flora giggled into his face. "The hangover where you had aspirin instead of bacon sandwiches for breakfast."

John nuzzled his face into her neck, his lips soft on her throat, a shiver of pleasure at the silky feel of hair on her skin. Flora took his hand and led him up to the room.

The sun created crazed patterns on the dirt on the window while they undressed each other in the bright light. Life with its many noises at the other side of the glass, voices, cars, doors, clashes, bangs, bells. All a separate world as they kissed warm moist skin.

They slept, Flora lifting her head to quiet. She sat up and checked her watch. "It's nearly seven. What time are we going out?"

John pulled her down to him. "Do you really want to go? We could always have fish and chips." He put a hand behind Flora's head and reached for her lips.

Flora pulled her head back. "But you said you wanted to see me in my red dress."

"You can always wear it here," said John reaching for her lips again. "I can lie on the bed and watch you walk up and down in it." He jumped at the nip at his waist, another jump at another try for her lips.

John gave up and sat on the edge of the bed. "The table's booked for eight thirty so we've plenty of time."

"When did you book the table?" asked Flora.

"Yesterday, while you were out," said John.

"But you said it was to celebrate Mr Gibson agreeing to the price for the MG," said Flora. "That was after I came back."

"I knew he'd agree," said John. He scratched at his chest and looked down at himself. "I need a shower."

"So do I," said Flora.

The room seemed even smaller while they both prepared themselves for their night out.

"I'll get the car out while you are finishing off." John pulled a dark maroon tie out of the wardrobe and put it under his shirt collar. It gave a stylish touch to his sober navy blue suit.

Flora stepped into her dress and turned to him to pull up the zip.

John lifted her damp hair and kissed the nape of her neck.

Flora turned her face to him, dimples in the pink of her cheeks. "Was it worth my while me taking it out of the wardrobe?"

"Well, I have seen you in it now." said John. He pulled up the zip, fastened his tie and walked out of the room, away from temptation.

Flora applied her powder and lipstick in the shower room mirror and looked down at her dress. It looked much the same as thousands of other dresses, a tight nipped in waist, no sleeves, a low scooped neckline, flaired skirt down to her calves. The colour set it apart from all of the other dresses. A red so bright it glimmered on the cotton sheen, and she and Caitlin found the perfect complement to its vibrancy, black patent leather high heeled shoes.

John parked the car out in the street and waited for Flora at the bottom of the steps. He watched her descend them with fingers to the wall with its years of scuff marks and ran up to her to give her his hand; a flimsy piece of paper drawn to a flame. A flip of his heart at her smile down at him, a strange new sensation.

He was pleased he chose the best for that night, heads turning while they were led to their table in the plush French restaurant, eyes following the flame red dress and black mass of hair.

John watched Flora enjoy the food and wine, her large brown eyes only for him. He smoked a cigar after the meal and while they finished their second bottle of wine

Flora looked at her empty glass and leant over the table to him. The low cut of her dress exposed her breasts, her skin milky white against the red.

"Has it all gone?" she asked.

"Yes," said John. "I think we've drank enough to celebrate my birthday." He saw Flora absorb this information; she'd drunk far more wine than he.

"I thought we were celebrating the price for the car," she exclaimed.

"We are, and the fact that when I'm twenty eight this time next year we won't be living in that hovel of a room."

Flora counted on her fingers. "That makes you…" she counted again, "seven."

John laughed. "Nearly there."

Flora leant over to him again. "But I haven't bought you a birthday present."

John leant over to her. "I've got news for you Flora Ballardine. When you lean over to me like that it's the best birthday present you could give any man."

Flora put her bottom lip between her teeth and sat upright. "Then you'll have to order me a whisky if we've finished the wine." She lifted her chin until her hair fell down the back of her chair and looked around the restaurant, turning her face to John with eyes so wide they looked surprised.

"I think a coffee would do nicely to end the meal with," he suggested thinking she might be a little drunk.

Flora opened her mouth in exaggerated shock. "Ach ye big jessie get yourself a drink of whisky, I'm having one. It's the least I can do, toast your birthday."

John reluctantly ordered a whisky for her. Flora held the glass to him and gulped it down, her skin flushing as far as her breasts.

"I think we'd better go," said John. He nodded at the waiter for the bill.

"Can't I give you another toast?" asked Flora. She blinked her eyes as though trying to focus them on him.

John ignored her and stood as soon as the bill arrived. He put the money onto the table. "You stay there until I help you up," he ordered hoping she wouldn't make a fool of herself while they walked out.

Flora took his hand, rose to her feet without a falter and with a meek look down followed John away from the table.

Again the eyes as they walked out of the restaurant.

John studied Flora's face in the cool night air; the breeze lifted her hair, the traffic swished by.

"Are you playing with me Flora Ballardine?"

"No, I love you too much to do that to you." She smiled at him. "Happy birthday John."

The people in the restaurant looked out to see the tall bearded man lean down and put a soft gentle kiss on the lips of the beautiful woman in red with the long black hair.

# Chapter Twenty Three

*John* lay on the bed with his head on a hand. "I suppose there's at least a dozen people down in the street taking a good look at you."

Flora splashed water into a cup and took some aspirin. "I doubt if there are many people around at six o'clock on a cloudy Sunday morning. And no one can see anything through this filthy glass." She gave a quick look out of the window and rushed back to the bed to snuggle into John under the covers.

He pushed her hair from her screwed up face, her eyes tight shut.

"I've a headache," she said, eyes still shut.

"Not a hangover?" A light enquiry followed by a kiss on her brow.

"I never have hangovers," snapped Flora. "And stop it."

"What do you expect when you insist on running around with no clothes on?"

"You shouldn't have looked," said Flora, after she responded to John's kiss.

A summer storm rumbled its way over them, leaving behind it a rattle of rain on the shutters. Below in the garage John engrossed with his work, Flora sat at the table watching him. She left him in the afternoon to kneel on the bed with her ear to the wall, humming along to the sweet voices of Esme and Shirley and their fellow worshippers.

# Chapter Twenty Four

*John* opened the shutters on Monday morning to see cobbles washed so clean every single one looked shiny and scrubbed.

The shutters down that evening following Paddy, Sunny and Reg's arrival. They left at 10; John closed the shutter after them and worked on until well after midnight, a pattern he was to continue over the following weeks.

Flora sat on her chair and watched the car materialize in front of her like a bright red phoenix.

Paddy worked at fitting the parts from the benches, always with his trilby rammed down on his head. Sunny constructed a wooden frame and assembled the body shell around it, always with a smile. Reg worked hard at looking busy; he behaved off-hand towards Flora and acted as though she was in the way whenever she took a mug of tea over to one of them.

John was so engrossed with the car nothing else was allowed to intrude into his life, including Flora. He'd follow her to bed hours later and out of it hours before her.

Neelam and Caitlin her only respite from her isolation, but Caitlin had finally been allocated her new house and she was busy decorating it with Danny.

Paddy and his constant talk cheered Flora. It usually concerned her physical attributes and babies and he'd often serenade her with his Irish songs. One night stood over her with his arms outstretched, his Adam's apple bobbing up and down to such an extreme Flora almost fell of her chair laughing at him.

"If you did less singing we might get more work done tonight," roared John. His glare wasn't at Paddy who had his back to him, his look at Flora.

"You have to give the ladies some attention John." Paddy winked at Flora. "And there's no need to be jealous of old Paddy. I've enough on my plate woman wise to keep me going for the rest of my life." Another wink at Flora.

John slumped down on the bed well after two that morning and asleep before he covered himself. Flora wrapped the bedclothes around him and held him in her arms.

On her return from the baker's the next morning she picked up the post off the office floor to find a letter addressed to her, in her aunt's handwriting.

"Are you going to eat your sandwiches before they get cold?" she asked switching the kettle on. Flora thought John intended to carry on working on the MG, but he walked over to the sink and washed his hands.

He sat on the steps and pulled the diary over to him, flicking through the pages while taking a bite out of a sandwich.

Flora made the tea, sat on her chair and opened her letter. "It's from Aunt Elizabeth," she said looking at John. She made it clear in her letter to her aunt that she and John were living together, unsure how she would react to this. A smile as she read the letter. Not a hint of censure from her aunt, her words full of love and warm wishes and a post script to say she'd visited Clairgowan and informed her father as to her whereabouts. Flora had a feeling her aunt omitted to tell him of her living arrangements.

"Why don't you pay your aunt a visit?" asked John still at the diary.

"You're not getting rid of me that easy," said Flora.

"I'm not trying to get rid of you." John looked at her with eyes dull with fatigue, his unsmiling face set for an argument.

"Am I in the way?"

"Of course not," retorted John. "It's just I haven't the space for anything else with a rush job."

"I'm helping aren't I?" asked Flora. "Answering the telephone, taking the paperwork off your shoulders."

"Yes," said John. "But I need to put all of my attention onto the car. If you were at your aunt's I could. Do you think I like it you sitting around all the hours God sends? We've hardly spoken over the past few days."

Flora supposed it was some consolation John had noticed. A shiver at the thought of sitting with the tea ladies. "I'm a big girl now John, I don't need you to hold my hand."

John at the diary again, Flora knew he was looking for space to spend more time on the MG.

"I've been checking some of the smaller jobs." She pointed to the ones she marked. "These are so small it's hardly worth your while for the small amount of money they bring in. If I booked in the worthwhile jobs for the mornings it would leave you the afternoons to work on the MG. You said the restorations were bringing the real money in." Flora looked at John and waited.

"It took a long time to turn this place around," said John looking at the diary. He shook his head. "I decided I wouldn't turn any work down."

"I'm not saying you should turn work down," said Flora." I can always use my charm to put them off until you've finished with the MG. And you were ages on the telephone yesterday talking to someone about his car. I can do that, all I need to do is ask your advice."

John studied Flora while he thought about it. "Right. Give it a try and I'll see how it goes. And remind me to telephone Sunny to tell him to chase up his cousin at the upholsterer's. I want the cockpit finished for Gibson's visit."

"I'll do that, " said Flora. "When would you like him to come?"

"Now!" said John pushing himself up from the steps as a car drove into the garage. He hadn't even finished his sandwiches.

Flora went over to John later that morning. "I've contacted Sunny's cousin." Talking down to the back of his head as he worked on a car. "I've arranged he comes in the day after tomorrow. It will give me time to rearrange the diary. And I've told him to come in the mornings so it will leave you with the afternoons free to work on the MG without having him under your feet. He said it would take three mornings to complete all of the upholstery." She waited for John's response. "I said I would confirm it with him if you agreed."

John stopped working on the car and stood over Flora. "I suppose you think all of that was a brilliant idea."

"Yes!" She gave him a steady look back.

"It was," said John, and gave her a quick kiss on the lips.

Sent away forgotten, the kiss the only physical contact they had in weeks.

"You'll need to see Jagroop to see if he has any chrome cleaner," said John nodding to the end of a bench and a jumble of chrome fittings. "Reg should be doing them but he doesn't seem to be making much progress."

Flora couldn't remember Reg going anywhere near them. "Can I do them?" She asked and waited to be told to leave them alone.

"Yes, if you want to," said John.

Flora a part of the team that night as she polished away and set out her gleaming trophies on the table.

"I hope he's paying you the going rate for that Flora," shouted Paddy, a wink at her inclusion in the workforce.

Sunny walked over to her and smiled down to her. "My cousin will be here with the upholstery. He asks me what country is your accent. I told him it is a Scotland accent." He beamed at Flora and waited for her confirmation.

"Yes, I'm from Scotland," said Flora.

"My cousin has never heard of it before," said Sunny.

"Scotland?" asked Flora.

"No. the way it is spoken," said Sunny still beaming.

Flora looked up from her polishing a few minutes later and saw Reg standing over her; he'd placed himself so the other men wouldn't see his face.

"I'm supposed to be doing that." His voice low so the others wouldn't hear him. "You must think you are clever taking the money out of my hand."

"I'll give you the money myself if you're so worried about it," responded Flora.

Reg stepped forward until he almost touched her; Flora pushed her chair back so she could stand. Reg turned to the roar of the engine.

Paddy let out a whoop.

The roar petered out, an anticlimax following the loud noise.

"You've done it John," shouted Paddy.

John grinned over to him. "Just about, a little more work tonight should do it."

"Then we can start fitting it into the car tomorrow." Paddy finished for him.

John nodded, still grinning.

"And it's all downhill after that," said Paddy "And you and Flora will be having more time together to be making babies."

"Paddy!" shouted Flora her cheeks heating up.

"What?" asked Paddy looking bemused with his screwed up smile.

John put his fists on his hips. "You are asking for a bloody nose you are Paddy."

"Now would you be doing that to a man supporting five children and another on the way?" asked Paddy.

"I would if he keeps on like that," said John.

"Well if that's the case I'd better be getting myself away." Paddy pulled off his overalls, winked at Flora and walked over to a shutter.

John hurried after him. "You're not walking out on me because of that are you?"

"No. I'm going to be chasing up those wheels," said Paddy.

"I need them on before Gibson gets here," said John shaking his head at him.

"If that is what you want, then that is what you shall have John," replied Paddy pushing up the shutter.

"I will be coming also," said Sunny to Paddy. He gestured at Flora. "You will show my cousin the doors? I will not be here tomorrow."

"Yes I will Sunny," said Flora who was delighted to be involved in more work on the car.

Reg appeared from the back of the garage with his jacket on. "I can come in early for that."

"No need," said John. "Flora's quite capable of dealing with it."

Flora prepared Sunny and Paddy's money for them at the end of each week, but whenever Reg was there he'd hang around John until he took his wallet out to give him a pound note for not doing much at all.

Reg waited for Sunny and Paddy to leave then stood over John who was back at working on the engine. John straightened up, looked at the grease and oil on his hands and turned around for a cloth to wipe them on.

"I'll get it," said Flora. She could have taken the money out of the tin box but she didn't, smiling at John as she unbuttoned his overalls. Conscious of Reg presence as she put her face to John's vest while reaching behind him. He hadn't showered for a couple of days, she breathed in his odour and another smile at him while she took the pound note out of his wallet.

Reg snatched it from her hand. "I might not make it for a couple of nights." He walked over to the open shutter, and at no reply from John. "I might have something else on."

"If you do, you do," snapped John. "I'm sure we can cope without you."

"I'll see how it goes," said Reg ducking under the shutter.

Flora looked at John. "Why do you put up with him?"

"I feel sorry for him I suppose." John put his hands up while Flora put the wallet back. Face down to her hair when she put her arms around him. "Do I deserve that?"

"You always will," said Flora.

John looked down at Flora as she fastened up his overalls. "If you stop tormenting me I should be finished in around an hour."

"OK, I'll stop tormenting you," laughed Flora.

John turned the engine over until he was satisfied with it. The shutter clashed down minutes later and Flora led up the steps. "I need a shower."

"So do I," said Flora. "Polishing chrome can be hot work."

# Chapter Twenty Five

*Flora* thought Sunny's cousin would have some family resemblance, such as being short and round or with a permanent smile on his face. She gulped at the tall, devastatingly handsome young man who walked into the garage. He had black glossy hair and eyes as large and luminous as Madhar's, and he wasn't dressed for work in a well cut light coloured suit. Two workers arrived with him, they carried in the cream leather seating and over the three mornings attached the hood and fitted out the remainder of the car. It started as soon as Flora took Sunny's cousin over to the doors. A show of white teeth the moment she spoke and him constantly flitting from the workers to Flora encouraging her to speak, and John was so busy he didn't notice a thing.

The last minute rush for Gibson's visit. Paddy fixed the wheels on the night before. The engine in the car, but not connected up, and the body work completed except for a lot of Flora's chrome work which still lay shining on a bench.

Flora in the office typing when he arrived. A polite, "Miss Ballardine," as she opened the door.

A smiling man returned.

"The car's looking lovely isn't it," said Flora.

"All the lovelier if you were sitting in it," replied Gibson. Eyebrows up at Flora as he went outside.

She finished her typing and took it into the garage.

John sat on the steps drinking tea in the lull before Paddy and Sunny's arrival.

"Mr Gibson seems happy," said Flora sitting at the table to check her letters.

"Very," said John. "And so am I at the price he's paying."

"He said something about me sitting in it." Flora looked at John for an explanation.

"Well…" John put his mug down and rubbed his beard while he thought about it. "He did want you to be included in the deal."

Flora tried to understand.

"He thought you'd go well with the car, sitting in it with your hair blowing in the wind." John tried to look serious. "But I said he couldn't have you because I needed you here to do the typing and answer the telephone. You know that sort of thing."

Flora gave a dismissive tut to the letters.

"But then I thought…" John couldn't stop a smile. "Why shouldn't you be sitting in the car while I deliver it?"

Flora sniffed. "You'll be going alone."

"But we've been invited to the party!" exclaimed John.

Flora studied his face. "If I am going, I am not going as a part of the birthday present."

"Would I do that to you?" John leant forward and put a hand behind her head.

"You might." Flora parted her lips.

"Will this convince you?" John pulled Flora's face to him and gave her a long heart jumping kiss.

"I think you should try to convince me again." Flora parted her

162

lips again.

John tried to convince her again and sat back. "Gibson asked me to look at a couple of cars a friend of his needs to offload. I'll take a look at them while I'm delivering the MG. One sounds roadworthy. If it is we could drive back in it and spend the night at a good hotel. Of course…" John looked very serious. "It will mean I'll have to give you a lot of money so you can buy suitable clothes. Something special for the party and the hotel."

Flora thought about it, turned her chair to John and put her face up to him. "I'm sorry, but you'll have to convince me again. I can take some convincing sometimes."

# Chapter Twenty Six

*Flora* turned her head away from the shower room mirror. "I've packed the suitcase and put your clothes on the bed for you John and I've polished your tan shoes."

"So I see."

Flora waited to hear the sounds of John changing before she applied her lipstick. "Everything OK?"

"Yes. I don't want any complaints from Gibson with the kind of money he's paying."

Flora looked at herself in the mirror, hair brushed down her back, subdued cheeks, brown eye shadow, mascara, bright red lipstick.

"Right, that's me ready," said John. "I'll take the suitcase down and park the MG out in the street. I'll leave the hood down; it's quite nice out there." He laughed. "And I'll give that poor sod some money and send him on his way. He's even put his overalls on to look busy."

"Reg is an expert at looking busy," said Flora fastening the large brown buttons on her jacket. The fur collar created a brown ruff around her neck. Her suit a silky tweed material, an open weave of subdued greens, yellows, creams and browns, her shape accentuated by the tight pencil skirt and fitted jacket.

Flora hurried out to the room as soon as she heard John run down the steps. She'd put her suit at the back of the wardrobe along with her dress for the hotel, all away from John's eyes until she wore them. Her dress wrapped up and hidden at the bottom of the suitcase. The now familiar roar of the MG below her in the garage while she took a paper bag out of her cotton duffle bag in the bottom of the wardrobe. Feet pushed into brown leather high heels, matching clutch bag snatched up, the paper bag put behind her as John rushed up the steps and into the room.

"What do you think?" She grimaced down to her legs. "I've even put stockings on."

John saw a small hat or a piece of brown fur pushed into the top of Flora's hair. He thought she might have worn a dress for the party, but she looked so beautiful and sophisticated she was sure to outshine anyone else there. Uncertain which he preferred, the stylish model in front of him or the Flora with shiny skin and red cheeks. He decided both, another flip of his heart.

"I thought you said you were ready." Flora shook her head at John's unfastened waistcoat and shirt collar.

He looked down at himself and grabbed his tie off the bed.

Flora had chosen John's clothes with great care. The tie dark gold, his suit the lightest colour she could find in the wardrobe, a dark oatmeal worsted. She waited for him to fasten his tie and button up his waistcoat before she took the paper bag from behind her back.

"I've bought you a little present." She took a cream and green paisley silk scarf out of the paper bag and draped it over John's shoulders.

"It's..." He stuck his chin in to look down at it. "It's a bit bright."

"It suits you," said Flora smoothing the cream fringe down his jacket. It did, the splash of green and cream went well with his suit. John had his hair and beard cropped for the day. He looked handsome and debonair, a man ready to conquer anything he put his mind to.

"Must I wear it?" asked John.

"Yes," laughed Flora. She grabbed his hand and dragged him out of the room.

The sky clear and blue, ideal for open topped driving. Flora waited in the car while John closed up the garage; a shout stopped him pulling down the last shutter.

Reg walked out of the back of the garage holding up his wrist. "Forgot my watch."

John watched him walk away down the street and turned his head to look at the back of the garage.

"Love the scarf John."

The shout from one of the dark recesses of the workshops.

Flora put a hand to her mouth and smiled.

John gave a warning look around him as he clashed the shutter down, locked it and concertinaed himself into the car. His turn to smile as the car bumped its way down the street.

Flora opened her mouth and looked down at the seat. "I can feel every cobble."

She clung onto her little fur hat as the car roared its way down the main road, and decided the paisley scarf would be best wrapped around her head instead of flapping around on John's shoulders.

They found the house where the two cars were for sale at the outskirts of Oxford, near to Gibson's address. It looked rather grand with a curved driveway leading to a large white door. Baxter, the owner, a tall pointy faced man who gave a forced laugh every time he said something. Flora waited in the MG while John followed him to the back of the house. He drove past her a few minutes later in a large blue open topped car with Baxter by his side. The car much more substantial than the MG; it had seats in the back and a silver eagle in flight on the top of the radiator.

Flora stepped out of the car to give her backside a rub. She walked to the side of the house and saw a woman at a doorway, hair a lank curtain over her face as she leant forward to look up to the back of the house. The woman's furtiveness hurried Flora away, she sat in the MG until John and Baxter returned.

John drove the car to the back of the house and returned to the MG a few minutes later.

"Well?" asked Flora.

John shrugged. "He agreed to my offer. He's tidying the Alvis for me to pick up later. Sunny will have to pick up the Aston Martin." He raised his eyebrows at Flora. "A Le Mans, quite a find."

If Baxter's house looked grand Gibson's was a palace in comparison. They followed a line of cars up a long sweeping drive to an elegant Georgian mansion with ivy covered walls. Two men waved the cars away to park on a field adjacent to the house. The elder of the two pointed at the MG and indicated they follow him; he led them to an empty courtyard, a hand up for them to stop.

John took the suitcase out of the car. The sounds of a band playing 'Stupid Cupid' drifted over the house as he put it down to the ground and watched with Flora while the man scrutinize every inch of the car and polished it from end to end with a duster out of his pocket. Inside and out, an extra rub on Flora's gleaming chrome work.

"Excellent," said the man to the car. He put the duster back into his pocket, picked up the suitcase and led them away. "Mr Gibson is waiting for you sir," to John, a nod to Flora, "madam."

Flora put the scarf into her bag, tidied her hair and gave a parting look back to the brash red and chrome.

The man led them into the house and along a long hallway awash with flowers and antiques. He put the suitcase down, gave a soft knock on a door and opened it at the response from the other side.

"Mr and Mrs Mason," announced the man.

Gibson rose from his chair behind a large ornate desk as the man led John and Flora into the room. Large French windows behind him gave a panoramic view of acres of sweeping lawns with people wandering over the grass or sat at tables beside a large white marquee.

"The car appears to be in excellent order sir," said the man. "Shall I inform Mrs Gibson of its arrival?"

"Good," responded Gibson. "And yes Thomas you may inform Mrs Gibson."

Thomas bowed and closed the door as he left the room.

Gibson motioned John and Flora to chairs at the front of the desk. His eyes appraised Flora, an imperceptible nod along with a smile to her. "Is it to be Mrs Mason or Miss Ballardine?"

She smiled. "Flora will do."

"Then Flora it will be." Gibson sat and took a prepared cheque from the desk and gave it to John. "I've had Baxter weeping down the phone. He did think you might make him a better offer for the cars."

"He needn't have accepted it," replied John.

"He will take any cash that comes his way," said Gibson. He sat back in his chair. "But you have obviously gathered that already. Whatever you give him it will be gambled away in a few days. The house will be the next to go. His poor wife is near to suicide with his behaviour."

A fair haired woman hurried into the room carrying streamers of white ribbon.

"This is Gloria my wife," said Gibson. "Who has been driven to absolute distraction all day organising the party."

His wife made a playful swing of the ribbons at him. "I'm here to tell you Thomas will drive the car up to the marquee as soon as we have decorated it." She went to the window behind the desk to gesticulate to someone outside with the ribbons. "I hope they can keep Sebastian inside the marquee for a little longer."

"It will be a wonder if he's still standing, leaving him beside all of that champagne," said Gibson. "And the gardener will love that, driving on his precious grass."

"Oh, you are an old fuss pot." Gloria Gibson kissed her husband on the top of his head and turned to John and Flora. "I'm afraid I will have to leave you, I've left Thomas blowing up the balloons. There's an ample supply of champagne in the marquee, help yourselves." She gave a devastatingly beautiful smile and left the room with a flutter of ribbon behind her.

Gibson stood and opened the windows behind the desk. "Would you like to watch the car's grand entrance Flora?"

The sounds of the band playing 'All I Have to Do Is Dream' came from the marquee.

Flora smiled at John and joined Gibson at the window.

A hand hovered over Flora's shoulders as Gibson pointed along a terrace at the side of the house. "You will have a good viewpoint at the steps a little further along."

Flora walked to the top of the steps and looked down to the marquee with her handbag held in front of her.

Gibson studied her for a few moments before he returned to his chair behind the desk. He leant over to John. "So you should be busy for a while?"

John had an idea the talk was the true reason for the invitation to the party and why Gibson encouraged Flora to leave. "The two cars should keep me going for a few months. The Aston Martin needs a bit of work. But the two of them are more in need of a revamp and a tidy rather than a full restoration."

"And the garage?" asked Gibson. "You did say you would be moving on."

"Yes," nodded John. "The garage is due to be demolished to make way for a new motorway. It will be a convenient jumping off point for me."

Gibson clasped his hands on the desk. "Gloria has decided we are to live in the south of France and has set her heart on a small châteaux we have seen." A hand lifted in the air. "So of course this old pile will have to go and I intend to off load a number of my business interests to start the slow decline into retirement. I like the way you work, you handled Baxter very well and you came through with the car. Would you be interested if I had any business to put your way? And more to the point, do you have the finances to take advantage of anything I might offer you?"

John considered this. "I wouldn't have the finance for a large business, but I would be interested in a small to medium sized business. It would all depend on the outlay of course."

Gibson nodded and gave John a gilt edged card. "This is my London office. If you move on before I have contacted you, or if you are no longer interested let me know. Otherwise, unless I have a change of heart I will contact you in six months or so. It will take me at least that to organize the property and business situation."

John knew the interview had ended; he put the card it into the breast pocket of his jacket and went over to the windows.

Gibson stood with John, the two men looking at Flora. "Of course the right kind of partner by your side can be one of your best assets. Especially if she comes with as good a pedigree as that young lady."

John about to tell Gibson to mind his own damn business when he saw admiration on the man's face, possibly envy.

It was as though she knew; Flora turned her head and smiled at John. He thought he'd never seen her look more beautiful. Drawn to her without the conscious effort of walking he heard Gibson's voice behind him.

"Find Thomas when you are ready to leave."

They stood at the top of the steps. John's hand on the soft material on Flora's hip, her smiling face to him separated from her body by a gossamer of downy fur, two heads turning together to the sound of the car horn.

The band started to play 'Happy Birthday' while Thomas drove the beribboned and ballooned car towards the marquee, leaving compressed lines of grass behind it. A gaggle of screeching girls dragged a younger version of George Gibson out of the marquee. Gloria Gibson took his hand, kissed him on the cheek and led him to the car.

"Come on, we'll join the party." Flora pulled at John's hand to go down the steps.

"Must we?" asked John. "I thought we might collect the car from Baxter and head straight for the hotel."

The girls squeezed into the car with Sebastian. Horn blaring, ribbons fluttering, balloons popping as he drove it around and around in front of the marquee, the patterns on the grass widening in ever increasing circles.

"We could at least have a drink of champagne," said Flora.

John flicked at the fur around her neck. "It's that stuff." He leant down to give her a quick kiss on the lips.

Flora pulled him down the steps. "But I want to see the band."

The two of them stepped back as the car roared past them, the labour of hundreds of man hours vanishing in a flourish of colour and noise.

Gibson observed the happy scene of his wife and son, his interest moving to the young couple at the top of the steps. He recollected the times he sought out Gloria at the conclusion of a successful business deal, their love making with that extra passion because of it. John Mason achieved two successful business deals that day. One circling in front of him, the cost of the expertise and delivery time at a premium, the other the pittance he offered Baxter for the cars. A chuckle at Flora pulling a reluctant John down the steps. Thomas knocked on the door and walked into the room with a bottle of champagne on a tray so Gibson could drink away the cost of the day. Not that it mattered, if his beloved wife and son were happy then so was he.

Thomas given instructions as to how 'Mr and Mrs Mason' would be transported to Baxter's house.

A few glasses of champagne and several tunes from the band later and jostled by the increasingly happy crowd, John finally persuaded Flora they should leave.

They found Thomas who led them through the house to the large main door, opening it to a silver Rolls-Royce.

John and Flora looked at each other.

"I have taken the liberty of taking care of your suitcase," said Thomas. He opened a door of the Rolls-Royce and stood waiting for them.

The house slipped by without a sound. John grinned over to Flora who sat on the edge of the large comfortable seat and fussed with her hair. Their taste of luxury soon over at Baxter's house.

The Alvis parked in front of the large white door with Baxter almost wringing his hands in anticipation of the money.

Flora sighed at the back of the receding Rolls-Royce while John paid Baxter and put their suitcase into the car. Looking up at the darkening sky as they drove away she took the scarf out of her bag and wrapped it around her head.

"Is the hotel far? Shouldn't we put the hood up or something?"

"I checked it, said John. "It wouldn't be much use. Anyway the hotel's not far."

The hotel was almost an hour far, the odd raindrop lashing into their faces by the time they drove up to 'The Castle'. It had two turreted towers on the two front corners which gave it some resemblance to a castle, reception not at the least put out by John's request for the car to be covered because of 'problems' with the hood. Flora hoped her nose and cheeks weren't as red as they felt as they were shown to their room.

"A bath!" she exclaimed. The four poster bed not such an attraction as the large sparkling bathroom. Flora tried the contents of various bottles and watched the hot water bubble up in the bath. She kicked off her shoes and pulled the tiny hat from her hair and gave it to John along with her jacket. "You said you were interested in that stuff." A trail of clothes left behind her as she returned to the hot water and bubbles.

"I didn't mean that," complained John.

"You took your time," said Flora with her head and shoulders above the billowing bubbles.

"I don't know what we are doing in here." John eased himself down into the scent and warmth. "We both had a shower this morning."

Flora splashed water over to him. "I'm sure we'll think of something."

# Chapter Twenty Seven

*John* checked his watch again. He hadn't taken long to change into his evening suit, sent down to the bar by Flora while she prepared herself for dinner. He was onto his third drink and second cigar as the last serving approached. A piano played in the dining room, a murmur from the diners.

"Stood up as well?" asked a man slouched beside John at the bar. His glass lifted in commiseration before he gulped his drink back.

Bleary eyes tried to focus behind John. "I take that back. That is definitely not for me."

John turned from the bar to see the vision in green.

Flora's dress a glossy silky material, a tight waist, skirt flared down to her calves, matching shoes and tiny handbag in her hand. Bare shoulders, soft white breasts cupped up to a daring exposure. Hair a mass of curls and waves and pulled back from her face with diamante clips. Her make up the same as that morning, this time with thick black eye liner to emphasise her large eyes.

John took her hand. "You look wonderful, Paddy would be proud of you."

Flora laughed, the clips flashed in her hair.

John's heart flipped and flipped again. It was the moment he knew Flora would always be there, in his heart.

They enjoyed their meal and decided to have another bottle of wine.

"So what did George Gibson have to say?" asked Flora.

"He might put some business my way next year," said John. "He seemed to think I need a partner, the right kind of partner." He didn't care about Gibson's opinion, but he still had the need to say it.

Flora's look to him steady while she waited for him to continue. Her lipstick gone, her lips soft, puckered, the colour of the wine.

"How long have we known each other?" asked John.

"Four months," answered Flora.

John shook his head. "No. It's six months."

"Before doesn't count," said Flora.

"Before doesn't count," repeated John under his breath. He filled his glass with the last of the wine.

Flora leant over to him. "Did you have much to drink at the bar?"

John gave an exaggerated wince. "Now that sounds very much like a nag to me." He held up his glass. "Do I have permission?"

Flora smiled and leant further over to him. "Yes."

"Don't do that!" exclaimed John. "Have you any idea what that does to me?"

Flora sat back her smile gone. "I think I will nag you."

John looked at his glass and put it onto the table.

"Not that," laughed Flora. "I'm going to nag you because you haven't asked me to dance." She looked over to a couple moving together on the small space in front of the piano.

John cleared his throat. "I was going to ask you something."

Flora by his chair, she took his hand. "I think if you are going to ask me something it should be at the end of a very busy day when you are stone cold sober."

She led John to the floor and yielded to him as he pressed his hand to her back. They barely moved to the music from the piano.

"Someone has to," said Flora.

John looked down to her.

She smiled up to him. "The tune. Someone to watch over you."

"I think it's me," said John. He put his face into Flora's sweet smelling hair.

The notes of the piano still in the air as they left for their room.

John quiet while they ate breakfast with no indication of how he was the night before. The day cold and windy, Flora sat in the car and wrapped the scarf around her head wishing she'd brought something more weatherproof than her suit.

John drove the car to the entrance of the hotel, stopped it and went inside. He ran out a few minutes later with a blanket.

"Stand up," he instructed.

He wrapped the blanket around Flora and sat her onto the seat.

She snuggled down to the warmth. "I think you've done this before."

"Someone has to watch over you," said John.

"Me," said Flora before she could stop herself.

"See. I wasn't that drunk," said John.

# Chapter Twenty Eight

*Flora* shook the blanket up into the air. It sighed down to the bed, the satin hem resting on the rumpled up rug. The soft plush wool and 'The Castle' emblazoned on it in large red letters brought a touch of luxury and colour to the room, and a constant reminder of that night at the hotel.

A quick run over to the baker's in the cold and dark November morning, John up hours before her to work on the engine of the Aston Martin.

"Breakfast," she shouted switching on a paraffin heater beside the table, and minutes later. "The tea and sandwiches are getting cold."

John responded to Flora's third call. He washed his hands and sat on the steps beside her. "How many enquires yesterday for the Le Mans?"

"Three," said Flora taking a sandwich out of her bag.

"You told them it will go to the highest bidder?"

"Yes," said Flora.

John took a sandwich out of his bag. "It should bump up the bank balance a good bit. I'll be starting on The Alvis Speed Twenty soon. It shouldn't take long."

Flora looked over to the long narrow car that was the current focus of John's life. Behind it loomed the stately Alvis, the next in line for his total absorption. She bit into her sandwich and questioned her presumption he was going to propose to her that night at the hotel.

"You've dropped some sausage on the floor," said John.

Flora looked down.

It took John a few minutes to bolt down his sandwiches. He drained his mug and walked over to the car. "You did keep the afternoon clear for me?"

"Yes," said Flora.

"I'm having problems finding some of the parts. I'll need a few hours to run around and find them."

"Right," said Flora who had planned to help Caitlin with her packing that afternoon.

"Paddy's off to Ireland to see the latest addition to his brood," said John at the engine of the Aston Martin. "And Sunny's busy tonight so it should give me a clear run through when I get back."

"Right," said Flora. She knew it meant another midnight finish for John and her coping with Reg if he turned up without Paddy to cheer her up.

John's 'few hours' turned out to be all of that afternoon.

The morning repairs were collected before he left so he switched the garage lights on and closed the two shutters near to Flora, leaving the one at the far end half way down to give access to any passing trade. The paperwork and the typing took no more than a couple of hours in the mornings once it was all up to date. Flora took the money out of the tin box and took it up to the room for something to do, and made a sandwich for herself while she was up there. Apart from that and taking the odd telephone call for a booking she sat at the table in the quiet watching the space under the half open shutter darken. She started to shiver despite the heater and wearing thick trousers and a jumper and tried to pull the shutter down to stop the freezing cold draught, but it wouldn't budge. So she moved her chair nearer to the steps, as far away from the draught as she could. Someone pushed the shutter all the way to the top while she was pulling the heater to the front of her chair. Thinking it was John she looked up to say what she thought about him leaving her for so long, and saw Freddie Thompson - Smythe walk up to her.

The closer he was the less he resembled the Freddie she saw in March, clothing dishevelled, his face sagging and sallow.

"Where's Reg?" No sign he recognised Flora. A stubby finger pointed over the heater at her. "Where is he?"

Flora had to swallow before she could speak. "I don't know where he is, but if I see him I'll let him know you are looking for him." Surprised at how normal her voice sounded.

"Don't come that with me," shouted Freddie. He moved to Flora's side of the heater. "I want Reg and I want him now."

"Then you'll have to go and find him," shouted Flora angry she had to heave for breath, a reminder of the dancehall.

Freddie hemmed her in between the heater and her chair at the bottom of the steps. All Flora could do was run up to the room. She picked up her chair but a leg caught on the bottom step, the extra second to lift it away gave Freddie the time to grab her wrist. He pushed her down instead of pulling Flora to him as she expected, the chair falling out of her hand and cutting into her side.

Freddie leant down and yelled into her face. "Look you bitch, I want Reg now."

A shout hurt Flora's throat, but it didn't sound the same as her voice. Freddie dragged at her wrist, pulled her up and yanked her away from the steps. Her chair clattered sideways to the floor, a metallic clang as it caught the heater. The hand let go of her wrist, the action so abrupt Flora carried on a couple of steps forward before she fell onto her hands and knees.

She looked up and saw John.

He continued to pull Freddie away and turned him around until he faced him. The punch appeared quite casual, a quick jab with little effort, but the crack on Freddie's nose said otherwise. His head jerked back, a howl, blood spurting. John marched Freddie away by the back of his collar and pushed him out of the open shutter, more howls out in the street.

Flora tried to stand but her knees wouldn't take her weight. Strong hands picked her up, strong arms held her so tight she couldn't breathe.

John's anxious face looked into hers.

"What am I thinking of leaving you here alone?" He rubbed his hands up and down her shivering body. "And you're freezing."

He helped Flora up the steps, switched the light on, sat her on the bed and wrapped the blanket around her. "Stay there," he ordered as he left the room, returning minutes later with a steaming mug of tea. "No more watching the garage alone unless you are locked in. Do you agree?"

"Yes," said Flora who would have agreed to anything to stay cocooned in the blanket with John's arm around her. She took a sip of tea.

"Thompson - Smythe got a few extra smacks for London," said John.

Flora looked up to his face. "You knew?"

He nodded and kissed her on the brow.

"And I think I knew then," said John. "Even though you were shouting and screaming at me and running off. And idiot that I am I still wouldn't accept it when you turned up here."

"Accept it?" asked Flora.

"That I love you," said John. He was going to ask Flora to marry him that night at the hotel, but the feelings he had that night without the clarity and intensity of that moment, loving Flora all the more for realising it.

Flora watched her tea as he pulled her to him.

"Has this been a busy day?" asked John.

"Yes," said Flora to the tea.

"And I'm stone cold sober?"

"Yes."

"Can I ask you that question now?"

"Yes."

"Will you marry me Flora Ballardine?"

"Yes."

"Are you going to put that mug down so I can hold you?"

Flora put the mug to the floor.

A shout came up from the garage.

"Reg," groaned John. "I should have shut the garage up."

"Freddie said he was looking for him," said Flora.

John jumped off the bed. "As soon as I saw the Jupiter I knew it was trouble."

Reg, who'd checked the tin box before he shouted, stepped away from the table as soon as he heard the door open above him.

"Is this something to do with that muck you peddle?" shouted John running down the steps

Reg licked his lips. "This has nothing to do with me John. Freddie's in with the big boys he owes them a fortune."

John grabbed the front of Reg's jacket, walked him backwards and slammed him hard against a pillar of bricks between the shutters.

Reg's hand went for his knife in his jacket pocket, but he needed John, or more importantly his money. Both hands up in supplication following another jarring thump against the pillar. "Freddie thought I could arrange to sell the Jupiter so he can pay them off." Reg waited for another thump, but John pushed him away and went outside to look up and down the street. Everything quiet, the other workshops closed with their shutters down.

"He's gone," shouted Reg who omitted to say he found the Jupiter around the corner at the top of the street. Freddie sat in it with blood down his front and blubbering on about the beating John gave him and Reg getting him out of trouble. Reg thought of a good way to get Freddie out of trouble, his knife, and Freddie wouldn't have to worry about anything again, but Reg knew it wasn't as easy as that. He was the one who introduced Freddie to the people he owed the money to; they'd be after him next if they weren't paid off and they were the kind of people who always found you in the end.

"What do you think John?" asked Reg. "He'll take anything thrown his way. The car's as good as the day you sold it to him. You could make a bomb out of it again."

"I think if he comes here again he'll be getting more of what he got before," said John. He started his car and drove it to the back of the garage.

Reg heard the car door slam shut, rubbing a hand over his mouth at the sounds of John moving around in the dark.

John eventually emerged with a box in his hands. He dumped it onto a bench and walked over to the open shutter. "Out!" he barked.

Reg shrugged so he'd look unconcerned and walked out to the street with his hands in his pockets. He fingered the knife. A surge of exhilaration at the power it gave him, imagining how he could slide it between John's ribs and do the same to the bitch up in the room, once he'd shown her a thing or two. But Reg's self induced sycophantic behaviour soon took over, he turned to John. "I would give it some serious thought John." Said with the reasonable tone of a helpful friend. "You'll make a mint out of it, a killing." The shutter screeched down, his face following the decreasing space. "Money in the bank," he shouted, twisting his mouth to the blank steel as the shutter clashed shut.

He ran to the top of the street and jumped into the car beside Freddie. "The bastard's not showing any interest. You'll have to try to sell the car on somewhere else, or get the money from the old bag who bought it for you in the first place."

Freddie's clothes and face were covered in blood, his lips and nose split and swollen, both eyes almost closed.

"My grandmother didn't have the money to start with," he wailed. "She sold off her jewellery whenever I asked for anything and now it's all gone and my parents have thrown me out because of it." Freddie put his head to the steering wheel. "What am I going to do?" His movement started the bleeding again; he pressed the corner of his jacket to the increasing flood. "I have to pay them by tomorrow. I told them to take the car but they said they want cash."

"I warned you about not crossing them," shouted Reg. "I'll work on him tomorrow, but the more this goes on the less he'll give you. He's a tight bastard; if he does agree to buy the car he'll do it for his own benefit, not yours. And I don't know what you did in there but you've just done me out of a night's money."

Freddie chanced his nose out of his jacket. "I was trying to get the bitch to tell me where you were."

"Don't you know who she is?" asked Reg.

The idiotic look on Freddie's mangled face said he had no idea what Reg was talking about.

Reg jumped out of the car.

"Where are you going?" cried Freddie.

"Where do you think?" snarled Reg. "Away from you." He walked away leaving Freddie with his nose in his jacket.

Flora heard the shutter close and peered around the door to look down to the garage.

John ran up the steps to her.

For all of their passion during their lovemaking it bore no comparison to the emotions they were experiencing at that moment, but John and Flora were both quite content to sit on the bed with their backs to the wall and hold each other.

"Why did Freddie want Reg?" asked Flora.

"He's trying to get him to sell on the Jupiter for him," replied John. "Most probably he needs to move it quick to get himself out of trouble and Reg will be in it just as deep as him."

"Will you buy it?" asked Flora.

"Hey!" John looked into her face. "Shouldn't we be discussing something else? Such as where we are going to be married."

Flora opened and closed her mouth.

"Do you mean to say we've been engaged for..." John looked at his watch. "At least fifteen minutes and you haven't decided."

Flora pulled her lips down so she'd look contrite.

"Scotland? Next door at the chapel?" John knocked on the wall by the bed.

"No," said Flora. "The registry office on the main road." She'd often stood and admired the old Victorian building with its marble pillars and stained glass windows.

"We'll go tomorrow," said John.

"Tomorrow!" exclaimed Flora.

"You aren't expecting a five year engagement are you?" asked John.

The harsh light of the bare electric bulb cast shadows down his face as he looked down at Flora, his eyes in darkness, slight creases between his brows.

She put a finger on the creases and ran it down his nose.

"I hope you are not going to say I have a bump on my nose," growled John.

"No," lied Flora. "I was going to say I love you and I love the bump on your nose."

"You must love me to want to stay in this dump with me," said John. He kissed Flora on the brow and pulled her to him. "Not much longer Flora. Next year and we'll be out of here."

"The motorway?" she asked.

John nodded and shrugged. "I gave myself six years at the most here anyway. I decided to leave everything the same so I wouldn't get comfortable." He laughed and looked down at the rug. "The only change I was going to make was to toss that thing out and it's still here."

"I'm pleased you didn't," mocked Flora. "That rug's alive. It scuttles around the room while we're asleep."

John jumped up and switched the light off. "There! That will stop you looking at the bump on my nose." He sat back on the bed and cuddled Flora to him.

"I thought you said you didn't have a bump on your nose," she laughed.

"Damn!" he exclaimed.

"Anyway I can still feel it with my finger."

John snapped at it with his teeth.

"I hope our children don't have go through their lives with bumps on their noses," warned Flora.

They sat in the dim light from the street lamps.

"No, not yet Flora," said John his tone terse. "Children will have to wait. I've worked long and hard to get to this point."

This didn't surprise Flora; John always used protection even in the most spontaneous of situations. "I'll give you ten years John Mason," she laughed. "And if you haven't impregnated me by then I'll have to nag you about it."

"You are making me feel like Paddy," laughed John. "And talking about Irishmen we'll go to the bar. I can't think of a better place to celebrate our engagement."

"I suppose I'll have to celebrate with my usual Babycham," moaned Flora.

John laughed and pulled her off the bed.

No sign of Caitlin behind the bar, John's arm around Flora while Patrick looked at her with a smile on his face and a twinkle in his eye.

"I expect you'll be wanting your usual young lady."

"Have I any choice?" asked Flora with a glare.

"I thought you might give Flora something stronger Patrick," said John. "Seeing as we are celebrating our engagement."

"And I expect you will be having your wedding reception here," said Patrick ever the one to grasp the opportunity to bring more money into the bar. "Now how many will be coming?"

"Ach, we've just decided to get married," spluttered Flora. "This is all getting a wee bit rushed."

Patrick leant over the bar and looked from one face to the other. "And is it rushed?"

"No!" They exclaimed.

"I'd better be telling Caitlin," said Patrick the smile gone. "You do know she will be moving out to live in her new house?"

"Yes, I do know Patrick," said Flora pressing her lips together at John.

Everyone in the bar crowded around to shake John's hand and

188

kiss Flora's cheek.

"Daddy's just told me." Caitlin rushed up to Flora and gave her a hug.

"Look at that," said Flora to the pints of beer lined up on the bar for John. "He'll be drunk by the time the night's over and I'll have to make do with drinks with cherries."

"Never mind about that, I want to know all about this big wedding," said Caitlin.

"Big wedding!" exclaimed Flora, "We haven't thought past the registry office."

"You'll have to go soon," said Caitlin. "They are closing it at the end of the year; they've built this horrible brick building in its place and it's miles away."

Later, much later Flora guided a very unsteady John through the garage and up the steps.

"Do you still love me even if I am a bit drunk?" he asked.

"Yes," laughed Flora. She always enjoyed it when John was more relaxed and less in control.

John staggered into the room and crashed down to the bed onto his back, one foot on the floor, arms above his head, eyes shut.

He wouldn't stir no matter how many times Flora shook him. She gave up and decided she'd have to undress him, but he flopped back down to the bed each time she sat him up to take his jacket off.

"John," she shouted into his ear. "You are going to have to stay as you are."

He opened his eyes. "There's no need to shout I was enjoying that."

Flora laughed and battered at him with her fists.

John rolled away, rolled back, grabbed her and rolled back with a shrieking Flora in his arms.

# Chapter Twenty Nine

*Flora* hadn't seen Reg in the garage so early before.

He ignored her and walked up to John who had his head down to a car. "Have you given the Jupiter any more thought?" A hand turned the knife in his pocket. "He says he'll consider anything you have to offer." The smooth surface of the hilt warmed with the friction.

John looked up, his red eyes and set face told Reg not to say anymore.

He paced around the garage until John finished with the car and slammed the bonnet down, opening his mouth to chance another try.

"Tea," called out Flora holding a mug up to John.

John wiped his hands, turned his back to Reg and walked over to Flora

She smiled at John, kissed her fingertips and touched his brow with them before giving him the mug.

Reg stared at Flora with the knife behind his back.

John sat on the steps and took a drink of his tea. "He can have half of what he paid me."

Reg open jawed at this. "Jesus Christ John, I know I said he'd consider anything you had to offer, but that's…"

"He was fool enough to pay over the odds to start with," said John. "And the car has to be in pristine condition. If anything needs doing it comes off the price. He can always go elsewhere if he's not happy with that."

"I'll go and find him and see what he has to say," said Reg putting the knife back into his pocket. He wasn't sure if it would be enough to cover the debt and he didn't need to find Freddie seeing as he was still around the corner at the top of the street. His crumpled and bloodstained clothes saying he'd spent the night in the car.

"I'll look at the car," said John. "But if Thompson - Smythe comes near he'll get the same as yesterday. I'm shutting up early so you'll have to be quick if you want me to take a look at it today."

Reg ran up the street and jumped into the car beside Freddie who'd changed into a clean jacket and shirt, his bloodstained clothes lying by the side of the car. His nose twice the size it should be, the nostrils caked with dry blood. Lips so swollen they protruded out from his face, both eyes busily changing to all the colours of the rainbow.

"Well?" he asked.

"He says he'll give you half of the price you paid him," said Reg.

"What!" screamed Freddie. "Well he's not getting it. I'll go somewhere else."

"Oh yea," said Reg. "And you'll find a dealer today who'll look at it right away and put the cash straight into your hand."

"It might not cover what I owe," cried Freddie "They're pushing up the interest everyday."

Reg jumped out of the car, opened Freddie's door and yanked him out.

"What are you doing?" protested Freddie.

"I'm taking the car so I can get some cash and get us both out of this mess," said Reg. He saw blood on the seat and turned to yell at

Freddie. "Couldn't you have taken better care of it?"

"I couldn't stop the bleeding," whined Freddie.

Reg went to get into the car praying there'd be enough time to clean it up before John took a look at it.

Freddie pulled at his arm. "My stuffs in the back," he shouted.

Reg pulled the bench seat forward and threw out clothes and bags from the boot of the car. About to throw a suitcase after them when Freddie grabbed it and held it to his chest.

Reg dragged it off him.

"Leave it," shouted Freddie. "They're only clothes."

Reg banged the suitcase onto the pavement and opened it. He pulled out the few clothes inside it and found a large brown paper bag in the bottom, opening it to see a mix of heroin and amphetamines. "You didn't pay them did you?" he screamed. "This is why they're after you."

"That's the second lot I haven't paid for," said Freddie. "They were very good. They if said I kept up with regular payments everything would be fine. Then I had to find somewhere decent to live. The rent was astronomical so I had to ask them for a loan..." His mouth opened and closed like a pouting fish.

Reg took closer look into the bag and saw a round brooch with sparkling stones. He took it out.

Freddie made a grab for it. "That's my grandmother's."

Reg pulled it way. "I thought you said she didn't have any jewellery left."

"It fell out of the old bat's blouse one day and she didn't even notice," sniggered Freddie. "I'm going to sell it when all of this is sorted out for some ready cash."

"You won't get much ready cash for this," said Reg giving the brooch a closer look. "It looks like glass to me."

"Are you sure?" asked Freddie. "My grandmother always wore diamonds."

"You might get a few bob for it," said Reg. He threw the brooch back into the bag, put it under his jacket and jumped into the car.

"Don't take the bag," wailed Freddie. "I was going to make a fresh start with that and I need some of it for myself."

"I'll try to sell everything on," said Reg. "You'll not get much, but if we put it in with the car money it might just about cover it."

"But I'll have nothing," said Freddie. He looked at his possessions strewn around on the ground. "Nothing."

"You'll be breathing," said Reg starting the car. "Wait here," he ordered. "If you show up at the garage you can say goodbye to everything."

Reg squeezed the Jupiter in between the Aston Martin and the Alvis and dashed to the dark at the back of the garage where John's old car stood, ostensibly for his overalls, his usual ploy. He opened a door of one the steel cupboards, very carefully so it wouldn't squeak, and put the brown paper bag beside a small box that was hidden behind old equipment and rubbish. The box contained a handful of amphetamines; Reg could rarely afford to buy more. Most of them to sell on apart from the few he kept back for his own use. He had to resort to using the garage when his room was trashed by the local gang to frighten him off their patch.

Reg searched around for a decent cloth while still pulling his overalls on. He found one at the sink and wet it under the tap. Sweat dripping down his face while he scrubbed at the large red stain on the seat, it wouldn't budge.

Flora appeared behind him to look inside the car.

"I've something that should move that. I'll clean up the inside while you do the outside."

Flora decided she could be magnanimous on the day she and John were going to arrange their wedding, even for the repugnant Reg. It took her some time but the seat finally shone like new. She washed away spots of blood off the floor and tidied and cleaned around her, thinking all the while of that time in London and the night she first met John.

Reg soon had the outside of the car gleaming. Flora stood beside him while he waited for John's inspection.

"He must be a mess with all of that blood," said Flora.

"He is," said Reg, with no sign of any gratitude for her help.

John gave the car a thorough check; he looked satisfied, and more amenable. "I presume he wants cash?"

"Yes," said Reg. "When…?"

"Finished?" asked Flora going up to John and putting her arms around him . "We can call into the café while we're out." She giggled into his face. "Seeing as you only had aspirin for breakfast."

John smiled and turned to Reg. "We're going to the registry office to set the date for our wedding."

Reg managed to crack a smile onto his face. "Congratulations! When…?"

"I'll see you back here in a couple of hours with the money," said John shaking his head at Flora.

His overalls off before Reg reached the back of the garage. He lied about the brooch; the stones looked like diamonds to him. With the combined value of the drugs and the brooch the brown paper bag was worth a small fortune.

Reg ran down the street with the paper bag hidden under his jacket, and the box from the steel cupboard in his pocket. He knew he wouldn't be seeing the back of the garage for some time.

The inside of the registry office fulfilled the promise of the grand outside. Stained glass windows splintering a multitude of colours onto marble, ornate plaster and mellow wood with the sheen of a hundred years of wax polish. John and Flora looked at each other as their particulars were taken and told they were lucky to find a space on the morning of the 23rd of December, the day before the beautiful building was due to close for ever.

They held hands in the bank, an arm around each other's waist while they chose a plain gold band for Flora in the little jewellers and sat in the steamy café with bodies touching while they ate mince and dumplings.

"Pass the salt Jacob."

"Very well Elizabeth. Or is it Betty?"

John's hand smacked. Half a dumpling in his mouth while he tried to talk. "I'm lucky; my father's middle name was Zachariah."

Flora snorting and giggling while John tried to laugh and swallow at the same time.

They returned to the garage and found Reg waiting who immediately ran off with the money.

John and Flora dragged their mince and dumplings up the steps.

Word soon got around about a tramp with a face like a squashed tomato sat on a suitcase with bags of rubbish around him. Freddie tormented by a gang of kids minutes after Reg left him. But Freddie was far superior to the usual tramp; he had the intellectual capacity to think of a way of keeping the hordes at bay. He gathered together bits of broken bricks and stones and threw them at the kids, not that he succeeded in hitting any of them. But the kids were far superior than Freddie, because they had the intellectual capacity to throw the missiles back, and hit him every time.

Freddie jumped up at Reg. "Where have you been?" he cried.

A boy darted past him, grabbed the suitcase and ran off with a bunch of friends.

"Look at that." Freddie pointed after them. "Why did you leave me here? They're a bunch of savages around here. I don't know how you can live in a dump like this. Of all the most uncivilised places…" He looked at Reg as hopeful as his bruised and battered face would allow. "You have the money?"

"Yes," said Reg. "And you are not going to see a penny of it. We're going to London right now to pay them off."

"That would leave me with nothing," howled Freddie. "What am I going to do?" He picked up his bags. They ballooned out at the bottom of each arm as he looked around him. "Where's your car?"

"There is no car," shouted Reg walking away.

"Then how are we going to get to London?" shouted Freddie.

"The same as all the other savages," shouted Reg over his shoulder. "The cheapest way, by bus."

Reg stood grinning outside a club in London; life was going to be very good for him over the next few weeks. The money he offered to clear Freddie's debt had finally been accepted, following the appropriate snivelling and grovelling in a back room. He hailed a taxi, the proceeds from the brooch and drugs in his pocket and waiting to be spent, along with his cut from the car money.

Freddie lumped and bumped his way out of the club with all of his belongings, a shove to help him on his way. He saw Reg in a taxi as it drew away.

It was a shame Reg just happened to be looking in the other direction, because it meant he missed Freddie's face shouting at him at the window.

# *Chapter Thirty*

*Rain* splattered against the window, the street lamps tired glows in the gloom. The bed unwilling to relinquish its warm embrace in the dark December morning.

"Coward," said John throwing the covers back.

Flora covered her head and heard the click of the light switch, the toilet flush, running water.

"It's that time," said John back in the room.

"What time?" Flora uncovered her head and squinted at the light.

"Bacon sandwich time," replied John who was dressed and at the wardrobe for a jumper, he needed the extra warmth under his overalls.

Flora covered her head again, for the cold to slip down her body along with the bedclothes.

John rushed out of the door.

The covers just out of Flora's reach. "I'm not running over to the baker's for your bacon sandwiches on a dreich morning like this," she yelled.

She did run over to the baker's because it meant she'd have to do

without her sausage sandwiches if she didn't.

Paper bags on their knees while they ate their sandwiches inches from the heater.

"I'm going to see Caitlin this afternoon," said Flora.

"She seems to have taken this wedding over," said John.

"I know," smiled Flora. She loved her friend for turning her wedding day into something special.

"Everything organised?" asked John.

"Just about," said Flora. She didn't say the most important part hadn't been organised, her wedding dress. Poor Caitlin had tramped around the shops with her to see her turn down everything they saw. Flora about to take a bite of her sandwich when realised she didn't need to go shopping for her wedding dress.

John looked at the diary. "I'll get Minx the Magnificent out and drop you off at Caitlin's. I should have some space later on this afternoon."

"No," said Flora, "I'll take the bus."

"You said it takes nearly an hour to get to her new house," said John.

Flora looked around the garage to think of something to divert John away from the subject of taking her to Caitlin's. "It looks empty since you sold the Jupiter and the Aston Martin." She nodded at the Alvis. It looked distinguished and regal with the new hood up, the gleaming eagle and chrome work a demonstration of her hard work. "Is it finished?" she asked.

"Just about," said John.

"I haven't seen Steve Allen lately," said Flora. "I thought he was going to buy it."

"He must have lost interest," said John trying to think of a way of diverting Flora away from the subject of the car. He looked inside the sandwich he was eating. "Not much bacon this morning." A look over to Flora's sandwich. "How's yours?"

She lifted the top of her sandwich and nodded at the amount of sausage inside.

They ate their breakfast in silence, so they wouldn't tell each other their secrets.

It was almost two before Flora could leave, she ran up the steps as soon as John started working under a car. "I'm going," she shouted running out with her secret, which was a parcel held to her chest under her coat.

Caitlin took Flora to see the nursery Danny had decorated and yet another new appliance in her shiny kitchen. They went into the colourful lounge with its low modern furniture on narrow legs.

Caitlin held onto her bulge as she sank down to a chair. "Now what have we here?" she asked eyeing Flora's parcel.

Flora opened it and draped her green silk dress over the back of the settee.

"You don't mean…" started Caitlin.

Flora nodded.

Caitlin pushed herself up and rushed upstairs as fast as her bulge would allow, returning with a long white veil. "I knew my wedding veil would come in useful one day. We could attach it to the bodice, and…" She put it under Flora's chin, draped it over the tops of her arms and gathered it together at the back.

Flora looked down to the delicate lace and saw it was covered with the tiniest of pearls. "It's lovely Caitlin."

Caitlin put the veil beside the dress; the white sparkled against the green. "Certainly unusual," she laughed finding a pen and her 'wedding list' as she called it and making a big tick. "At last! Trust you to leave it until two weeks before your wedding. Now we can buy all of the trimmings." She sank down to her chair and worked her way down the list. "You haven't mentioned your family, or John's. Daddy's ordered enough food to feed half of Birmingham so it doesn't really matter how many will be going to the reception."

"No," Flora shook her head. "John and I decided we just want our friends with us at the wedding."

"And you've booked The Castle for your honeymoon," said Caitlin at her list, and with a look over to Flora. "And Danny's arranged a stag night at the bar for John."

Flora pulled a face.

"No women allowed," laughed Caitlin. "Anyway you are not supposed to see the bridegroom before the wedding so you'll have to stay here the night before. We can have our own party here, we'll ask Neelam to come along." She checked her list again. "And you couldn't possibly prepare for your big day in that flea pit. It's a wonder you haven't broken your neck on that old mat thing on the floor..."

Caitlin forced her head up to see if Flora understood the meaning of her words. The flame red cheeks said her little world wasn't so safe anymore.

Flora jumped up and rushed out of the house.

John sat on the steps with his overalls off and drinking a mug of tea when she stamped into the garage. Surprised at Flora returning so soon he opened his mouth to say so.

Flora stuck her face in front of him. "You and Caitlin must be having a really good laugh at me. A really good laugh at silly stupid Flora." She pushed by him, ran up the steps and slammed the door behind her.

John put his mug down and trudged up after her.

Flora sat on the bed staring at the opposite wall. "Not for a long time Flora," she panted, furious at herself for being such a fool and ignoring her own instincts. "No wonder you said you didn't want children, you and Caitlin…"

John opened his mouth. "You don't think Caitlin's baby's mine do you?" he asked incredulously.

"What am I supposed to think?" shouted Flora. "I do know she's been in this bed." She jumped up and paced up and down the room with her arms around herself. "Go on," she yelled leaning over to John. "Deny it!"

"Yes, I will deny it's my baby," shouted John. "It was over two years ago, before she married Danny. I had a good night at the bar and there she was at the doorway, and before I knew it we were in bed."

"And of course you couldn't resist her," shouted Flora.

John was in such a drunken haze he could only recollect Caitlin saying she needed to know before Danny. She left before he woke, that night at the bar with Flora the first time they spoke of it. He pulled Flora to him, relieved when she didn't resist. "All I know is Caitlin married Danny a couple of days later and this baby's very important to her. If Danny and Patrick found out it would devastate her."

"I'm not going to say anything am I?" said Flora. She put her face to John's jumper.

"It's you I love, it's you I'm going to marry," said John. "No one's laughing at you; no one's trying to make a fool of you."

"You should have told me," said Flora. She wanted to stop but she couldn't.

"Right!" said John. He led Flora to the bed, sat her down, pulled the chair up and sat on it. "You start," he ordered.

"Start?" asked Flora confused.

"You said I should have told you. And if I have to tell you who I've been to bed with you should do the same."

Flora licked her lips. "I…I…" she stammered wishing she hadn't started it all. "I've made such a fool of myself," she cried.

John put his head down, he hadn't realised the implications of his words until he said them. Who Flora slept with before him something he didn't want to know or think about.

"Caitlin!" exclaimed Flora. "The baby, I can't leave her like that John. I'll have to go to her and put her mind at rest."

John pulled her off the bed. "Come on, I'll take you."

"It looks like Danny's back from work," said John at the tiny Austin A35 parked outside the house

"I'll be careful," said Flora, "I can't leave it until tomorrow." She ran up the garden path, her knock answered by Caitlin's white face. Flora put her arms around her. "I'm so, so sorry," she whispered.

"Oh, it's you Flora." Danny appeared behind Caitlin.

Flora gave him a bright smile. "I had to see your lovely wife Danny and give her a big cuddle for doing so much for my wedding."

Danny saw John's car and walked down the path shaking his head at the things women do.

"You are the best friend I've ever had and look at what I go and do to you," said Flora.

"It was ages ago," said Caitlin. "Before I married Danny and..."

Flora put a hand over her mouth. "Not another word about it... Ever," she ordered.

"John loves you very much Flora," said Caitlin.

"I know," said Flora, "and I love him." She gave Caitlin another hug and hurried down the path. Danny's head bobbed up from the car window, his resemblance to Patrick always surprised Flora. "I suppose you've been talking about this stag night," she accused.

"Something like that," laughed Danny.

Caitlin joined him; they waved the car away with their arms around each other.

"I know I said I didn't want my family near the wedding," said John. "But it doesn't have to be the same for you." He gave Flora a quick look. "Have you written to them?"

Flora turned and looked out of the window.

"Are you afraid your father might not approve of you marrying me?"

"No," said Flora, "it isn't that. I still want it to be just our friends at the wedding but if I tell Aunt Elizabeth she'll tell father and I'm so happy and he's…"

"Is this because he might lose the house?" asked John.

Flora nodded. "This might be his last Christmas and Hogmanay at Clairgowan House."

"Where do you want us to spend our honeymoon?" asked John. "The Castle or Clairgowan?"

Flora looked at him. "Clairgowan," she whispered.

"Then you'd better write to your father and let him know."

The door Flora had locked and bolted for so long suddenly swung wide open.

"We'll set straight off after the reception." John laughed. "I'm sure Minx the Magnificent can make it all the way to Scotland."

Flora sure she could feel the breeze from the mountains. A sudden yearning came over her, for the quiet, the black nights, the green fields, the pure white of the snow, the trees, the house, the oil lamps, the roaring fires…

"I can take a look at this money your father owes while we're there," said John. "He shouldn't be losing the house for the sake of two thousand pounds."

Flora blinked her eyes and put a hand to her mouth. "Aunt Elizabeth! She always visits for Hogmanay."

John raised his eyebrows. "This honeymoon's becoming more

crowded by the minute and a lot longer than a few nights at a hotel."

Flora put a hand to the side of his face and stroked his beard. "I love you John Mason."

John turned his head to kiss Flora's hand. "I should hope so. I've an awful feeling I'm going to loose the deposit for the bridal suite at The Castle."

Flora sat at the table and wrote her letters to her father and Aunt Elizabeth while John parked the car in the back of the garage. Looking up when she finished them to see he was still there, she found him in the shadows.

"I've been meaning to check," said John. "Reg always seems to be disappearing back here."

"I've noticed," said Flora. "Anything?"

John shook his head. "Nothing, it must be my suspicious mind."

"It's ages since we've seen him," said Flora.

"Knowing Reg he'll have helped himself to a good chunk of Thompson - Smythe's car money," said John. "He'll be back as soon as he's spent it all."

# Chapter Thirty One

"*That's* Minx the Magnificent all prepared for the long haul," said John at the engine. The old car parked facing a shutter, all set for the following day. He slammed the bonnet down and took the bags of shopping off Flora to put them into the boot. He laughed. "Are you sure we're taking enough food with us?"

"Auld Mungo wouldn't think of getting anything in for us," said Flora checking she bought everything they needed. She looked at John. "I thought you were going to the barber's," she cried.

John ran his fingers through his untidy hair, definite curls now. "It's only a few minutes at the registry office Flora. I don't know what all the fuss is about." He rubbed his beard, a grimace at how thick it was.

A car drew up outside the garage.

"You aren't taking more work today are you," wailed Flora. "I've all the packing to do before I go to Caitlin's and…"

"Nobody pays me when I'm not working," said John walking out to the car.

"But we're getting married tomorrow," she shouted after him.

"Ah!" Reg walked into the garage. "I'm just in time." He had a camera in a leather case. He smiled at Flora and lifted it up to her. "Have

you sorted a photographer out?"

"No," said Flora. About to say she intended to choose the best of everyone's snaps when she saw John nod at the driver and take the car keys from him, lifting her hands in the air and slapping them down against her thighs.

John drove the car into the garage, leaving a trail of oil behind him. He jumped out to find something to catch the oil which had already formed a black puddle on the floor.

"I've been busy for the last few weeks," said Reg. "That's why you haven't seen me."

John pushed a tray and himself under the car.

Flora ran up the steps to start her packing. Running back down later to put it into the boot of the car and relieved to see Reg wasn't there.

John was still under the car. "I told Reg the time for the registry office."

"Why?" asked Flora.

"For the photographs," said John. "And I told him to take some money out of the box. He said he's seen a couple of badges that should come in handy for the restorations."

Flora checked the box to find Reg had taken 10 pounds, an exorbitant amount for a couple of badges. She slammed the drawer shut, more angry at Reg inviting himself to the wedding than the money.

Two hours later pacing up and down in the room waiting for John to take her to Caitlin's.

He dashed in, pulled his jumper off and grabbed a shirt and his leather jacket from the wardrobe. "Right, that's me done. I hope you're ready Danny's waiting outside."

"Ready!" exclaimed Flora. "I've been waiting for hours and I thought you were taking me."

"Patrick's opening the back room for us early," said John fastening his shirt. "I'll be late if I take you all the way there."

"You'd better not sleep in after your night out," said Flora. "And the ring…"

"Sunny said he would come and look for me if I'm late," said John. "You know me, it only takes me five minutes to dress, and we can always borrow a ring if I forget it." He shrugged his jacket on, grabbed Flora's arm and pulled her out of the room.

"And your buttonhole…" She pointed over her shoulder.

"If I remember Flora," said John. He checked his watch while hurrying her down the steps. "I've missed five minutes of it already."

Flora rushed out to the street and pushed into Danny's car. "I'm pleased you know what is more important," she shouted.

John slammed the door shut and made a circle with his finger.

Flora wound the window down, her upturned face waiting for a kiss or a few words concerning the following day.

John rubbed his hands together and spoke past her to Danny. "Make it a quick turn around Danny. They say it's going to be the best night at the bar for a long time."

"Right John, have the drinks all lined up ready for me," laughed Danny who seemed to find it all very funny.

The car drew away, taking with it the stiff face of Flora. Danny stopped it at the shout behind them. John ran up, put his head inside the window and gave Flora a long heart stopping kiss.

"Do you still love me even if I am a heartless bastard?" he asked.

"You make it difficult at times," answered Flora. She put her hand up, but the car pulled away before she could touch the silky hair.

John waited until the car turned the corner, slammed the shutters down and ran down the street, in the opposite direction to the bar.

# *Chapter Thirty Two*

*Flora* put a hand to her cheek. "I can feel my face burning. Are my cheeks red Caitlin?"

Caitlin turned away from the window.

Flora looked wild and beautiful, hair a black mass of curls, eyes wide, cheeks flame red. The green silk dress shimmered against the soft white cloud of pearls across her throat, the veil at the back of the dress a sparkling cascade down to the hem. Her wedding outfit complete with white satin high heels and a posy of tight white rosebuds.

"You look lovely," said Caitlin. She looked at Flora and understood why John was going to marry her, and with a hint of envy and memory she thought she locked away understood why Flora was going to marry John. "Don't do a thing," she ordered, "you look perfect."

"Oh Caitlin, I shouldn't have expected you to do so much," said Flora. The flowing peach coat hardly hid Caitlin's bulge which seemed to have grown to gigantic proportions over the last few weeks.

"I'm fine," laughed Caitlin, "I haven't enjoyed myself so much in ages." She dashed to the bottom of the stairs. "Danny O'Brien," she bellowed, "get yourself down here, we're ready."

A pasty faced Danny came down the stairs a few minutes later

211

fastening his tie. "I don't know why you have to shout so loud Caitlin." he complained.

"It's your fault for drinking so much," said Caitlin without a hint of sympathy.

Danny picked up the car keys and hurried out of the door.

Flora went to follow him, heart beating hard in her chest.

Caitlin stopped her with a hand. "No, not yet."

"But we are all going in your car!" exclaimed Flora.

"He must have to move it nearer to the house or something," said Caitlin. She looked out of the window again. "At least it's not raining

The longer Flora waited the more her heart galloped away, taking her along with it. She licked her lips to moisten them. "You know Caitlin, John doesn't seem to think today's all that important."

Caitlin turned from the window her face radiant. "Come on Mrs Mason to be." She led Flora to the door and opened it. "Your chariot awaits."

Flora gasped at the Alvis. White ribbons fluttered over the long bonnet, a large white bow tied to the eagle. Sunny, impeccably dressed in a dark grey suit, opened a door his beaming smile broader than ever.

Caitlin walked Flora down the garden path. "And John doesn't think today's all that important."

Flora helped into the car, the inside full of the heady scent of freesias, their colourful blossoms strewn along the back of the seat.

Caitlin dabbed Flora's wet cheeks with a handkerchief and kissed her. "Danny and I will follow behind you."

Sunny closed the door and sat behind the wheel. "You are a vision of loveliness Flora. I am to take you to John to give you to him. It is a busy day for Sanjeev. I am the best man and I give him the ring." He turned and beamed at Flora. "John has been busy, has he not? He rushes here; he rushes there, all for you."

Flora saw her wonderful handsome John waiting for her outside the registry office. His eyes as full as hers and the smartest she'd ever seen him, hair cut, beard trimmed, white rosebud on his navy blue suit. He helped her out of the car and gave her a soft kiss on her lips.

"You look beautiful," he whispered, a catch in his voice.

A ray of sunshine slipped between the clouds and shone on the stained glass windows. John and Flora bathed in colour and light as they went hand in hand to be married.

The sunshine a short-lived break in an otherwise grey December day. Reg clicked away with his camera at the small group outside the registry office. Paddy, Danny and Caitlin stood at one side of John and Flora. At the other side Sunny, Madhar and Neelam who jingled with gold and almost outshone Flora in her blue sari. Someone threw confetti for a bluster of wind to whisk it up to the sky, heavy spots of rain chasing them to the cars, laughing all the way up to the bar.

Patrick stood waiting for them at the door. The bar festooned with streamers and balloons, the tables covered with white tablecloths and laden with mountains of food, one with a beautifully decorated cake. Paddy serenaded the newly married couple with "I'll Take You Home Again Kathleen' in honour of the latest addition to his family, an empty glass at the side of his mouth to give resonance to his beautiful voice. Sunny stood after they'd eaten, cleared his throat and started to read out his 6 sheets of paper, word by word.

Paddy saw people starting to nod and decided to intervene, shouting over. "You should tell them the story about John and those six girls Sunny."

Flora pretended to glare at John.

"You are a liar Eamon Goggin," shouted John. "I only counted five."

A roar went up.

It was open house, the reception really a continuation of the party from the night before, with the incidental break of the wedding a small interruption. Paddy held up a pint of Guinness to John and took a deep draught. Sunny about to give up and sit down when John handed him two light pieces of paper.

"Ah, two telegrams," said Sunny to a sudden hush. He read the telegrams, lips moving before he spoke. "To John and Flora. Best wishes from the laird. And all at Clairgowan."

A hushed mutter before Sunny read out the other telegram.

"To John and Flora. Love and good wishes on your wedding day. Aunt Elizabeth."

"A speech from the bridegroom," someone shouted.

Whistles and banging on the tables until John stood. He pulled Flora up with him and thanked everyone with his arms around her waist.

Flora held onto his strong arms, she knew by the wording on the first telegram that her father hadn't sent it.

John sat down to cheers and clapping. Flora sat on his knee and pulled his arms around her.

Reg continued to act out his role as the photographer, flashes as he worked his way around the bar.

"John, Flora," he shouted.

The flash in their faces, another flash while they cut the cake.

"There!" Patrick plonked down a brown paper bag in front of Flora. "Now if you tell anyone I will deny it."

Flora opened the bag; it contained a small bottle of Scotch whisky.

"We are going now," said Neelam giving Flora and John a hug. "I am taking Madhar home and Sanjeev has to tidy the car for Mr

Allen."

Flora looked at John. "So he did buy the car after all."

"Yes," laughed John. "He said he didn't mind hanging on until after the wedding."

A grinning Reg stood in front of them a couple of hours later. "What do you think of your wedding photographs?" He threw them onto the table.

"That was quick!" exclaimed Flora.

"Yea, well my mate developed them straight away as a special favour," said Reg.

He leant over John and Flora while they looked at the small black and white photographs.

Most of them were blurred and smudged, the two better ones of John and Flora. One with their heads together while they cut the cake and smiled at the camera, no sign of the cake, or their bodies. The other when Flora was sat on John's knee, her mouth slightly open in the start of a smile, John's arm around the lace with his eyes looking down to her.

"Thanks Reg," said Flora appreciating the effort.

"Yea, well…" said Reg. "The trouble is it all turned out more expensive than I thought."

"How much?" asked John going for his wallet.

"Five should cover it," said Reg. He snatched the notes out of John's hand and hurried over to the bar.

John and Flora laughed at each other.

"He had me worried there," said John. "I thought he was going to do something for free." He pulled Flora to him and kissed her. "Are we going to sit here until we have to start the long trek north? Or…" He kissed her again. "Are we going to do something else?"

Flora giggled into his face. "The something else sounds very

215

interesting."

They tried to make a discreet exit, the shouts and hoots said they didn't succeed.

Flora leant against John in the cold night air.

"How much of that whisky did you drink?" asked John.

"Just a couple of sips," hiccupped Flora.

They ran hand in hand, Flora carrying her posy, her veil floating behind her.

John unlocked the door, grabbed Flora, slung her over his shoulder and crashed into the office. He plonked her feet on the floor and pulled her to him.

"You've left the door open," said Flora.

John dashed over to shut it, and turned back in time to see the garage door closing.

The lights on, no sign of Flora in the garage, John thought she hadn't the time to go up the room. "Where are you?" he shouted. He heard Flora's voice above him and ran up the steps two at a time.

She was lying on the bed, head on her hand, bedclothes lifted up high, naked body temptingly stretched out, an inviting smile...

# Chapter Thirty Three

*Flora* looked at her posy and breathed in the delicate scent of the rosebuds. "I'd like to put it beside my brother's stone. He's not there, but I'd like Alasdair to know I haven't forgotten him."

"We'll put it in the boot," said John. "It should be cool enough to keep it fresh."

"Where are the wedding photographs?" asked Flora.

"Still in my jacket." John went to the wardrobe, took them out of the pocket and gave them to Flora. "You're not taking them are you? They're not very good."

"I'll take the two of us at the bar." Flora shuffled through them. "We've plenty of old frames at home." Her mother's photographs torn out and thrown on the fire, Clairgowan House hours away, memories and emotions all rushing towards her.

They set off later than they intended, at 5 o'clock in the morning, and soon the only car on the new motorway and apart from the delay of a short lived blizzard at the Borders made a steady progress north in the sturdy old car. Daylight a dull intermission between the long winter nights, in darkness as they drove through the snow covered glen surrounded by the vast pale wraiths of the mountains.

John stopped the car at the gate set in the stone wall surrounding the kirk and graves.

Flora looked at the rosebuds and remembered holding them before her wedding, and her uncertainties about John. The firm grip of his hand warm, loving and safe as he walked by her side up the dark path and over the snow covered ground. She stopped at a small squat stone amongst the sentinels of larger ones and leant down to prop her posy against it.

They stood looking down; the roses a white glow against the black.

A breeze sighed down the mountains. It played with Flora's hair; soft fingers lifted it and let it fall.

They turned and walked to the path.

A sudden blast of cold air whipped Flora's hair over her face and pushed them down to the gate. Shrieks of icy wind snatched at the car doors and chased them up to the gates spitting flurries of snow at their rear. John took the car to the side of the house and stopped feet from the door. Above them a howling maelstrom of thrashing branches and the rattle of snow on the roof of the car, the kitchen window a square beacon of light beckoning to them with the promise of warmth and shelter.

John and Flora laughed at each other, opened the car doors and ran.

The wind blew them into the house along with a scatter of snow. They changed to pin pricks of water on the flagstones by the time Flora pushed the door closed and hung their coats behind it. She took John's hand to lead him to the fire, and the high backed chair.

Mungo Ballardine slept on despite their noisy entrance. With Flora's healthy exuberance John presumed her father would be a stocky red faced man with a shock of black hair. He looked down at the sleeping man and understood why she referred to him as 'auld'. Lips loose and wet at the corners, hair grey and thinning, face lined, grey stubble. Wearing an old waistcoat and shirt, legs spread out in front of him in old faded corduroy trousers, feet in scuffed shoes.

Flora shook his shoulder. "Father... Father... It's Flora."

The eyes opened and looked behind Flora to John. They reminded John of cold still waters, their colour unfathomable. Mungo Ballardine up on his feet without hesitation, he was a tall man, but not quite John's height.

"Father, this is John," said Flora, a smile to John. "My husband."

John stepped forward. "John Mason, Mr Ballardine." He put his hand out.

"It will be Mungo."

A smile accompanied the tight grip on John's hand. It lit up the eyes, the expression of pleasure with lips open and relaxed.

"Thank you Mungo," said John with some relief. He wondered how he would address his father-in-law, and his reception.

Flora breathed in the odour of the oil lamps and looked around her at their mellow light, the wooden table and chairs, the cupboards, benches, dark corners, the pot sink with the window above it, the large black range, high cluttered mantelpiece and ticking clock. She released her breath the same moment the fire collapsed in the grate; the feathery mass pulsating with heat.

"So you've wed my Flora."

The statement without rancour, but John noticed a change in the pale eyes.

The handshake complete, John stepped back so Mungo could greet Flora.

"I would say this calls for a celebratory dram," said Mungo. He motioned John to a smaller chair opposite his. "You will be getting the whisky out Flora?"

"That sounds good, but I'll empty the car first if you don't mind Mungo," said John.

Flora picked up a log from the side of the range and threw it into the grate; flames curled themselves around it, sparks roared up the chimney.

Mungo looked at Flora. "Then Flora will be getting it out while you are busy."

Flora threw another log into the grate. "I'll have to help him father, there's a lot to be brought in."

"No," said John going over to the door. "You stay in the warm, I'll bring it in." He opened the door and braced himself with his head down to the stinging snow and howling wind.

The door slammed behind John, leaving a vacuum of quiet. Flora filled the grate with more logs, took the tray out of a cupboard with the whisky and glasses and put it onto the table. She thought of the years she did that for her father and the evenings they sat alone by the fire, and how the last six months might have been a dream if it wasn't for the wedding ring on her finger.

John crashed through the door with luggage and bags of shopping in his hands, the howling wind and snow following him in.

Flora rushed over to the door; it resisted her efforts to push it shut.

"No! I've a helper." John dropped everything to the floor and held onto the door. Someone staggered in with more bags of shopping. "Done it all in one go thanks to you," said John. He closed the door and took the bags from the small bulky person.

Coat almost to the floor, mittens and boots, a long woollen scarf mummified the head leaving no more than the eyes exposed.

The scarf unwound to reveal the thin smiling face of Jeannie

Drummond, or 'Simple Jeannie' as the villagers called her. "I've been keeping an eye so I could come up to help ye Flora." Mittens off, scarf and overlarge coat hung behind the door, boots kicked off to reveal wrinkled and darned stockings.

Jeannie was a very late baby of a very large family, her clothes hand me downs many times over. A straight skirt flapped around her ankles, the front kneed by someone much taller, a hand knitted jumper hung around her thighs, wrists rolled to a thick wad. She was small and thin, some unkind people would say scrawny and at 15 years old appeared barely in her teens, a long brown pigtail down her back a help to her childlike appearance.

The girl looked at the clutter on the floor, her face pointy with eagerness. "Where would ye like these Flora?"

"These can go up to my bedroom, thank you Jeannie," said Flora to a suitcase and travelling bag.

Jeannie picked them up in one hand and lurched to the other end of the kitchen. She opened the door, picked up an oil lamp and disappeared into the black leaving the door swinging behind her.

"And where would the whisky be Flora?" asked Mungo with a keen look over to the tray.

Flora laughed and shook her head. She led John over to the fire. "I'll deal with the unpacking; you've been driving all day, rest yourself for a while."

"Aye, leave the women to women's things," said Mungo who decided he'd waited long enough and was at the table pouring the whisky out. He gave a glass to John and Flora and held his in the air. "To you both… Flora and to you…" He tried to grasp John's name.

"John," said John with a smile. He held his glass to Mungo and let the fiery liquid slip down his throat.

Jeanie dashed back into the kitchen and closed the door. "It's lovely and warm in your room Flora, I've had the fire on all day."

"Come and join us Jeannie." Mungo splashed whisky into a glass and gave it to the girl.

"Ach, I don't know if I should," said Jeannie. The glass jabbed up to her mouth; the whisky didn't even touch her lips.

John and Flora were wearing jeans and jumpers, but Flora thought how sophisticated they looked compared the gauche girl. "You haven't been introduced have you?" She smiled at John. "John this is Jeannie Drummond." Flora turned to Jeannie. "Jeannie, this is John my husband."

John put his hand out. "Thanks again for saving me another trip in that lot." He nodded to the howling wind outside the window.

Jeannie's red face down to her glass, John's hand given a quick grab.

Flora drank back her whisky and smiled at the girl's shyness.

"It is surprising what that little body can do," said Mungo refilling his glass and sitting on his chair. "Jeannie never misses coming to clean and cook for me whatever the weather." He leant around the wing of his chair to give the girl an exaggerated wink. "Jeannie always keeps me right."

Flora saw Jeannie return the wink and felt her smile stiffen, her lips draw back in rigid lines.

"Come on lad, sit yourself down." Mungo motioned to Flora's chair again, downed his drink and held up his empty glass to John. "Though if you refill them now it will save you the bother of having to get up again."

John laughed and took the glass. "I'll drink to that Mungo."

"Would ye like me to put the shopping away Flora?" asked Jeannie. She put her glass onto the tray and rushed over to the bags.

What Flora would have liked was for the girl to go, get out of the house. A bluster of wind lashed snow against the window, a rush of shame at the thought of Jeannie walking up from the village in the dreadful weather to help.

"Yes, you can put it into the cupboards Jeannie," said Flora. She put her glass down and went to open the door to go up to her room. "I'll go and unpack."

Jeannie scuttled around with the bags. "I've left a lamp lit in your room Flora, if ye leave the door open it will guide ye up."

"I do know that," snapped Flora, angry she forgot to take a lamp. She opened the door pretending she intended to go without a one, the light from the kitchen soon gone, feeling her way up the banister and along to her door. The flickering fire and lamp on the table at the side of her bed welcoming her into the room.

Flora opened the wardrobe to unpack and stood back at the cheap, tatty clothes she left behind. She emptied the wardrobe and chest of drawers and pushed all of her old clothes into a pillowcase. The suitcase unpacked and unzipping the travelling bag when a knock came at the door.

Jeannie's thin face peeped through the gap. "I've put the food away Flora. I think this is yours." She brought in Flora's cotton duffle bag and put it onto the bed.

"Thank you Jeannie," said Flora, and meant it. The travelling bag contained her suit with the fur collar and her red dress John asked her pack. She closed the zip not wanting to flaunt them at the girl.

"Shall I put the tea on?" asked Jeannie. "There's sausage and cold potatoes to fry, and fresh bread and scones from Mrs Brown. She sends them up every day."

"Yes, that would be lovely Jeannie," said Flora.

"Your new man's nothing like Robert Brown," said Jeannie. "He's so tall, and his hair is so..." She looked up trying to find the right word.

"Red!" said Flora. She didn't know whether to laugh at the girl or snap at her for comparing John with Robert.

"We all think ye were very brave Flora," said Jeannie. "To run away to be married. Who'd have thought Flora Ballardine the laird's daughter would do such a thing. It is all so romantic."

So that was the story. Flora looked at Jeannie in her cast off clothes and knew no matter how poor the Drummonds were they would fight the world to protect their children. She was so happy to return, the real reason for her leaving an inconvenient memory she chose to forget.

"There's a letter from Miss Montgomery on the mantelpiece to say she'll be on her usual train for Hogmanay Flora," said Jeannie. She turned to go. "I'll be away down to make the tea."

"Wait," said Flora. She gave Jeannie the pillowcase. "I know they'll be too big for you Jeannie…"

Jeannie looked inside the pillowcase. "Oh Flora," she gasped.

"They're only old clothes Jeannie." snapped Flora.

"But they're new to me Flora," said Jeannie. The girl rummaging through the clothes as she left the bedroom.

Flora put a hand to her chest, took a deep breath and finished her unpacking. Her wedding photographs were in her duffle bag; she took them out and took the lamp with her to go the room at the top of the stairs. It was full of rubbish and clutter but she soon found two dark wooden frames with glass in them. The small photographs looked a little better in the frames, Aunt Elizabeth to have the one with their heads together while cutting the cake. Flora put it onto the chest of drawers in her aunt's room with the flowery bed quilt and returned to her own room to sit on the bed and look at the other photograph. John's expression as he looked down to her saying what the day had been all about, his face full of his love for her. She kissed the glass over his face and left her bedroom to put the photograph onto the desk in the study next to Alasdair's, and forgot to take a lamp again.

Jeannie cursed for closing the kitchen door, the windows in the corridor vague shapes covered with snow. Flora annoyed she had to feel her way down to the study door thinking of the time she didn't need a lamp. She scrabbled for the door handle, walked into a table, shivering in the dark until she found the desk and the cold leather chair behind it. A pale glint on glass her guide, her wedding photograph placed next to it.

More confident on her walk to the kitchen, her eyes on the strip of light under the door. The warmth, light and smell of Jeannie's cooking enveloped her, drew her in.

Her father sat on his chair with a glass of whisky. John sprawled out on her chair with an empty glass in his hand, asleep. Jeannie stood between the two men with a foot over John's long legs frying sausages in a large black frying pan on the hob. Flora took the glass from John's hand and thought how peaceful and vulnerable he looked and if she didn't have an audience she would have kissed him.

"Yon lad cannot take his whisky," chuckled her father.

"You've spent many an hour sleeping by the fire father," replied Flora. "And yon lad's been driving since the early hours." She decided she didn't care if she had an audience and kissed John on the brow.

He opened his eyes before she lifted her face away and gave her a quick kiss on the lips.

Jeannie's face reddened as she turned for the bowl of boiled potatoes on the table.

"I'll fry the potatoes," said Flora.

She fried the potatoes and invited Jeannie to stay for the meal. Laid the table, served the food and insisted she make and pour the tea. John laughed at Mungo's barbs over his inability to drink the whisky and retaliated by saying he would have to get more practise in. Jeannie blushed and looked down to her plate each time John spoke to her. Mungo couldn't quite grasp John's name despite the constant prompts from John and Flora. John found this funnier and funnier and decided he'd have to accept 'lad'. Flora marvelled at how she could forget the wonderful taste of Mrs Brown's bread and scones.

She was sat with her back to the fire. The food, heat, tiredness, they all conspired together to pull her eyelids down.

"Why don't you have a nap upstairs?" asked John. "I'm feeling a lot better for closing my eyes for a few minutes." He helped Flora up from her chair, put a hand around her waist and walked her to the door.

Jeannie jumped up from the table, lit a lamp and put it into John's hand. "I'll clear away Flora, and if I'm no here when ye come down I'll be here in the morning to help with the Christmas dinner." She opened the door for them. "I'll prepare the meat so ye can put it in the oven early."

Flora opened her mouth to tell the girl not to come but John led her through the door and up the stairs.

The fire was almost out in the bedroom; John took a log out of the basket at the side of it and pushed it into the dying embers, turning to Flora wiping his hands to see her lying on the top of the bedcovers. "Oh no you don't." He pulled her jumper over her head, slipped her shoes off and eased her jeans down her legs. "And as much as I'd like to stay I'm going to leave you alone so you can have a rest." A kiss on her belly button before he lifted the covers so she could slip under them. Then he picked up his lamp and closed the door quietly behind him.

The bed held Flora in the soft warm hold of an old friend. It pulled her down into a deep sleep to waken an hour later feeling fresh and relaxed. She dressed, put more wood on the fire, and this time remembered to take the lamp with her down the stairs.

She saw a light under the study door and heard John and her father talking, and another voice, Bob Brown. A check in the kitchen, empty, no sign of Jeannie, the roaring fire illuminating the room with its flickering light. The bathroom freezing, her breath spurts of steam. Flora washed her face, brushed her hair and left the lamp behind her to take the cold off the air.

She opened the study door to the convivial scene of lamps lit around the room and the smell of cigars. John, her father and the broad shouldered figure of Bob Brown sat beside the crackling fire with a glass of whisky in their hands.

"Flora!" Bob Brown put his glass down and rose to greet her. His face down to her as he took her hand, his brown hair almost a tonsure around his head. "I have wished your man the best for your marriage and I do the same to you."

"Thank you Mr Brown," responded Flora and looked for another chair to join them.

"I am afraid I have to go Flora." Bob Brown picked up his heavy overcoat and put it on while checking his watch. He turned to John. "I might see you again before you return to Birmingham John?"

"You might," said John raising his glass.

"And I will be seeing you when I see you," chuckled Mungo raising his glass.

Flora shook her head at him and saw Bob Brown at the door waiting for her to see him out, something not expected before. He followed her through the kitchen and stepped forward to open the outside door. The snow had stopped, the night still and dark, stars twinkled in a clear black sky, the ground a carpet of sparkling white. A car that could only belong to Bob Brown stood beside John's car. It had a small Egyptian head on the front of the long bonnet and it looked as large as George Gibson's Rolls-Royce.

Flora folded her arms against the cold while Bob Brown fussed with the buttons on his coat.

"I have to pick up Robert at the station. Trust him to leave it until the last minute." Gloves taken from his pocket and looked at. "I wrote and told him you had left Clairgowan Flora. His mother took the call from Robert only this morning to say he intended be here for Christmas. She didn't think to tell him about you marrying and you visiting. I expect she didn't want to put him off." He looked at Flora. "His mother misses him Flora; this will be the first time she has seen him since he left for America."

"I didn't send Robert away," said Flora, "or make him stay away." They hadn't spoken of Robert since he left and Flora realised his parents blamed her for him leaving, the same as her father.

"Your man says he works in a garage."

John's car scrutinized. It looked old and weary beside the large expensive car.

"Yes," said Flora. "And it happens to be John's own business." Irritated she had the need to say so.

"Well I had better be going for Robert." Bob Brown's shoes crunched on the frozen snow. "You received the telegram?" His enquiring face looked over the huge bonnet of the car.

"Yes, thank you Mr Brown," replied Flora, a catch in the back of her throat. The person who did send her wedding telegram the one with the most to lose when she married John.

She watched the car make a sedate reverse around the corner, closed the door and returned to the study.

The whisky flowed freely for the remainder of the evening with Mungo helping himself to John's cigars and entertaining him with his long tales of the happenings in the glen. John noticed the only enquiry concerning him came from the other man Bob Brown.

"Ah," said Mungo. It was almost midnight, more effort needed to rise from his chair. "I think I should be off to my bed." He picked up a lamp. "Have you far to travel?" A sympathetic smile to John.

"A far as up the stairs Mungo," laughed John.

"How much whisky have you drank tonight father?" shouted Flora jumping up and standing beside John. "You know John's staying here, and you could at least try to remember his name."

The smile changed to open mouthed comprehension. Mungo shook his head. "Take no notice of me lad. I am an old man who has had too much to drink."

"I wouldn't worry about it Mungo," assured John. He stood and put his arm around Flora. The pale eyes met his, the message they conveyed ambiguous. John thought Flora might be right about the drink and returned the nod before Mungo turned to go.

"I hope he's suffering in the morning," muttered Flora. "The trouble is he'll be as fresh as a daisy."

John sat down to his chair and pulled Flora onto his knee. She put her face to his neck, her love for him wiping away her uncomfortable feelings. They sat with arms around each other until the clock on the mantelpiece chimed the hour.

"Come on." Flora dragged John off the chair. "Auld Mungo should be well out of the way by now."

She extinguished the lamps except for one and led John out of the room with it.

He hesitated at the bottom of the stairs. "I'll have to pay a visit to the bathroom first."

"I've left a lamp on inside to warm it up," said Flora. She gave John her lamp. "Use this one to guide your way up."

She felt her way up the stairs and along to her room, undressing in the light from the flickering flames. Waiting for John under the bedcovers when he came into the room and shook his head.

"I think the honeymoon's over before it's started Flora." He put the lamp down and sat on the bed.

Flora sat up startled at this change.

John took his clothes off and threw them down to the floor. "That lamp didn't work." His grim face looked over his shoulder at her. "The important bit's just fallen off in that ice box you call a bathroom."

Flora pulled him under the covers, snorting and giggling while she repaired the important bit.

John thanked God his fear wasn't true.

# Chapter Thirty Four

*Flora* opened her eyes to soft black velvet. John's sleeping body by her side, his breath warm air on her cheek. The oil lamp out, the fire long dead, Clairgowan House mantled under the special quiet the snows brought with them. No street lamps outside the window, or rattles, cats, cars and people, the room above the garage always invaded by light and noise.

She kissed the bump on John's nose and slipped out of the covers, the air tingled with the cold.

Her hand connected to the heaviness of a jumper, the size saying it was John's. She pulled it on and tugged it down to her knees. A drawer found without a falter, opened and closed without a sound, the door where it should be, a token brush of fingertips on the banister, instant contact with the kitchen door handle. Warm bare feet ran over cold hard flagstones in the soft glow from the fire, the triumph of catching it minutes before it died and had to be relit. Her father's Christmas present, a beige moleskin waistcoat, put onto his chair. Backwards and forwards to put legs into the grate, the red embers flaring into life with crackles and sparks.

Flora sat on her chair with feet up and jumper pulled over her

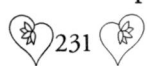

knees, the heat on her face as the flames licked their way through the logs and roared up the chimney. She might have wrapped up in the past and put her boots on to walk in the white of the snow and black shadows of the trees, but not that Christmas morning, not with John upstairs.

A large roasting tin was stood on a bench covered with a tea towel; she lifted it off to see the giant piece of beef she brought with her covered with inches of fat, 'God bless Jeannie.' Flora lifted the oven latch with the towel, pushed the roasting tin inside and watched the fat melt and ooze down the meat. She slammed the oven door shut, made a quick visit to the ice cold bathroom and ran up the stairs, back to John. Teeth chattering and shivering by the time she arrived back in the bedroom.

She pulled the jumper over her head, slipped under the covers and put her arms around John, pressing her cold skin against the throbbing heat of his body.

He jumped. "You're freezing!" he exclaimed putting his arms around her. "I thought I was having a nightmare. I thought a block of ice rolled down a mountain and latched itself onto me." He kissed Flora and pulled her to him, the two of them responding to the other's exquisite embrace.

They dozed with arms around each other until a diffuse of pale light replaced the black.

"I'll have to make the ten mile trek to the ice box," said John lifting the covers.

"You can put the heater on while you're up," said Flora pulling the covers around herself and snuggling down to the warmth.

"You mean light the fire," said John. He dressed and went over to the basket of logs by the side of the fireplace. "There's no sticks and paper."

"You'll find them at the side of the range in the kitchen," said Flora snuggling further down. "You can check the meat in the oven and feed the fire while you are down there."

"Anything else?" growled John.

A soft kiss on Flora's brow.

"I wouldn't mind a drink of the coffee we brought with us. You'll find it in one of the cupboards."

A nudge in her back this time.

Flora waited until the door closed behind John before she jumped out of the bed. A hand in the back of a drawer to find a small box with a ribbon on it, she put it onto John's pillow and snuggled into the warmth.

John was so long she fell asleep, woken by the door opening and the wonderful aroma of coffee. John put the cup and saucer on the bedside table next to her and went back to the door to pick up the sticks and paper. He carried them over to the fireplace and knelt down to push them into the soft grey powder that was residue of the previous night's fire.

Flora sat up and sipped at her coffee. The small box had fallen under the covers, she found it and put it back onto the pillow. "Did you check the meat?" Really wanting John to turn to her and see the box.

"No need," said John. He struck a match and leant back on his haunches to watch the fire take hold. "That Jeannie arrived and cooked a hearty breakfast for me. I think she was here before by the looks of the kitchen and she said she'd already cooked your father's breakfast. There's no sign of him, I think he's out somewhere. Anyway she said you needn't rush down because she has everything ready. All you'll need to do is prepare the table."

Flora smiled, 'God bless Jeannie' again, and she knew where her father would be, at the kirk. He wouldn't go to the Christmas Eve service in town, because he didn't have his own pew. Surprised at how late it was when she checked her watch, her father would have usually returned by then.

John took two logs out of the basket and pushed them into the crackling flames.

"Your hands will be filthy doing that," said Flora, her voice high to attract his attention.

John checked his hands, rubbed them together, turned to Flora and followed her eyes to the box on the pillow.

Flora put her cup and saucer down and sang out, "Merry Christmas."

John pressed his lips together, pushed himself up and sat on the bed. "With the wedding and everything I didn't think you'd want to bother with Christmas presents." He pulled off the ribbon, opened the box and took out the gold signet ring with the boldly cut initial.

"It's supposed to go on your little finger," said Flora, a tinge of disappointment at John not buying her a Christmas present.

John put the ring on the little finger of his left hand, it was a perfect fit.

A quick kiss on Flora's cheek before he opened the wardrobe. "I see you packed your red dress." He put it onto the bed. "Are you going to wear it for Christmas dinner?"

Flora threw the covers back and stood with her back to John while she dressed in the jeans and jumper she wore the night before.

"What about your frock?" asked John. "Aren't you going to wear it?"

"It's a dress," snapped Flora brushing her hair. "And I have to help Jeannie and have a bath before I put it on." She threw the brush down and looked in a drawer for the silks and ribbons she bought for Aunt Elizabeth's Christmas present, choosing a blue ribbon with silver threads. The ribbon for Jeannie, Flora sighed at everyone receiving a present except her. Her father always proclaimed he didn't believe in the silly practise of buying birthday or Christmas presents, but he'd gladly accept anything bought for him.

"Are you angry with me?" asked John, he sounded surprised. He turned Flora around to face him. "Do you still love me?"

"Yes," whispered Flora. She knew she always would, Christmas present or no.

"And I need a bath before I change," said John.

Flora smiled up at him. "You'll have to join me in my bath unless auld Mungo left behind his dirty bath water."

John winced.

Flora laughed. "I'll turn the taps on, the bath takes ages to fill."

She ran down to the bathroom. The squealing bath taps turned on, boiling water splashing and bubbling down into the deep space, opening the kitchen door to the wonderful smell of Christmas dinner.

Jeannie jumped up from Flora's chair. "Everything's ready Flora, except for the table. I thought ye would want to do that. Would ye like me to cook your breakfast?"

The girl was almost crouched, ready to jump at Flora's command.

"No thank you Jeannie. It's late for breakfast now," said Flora. She looked at the ribbon thinking it was such a small gift for all of Jeannie's hard work. "It's not much Jeannie..."

Jeannie gasped, she wore a cream woollen flared skirt down to her ankles the waist almost slipping off her hips, socks, black laced up shoes, a short sleeved pink jumper three times overlarge for her. The skirt and jumper pushed into the pillowcase the night before.

"Do you want me to tie it onto your pigtail for you?" asked Flora holding up the ribbon.

Jeannie nodded and brought her pigtail to her front, tears splashing down her thin cheeks.

Flora clenched her teeth at the girl's overt reaction to such a small gift. She tied an elaborate bow on the end of the pigtail and hugged the bony shoulders. "Merry Christmas Jeannie."

"Ach, we're not finished yet," said Jeannie running over to a pile of knitting on one of the benches. "I've already given the laird his scarf." She ran back to Flora with a scarf on each hand, her thin face pink with pride. "One for ye, and one for your new husband. I haven't shown them to Mr Mason yet, I'm giving ye first choice."

Flora knew Jeannie would have laboriously unpicked old knitting and stretched out the precious supply of wool by knitting the scarves on the largest needles possible. One scarf pink and green stripes, the other black and red. She chose the pink and green, her one Christmas present from one of the poorest people in Clairgowan.

John duly presented with his scarf when he entered the kitchen, a quick peck on Jeannie's cheek in return. Flora sure she heard a squeak from her.

"I'll wear it to go and check on Minx the Magnificent," grinned John wrapping it around his neck. He gave an obvious look to Flora. "I'll turn the engine over then I'll have a bath. I've put my clean clothes in the bathroom."

"I think I'll have a bath myself Jeannie," said Flora trying to think if she should go first so Jeannie wouldn't guess that John and her were having a bath together.

"But the laird had his bath before the kirk!" exclaimed Jeannie. "There'll never be enough water from the range for three baths in a row."

"I do know that Jeannie," snapped Flora. She escaped to the bathroom before she took hold of the girl and pushed her out of the house.

John followed her in a few minutes later while she was undressing.

"There's no lock on the door." He didn't look very happy about it.

"You can always whistle very loud if you think Jeannie might come in and see something she's not suppose to," laughed Flora stepping into the bath. She sat in the steaming water and put her head back, hair floating up around her.

John followed her into the bath, pulled at her feet, grabbed her and lifted her up. Tickling and tormenting Flora until her shrieks echoed around the room.

"It was better than whistling," he grinned drying himself later.

A wet towel flicked at him.

John put on a white shirt and slacks, Flora her jeans and jumper.

"What about your red frock?" asked John.

"I'll change into it before the meal," said Flora becoming more exasperated at him insisting she wore the dress.

John followed Flora into the kitchen. Mungo sat in his best tweed suit by the side of the fire, the moleskin waistcoat under his jacket. "You were making plenty of noise in there," he remarked.

John grinned at his ploy working.

Flora giggled behind her hand.

Mungo rose from his chair and smiled at John. "Jeannie has lit the fire in the study. Would you care to join me for a companionable few minutes while the women take care of the Christmas dinner?"

"That sounds good to me," replied John flashing a smile at Flora as he followed Mungo through the door.

Jeannie scurried over and grabbed the wet towels and John's clothes out Flora's hands and ran over to the sink with them.

"You are making me redundant Jeannie," laughed Flora.

"Ach, it is your honeymoon Flora," said Jeannie scrubbing at the sink. "It's lovely outside. The clothes will dry in a crack if I put them on the line now." She ran outside with the dripping clothes, the towels and clothes washed and on the line within minutes.

Flora arranged one of Aunt Elizabeth's embroidered table clothes over the table and set out matching napkins. She remembered seeing an old battered silver candelabrum the night before in the room at the top of the stairs, sending Jeannie up for it. The girl ran into the kitchen with it, put it on a bench and started polishing it, but not before she put her pigtail down her back so she wouldn't dirty her new ribbon.

"Would you like to stay for Christmas dinner Jeannie?" asked Flora. It was the least she could do seeing as the girl did all of the hard work.

Jeannie turned and clapped a hand to her mouth. "Me!" she exclaimed. "A Drummond staying for Christmas dinner at the laird's house."

"Yes," laughed Flora.

The candelabrum put in the centre of the table; an old silver cruet set polished and set out with the cutlery.

Flora stood back to look at the table. "I think it needs a little extra something to finish it off."

"There's a big holly bush full of berries by the wall down in the village, a few pieces here and there on the table would look nice," said Jeannie. "I noticed it coming out of the kirk this morning." Keen eyes looked at Flora. "I see Robert Brown came for Christmas. I saw him at the kirk with Mr and Mrs Brown. The laird took a ride with them up to the farmhouse in Mr Brown's flash new car."

"Yes. I knew Robert intended to be at Clairgowan for Christmas," replied Flora smoothly. She checked the food, for something to do, everything looked perfect. "You've been really good Jeannie. Thank you for cooking the dinner."

"Ach, it was no bother," said Jeannie. She took a large pair of scissors out of a drawer and ran to the door clicking them in the air. "I'll go and get the holly Flora."

Flora checked on the men before she changed. John and her father stretched out by the side of the fire drinking whisky and smoking cigars.

"I hope you two will be sober enough to eat your Christmas dinner," she warned, secretly pleased they seemed to be getting along together, and with a look at her father. "And I see you have a good supply of whisky in."

Mungo had taken his jacket off because of the heat of the fire; he looked down to his new waistcoat. "I found this on my chair, drunk or sober I am ready for the big event." And with a look at his glass. "Bob Brown kindly provided the whisky as an early Christmas present."

"And thank you for the thank you for your other Christmas present," retorted Flora with a nod at the waistcoat.

Mungo smiled and puffed at his cigar.

"I'm off upstairs to change so the dinner shouldn't be long," said Flora.

"I'll be up in a minute to pull the zip up on your frock," said John.

"And I will top up your glass for your return," said Mungo.

Flora ran up the stairs shaking her head at John going on about the dress and her father's profligacy with the whisky. She threw her jeans and jumper onto the bed, stepped into the dress and looked at the mirror, her cheeks scarlet from the heat in the kitchen, her drying hair a wild black mass around her head. John appeared behind her; he pulled the zip up and looked at her in the mirror.

"You look beautiful."

"Like this?" laughed Flora a hand to her hair.

He nodded, looked down and put a hand into his trouser pocket.

Flora heard a chink and saw John's hand come up with a row of even sized pearls. He placed them across her neck, the pearls warm against her skin.

"I knew they would look perfect with the frock."

Flora lifted her hair so John could fasten the clasp.

"You didn't think I would let our first Christmas go by without something special."

A kiss on the nape of her neck, soft lips, the silky feel of hair.

"They're beautiful," whispered Flora with fingers to the pearls.

John shook his head at her in the mirror. "No. You are beautiful." He put his face down to her hair. "I suppose you are going to tame this wild beast." Hands cupped her burning cheeks. "And I suppose you'll be covering these beautiful creatures."

Flora nodded at the mirror.

John sighed. "I thought you might." He raised his eyebrows to her in the mirror. "I'd better go or your father will work his way through all of my cigars." He kissed the top of Flora's head and left her looking at the mirror.

Flora stood looking at the pearls, took a deep breath and brushed her hair until it lay down her back shiny and still. A careful application of make up, cheeks toned down, eyes lined and coloured, lipstick, determined to look as beautiful as she could for John. High heels on before she turned full circle to look at the room then back to the mirror, and her. She'd lived in that room since she was 9 years old and not once did it occur to her she would stand there and look as she did.

Face to the stairs to watch the skirt of her dress flounce up in front of her.

The kitchen empty, except for the man sat in her father's chair. Robert! His mouth open as he stood. "Flora you look…Beautiful."

He was dressed in a hand knitted jumper and check slacks. Flora looked at the familiar brown hair and eyes; if they had married their children would have had dark hair and brown eyes.

She put a hand to her pearls. "It's because of these. They're from John. They'd make anyone look beautiful."

"No!" Robert shook his head, a vehement disagreement. "I mean you Flora, the way you look."

Flora smiled, her hand still on the pearls. "Thank you Robert."

"You sure have changed Flora."

Flora noticed the trace of an American accent.

Robert walked up to her. Familiar fingers took her hand away from the pearls, she pulled it away.

"Why did you do it Flora?"

The familiar petulant look.

Flora knew the meaning of his question, irritated Robert presumed to ask. "You have no right to ask me why I do anything Robert." She stepped back, remembering his tactic in an argument would be to stand close to her so she had to breathe in his anger.

Robert stepped forward. "If anyone has the right it's me Flora."

"No Robert," shouted Flora. "You lost that right the moment you decided to go to America."

"There you go," shouted Robert. "You run off in a temper and marry some guy who works in a tin pot garage."

Flora looked around her. She saw pieces of holly scattered over the table, glossy green and scarlet berries amongst the bright embroidered flowers. "Where is everyone?" she cried.

"I sent that Jeannie off to get more holly," said Robert. He flicked the back of his fingers to the direction of the study. The laird said he'd keep this whoever he is out of the way so we could talk."

The dismissive hand, John discarded as an irrelevance.

"Talk!" exclaimed Flora. "I have nothing to say to you Robert. And my husband's name happens to be John. And I will answer your question. I married John because I love him."

"I can't let you go and ruin your life on some loser just because you married him on the rebound," shouted Robert. "And off you go again with your temper Flora. No wonder I left."

Flora needed to be beside John, she ran out of the kitchen.

John's concerned face at the study door, her father sat by the fire taking a great interest in his glass of whisky.

John took her hand. "Are you OK? I thought I could hear shouting."

John was so different to Robert, his hand reliable, secure, his face full of love. Flora looked past him to her father, a laugh. "You know me I always get flustered over the Christmas dinner." She pulled at John's hand. "Come on, I'll introduce you Robert, Mr Brown's son."

They found Jeannie stood on a chair arranging holly over the mantelpiece. "Ach, ye have just missed Robert Brown." She jumped down, wiped the chair and pushed it to the table with the wooden legs screeching over the flagstones.

Mungo walked into the kitchen, sat at the head of the table and smiled at everyone. "And where would this Christmas dinner be?"

The meal just as it should be, chatty, laughs, the food wonderful. Flora sat next to John at the table; her chair so close to him she could feel his every move.

Jeannie scurried around after the meal. She cleared the table, washed the dishes and brought in the washing. Eventually packed off to her family with a mountain of food. Mungo sat by the fire in his old comfortable clothes and asleep within minutes.

The day already dark as John and Flora plodded up the stairs with an oil lamp.

"This Robert?" asked John. "The reason why your father hid me away in the study."

"Everyone thought we were going to be married," said Flora.

"He must be a bit of an idiot," said John.

They lay side by side on the bed, sated, happy to be alone.

"An idiot?" asked Flora.

John pulled her to him. "Yes, he must be an idiot to have let you go."

They extinguished the lamp, undressed and slept away the meal under the warmth of the covers, John opening his eyes to see Flora pushing logs into the fire.

"Have I got to lie here all night and look at your back?"

She stood and turned to John.

"I see you are still wearing your pearls."

"A girl has to keep something on to keep her warm," replied Flora.

She stood with legs apart, hair pushed from her face with a hand. The vision of Flora with the sparks and flames behind her to stay with John for ever. Her wonderful shape, full breasts, black pubic fuzz, eyes dark moons in her face, cheeks smudged with red, lips open with the start of her glorious smile. He lifted the covers; Flora floated over to him in the dancing light.

John covered her, pulled her to him and let her carry him to paradise.

# Chapter Thirty Five

*Stars* lingered in the dark, the long winter night reluctant to leave. A luminous streak appeared; it grew in size and strength like a radiant flower unfolding across the sky. The colourless sparkles swept aside by the light of the coming day.

"That block of ice paid me another visit last night."

"Someone has to keep the kitchen fire going," laughed Flora. She turned from the window and jumped onto the bed.

John's strong arm grabbed her and pinned her to him. "Why have you put your clothes on?" He sounded disappointed.

"Because I'm going down to the kitchen to cook breakfast."

Before Jeannie arrived.

"Not more food," groaned John.

Flora rubbed her nose into his beard. "I'll take you on a good long walk to work it all off."

"I can think of a better way to work it off." John's voice low, husky.

His other arm left the covers, warm air escaped from the bed. Flora breathed in his moist odour, the sweet smell of the night before. She let John undress her and joined him under the covers.

She hurried into the kitchen an hour later to the smell of bacon, eggs and toast and her father sat at the table eating his breakfast. Jeannie sugaring and stirring his tea, new ribbon down her back.

"The fire was fair away this morning Flora." Jeannie clattered the frying pan onto the hob, put in rashers of bacon and watched them sizzle over the heat.

"Of course the fire was on. I always feed it during the night," snapped Flora. "And I'm quite capable of cooking the breakfast myself Jeannie."

Mungo smiled at Jeannie. "Flora will have to be up a lot earlier than this to beat you into the kitchen Jeannie." He looked at a forkful of bacon. "Perfection Jeannie, perfection."

John walked into the kitchen eyeing the food.

"I thought you weren't hungry," accused Flora.

"That was then," said John.

Mungo pulled out a chair. "Sit yourself down lad." He smiled at Jeannie. "Three eggs for the lad Jeannie, he looks as though he needs your good cooking inside of him."

Flora put her hand out for the bowl of eggs; Jeannie grabbed it and cracked the eggs into the frying pan.

Flora clashed a chair back and sat at the table opposite John.

Jeannie fried the bacon and eggs, put Flora's food in front of her and scurried over to John with his plate.

Flora stabbed at her bacon and egg.

Mungo picked up the last piece of toast. "We need more toast Jeannie." He smiled at John and nodded down to his plate. "If you think that is good wait until you have tasted Jeannie's toast."

"Toast Flora?" Jeannie stuck a slice of bread onto a toasting fork and held it to the fire.

Flora shook her head.

Jeannie buttered the toast, put it onto John's plate, made a fresh pot of tea and rushed around the table refilling everyone's cup.

Mungo waited for Jeannie to put the milk into his tea and sugar and stir it before he stood and picked up his cup. He smiled down to John and nodded at Flora's chair by the fire. "Are you sitting on a more comfortable chair to finish your tea?" He smiled at Jeannie. "Though you had better ask Jeannie's permission, she usually sits with me by the fire after breakfast."

Flora's hands gripped her cup.

Jeannie lifted her chin at the unused to complement of anyone asking her permission to do anything. She clattered the empty plates together at the table and ran over to the sink with them, pigtail and ribbon bobbing behind her. Chin even further up at the importance of her response. "Ach, I don't mind anyone taking my place by the fire."

Flora sure she felt the china bend under the pressure of her hands.

John shook his head and swallowed back his tea. "I'd better check the car." He stood up from the table. "I'll turn the engine over and I'd better wipe the snow off. The old lady needs a bit of pampering to keep her going."

"Yes." Mungo sat on his chair by the fire and took a slurp of his tea. "That is how it is when you cannot afford better."

John grimaced at the jibe, walked over to the door and put his coat on. "Is there an old cloth I can use Flora?"

"I'll get it," shouted Jeannie before Flora could respond.

She looked into her cup while she heard John thank Jeannie and open and close the door.

Mungo stood and drained his cup. "I might as well tell the lad he is wasting his time clearing the snow away, we are due a lot more of it yet." He waited for Jeannie to run over for his cup, and followed her to go outside.

Jeannie hovered over Flora. "Are ye finished with your cup Flora?"

Flora looked up at her. "No Jeannie, I'll see to it. And I'll see to everything else, so you needn't come up to the house while I'm here." Her calm voice belying the anger about to erupt out of her mouth.

Jeannie's face sharp lines of hurt, but she went to the door for her coat and scarf and put them on. "When will ye be going back?" Head down to fasten her coat buttons.

"We haven't decided," said Flora.

The thin face up from the buttons, a smile. "I might be seeing ye at Hogmanay."

"I doubt it, it's many a long year since we had a Hogmanay party at Clairgowan House," said Flora so the girl wouldn't feel invited.

Jeannie wound her scarf around her neck and pulled her pigtail over her shoulder so the ribbon hung down her front. Her coat a dirty brown colour, a slight flare after the nipped in waist. It hung on the thin body, the waist somewhere on the hips, the hem almost touching the flagstones.

The girl fiddled with the ribbon, as though she was waiting for something.

"Are you due any wages Jeannie?" Flora couldn't remember the amount of money she brought with her. She knew she'd have enough, but decided to ask John for it rather than go all the way up the stairs for her purse.

"Ach, I couldn't take anything from the laird Flora, we all know how strapped he is."

Scolding eyes at Flora, thin lips stretched over wet teeth, the same as a fox or weasel.

Jeannie ran out of the door before Flora threw the cup at her, and

almost ran into Mungo who was stood with his hands in his pockets watching John crank start the car. It took several tries; the engine wheezing and spluttering a couple of times before it roared into life.

The sun shone out of a clear blue sky, the ground a mosaic of puddles and melting snow amongst the gravel.

"Laird." Jeannie looked up to him. "Flora says she has no need for me to come up to the house while she is here."

Hands still in his pockets Mungo smiled and leant down to Jeannie shaking his head. "Then that is how it will have to be Jeannie."

Jeannie put a hand to her mouth and rushed away.

John looked after her, steam rising from the melting slick of snow and ice on the bonnet of the car. He leant down to wipe it away with the cloth.

Mungo looked down to the back of John's head. "And when do you intend to return to…"

"Birmingham," said John to the car. "We haven't decided. But I can't stay away from the garage for too long, I'm losing money when I'm not working."

"And Flora, how does she occupy herself while you are working for this money?"

"She helps." John didn't elaborate because he knew Mungo had no interest in the garage, or anything he did. He straightened up to wring the cloth out, in time to see the look to him; Mungo rearrange his face into a smile. It took John a few minutes at breakfast to realise the smile had various uses. To upset Flora and to put him at ease the first night they arrived at Clairgowan House. The pale eyes looked at him with the colour of frozen water, no whisky this time to confuse their meaning.

John turned the engine off and continued to wipe down the car.

"If you are worried about this money you should be getting yourself away as soon as you can," said Mungo. "Flora can stay on for a while and follow you later."

The two men hadn't seen the kitchen door open and Flora walk out pulling her coat on.

"Father!"

Flora laughed and ran over to John. "A few days married and he's trying to chase you away from me."

"I am trying to help the lad," smiled Mungo. "We are due a heavy snowfall anytime now and he is worried about his work." He nodded at the car. "You will struggle to find that in a few hours, you could be stuck here for weeks."

Flora squinted up to the sun. "You don't always get your predictions right father." She took hold of John's hand. "Come on, I'll take you on my favourite walk."

John threw the cloth down and followed her to the trees.

"I've told Jeannie not to come while I'm here father," shouted Flora over her shoulder.

"Aye, and she will be back as soon as you are gone," muttered Mungo watching Flora pull John into the shadows of the trees.

"It's dark," said John, "and wet." He jumped away from a soft splash of melting snow.

Flora laughed. A minute after Jeannie left humming to herself while she finished washing the breakfast dishes, happiness bouncing her over the thick carpet of pine needles. She put a hand out to touch the trees, old friends she walked amongst all her life.

They walked further into the dark.

"Is it always like this?" asked John.

Flora saw how John was tolerating the walk to please her and for a moment saw the trees in his eyes, the black shadows and dripping water, the musty smell.

A brilliant shaft of sunlight probed into the dark. Both drawn to the light to see a haphazard circle of fallen trees, a mist of moisture and decay drifting up in a haze of colours.

John leant down to some moss covered stones. "There must have been another building here at some time."

"They're just stones," said Flora watching flimsy clouds of midges perform their complicated ballets in and out of the sunbeams.

"No," John rubbed at the edge of the cut stone, his hands suddenly at his hair, beard and face, a dancing cloud around his head.

"It must be your red hair," laughed Flora.

They ran hand in hand, laughing, Flora leading the way, running out of the trees to the back of the house. Between the two wings a tangle of young trees, weeds, tall unkempt bushes.

"It used to be a garden once," said Flora, a vague memory of green and flowers and clipped bushes.

The sun dipped behind the trees, an ominous black ridge of clouds from the north loomed over the grey tiles and chimneys at the front of the house.

"It hasn't been touched for years," said John.

"Fourteen," said Flora. Since Alasdair died, another memory, so clear and sharp it hurt. Thrown into the air, her screams of delight and fear bouncing off the walls while she looked down to a young man's laughing face.

She looked to the east wing, where she lived as a child, ornate chimneys and windows with curtains.

John looked at the wing opposite, a long expanse of grey tiles without chimneys, and a long grey stone wall without windows. "Why on earth did they build that?"

Flora laughed. "For show, they ran out of money. It's a sham, a shell, there's nothing inside."

They took a slow walk around the house, finishing off at the gates with arms around each other for warmth.

"Right!" John put his face to Flora's hair. "We didn't decide how long this honeymoon was going to last."

Flora looked up to him with eyes wide with worry, face white in the gloom. "We did John." Words out in a rush. "You agreed we'd stay for Hogmanay and Aunt Elizabeth. And you said you'd look into father's debts. I don't know how he'll cope if he loses the house. It would kill him if he had to live elsewhere…"

"O K… OK…" John kissed the top of Flora's head and pulled her to him. "We'll stay on until your aunt arrives." Easy promises made without a thought to their consequences. "This money your father owes, is it because of the house? Big old places like Clairgowan House can cost a lot to maintain." Checking the house with the eye of a builder's son during their walk. John knew his father would be proud of him. "The exterior's quite sound and I haven't seen signs of any recent building work. I'd take a look at inside the main house but that door at the end of the corridor's locked."

Flora shook her head. "No, it isn't the house John. Father's always in debt, the problem this time is he hasn't any more land to sell to pay them off. All I know is he owes Mr Brown a lot of money, as for the others…" She shrugged. "The solicitor Mr Boyle has the details."

"It's dark early." John lifted his arm behind Flora, the air around them black and heavy. He peered at his watch, it wasn't even midday.

High above them, something, someone, released a handful of pure white feathers. Faces up to their slow, lazy descent, heads, shoulders and everything around them covered with a soft blanket of white within seconds. They rushed to the corner of the house, the car already a misshapen hillock of snow by the kitchen door. The two of them brushing the snow away at the front of the fire while trying to ignore the triumphant look from the figure in the high backed chair.

A meal of Christmas dinner leftovers, Mungo sat by the fire for his afternoon nap. Lamps filled and lit while he slept, fires built up, more leftovers left on the table for his supper, platefuls of food taken up the stairs. John wedged a chair against the bathroom door for their bath. Then to the bedroom, hot damp bodies on the cool smooth quilt, the fire a hot flickering light. John and Flora gazed at the fire, loved, slept with limbs entwined, loved, gazed at the fire, ate, loved again and slept again, beyond the window a constant curtain of white.

The snows continued without a break for the next three days. John would start the day with his complaints concerning blocks of ice and Flora would placate him the way she knew best. Breakfast with Mungo, the three of them sat together in the kitchen or the study until the midday meal. Mungo appeared to be more amenable with their enforced confinement. He stopped goading Flora and continued to tell his stories of past happenings in the glen, some of them quite funny.

John laughed and shared his cigars with him; it was a much better option than sitting in silence willing the snow to stop.

Mungo asleep by the fire following the midday meal, chair wedged against the bathroom door, John and Flora to the bedroom, to their own small world of love and desire.

# Chapter Thirty Six

*Flora* looked out to a tranquil world of white. Mountains and glen a glittering sweep, gates an intricate lattice of ice and metal, fountain a gentle peak emerging out of the deep snow. The tree's heavy loads curving their limbs to the ground, the house surrounded by gigantic catatonic dancers waiting for a thaw to release their frozen poses.

John looked over her shoulder and rubbed his fingers over the misted window. "Thank God it's stopped."

He went down the stairs and opened the kitchen door to a waist high wall of powdery snow, the car a gentle mound at the side of the house.

Mungo sat at the table and smiled over to him. "I did warn you."

John opened the door again following a silent breakfast, this time with a brush and shovel to clear away the snow.

"You will need more than that to get out of here," said Mungo drinking tea by the fire.

"Stop it father," retorted Flora. "You know Mr Brown will clear a way for us as soon as he can."

"As soon as he can might not be this side of February," chuckled

Mungo.

It took John most of the morning to reach the car, and he was freezing cold despite the hard work, his heavy coat, gloves and Jeannie's scarf.

"Come inside and warm yourself by the fire for a while," said Flora at the door.

John looked down to the corner of the house. It would be dark by the time he worked his way down to it, and another day's work to clear a path to the gates. He propped the brush and shovel beside the door and hurried into the warmth.

Flora made the two men a cup of tea and left them drinking it at the side of the fire while she peeled potatoes at the sink for the midday meal. Head down to the potatoes remembering the times she and her father were cut off by the snow. How she used to feel safe and snug, the worries of the outside world kept at bay by the wall of white. She carried her pan of potatoes over to the fire and sighed at the silence between John and her father, the friendly atmosphere dissipating the moment the snows stopped.

"And what would we be having with the potatoes?" asked Mungo.

"Ach, that's all you men think about, your bellies," laughed Flora. She balanced herself between the two men and plonked her load onto the hob.

Three heads turned to the sound of the tractor.

"It will be Bob Brown," said Mungo hurrying over to open the door. The loud roar of the tractor bouncing around the kitchen as it past him, followed by the silence of the switched off engine.

John and Flora followed Mungo and stepped outside to see Bob Brown in an open topped tractor. He handed a basket down to Mungo who hurried back into the kitchen and closed the door, leaving behind him the wonderful smell of Mrs Brown's bread and scones.

The tractor had cut a deep swathe down the side of the house and around the car. It stood several yards past the door with a small mountain of snow at the front of the broad shovel.

"Thank you Mr Brown," said Flora.

"You know I would not leave you snowed in if I could help it," said Bob Brown jumping down from the tractor. "The road through the village is clear and they say you can travel all the way into town now." He was dressed for the weather, thick gloves and a long heavy coat, trousers pushed into high fur lined boots. The flaps of a peaked fur hat fastened under his chin, his cheeks raw with the cold.

Flora looked at John. "I can go down to the village now and telephone Mr Boyle the solicitor."

"I doubt if his office will be open over the holidays Flora," said Bob Brown. He looked puzzled. "Why do you wish to telephone Mr Boyle?"

"To speak to him about father's debts," said Flora. "Mr Boyle said father has to make payments towards the money he owes or he might lose Clairgowan House."

Bob Brown looked at the kitchen door. "The laird has not mentioned this to me. He persuaded me to loan him two hundred and fifty pounds in September even though he knew it would cause trouble between me and Mrs Brown. But I have told him he must not ask me for more." He looked at the ground then lifted his head to Flora. "I suggest you try old Charles Boyle the father. He still lives in the same house at the other side of town. And if you do contact old Mr Boyle you can tell him I will cancel the laird's debt to me. I have no wish to see him thrown out of Clairgowan House."

"Thank you Mr Brown," enthused Flora. "You have always been a good friend to father." She smiled at John.

"I do not know what Mrs Brown will say about it. But I will always remain a friend to the laird whatever the circumstances," replied Bob Brown. He heaved himself back into the tractor and nodded in the direction they took their walk. "I see some trees have fallen, I will cut them as soon as I can and bring the logs for the fire." His head down to start the tractor. "Robert left before the snows." A quick look over to Flora. "It pleased his mother to see him but she was a mite upset he left so soon."

The tractor started with a roar and reversed away from the mountain of snow. It made a tight circle, a salute from Bob Brown with a gloved finger to his brow before it disappeared around the corner of the house.

Flora turned to the kitchen door. "I'll tell father then telephone old Mr Boyle when we've eaten."

"No!" John caught her arm. "Wait until we've spoken to this old Mr Boyle. And we'll go and see him; these situations are best dealt with face to face." He grabbed the brush. "I'll clear Minx the Magnificent to see if she's still alive under this lot."

A snowball hit Flora as she opened the door. She laughed and threw one back. John skimmed the snow off the car towards her with the brush. Flora shrieked, jumped away and made another snowball while eyeing John with a determined look.

Mungo's voice shouted from the depths of the kitchen. "Someone close that door and stop the draught. And get yourself in here Flora the potatoes are turning to mush."

Flora dropped her snowball and turned to the door.

John ducked his head down and concentrated on the car.

Flora put her head through the door. "Pull the pan off the hob father." She closed the door and ran up to John, picking up a handful of snow on the way.

258

John dropped the brush, grabbed Flora by her waist and swung her around and around. Her head back, hair swinging out, cheeks burning red with the cold. She dropped her snowball as her feet fell to the ground, both panting spurts of steam at each other's face.

John cupped Flora's cheeks in his hands; he could have stood there for ever looking into her eyes.

"Are we going to stay here and freeze?" she asked, lips pouting from the pressure of his hands. "If you insist on cutting our afternoon short by going out, you'll have to promise me an extra long bath later on."

"What about Mungo?" asked John. "He'll be awake by then."

Flora looked up while she thought about it, cheeks still in John's hands, lips pouting. "No." She shook her head. "The bath's not big enough for the three of us."

Her laughing face left John's hands. A snowball thrown at him and Flora inside the kitchen with the door closed before he could retaliate.

John cleared the snow off the car, the engine started at the first crank.

The last scrapings of Christmas dinner and mushy potatoes eaten with the three of them eyeing Mrs Brown's bread and scones.

John and Flora up to the bedroom immediately after the meal to tidy up for their outing. They changed into dark slacks, John with a shirt and tie under his jumper.

Flora looked in the mirror; her pearls a soft glow against her black jumper. "I remember asking my mother once why she was crying. I was very little so I started to cry." She touched the pearls with her fingertips. "Mother said it was because we'd lose Clairgowan House one day. Then Alasdair died, and mother left and father closed up the main house."

John came up behind her and put his hands on her shoulders.

Flora smiled at him in the mirror. "I wondered why we'd been living in those big draughty rooms when we could have been more warm and comfortable here." She turned to John. "I should have made more of an effort to involve myself with all of this before now but father's so secretive about everything. And when you are young and you are told something often enough you accept it, you even sit back and wait for it to happen. And later on I thought I could help with…"

"Robert?" asked John.

Flora nodded.

John pulled her to him and held her in his arms. "I need whatever money I have Flora…"

Flora put her fingers to his lips. "Don't you dare John Mason. I've seen how hard you work and I'm not going to let you spend a penny of your money on Clairgowan House. This place has been nothing but trouble for the Ballardine's since they set down the first stone. All I want is for father to spend the last of his days here."

John kissed her on the brow. "We'll see what this old Mr Boyle has to say." He didn't say he had no intention of volunteering any of his money to help Mungo Ballardine.

John and Flora made a quiet exit past Mungo who was fast asleep in his chair.

They drove past high banks of snow, the road through the glen a narrow black ribbon snaking through eye hurting white, everything around them featureless apart from the odd tree and huddle of houses. The town looked dirty in comparison to the pristine snow, the noise and busyness a welcome respite following the quiet stillness of the glen.

Flora often visited Mr Boyle's house as a child, her memory of a large imposing stone building in fact a medium sized house with a tiny front garden.

John used the large door knocker.

Bolts drawn back, the enquiring face of Charles Boyle looked out to them.

"Well if isn't little Flora Ballardine," he exclaimed. The door opened wider as an invitation for John and Flora to enter.

Flora smiled. "I'm not so little any more Mr Boyle, and I'm Flora Mason now," she stepped into the house with John and turned to him. "This is my husband."

John took the frail hand. "John Mason Mr Boyle."

"And you are not from around these parts are you John?" asked Boyle.

"Shropshire," replied John.

"Ah! A Shropshire lad!" exclaimed Boyle. The old man well in his eighties, but his eyes bright, his manner alert as he shuffled along in a pair of old carpet slippers. He ushered John and Flora into a room and insisted he leave them to make tea.

John and Flora sat on an old settee, the brown leather cracked with age. Around them a clutter of old photographs and ornaments and dusty old paintings on the walls. A Victorian jardinière stood at the window with a giant aspidistra inside it, the huge leaves stopping most of the daylight from entering the room.

Boyle returned with a rattle of bone china tea cups and saucers on a tray along with a silver tea service and a plate of biscuits.

"And I expect you are here to see me because the laird is in his usual kind of trouble," said Boyle pouring the tea. He handed John and Flora a cup and sat back at the silence, years of waiting for clients to tell him their problems still a part of him.

Flora looked at John.

He leant over to Boyle. "Flora's concerned her father might be put out of Clairgowan House Mr Boyle. Your son informed him six months ago that there's a threat of him losing the house if he fails to contribute payments towards his debts."

"And the amount of these debts?" asked Boyle.

"Two thousand pounds," replied Flora. "And father also owes money to Mr Brown, but he says he will cancel this debt to him."

The old man shook his head. "I am retired now Flora, you should be speaking to my son. But I am afraid he is away with his family at the moment."

"The problem is father has no more land to sell Mr Boyle," said Flora.

"And my concern," said John. "Is the value of Clairgowan House far outstrips the amount of money owed."

"Yes, I agree," said Boyle. He looked at Flora. "Are you sure the sum mentioned was two thousand pounds Flora?"

She nodded. "Yes. And father has no money to make these payments."

"And we can't wait until your son's office reopens," said John. "I have to return to my business within the next few days." He saw the quick look from Flora

Boyle thought about it, gnarled fingers on his chin. "See me tomorrow afternoon, I will make enquiries and see if there is anything I can do." A warning look to John and Flora. "But I cannot promise anything."

The old man reluctant to let the young couple leave, visitors rare at his age, but he was happy they had given him something to occupy his empty hours with. A pen and paper first, before the commencement of the long search for his spectacles.

John and Flora shopped for fresh food, the short day and cold chasing them away from the town and along the glen to Clairgowan.

Mungo peered around his chair on their return.

"Good news father." Flora emptied the bags of shopping and rushed around setting the table and arranging thick slices of cooked ham onto the plates. "Mr Brown says you won't need to pay back the money you owe him."

"Yes, I know," retorted Mungo. "I took a walk up to the farmhouse for some company and Bob Brown took me aside and told me. The man was obviously too frightened to tell me in front of his wife." A snort of disgust at the fire at this before the grey eyes darted over to Flora. "And Jeannie would not leave me for hours sitting alone."

Flora shook her head at John and put buns and cakes onto plates. "Yes, but there's more good news. John and I have been to see old Mr Boyle and he asked us to go and see him tomorrow. He said he can't promise anything, but he'll see…"

"Old Boyle," snorted Mungo. "He will not be of any use, the man retired years ago. I need money not promises." He looked over to the table. "And I do not want any of that. A man needs warm food inside of him this time of the year not that cold stuff."

Flora turned to him, cheeks flushing up. "Then do without," she shouted.

Mungo smiled at the fire. "There you go with your temper again."

Flora threw food onto two plates, picked them up and looked at John. "We'll eat upstairs. I'm sure father will be happier with his own company than having to put up with my temper."

# Chapter Thirty Seven

*Flora* cleared away the breakfast plates and took them over to the sink. "Why don't you come along with us to see Mr Boyle father?"

"And be humiliated again," grumbled Mungo.

Flora poured him another cup of tea. "You never know, he might be able to think of something to help." She smiled at John as she leant over the table to fill his cup.

"Old Boyle retired years ago," retorted Mungo. "What can the man do in a day?"

Flora refilled her own cup, sat at the table and picked it up to drink her tea.

Mungo threw sugar into his cup and splashed milk in, his chair screeching back on the flagstones as he stood. "And while you are filling yourself with tea your aunt's room needs seeing to. In case you have forgotten she will be arriving on the three o'clock train this afternoon." He picked up his cup and sat on the high backed chair. "Jeannie would not need telling."

"I'm sure she wouldn't," said Flora. "And no, I haven't forgotten Aunt Elizabeth." She smiled at John. "We can meet her at the station after we've seen Mr Boyle."

Mungo took a slurp of tea. "Jeannie would have had the room cleaned and tidied long before now."

Flora took a drink out of her cup. "I'm going to see to it as soon as I've drank my tea."

Mungo nodded and smiled over to John. "Jeannie would know that bed needs a good airing. She would have had the fire lit days ago."

Flora clashed her cup down.

John stood up from the table. "I'll light the fire." He looked at Mungo. "It's the room next to yours?"

Mungo nodded and smiled at the fire.

The fire set and ready to light; John struck a match and watched it take hold. Flora followed him into the room carrying clean bedclothes, a brush, dustpan, duster and polish. He turned his head to her. "Your father certainly knows how to get you going."

She sighed and sat on the flowery quilt. "I know. But he might be right John, what can Mr Boyle do in a day?"

John sat on the bed and put his arm around Flora. "Let's see what he has to say first."

Flora shook her head. "I think we might have to wait until his son's office opens."

John pulled her to him. "I can't leave the garage for that long Flora. I'll lose too much money."

Flora nodded and put her head down.

"Unless…"John shrugged and questioned his need to test Flora. "I go back and leave you here until the office opens."

Flora took a deep breath.

Her hesitation brief, a minuscule passage of time, but it was enough to confirm to John that Flora had considered this herself.

"You're as bad as father," laughed Flora. "A few days married and you are trying to get rid of me already." She pushed John down to the bed, kissed him, put her hands under his jumper and shirt and caressed his skin.

They undressed each other and loved each other on the top of the flowery quilt, lying in each other's arms until the fire stopped crackling and they started to shiver.

"I wonder what my maiden aunt would say about this?" laughed Flora.

"You can tell her we've given her bed a good airing," responded John.

Flora gave a snort of a giggle, rolled away from him and grabbed her clothes. "I have to tidy this room. Of course you can always help me."

John winced and rushed around pulling his clothes on. "I think I'll check on Minx the Magnificent."

Flora laughed. "I thought you might think of something else to do." She put her arms around John's waist and kissed him. "And I packed your oatmeal suit so you can wear it for Aunt Elizabeth; we are going to look our very best for her when we meet her at the station."

John raised his eyebrows. "And bossy as well."

Flora put her head to his chest. "I love you John Mason."

John put his face to Flora's hair, breathed her deep into his lungs and prayed for the snow to stay away.

The dry cold air suited the old car, the engine roaring into life at the first crank. John chipped at the frozen snow around the door and the car with the shovel to pass the time. But he forgot his gloves, hurrying to the pot sink in the kitchen to put his freezing hands under the hot water tap to thaw them out.

"I cannot see of what use old Boyle will be."

John picked up a towel and turned to the high backed chair. "He might be able to put a stay on this threat of you being evicted."

Mungo peered around the chair to John, no smile, the pale eyes without colour. "I do not need favours from an old man," he shouted. "I need money."

John dried his hands and threw the towel down. "As you have pointed out yourself Mungo. I can't afford to be of much use to you in that department."

Flora hurried into the kitchen. "We are going to have cooked ham for dinner again so no complaints father. I'll cook us all a hot meal tonight."

Mungo quiet during the meal and he left the table without waiting for a second cup of tea.

John and Flora left him glowering at the fire.

John soon changed and sat on the bed to watch Flora change into her suit with the fur collar.

Hair brushed down her back before she put on her little fur hat, face to the dressing table mirror to apply her makeup, buttons fastened, fur collar fluffed up around her pearls. She'd packed brown high heeled ankle boots and a brown wool wrap, putting them on and picking up her handbag and turning to John.

He stood and put his arms around her and nuzzled the fur.

Flora laughed. "Oh no you don't. We haven't the time."

"Flora," started John, "we have to start to think of when we …"

"I almost forgot." Flora's large brown eyes up to him, John wanted to wipe the make up off the cheeks, see the lovely pink bloom. She pulled him to her aunt's room to show him the embroidery silks and ribbons around their wedding photograph. "They're lovely aren't they." Her happy face waited for him to agree.

John nodded. "Yes…Whatever old Boyle comes up with, we'll have done what we can Flora."

Her head rejected this nuisance. "I know... I know..." Irritation in her voice, arms around him, a smile. "This is going to be the best Hogmanay ever. All of my favourite people together. You." A kiss on John's lips. "Aunt Elizabeth and father."

John pulled down the stairs and into the kitchen, Flora's boots clicking on the flagstones.

The sound drew the pale eyes away from the fire. Surprise opened the mouth, a definite colour in the eyes, a wash of pleasure, admiration, pride.

It was the first time John saw Mungo Ballardine show any sign of warmth for his daughter.

"We're away now father." Flora's boots clicked past him. "Wish us luck with Mr Boyle."

Her reply a grumble to the fire. "I need money not luck."

Boyle opened the door before John had the chance to use the door knocker. It was the man who Flora remembered from her childhood. Highly polished shoes replaced the carpet slippers, spectacles on, dark blue tie, pale blue shirt with a white starched collar, a small rosebud in the lapel of his smart grey suit. It always fascinated her, at how he could obtain a rosebud in the middle of the winter, this one the palest of pink.

"Good news," proclaimed Boyle. He ushered John and Flora into the room with the aspidistra and waited for them to sit on the cracked settee. "My son's secretary kindly provided me with the laird's file." The old man settled himself into a chair and smiled at Flora. "You have Mr Brown to thank for setting a precedent Flora. I have contacted all of the laird's local creditors and as soon they knew Mr Brown cancelled his debt they agreed to do the same. The laird is still held in very high regard in these parts."

"Oh, thank you Mr Boyle!" exclaimed Flora. She smiled at

John.

John leant forward. "You said the local creditors."

Boyle bowed his head. "I did indeed. I am afraid the taxman cannot behave in such a charitable way. The laird has not been paying his land taxes."

"And the amount?" asked John.

"Two hundred and fifty pounds," replied Boyle.

"You mean father's going to lose the house because of two hundred and fifty pounds," cried Flora.

Boyle nodded his head. "The laird has always been remiss in paying his land taxes Flora. I expect it will be for land he sold years ago and the taxman has lost his patience with him."

"If only father had more land to sell," said Flora.

"He has," said Boyle. "The land on which the trees stand. But whoever owns the land controls access to Clairgowan House. That is why the laird cannot sell it." He shook his head. "And the land is almost worthless Flora, it is not worth two hundred and fifty pounds."

John took a cheque book out of a pocket and felt around himself for a pen.

Boyle took a fountain pen out of his breast pocket and handed it to him. "You are going to pay the laird's tax bill for him?"

John shook his head. "No. I'm offering to buy the land on which the trees stand for the sum of two hundred and fifty pounds." He filled the cheque out and gave it to Boyle along with the pen. "I've made the cheque payable to you Mr Boyle with a little extra for your fee. Mungo Ballardine must not see one penny of this money. It must be used to pay his tax bill or I withdraw my offer. And if he does accept my offer the title deeds to the land are to be in the name of Mrs Flora Mason."

Charles Boyle admired quick John's grasp of the situation. Clairgowan House would be impossible to sell without access, and

Mungo Ballardine could not refuse his offer because his daughter's name would be on the title deeds. He saw his son recommended Flora leave Clairgowan House, her pearls, stylish clothes and clever husband said it was the best advice she would ever receive.

Flora put a hand on John's knee, cheeks flame red. "Thank you," she whispered.

John took her hand. "I'm trying to protect your inheritance Flora."

It was true what he said, but not the main reason why John relented and paid the money. He did it because he knew it would be the only way to persuade Flora to leave Clairgowan House with him.

Flora looked at her watch and jumped up. "Aunt Elizabeth!"

John shook Boyle's frail hand. "Thank you for your assistance Mr Boyle."

"Yes. Thank you Mr Boyle," repeated Flora.

They made their farewells at the door, John and Flora hurrying to the car in the half light of the winter afternoon.

Charles Boyle closed the door on the cold and hurried to warm himself by the fire. He returned to the door with a click of his tongue at his memory. His hand hesitated at the handle, puzzled as to why he was there. The sound of the car driving away reminded him of his intention to give his good wishes to the young couple for the new decade, 1960 a few hours away. Another click of his tongue, this time with a shake of his head at him missing a year, 1959 a few hours away, or it might be 1958...

John and Flora quiet in the car, both concentrating on arriving at the station in time. The lumbering puffing train leaving as they ran onto the platform, all of the passengers rushing past them with the Hogmanay celebrations in mind, except for one.

"Aunt Elizabeth," shouted Flora. She ran up to her aunt and

hugged her so tight her feet almost lifted off the platform.

"Flora," laughed Elizabeth holding onto her hat. She stepped back to admire her. "Look at you. You look beautiful."

Flora put her fingers on the pearls. "It's the pearls; they'd make anyone look beautiful. They're my Christmas present from John." She turned to John. "John, this is Aunt Elizabeth."

A laugh from John. "I thought it might be." He put his hand out to the elderly lady with the look of Flora about her. Smaller, slimmer, but with the same large brown eyes and greying hair that must have been as black as Flora's one day.

Elizabeth shook her head at his hand. "And you are not getting away with that young man."

She put her hands on John's shoulders to pull him down to her, a kiss on his cheek, and a whisper in his ear. "You have turned my beautiful Flora into a princess."

Elizabeth saw the look of pleasure on John's face as he leant down to pick up her suitcase, linking John and Flora's arms as they walked along the platform.

"You wouldn't believe what John has done Aunt Elizabeth," said Flora. "He's bought the trees around the house for me. They belong to me now."

They reached the car; dirty humps of cleared snow lined the quiet road.

John opened the boot of the car and put the suitcase in. "Your father has to agree to the sale Flora."

"He'd better," retorted Flora.

John helped Elizabeth into the back of the car, started it and jumped into the front with Flora.

Flora turned to Elizabeth. "I told John I didn't want him to spend any of his money on Clairgowan House Aunt Elizabeth." She pretended to glare at him.

John gave an exaggerated sigh. "Are we going to have our first argument in front of your aunt?"

Flora giggled and put her hands to her face.

The car full of laughter and talk all the way to Clairgowan with John and Flora answering Elizabeth's questions about their life in Birmingham and Flora chattering on about the meeting with old Mr Boyle.

Elizabeth saw the way John looked at Flora and knew his love for her was steady and true. His love turning her into the stunning, happy young woman who almost hugged the life out of her on the platform. She regretted the way Mungo and herself exploited Flora, the need to save Clairgowan House superseding her happiness. Robert Brown was spoilt and selfish, Lady Derman's reticence concerning her grandson explained with a whisper from Bernice. John Mason far outstripped Robert Brown and Freddie Thompson - Smythe. Elizabeth smiled at clever Flora outwitting them all.

The car stopped by the kitchen door with Elizabeth noticing the dearth of information at Mungo's reaction to Flora's marriage. She left John and Flora at the car to collect her suitcase and entered the house alone to see the figure rise from the high backed chair.

Mungo Ballardine was an imposing figure when he wore the tartan, his smiling face reminiscent of the handsome looks of his younger days. He stood so tall and straight the last 46 years might have been an imagination for Elizabeth, a cruel dream of a teenage girl at the beginning of her journey of infatuation and pain.

"A dram after your long journey Elizabeth?" Mungo went to the tray on the table and poured whisky into two glasses, turning his back to Flora as she came through the door.

John followed her in with the suitcase.

"Would you mind taking my suitcase upstairs for me John?" asked Elizabeth. She took off her coat, put it on a chair by the table and unpinned her hat.

"Yes, of course." John knew Elizabeth meant he take Flora out of the room. He put an arm around her and led her away.

Flora's cheeks flared up, her face over a shoulder. "You could at least ask about Mr Boyle," she shouted.

Elizabeth waited until the door closed behind John and Flora and turned to Mungo. "She has a right to be angry with you."

"It will only be bad news," grumbled Mungo. "I have no wish to know about old Boyle." He offered Elizabeth her glass his eyes saying otherwise.

Elizabeth took off her hat and stabbed it with the pin. "Then I will tell you what you do not wish to know Mungo." She put her hat onto the table and took the glass. "Mr Boyle has persuaded others to do the same as Mr Brown and cancel your debts, and John has offered to pay two hundred and fifty pounds for the land around the house to pay your tax bill."

"He can offer what he likes," shouted Mungo. "That land is not for sale. I cannot sell it even if I wanted to."

"John has arranged the title deeds go in Flora's name, so access to the house will not be a problem." Elizabeth sat on Flora's chair and took a drink out of her glass, the fire and whisky soothing and warming her body.

Mungo thought about it. "That is different." He emptied his glass and poured himself another drink muttering down to the glass. "And him making out he has no money."

"Why do you say that?" asked Elizabeth.

"That car he uses." Mungo sat himself down on his chair. "Most probably he had to borrow the money to dress Flora up in her fancy clothes and jewellery so he would look good. And I expect he will have to do the same for the land." He raised his glass to Elizabeth, a smile. "I will consider this offer as soon as I have the money and not before."

Elizabeth shook her head. "Do not measure Flora's husband the same as yourself Mungo. Using that car might be called thrift, of which you know nothing about. And you will not see one penny of this money. John has lodged the cheque with Mr Boyle on the strict understanding it is to be used to pay your tax bill."

"I expect it will have to do for the time being," muttered Mungo.

Elizabeth leant over to him. "It will have to do for the foreseeable future Mungo. I doubt the people you owed the money to will allow you a repeat of the same situation."

"I am the one to decide my situation," roared Mungo. He jumped up, drank his whisky and splashed more into his glass. "I need money," he shouted, "not this tinkering around." His pointed his glass at Elizabeth. "I am in this situation because of Flora. She sent Robert Brown packing with her temper. She runs off in a temper and comes back with…"

Elizabeth pushed herself up off the chair. "I hope you have not been causing mischief Mungo."

Mungo held up his glass and smiled. "You know me Elizabeth; I can be civil to anyone if I need be."

"Yes, I do know you Mungo," said Elizabeth. "Leave Flora alone; let her live her own life. And you should be grateful to John for helping you."

Mungo's face creased up in puzzlement. "Who?"

Elizabeth gave an exasperated shake of her head. "John!" she exclaimed, "Flora's husband, your son-in-law."

Mungo raised his glass. "Of course I am grateful to the lad." The whisky swallowed. "And I accept his offer." His face down to Elizabeth, inches away. "How can I refuse my daughter the opportunity to own her own piece of land?"

Elizabeth looked at the smile, stepped back and put her glass onto the table. "And that is all Flora will have by the time you are finished Mungo Ballardine."

She went to her room to unpack and sat on the bed to look at her presents.

Flora put her head through the door, John behind her. "Do you like them?"

"Off course I do," replied Elizabeth. "The silks and ribbons will be put to good use and your photograph will have pride of place in my little flat." She opened her suitcase, took out an embroidered tablecloth and gave it to Flora. "A wedding and Christmas gift for you both."

"Thank you Aunt Elizabeth, it's lovely," said Flora looking at it. "But we haven't anywhere suitable for it at the moment."

"Put it in a safe place until you do," said Elizabeth. She shook her head at the jeans and jumpers John and Flora had changed into. "You are not going to spend Hogmanay dressed in those clothes are you?"

Flora looked down at herself. "But everyone will be at Bob Brown's. The villagers know father can't afford to put on a party."

"Whether anyone comes or not I think it is about time Clairgowan House celebrated Hogmanay in style again," said Elizabeth. "Go... Change," she ordered shooing John and Flora away with a hand. Smiling at them obediently leaving the room she followed them to the door. "Mungo has accepted your offer for the land John, and he his grateful for your help. Flora will tell you, he would never think to say thank you, but he is grateful for what you have done."

The narrow corridor lit by two oblongs of muted light from each of the bedrooms. John and Flora turned to her in the shadows.

"Let us enjoy tonight," said Elizabeth. "And celebrate what has happened and look to the future. I was so looking forward to spending Hogmanay with you all. Let us be happy and make this a night to remember."

Elizabeth saw John and Flora smile at each other. A reminder of the times she had to appease her sister Beatrice because of Mungo and his selfish behaviour. She returned to her room and took a blue satin dress out of her suitcase. The style told it all, ankle length, heavy on the shoulders, a nipped in waist. A dress to party in, her partying more frantic as time and opportunities slipped quickly by.

Her appeasement continued in the kitchen while she helped Flora prepare the meal, the room full of laughter and talk by the time they all sat at the table to eat. Flora looking radiant dressed in her red dress and pearls, John smart in dark slacks and a white shirt.

They all left the table and sat at around the kitchen fire to watch the clock go round. The happy atmosphere continuing for the remainder of the evening, and helped by Mungo topping up everyone's glass with whisky at frequent intervals. John in keeping with the convivial mood shared his cigars with him, Mungo in turn offering him a flaming spill. John looked into the pale eyes each time he leant over to light his cigar, and knew whatever was in them it certainly wasn't gratitude.

Flora jumped up a few minutes to twelve. "What do you think Aunt Elizabeth?" She looked at John.

Elizabeth looked doubtful. "He is supposed to be tall, dark and handsome." She laughed at Flora. "But I suppose we will have to make do with a tall, handsome red headed Viking."

Flora spluttered and giggled.

John's glass taken from his hand by Elizabeth, cigar snatched from his mouth by Flora and thrown on the fire. Pulled from his chair and marched to the outside door by the two women.

He looked at Flora. "Where are we going?"

"We aren't going anywhere," giggled Flora. "You are. And you have to stay where we put you until we give you permission to come back into the house again."

Elizabeth opened the door, the icy air a shock.

John placed outside facing the door, a gust of wind billowed his shirt out. "Is this absolutely necessary?" He folded his arms against the cold, the door closed on a shivering figure with a very aggrieved face.

"I think we might have put him outside a little early," laughed Elizabeth.

"He will need more than red hair and a beard to turn him into a Viking," said Mungo refilling the glasses again. "We should leave him out there for a good hour to toughen him up."

"I didn't see you rushing to go outside," retorted Flora.

Three faces to the clock, the door crashing open exactly on midnight. John almost fell into the kitchen, with his arm around the blushing Jeannie Drummond.

"That girl just can't leave us alone," snapped Flora.

"It is only a little bit of fun Flora," laughed Elizabeth.

"Jeannie," shouted Mungo. "I thought you had abandoned me to Flora's ministrations."

Flora's angry face at Elizabeth. "See!"

Elizabeth sighed and shook her head at Mungo.

The moment lost in toasting in the New Year, and greeting Bob and Mrs Brown, and Tam and Morag Fraser from the village post office along with their three girls. A crowd of Drummonds, Andy McManus with his wife and son Alex, Tom and Fiona MacDonald who went to school with Flora and Mr and Mrs Stewart from the village shop.

They all crowded in along with the other villagers. Everyone bringing with them their contribution of food and drink for the festivities until there wasn't an inch of space left on the table. Mungo greeted them all as the laird should, loud and expansive. Elizabeth, Flora and Jeannie rushed around providing everyone with food and drink. John in the centre of the laughter and noise, his back slapped, hand shook, people queuing with drinks for him while he tried to talk to everyone at the same time, the three Fraser girls gazing up at him with open mouths.

Flora shouted through the crowd to Elizabeth. "This is wonderful. What are they all doing here tonight?"

Elizabeth laughed. "They are doing what they do best Flora. Giving your new husband a good old fashioned Highland welcome."

# Chapter Thirty Eight

*Flora* turned her head on the pillow, which set off a painful throb behind her eyes. Her recollections of the night before didn't quite stretch to going to bed, or undressing, or finding her way up the stairs. But she could remember the screeching sound of the table legs as they moved over the flagstones and the magical appearance of a fiddle and accordion. Her crossed hands held by another pair of crossed hands and spinning around faster and faster to the quickening music. Sat on someone's knee or a chair and screaming with laughter at John who was dancing a disjointed waltz with the youngest of the Fraser girls who was at the most three foot tall. Slipping off the knee, or chair, and deciding with the logic of the moment to stay sitting on the floor because she knew she'd slip off the knee, or chair, again…

Sitting up changed the painful throb into a very painful hammering, and she needed the toilet, and a drink, water, tea, anything to take away the taste of stale whisky. She eased herself off the bed with a scowl at John's peaceful state as he lay sprawled out with his face down to the mattress. The difficult manoeuvre of dressing while she kept the painful hammering down to a minimum achieved. Brushing her hair a step too far, the brush thrown down and cursed, the whisky cursed and Flora cursed for drinking so much.

John's voice came up from the mattress. "Some of that coffee wouldn't go amiss."

"If you think I'm running up and down those stairs being your servant you are very much mistaken," snapped Flora. She snatched the door open and slammed it shut behind her.

John jumped an inch off the bed while Flora stamped down the stairs cursing the door, her head, and the whisky again and herself again and the freezing cold bathroom and having to lean over the sink to brush her teeth and wash her face.

She slammed the kitchen door back. The fire roaring and everything tidy. Food from the night before stacked neatly along the cupboard tops, the table returned to where it should be in the centre of the room.

Elizabeth, who was sat on Flora's chair drinking tea, winced and turned away from the matted hair falling over the slit eyed face.

A noisy clatter at the sink, Flora saw the pigtail and new ribbon.

Jeannie put the last of the dishes onto the draining board. "I will start the breakfast now Miss Montgomery."

"You will not start the breakfast, you will get out," shouted Flora, and wished she hadn't. The pain she'd inflicted upon herself no help to her mood. "I told you before not to come. Or can't you understand something as simple as that?" Her voice rose to a screech. "Or are you as simple as they say you are?"

"Flora!" exclaimed Elizabeth. She put down her cup and hurried over to Jeannie to put an arm around the thin shoulders. "We will have to excuse Flora's bad temper Jeannie; I think she is feeling a little frail this morning. You may go home now; you have helped quite enough for one day."

Jeannie dried her hands, her face up to Elizabeth. "But the laird said I had to come up this morning to tidy away Miss Montgomery. He said Flora would be in no fit state to do anything."

"And you have made excellent work of tidying away Jeannie. You should be commended for arriving at such an early hour." Elizabeth gave the girl her coat and scarf and opened the door. "Thank you Jeannie."

Jeannie stood at the doorway with the coat and scarf in her hands. "But I came early so I could make the laird's breakfast for him Miss Montgomery." She gave Flora a dart of a look. "He said I fry his bacon to perfection, and Flora's always late with the meals, and he has to sugar his tea, and he's been missing me, and no one can better the way I look after him."

Elizabeth gave an impatient nod. "I am sure the laird appreciates you being such a willing lackey Jeannie." She shooed the girl out of the door with the back of a hand. "Go... Go... I will prepare the laird's breakfast for him."

Jeannie backed out of the door. "But the laird's toast Miss Montgomery."

Elizabeth leant down to Jeannie and gave her a sweet smile. "And I promise I will try my very best to meet your high standards with the toast Jeannie." She closed the door on the girl's face and turned to Flora who was slumped at the table with her head in her hands. "I think tea and aspirin for your breakfast young lady."

A cup of tea put in front of Flora, the aspirin put into a hand and taken with a large gulp of tea.

Elizabeth sat at the table with her. "When do you and John intend to return to Birmingham Flora?"

"I don't know," complained Flora. She put her hands to her brow and looked down to the table.

"Your father will need Jeannie when you do leave Flora," said Elizabeth.

"I know," said Flora. "But she comes and goes as she pleases. And she doesn't take a bit of notice of anything I say. And when she is here she pushes me out." She looked under her hands to her aunt. "It's as though I don't belong here anymore Aunt Elizabeth."

"And I wonder who has encouraged all of this," commented Elizabeth up from the table. She searched the mantelpiece for a pen and paper and sat beside Flora. "Has Jeannie received any payment for coming and going as she pleases?"

"No," said Flora. "She said she couldn't take any money from father."

"I doubt if your father would think to offer payment to Jeannie in the first place," said Elizabeth. "Now if you employed Jeannie for one pound a week for her services you could dictate to her when she comes and goes."

"A pound a week isn't much," said Flora.

"A pound a week will be a fortune to the Drummond clan," replied Elizabeth. "Jeannie would not dare put that in jeopardy. She will be your hired help and do exactly as you say, not a silly girl fawning around the laird."

Several cups of tea later and the paper had a list of Jeannie's duties and a the times she was to arrive and leave Clairgowan House, and the telephone number of the garage along with the instruction to report to Flora once a month.

"There," said Elizabeth. She put the list into her pocket. "Now you can return to Birmingham with an easy mind. Your father can be rather forgetful concerning the payment of money so I suggest you leave that side of it in Mr Brown's safe hands. Forward the money to him monthly and ask him to give Jeannie's wages to her mother at the end of each week."

"You've thought of everything Aunt Elizabeth," laughed Flora.

"Except for the coming month," replied Elizabeth. "But I am sure you and John have the money between you."

"John!" exclaimed Flora. She jumped up, winced and held her head.

"Still a headache?" asked Elizabeth.

"It's a little better," said Flora. She grimaced. "I was horrible wasn't I?"

"No." Elizabeth kissed her on the brow. "I love you too much for you to be horrible." She looked into Flora's face. "You must always remember your loyalties belong to John. He loves you very much Flora. You are very lucky, treasure every moment of it."

"I will." Flora gave her aunt a hug. " And thank you Aunt Elizabeth."

"So I expect it will be tea and aspirin for John's breakfast," laughed Elizabeth going for the kettle.

"I think he'd rather have coffee," said Flora.

"Then I will make a pot of coffee for you both," said Elizabeth. "You still have some recovering to do."

Flora put cups and saucers, and the aspirin onto the tray while Elizabeth made the coffee. "You seem fine," she huffed.

Elizabeth laughed. "Maturity teaches you to ration the whisky Flora." She put the pot of coffee onto the tray. "Now go to your new husband before he dies of dehydration."

Flora picked up the tray and tried to balance it in one hand, push her hair back from her face and open the door at the same time.

"And ask John to wash that mop of yours and put the brush through it." Elizabeth put the frying pan onto the hob and went for the bacon and eggs. "Or even better still tell him to put you in the bath. Then you might start to resemble a human being instead of a mad scarecrow."

Flora screwed up her face, and stepped back from the opening door and her father. She put her head down to the tray, sidled past him and ran up the stairs.

Elizabeth smiled over to Mungo. "I have decided to take on the honour of taking care of you today Mungo so I have sent Jeannie home." She put rashers of bacon into the frying pan. "Though I doubt if I can better the high standards you have become accustomed to."

Mungo rubbed his hands together, a smile as he sat on his chair by the fire. "No one can better your standards Elizabeth."

Another smile from Elizabeth. "Wonderful news Mungo. Flora has decided to put Jeannie's employment on a proper footing."

"Employment! Proper footing!" spluttered Mungo with a laugh.

Elizabeth nodded down to the frying bacon. "Flora will pay Jeannie one pound at the end of each week." The bacon turned over. "I have a list of the girl's duties. It is quite comprehensive; it will stop her sitting in front of the fire and drinking tea all day." She turned her head and smiled at Mungo. "And I will ask Mr Brown to pay Jeannie's money to Mrs Drummond." The bacon turned again. "It will take the burden off your shoulders Mungo; the laird has plenty of other considerations to occupy his mind."

"I can think of a better use for this money," snorted Mungo.

"It is a small price for Flora's peace of mind," said Elizabeth as she picked up the bowl of eggs.

"Conscience money you mean," smiled Mungo. He leant over to Elizabeth. "Flora knows her responsibilities lie with me, the laird. She knows her place is here." The arm of his chair slapped. "Here at Clairgowan House. She knows she should be taking care of me, not the village simpleton."

"Ah!" Elizabeth stood with the bowl of eggs, opened her mouth and put her head back. "So that is what it is all about."

Mungo sat back smiling.

Elizabeth gave him a sweet smile and lifted up the bowl of eggs. "Two eggs and your bacon nice and crispy."

Mungo smiled and shook his head. "You know me so well Elizabeth."

"How true," mused Elizabeth cracking eggs into the frying pan. "How true."

Mungo leant over to Elizabeth again. "And I expect it will be the lad throwing this money around to look good." He shook his head. "I cannot abide scheming people Elizabeth."

Elizabeth shook her head in sympathy. "Nor I Mungo... Nor I." She fried the eggs, put the food onto a plate and took it to the table her brow creased with concern. "I hope I am not late with your breakfast Mungo."

Mungo followed her and sat at the table. "Right on time Elizabeth." He stabbed the bacon with his fork and looked at it. "Perfection Elizabeth, perfection."

Elizabeth bustled around making the tea and pouring a cup for Mungo. Milk and sugar, a brisk stir of the tea with the spoon rattling against the cup. She stepped back with a hand on her chest. "The toast!" she exclaimed. "I almost forgot!" Another bustle, the bread sliced and stuck onto the toasting fork and held to the fire, a thick coating of butter. The plate of toast placed on the table. "Is that to your satisfaction Mungo?" A tentative enquiry with another crease of concern.

Mungo took a bite out of the toast and gave it a thoughtful chew before he swallowed. "Perfect Elizabeth, perfect." The lips twisted. "That Jeannie always holds it too close to the fire and burns the corners." A smile to Elizabeth. "You are not joining me for breakfast?"

Elizabeth laughed. "We cannot all be as hale and hearty as you following the Hogmanay festivities." A sweet smile to Mungo. "But I will join you for cup of tea." Another bustle around to pour her tea, more for Mungo along with another noisy stir with the spoon before Elizabeth sat at the table.

"It could be old times Elizabeth."

Elizabeth looked past Mungo to the door, beyond it the corridor and the door to main house. Sure she heard a clamour of voices echo towards her, Beatrice, Alasdair, little Flora.

The knife and fork clattered onto to the empty plate, a finger pointed at Elizabeth. "And you will notice Flora is in no haste to leave Elizabeth."

Elizabeth sighed and took a deep breath. "I think you should ask the Browns to dinner Mungo."

"I should?" asked Mungo surprised. He emptied his cup, looked into it and put it down.

Elizabeth bustled around making a fresh pot of tea. "You will have to deliver the invitation yourself." She laughed. "Flora is in no fit state to take a walk to the farmhouse." The tea poured, another brisk stir with the spoon. Elizabeth sat at the table. "And stay at the farmhouse until it is time for dinner Mungo." She leant over to him, eyebrows raised, conspirators together. "You know I prefer to have the house to myself when I am making one of my famous stews."

Mungo sat back, shook his head and smiled at her. "You are spoiling me Elizabeth."

Elizabeth gave the sweetest of smiles. "Mungo." She allowed herself to touch one of the hands at the side of the plate with her fingertips. "It is the least you deserve."

John took the aspirin and drank most of the coffee, and took Flora to the bathroom when he'd sufficiently recovered. He washed her hair in the bath. Flora between his legs with her back to him, her head up while rinsed the suds away and gently, so gently brushed her hair away from her face.

He put his arms around Flora, pulled her to him and put his face to the smooth black sheen down her back. "Flora we have to think of when we…"

Flora stood, water splashing. She looked wonderful, a pink wet Venus. "Oh no you don't," she laughed jumping out of the bath. "You forgot to push the chair against the door."

John followed her out of the bath and rubbed himself with a towel. "It's no good ignoring it Flora."

"I know…I know…We'll discuss it later." Flora dressed and with the towel wrapped around her hair before John had finished drying himself. She turned to him at the door, eyes wide, cheeks flame red, her glorious smile daring him to spoil her happiness. "You'd better hurry or Aunt Elizabeth might see something she's not supposed to."

John dressed and followed her into the kitchen several minutes later. Flora sat with her hair down in front of the fire. No Mungo, Elizabeth stood at the table with a pinafore on, raw meat on a cutting board, potatoes, onions and carrots beside it.

Flora ran her fingers through her hair, whipped it up and down her back. "Do you want anything to eat John? I'm going to wait for Aunt Elizabeth's famous stew, wait until you've tasted it."

"You seem to have recovered young lady," laughed Elizabeth. "And you should be drying your hair upstairs in your bedroom, and I see you haven't brought the tray down."

"I know," said Flora. "You want us out of the way while you are making the stew." She took John's hand. "If you don't want anything to eat we could take a walk through my trees." A laugh at Elizabeth. "You did notice I said my trees Aunt Elizabeth."

"I did," replied Elizabeth. She took a large pointed kitchen knife out of a drawer.

"And I think John would do better with another warm drink

inside him instead of wandering around in the cold."

Flora put her fingers to his brow. "Still suffering?"

"No. I'm fine," replied John. "And I don't want to take a walk or have anything to eat." What he did want to do was take Flora upstairs and discuss them leaving.

"Go Flora," said Elizabeth. "You go and catch pneumonia while John stays in the warm."

"Right," said Flora, "I will. I'll go and catch pneumonia all by myself." She gave John a quick kiss on his lips. "Watch the knife John, Aunt Elizabeth hates anyone around her while she's making one of her famous stews." A laugh to him at the door before she closed it. "I think it's to protect her secret recipe."

Elizabeth smiled and shook her head at John. "Young women these days, running around outside in the middle of the winter with no coat on and damp hair." She pulled out a chair from the table for John and made a pot of tea.

John sat back while Elizabeth filled his cup. He shook his head at the milk and sugar.

Elizabeth picked up the knife. It sliced through the meat with little effort, a scatter of soft red cubes building up at the side of the board. "Has Flora discussed Jeannie with you?"

"Yes." John stood and took his wallet out of his back pocket.

Elizabeth stopped cutting the meat and held up the knife. "Four pounds John."

John counted out the notes onto the table.

"There," said Elizabeth. "That is everything in order." Her head down to the meat while the knife sliced through it. "Return to Birmingham today John. Take Flora with you and go."

"I would like to," said John. He shrugged. "But she doesn't seem in any hurry to leave."

Elizabeth smiled and nodded her head. "I will see to Flora."

Flora came crashing through the door and rushed over to the fire to put her wet hair down to the heat. "The trees are still there, they haven't changed a bit since they became mine." She laughed. "And it's started to rain."

"Oh!" exclaimed Elizabeth looking up. "I would pack immediately and go."

Flora straightened up and pushed her hair away from her face. "Why?"

"Because the rain could change to snow at any moment, that is why," replied Elizabeth.

John put an arm around Flora. "We have to go back to Birmingham at some point Flora."

She shook her head at him. "But I can't go without saying goodbye to father."

"It could be hours before he returns," said Elizabeth. "I will give your father your fond farewells."

"But we haven't had anything to eat," protested Flora.

Elizabeth nodded over to the food from the night before. "There is more than sufficient for your journey." She motioned at John and Flora with the knife. "Go! Pack while you still have the daylight to travel by. If we have a heavy snowfall you could be trapped here for weeks and John will have no business to return to."

Flora put her hands on her waist and glared at Elizabeth. "And Jeannie?"

"I will see to Jeannie." Elizabeth looked at the notes on the table. "I will give the money and list to Mr Brown and tell him what you have decided."

"You've thought of everything," laughed Flora. She rushed over to her aunt and gave her hug.

Elizabeth stood with the knife in the air while Flora rocked her from side to side.

"If you think for one moment there's any competition between my lovely John and Clairgowan House you are very wrong Aunt Elizabeth." Flora looked over to John and shook her head at him. A smacker of a kiss on her aunt's cheek before she let her go. "John and I were going to discuss it later, and I was going to say we should go tomorrow. But you are right; the rain might change to snow." She grabbed John's hand. "Come on we'd better pack and go before Aunt Elizabeth chases us out of the house with that knife."

# Chapter Thirty Nine

"*It* says we have to vacate the premises on or before the last day of August."

John read the letter over Flora's shoulder. "Four months. I should have something organised well before that."

Flora turned to John to see him walk away, anger bubbled up in her stomach. The ringing telephone stopped her shouting at him and telling him he could organise anything he wanted but it wouldn't be much use if he didn't talk it over with her. She threw the letter down and snatched at the telephone, slamming it down after she scribbled a booking in the dairy. A car drove into the garage. John walked over to it to talk to the driver, discussing someone's car with him far more important than discussing the minor matter of his wife's future with her.

Flora kicked at her chair to turn it around and sat on it with her back to John.

Her bravado at Clairgowan House lasted as far as the gates, looking back at the trees and wishing she didn't have the feeling she was running away from her father again. They arrived at the garage in the middle of a freezing cold night, running away from Clairgowan House far, far different in the winter. Flora stood in the tiny grim room yearning for the roaring fires, mellow oil lamps, the space, her large soft bed.

John knew, he put his arms around her. "We won't be here for ever Flora."

His understanding some comfort, but the bleak winter days pulled Flora's mood further down, and John returning to his old routine of working in the garage from early in the morning until late at night. She didn't complain because she knew he was making up the money for buying the land and trying to accumulate as much as he could before the garage closed. The motorway seemed so far away before Clairgowan, her honeymoon a line between bustling normality before to a slow decline on their return. It started with the appearance of a scatter of blank shutters in the cobbled street and Esme and Shirley ringing the office bell one day to tell her they wouldn't be holding their services in the room next to the garage anymore. A heavy black mood slipped across Flora's shoulders at the thought of not hearing their joyous voices again. No Paddy to cheer her up because John didn't have a car in the garage to restore. Reg called in most evenings and hung around looking busy until John gave him his pound note. His presence another burden for her to carry and chasing Flora to bed earlier and earlier to shorten her miserable days.

She answered another of Jeannie's ordered telephone calls that morning. As usual no preamble, Jeannie's stilted voice. "Everything is fine Flora." A clatter and the dialling tone before Flora could respond, cursing the girl as she slammed the telephone down.

Cars started to stack up outside the garage. The other garages in the street had closed down the month before which meant John worked even longer hours to keep up with the extra business coming his way.

Mr Singh moved out the week before. The scatter of closed shutters slowly changing to a scatter of open shutters, the clamour, industry and friendships around the garage moving on to the new industrial estates. Flora missed the shy Madhar and her chats with Neelam over a cup of tea. Neelam had tried to stay in her beloved home as long as she could but the fires in the empty houses around her frightened her away. Her new home over an hour's bus ride away. Sunny called in for the washing and brought the curry back with it, cold.

Flora looked at her watch again, watching the afternoon crawl towards her better than answering the telephone, taking the customers money and chatting to them. Or the pile of typing sat on the table waiting for her and her neglected paperwork. Midday! She gathered her work together, ran up the steps with it, back seconds later with her purse and running out to the street without bothering to enquire if John needed to go out anywhere. "I'm going," shouted over her shoulder.

Patrick O'Brien (Caitlin didn't surprise anyone when she named her baby after his grandfather) brought so much colour and excitement into Flora's life she was sure she saw bright fireworks fizzing and popping around her. She couldn't stay away from him, her lips drawn to the new bloom on his cheeks, his tiny fists grabbing at her heart.

Flora waited two long patient months for her precious afternoon alone with Patrick …and Caitlin of course. Danny and Caitlin's families at last accepting Caitlin could care for her baby without their help, Danny at work, the doting grandfather reluctantly acknowledging the bar needed his attention. Perfect!

Caitlin opened the door and stepped back so Flora could hurry into the lounge.

"He looks like an angel now," laughed Caitlin following her. "The little monster's been crying all morning. I've hardly had the chance to wash my face."

Flora looked into the cot, long blond eyelashes rested on pink plump cheeks. "Why don't you have a soak in a nice hot bath while he's sleeping Caitlin? I'll watch over him for you." She held her breath.

"Great!" exclaimed Caitlin. "I'll do that. Thanks Flora." She started to go up the stairs.

"Oh! He's got a little bit of sick on his cardigan Caitlin." Flora tried her very best to sound irritated.

Caitlin smiled and continued to go up the stairs. "He must have been saving it up for you so you'd have to pick him up and change him. Go ahead, you know where everything is."

Flora changed the tiny cardigan, slowly, very slowly to prolong the pleasure. Patrick didn't stir; she stood to put him back into his cot, but decided to prolong the pleasure a little longer by holding him for a few minutes.

Caitlin came down from her bath to Flora cooing at the sleeping baby in her arms. "You have a definite broody air about you Flora Mason," she grinned.

Flora leant down to put Patrick into his cot, and to hide her burning cheeks.

"Danny and I had to wait over two years for our little monster. How long do you think John and you will wait?" asked Caitlin. Fresh and relaxed from her bath she sank down in a chair, a soft veil of contentment falling around her.

Flora sat on the edge of her chair and fiddled with her wedding ring. "We have to find somewhere to live first." Her joke she would wait ten years for a baby not so funny anymore.

"See if you can rent a house on the estate." Caitlin raised her eyebrows and nodded at Flora. "Then I'll have a handy baby sitter."

It was so tempting. Flora tried to imagine John amongst the sameness, the uniformity of the houses, the gardens, the doors. But however hard she tried she couldn't see him walking up one of those paths at the end of a working day. Patrick woke and started to cry. She sat back in her chair, so she wouldn't pick him up and see herself behind one of those doors with a baby in her arms.

The moment passed and Flora stayed on as long as she dare. But Caitlin didn't seem to mind, in fact she asked Flora to feed Patrick his bottle while she made a meal for Danny coming home from work. Flora bounced out of the house following three glorious hours with Patrick and Caitlin and decided to prolong her wonderful afternoon by going into town to shop for more baby clothes.

She didn't realise how late it was until a shop assistants asked her to leave because she wanted to close up the shop, and the buses were full because all of the shops and offices closed at the same time. The road works that would overtake the garage one day another hold up, Flora alighting from the bus well after 7 o'clock.

She hadn't bought any food so she walked up the shopping street to check the fish and chip shop hadn't closed. The wind whisked paper into the air and rolled it down the quiet street. Piles of rubbish were building up outside the doorways of the empty shops. Some of them with their blinds down as though ready to open the next day, others boarded up. Several with no doors and the insides stripped of their contents, one with a blackened door and sooty windows where someone had set fire the rubbish.

The clothes shop the first to close in January, a week later the jewellers where she bought her wedding ring and John's signet ring. March with a flurry of closures, the cobblers, the little café, a butcher, a greengrocer, the haberdashery shop. Most of the food shops remained open which included the baker's thank goodness, and she saw the fish and chip shop hadn't closed, another thank goodness. Flora crossed over to the office door; buying the baby clothes for Patrick had nearly emptied her purse, she'd need money out of the tin box.

Her first try at the bell didn't bring any response, or the second.

Her third try did because she kept her finger on the bell until the door opened. All she saw was the back of John's head, his overalls and the garage door closing behind him.

She followed him into the garage determined nothing and no one was going to spoil her good mood. Reg wasn't there which helped; most probably he'd already been and scurried off with his pound note. Flora plonked herself onto her chair with the bags of baby clothes on her lap.

John down to the engine of the car he must have left to open the door, silent. He must have worked non stop since she left, the shutters down which meant the street had been cleared of cars. Three cars were inside the garage apart from the one John had his head down to; sometimes he squeezed more in so he could work on them overnight.

"I thought I'd buy something for when Patrick's older." Flora took a powder blue romper suit out of a bag.

John lifted his head to look at her. The harsh garage lights cast deep lines down the side of his nose, brows over two black voids.

Flora put the softness to her face. Head down to put it back into the bag, jerking it up in response to the loud clash of the car bonnet and in time to see John throw a long handled spanner to the floor. The throw so ferocious it gouged a chunk out of the concrete, rebounded up in the air and fell back down to the floor with a metallic clangour.

"You know what we decided about babies," shouted John. He went to another car, his face twisted with the effort of opening the bonnet.

A lid flew off and spun away, Flora's unhappiness free at last to burst out into the open. "What's the matter?" she shouted. "Are you so sorry to see me enjoy myself you have to spoil it?"

"The phone hasn't stopped ringing while you've been out for most of the day enjoying yourself," shouted John, at last he opened the bonnet.

Flora clashed her bags down onto the table, walked over to John and stood with her hands on her hips. "And while you are shouting at me do you think you can bring yourself to tell me when you intend to close the garage?"

John put his hands on the side of the car and looked down at the engine.

Flora pushed her face to John's, hands still on her hips. "And while you are actually communicating with me can you tell me where we are going to go when you do close the garage?"

John leant down to the engine and started to work on it.

Flora grabbed his arm, John's studious disregard of her incited such a flash of fury she wanted to hit him, hurt him. He tried to shrug her hand away; Flora hung onto his overall sleeve with both hands, jaw tight with the effort. She wanted to turn John around so he'd look at her and pulled him sideways away from the car.

His head hit the bonnet with a loud crack.

Flora let go of the sleeve and gulped at a face she hadn't seen before, eyes blackness, face rigid lines.

Both caught in a frozen state for less than a second.

John's hands moved so quick Flora jumped. Her arms grabbed and pinned to her sides.

John took a deep breath. "I haven't decided anything yet."

"Oh," said Flora, eyes wide in mock curiosity. "And when will you decide?"

John moved his head. Flora thought he was going to kiss her. Angry he didn't she shrugged his hands away. Angry it was so easy, angry John didn't pull her to him and put his arms around her.

She dashed over to the table, picked up the bags and ran up the steps shouting over her shoulder. "When you do decide, we'll discuss it then shall we? And as usual Flora will have to agree with John. This is what we will do Flora, because I have decided. Do you agree?" Stood at the top of the steps and screaming down to the garage. "Because there's no other option Flora. Because if you don't agree this is what we are going to do anyway."

Flora slammed the door shut and threw the bags down. She lay on the bed and closed her eyes, missing Clairgowan House, missing the happiness she and John shared there.

The door opened, Flora turned to face the wall.

"We could do with a break."

Flora stared at the wall.

"I'll finish early tomorrow. A woman rang this afternoon, she has a Hornet for sale. She had me on the phone for over an hour."

The reason for his bad mood, someone dare stop him working for over an hour. Flora didn't move.

"It's out in Tamworth. I'll cancel the bookings for tomorrow afternoon so we can have a run out to take a look at it and go for a meal. The car shouldn't take long to sort, a couple of months at the most by the sounds of it. Then I'll close up the garage. We could stay at your Aunt Elizabeth's while I chase up a few of my contacts in London. If something turns up we could look for a flat, somewhere to live."

"There!" spat Flora. "I knew." She pushed her hair from her face and turned to John cheeks burning. "I knew you'd decide without asking me. You know I hate London, you know that." Voice so thick with her anger she could barely breathe. "Well I'm not going so that's that with your great plans. And I'm not going tomorrow either because I'm going out."

"I don't know how long I'll be and idiots are stripping and torching everywhere." John stopped trying to pacify Flora. "I'm not going to have you coming back to an empty garage; you are going with me."

"I'm not." Flora pushed herself off the bed and stood with her face to John, his breath on her skin. "I'm not." Her voice quiet, eyes wide, a smile. "I'm not."

"You are," said John.

"I'm not," screamed Flora, head shaking, hair flying.

John knew his fatigue started it all. He wished Flora would put her arms around him and pull him to her so he could be inside her and the harder he pushed against her the more she would pull him to her and the future with its uncertainties be certain and Flora's chaos replaced by calm.

Flora's screeching voice in his face. "You can do what you want but I'm not going."

John took hold of her arms, walked her backwards and sat her on the bed.

"You'll have to pick me up and throw me in the car," screamed Flora up to him.

"And that is exactly what I will do," said John. He turned his back on Flora, left the room and closed the door.

Flora jumped up and snatched the door open. The back of John's head as he went down the steps begged her fingers to touch it, but her temper pulled her along in its frenzied wake, screaming down at him. "And if you think I want any of your babies you are mistaken because they might turn out just like you. Bad tempered, uncaring, mean, no sense of fun." Spluttering with spit flying out of her mouth. "So cool you think you know it all, bad tempered."

John back at the car, his head down to work on the engine.

Flora clenched her fists, screeched down at him, slammed the door after her and threw herself onto the bed. Still curled in in a ball and staring at the wall when John returned to the room hours later.

They lay back to back, Flora on top of the covers fully clothed,

John undressed and under them. John asleep within minutes, the room full of daylight before Flora closed her eyes.

# Chapter Forty

*The* telephone woke Flora; she looked at her watch, 11 o'clock. John's voice below her in the garage. He must have thrown the bedclothes back, the blanket over her with the sheet on top.

Flora pulled the clothes around herself and lay looking at the wall. Caitlin said she and Danny were going shopping together so she couldn't go there. Neelam! She could run out of the garage and stay with Neelam all afternoon, even stay the night if she could, anything rather than go with John.

His boots on the steps said she'd left it too late. The door opened behind her.

"We are leaving in an hour."

No argument in his voice, the door closed, his boots on the steps.

Flora listened to the preparations below her. Two of the shutters clashed shut, the old car started at the back of the garage and driven out to the street. She showered and dressed, and sat on the bed to wait. It was better than John picking her up and throwing her into the car, which she knew he would do.

John came into the room minus his overalls and boots, straight

to the wardrobe to put clean jeans and a shirt on. Flora silent while he dressed. His face down to fasten the buckle on his belt. "So you've decided to come."

"Have I any choice?" retorted Flora.

John put his leather jacket on and took hold of her arm to pull her off the bed. Flora in her red trousers, flat shoes, pearls a luminous curve against her black jumper, wet hair scraped back in a pony tail, no make up, lips full and red, cheeks ablaze, eyes large and angry. She looked wonderful.

He slipped his hand down her arm and took her hand to lead her out of the room.

Flora started to feel a little bit better at the thought of spending an afternoon away from the garage, until she saw Reg sat in the back of the car.

John opened the car door for her. "Reg can drive the Hornet to the garage if it's roadworthy." About to add they'd follow Reg and catch up with a meal later when Flora sat in the car and slammed the door shut snatching it out of his hand.

Reg sniggered at the two rigid bodies sat in front of him and thoroughly enjoyed himself by ignoring Flora and chatting non stop to John all the way to Tamworth.

They arrived at the house with the stony faced Flora refusing to get out of the car, and John just as stony faced slamming the door shut.

Reg swaggered up the path to the house with John. He pressed the door bell and smirked back at the car. "You should give the bitch a good slap about the face. That would teach her a thing or two." Reg knew he could say this because he was on John's side.

"You call her a bitch again, and you'll be the one to get the slap about."

John's face to Reg a frightening mask of intention

The day couldn't decide if it was spring or winter, the sun finally giving up its struggle with the grey clouds and disappearing behind them taking any warmth with it. Flora sat shivering in the car and watched a fine drizzle dribble down the windows. A sigh at John hurrying towards the car with no sign of Reg which meant she had longer to wait.

He opened the car door. "You must be freezing." Care in his voice, a hand to her. "Come inside with me, we've been offered a hot drink."

Flora took John's hand. It hadn't changed, the same warm grip full of love for her.

"The car's not good enough for the road; Sunny will have to pick it up." John led Flora up to the house and spoke to the approaching door. "Do you still love your thoughtless husband?"

"Yes," whispered Flora to her feet.

The back of her hand pressed against John's lips, the silky feel of hair on her skin.

Flora sat in front of a fire and grateful for the cup of tea from the chatty but pleasant lady. Her husband bought the Wolseley Hornet to keep himself busy during his retirement.

"It's over a year now since he died," she said. "He would never forgive me if I left it to rust. He promised to take me on a motoring holiday as soon as he finished it."

The sadness of the unfulfilled promise followed them back to the car.

Reg astounded at the change in front of him, bodies relaxed and leaning towards each other, Flora's soft profile smiling at John.

John turned his head. "I'll drop you off at your place Reg."

Reg grunted a reply and festered in the back of the car at no sign of any money for his time and John's reaction when he tried to help him to put the bitch in her place. He took his knife out of his pocket and turned it in his hand all the way to Birmingham and only spoke to give John directions to his lodgings, stopping him at the top of a row of neat terraced houses.

John and Flora watched him walk away.

John turned to Flora. "All the years I've known Reg and I never knew where he lived."

"What will happen to him when you close the garage?" asked Flora.

"I think any favours Reg did for me have been repaid many times over," said John. He put his brow to Flora's. "More to the point is where can we find some food? For some reason I didn't get my bacon sandwiches this morning."

Flora giggled into his face and kissed him.

They went in search of food with an air of reprieve and celebration about them.

Reg heard the car drive away. He checked over his shoulder and ran back up to where he left the car, and around a corner to a street of dilapidated houses and the slum he called home.

They found a restaurant near to the garage.

Flora looked down to her plate. "I will go to London with you."

"And what about this baby thing?" asked John to his plate.

Flora chewed her food and looked over John's shoulder. She swallowed and gave a shrug. "Patrick will grow up looking like Danny and I think Caitlin would like to keep him so I suppose I'll have to wait until it's the right time to have our babies."

John lifted his head. "Babies?"

"Three," nodded Flora. "All girls." She tried not to giggle at John's worried face. "And of course they will all take after their mother and never ever lose their tempers."

John didn't dare argue with that.

They loved each other all that night, and in the way they knew best, passionate and tender and careful of each other's needs.

# Chapter Forty One

"*So* you'll soon be on your way John," said Paddy.

"Yes." John nodded down to the Hornet. "It shouldn't take long to finish it off. I'll start advertising it tomorrow."

The diary was full of bookings for the next two weeks, the following blank pages a demonstration his life of physical grind had almost ended. The radical change, the giant stride days away and John ready now to take that stride.

"I'm surprised you took on another car this late," said Paddy.

John smiled.

"Not so easy is it?" said Paddy.

John shook his head. "I thought I would run out of this dump without a backward look and here I am hanging on. It's just as well they're mowing the old place down or I might still be here in ten years time."

"No you wouldn't John," replied Paddy. "That's why you've worked so hard, so you could get out of here." He screwed his face up into a smile. "Remember that Daimler? It was sitting in the garage like a bloody big bus for months."

John laughed. "I thought I was never going to shift it. And I had

to stop eating at one point to pay for the parts. I soon found out the smaller cars with some panache about them had more appeal."

"And that's enough of the serious talk," said Paddy. He turned to shout over to Flora at the table. "Seeing as me and Sunny are done after tonight I want to see what the chief polisher has to say about having a closing down party."

Flora looked up from a piece of chrome she was polishing. "A party, here?"

"We'll have a party at the bar," said John. He looked over at Flora. "We'll arrange it with Patrick tomorrow night."

Flora smiled at him.

John continued his work on the Hornet. He didn't need to lift his head to see the rusted metal and discarded car parts piled up in the corners, the detritus of his years of hard work all around him. Tools hung on the walls and scattered about, all old friends fitting comfortably in his hands. The well used machinery, every nuance known by heart so he could coax the best out of them. Worn benches, shelves with their oily clutter, and the sink he stood in front of thousands of times and the shutters which he opened and closed almost as many times. The wooden steps leading up to the stark room behind the door. A daily prompt it was a temporary stay and John Mason didn't belong there, any sign of the real man hidden behind the wardrobe doors.

That night the same as any other night, the industrious Sunny working without a break in his beaming smile, Reg behind him pretending to look busy, Paddy with his trilby hat and non stop talk and songs. Flora sat on her chair at the table with her head down to her polishing, the diary beside her which had controlled John's life for so many years. The small world inside the garage continuing on as usual while a new world waited outside the shutters, John's next challenge both frightening and exhilarating.

The telephone rang after 9, which was unusual. The calls usually petered out to a silence as the evenings wore on.

"Mason's garage." Flora's voice echoed around the garage, a pause. "Oh, hello Mr Gibson."

John's neck stiffened over the car. His head full of the contacts he made over the years and his intention to chase up everyone of them. Gibson included if he was still in the country, and his promise to contact John well over the 6 months he mentioned.

"He's very busy at the moment Mr Gibson. Can I take a message?"

Sebastian had wrecked the MG and Gibson needed him to put it together again. John waited for Flora's confirmation.

Flora put a hand over the mouthpiece, her face to John. "He says he needs to speak to the man."

John walked over to her his usual reflex to pick up a cloth to wipe his hands forgotten. Flora exclaimed at his oil smeared hand and put the telephone to his ear, her face inches from him.

"Hello George."

"Hello old man," replied Gibson, "still busy I see."

"You are lucky to have caught me; I'm closing the garage down in a couple of weeks," replied John, dashing any hopes of him repairing the MG.

"Just the ticket," responded Gibson. "I did mention last year I might have something to put your way. A couple of businesses actually, both near Hounslow in London. They are ticking along nicely but in dire need of a good kick up the backside. Just the thing for you to get your teeth into. I'm rushing between here and France at the moment, so time is of the essence. I have a gap over the next few days while I'm in old Blighty. Are you interested in taking a look?"

John looked into Flora's eyes. "It depends on what you are offering

George."

A chuckle from Gibson. "I thought as much. I'm in your direction tomorrow and I should be finished my other business by seven. I'm running around like a blue arsed fly trying to fit everything in. If you are interested I could meet you at your place and you could follow me down to a small flat I have near a garment factory I would like you to take a look at. I'll gather the paper work together so you can take a good look at the accounts overnight and you could view the two factories with me the following day. You could stay at the flat while you are deciding. It will be the sofa the first night, then I'll be off to France so you will need your own transport."

John looked at the unfinished Hornet, the diary, Flora.

"Are you interested?" asked Gibson with a hint of uncertainty at John's silence.

"I'd be very interested in taking a look George," asserted John.

"Good!" exclaimed Gibson his voice booming down the telephone. "I will see you at seven tomorrow evening."

"Right!" said John. It would take more than a few days to take a good look at these two businesses. He'd have to close the garage down two weeks earlier than he anticipated, and he had less than a day to do it. About to take his ear away from the telephone.

"By the way," Gibson again, "is the pink cheeked beauty still around?"

"She's Mrs Mason now George," replied John.

Flora pulled a face at him and pretended to look bored with a hand on her hip.

"Congratulations!" exclaimed Gibson. "But I am afraid you will have to find a hotel for the first night if you decide to bring her along, and it will severely reduce our time together. If you followed me down to the flat we could have had a good session together to view the accounts.

You will need a clear field John," warned Gibson. "Whatever you decide I will see you tomorrow evening with the paperwork."

John moved away from the telephone his mind full of the hundreds of things needed to be done. He knew Gibson was trying to rush him and the need to approach this opportunity in a calm and methodical way, and with his mind clear of all concerns and distractions.

Flora put the telephone down and looked at him.

John nodded up to the door at the top of the steps.

"I said I would go to London with you," complained Flora. "Now you say you want to go without me."

They stood in the room looking at each other.

"It's only for a few days Flora, a week, two at the most."

Flora sighed. "I suppose someone has to stay behind to close up the garage."

John licked his lips. He'd waited for that part, for Flora to accept he went without her.

"I can't leave you here, it's not safe, I can't leave you here alone." Flora alone in the garage would be the biggest distraction of all.

"Where am I to go?" A plaintive question followed by a spark of anger. "I'm not going to Aunt Elizabeth's; she'll parade me in front of her friends and expect me to take afternoon tea with them."

Relief, Flora would expect him to telephone her and visit her at her aunt's, distract him.

"Clairgowan?" John shrugged his shoulders, a casual enquiry.

Flora looked surprised, and pleased. "I was thinking of Caitlin or Neelam."

Near enough for her to expect him to drive up and see her, or telephone her, distract him.

"I'm sure your father would be pleased to see you and you can see if Jeannie's been behaving herself. And I'll give you plenty of money to see you through."

Flora laughed. "Be careful," she warned, "that sounds like bribery to me."

"I'd start packing now," suggested John. "We'll have to set out in the early hours if I'm to back in time for Gibson tomorrow."

"Tomorrow!" exclaimed Flora.

# *Chapter Forty Two*

*Flora* dropped her pearls into her cotton duffle bag, pulled the drawstring tight and looked around the room for the last time.

John hurried in, the long day ahead of him set on his face.

"I could have caught the train," said Flora.

"No." John locked the cabinet, led Flora out of the room and locked the door behind them. "I need to know you arrived safe and sound."

It was almost midnight, the car parked in a square of light in the street from an open shutter.

John hurried Flora down the steps and into the car. He slammed the door shut and returned to the garage. Flora's luggage stored away in the back of the car, John's luggage on the bed in the room.

Flora peered into the garage and wondered at the delay following the dash to pack and get her away. John hurt her by his need to separate her from that special point in his life, but Flora was determined not to spoil it for him. She knew his hard work had been all about that moment, and she loved John enough to allow him to enjoy it without her.

Someone ran up the street out of the dark with a large bag or

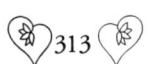

sack over his shoulder, Reg. He ran past the car and into the garage and followed John out a few moments later, stood with his hands in his pockets watching him crank start in the car.

John sat beside Flora and returned her look. "I couldn't leave the place empty with the Hornet."

"Can you trust him?" she asked.

"I've asked Sunny to keep an eye on him." John didn't say Sunny had enough to do without having to check on Reg.

The old car bounced down the cobbled street, turned into the cut and hesitated at the junction with the shopping street. A few of the streetlamps had escaped the stone throwers, each one a spotlight in the dark highlighting the dereliction and abandonment of that once vibrant place.

The car left the cut to head for the main road. It was exactly a year to the day since Flora walked through that cut looking for John. She didn't tell him, her mind on the people she left behind and not saying goodbye to them. Sunny and the lovely Paddy, both gone by the time she went down to the garage. Neelam and the shy Madhar, Patrick and her friends at the bar, Caitlin and Danny, and their beautiful baby Patrick who she wished she could have given one last kiss.

They stopped once for petrol, the short night gone before they reached the Borders, arriving at the lush green glen on a lovely summer's morning, the snow on the peaks of the mountains glistening in the sun.

Flora leant forward for her first glimpse of the village and the trees, a smile at the gates as the car went up the incline.

John circled the car around the fountain and parked it facing the gates with the engine left running.

Flora opened the kitchen door to see Jeannie jump up from her chair with a hand to her mouth.

John clattered in after her, his hands full of luggage to save him wasting time on two journeys to the car.

Mungo peered around his chair and watched John hurry through the kitchen.

"I'm staying for while father." said Flora. "John has important business he needs to see to in London."

John ran up the stairs, dumped the luggage in the bedroom and raced back down to the kitchen.

"You are in a rush," remarked Mungo.

John strode past the smiling face.

"There again clever people are always in a rush," continued Mungo with his smile to the fire.

John was in no mood to justify his actions; he took Flora's arm and led her outside.

They held each other at the gates, the throbbing car engine telling of John's haste to get away.

He put his face to Flora's hair. "I'll drop you a note to let..."

Flora put her fingers to his mouth. "No letters," she ordered. "Only you, nothing else will do."

A kiss that went on forever before John jumped into the car, slammed the door shut and drove through the gates.

Flora returned to the house to unpack, and send Jeannie away.

John wound the window down and breathed the pure air from the mountains deep into his lungs, Flora safely ensconced within the confines of Clairgowan House giving him the freedom to fully enjoy the challenge ahead. He pushed the old car as hard as he could and arrived at the garage with time to spare before Gibson arrived. The shutters down and the telephone off the hook.

"I got sick of the noise," snivelled Reg. "And they were queuing up with the cars at one point. I got sick of batting them away so I pulled the shutters down and they'll stay down tomorrow."

John didn't say anything; he went up the steps to shower and change into a suit. He packed the car with his belongings, including the contents of the cabinet; he didn't intend to leave anything to chance, and Reg. The car parked outside the office door ready for Gibson. It looked like the old workhorse it was, but a new car would have to wait. John knew Gibson wouldn't be offering him anything on the cheap; he needed to conserve every single penny he had in the bank.

He rang around the find a buyer for the Hornet; a specialist car sales firm agreed to sell it on for him for a commission. It meant his profit margin would be severely reduced but it was the best he could do in the time available, and John would have to depend on Reg to deal with it for him.

"It's roadworthy now. If you put the finishing touches to it and deliver it for me I'll give you a good cut out of the price," said John who knew it wouldn't occur to Reg to do it as a favour to a friend.

"Yea, right," said Reg. "When will I catch up with you?"

John checked his watch; Gibson was due at any moment. "I shouldn't be more than a couple of weeks. I'll see you back here."

"Yea, but what about after that?" It sounded like a whine, it was.

John threw a spare set of garage keys onto the table. "You can have the use the garage until the end of August; you won't be short of business. And you can have all of the gear to set yourself up in your own place. It's all yours, I'm giving it to you."

"You know it's all clapped out," snorted Reg. "And I can think of better things to do than slaving my guts out all day."

The office doorbell rang.

"Then you'll have to do these better things without me," said John.

He found Gibson waiting for him and followed him to Hounslow and a thirties style block of flats.

"I'm letting this flat go as well old man. On a lease of course, but near to the garment factory I want you to view." Gibson put two large files onto a table. "Now down to business."

Papers flashed under John's nose and drinks pushed onto him, confirming Gibson wanted him at the flat to himself so he could hustle him into a commitment without disruption.

John turned down the drink and gave Gibson a couple of hours. "Thank you George." He sat back and at smiled at him. "Now I'll take a look for myself."

Gibson demurred by pursing his lips, but he didn't argue. "Then I shall leave you to it John." He left John at the table and retired to the bedroom.

John worked his way through the two files. The two businesses consisted of an engineering works and a garment factory, neither of them particularly dynamic and lucky at times to achieve a profit margin, the engineering works often operating at a loss. He looked at his watch when the figures started to blur. It was over 24 hours since he and Flora set out for Clairgowan.

He looked around him at the flat. It was quite palatial compared to the room above the garage, the one bedroom, bathroom with a bath and shower, a kitchenette, a fair sized lounge with a long comfortable looking sofa, his bed for the night. John crashed into sleep with statistics swimming around his head, cash flows, graphs, pie charts…

# Chapter Forty Three

*Gibson* drove John to the engineering works. The massive old building appeared quite substantial, but it had a tired neglected air about it, and once John was inside he saw most of the machinery needed updating, a lot of it pre war.

Gibson saw his lack of interest. "I thought it would be up your street following the garage old man."

John shook his head. "Your asking price is way too high for a start George. And it would need a considerable amount of investment on top of that to make it a viable proposition."

The garment factory consisted of a giant Nissen hut with a round corrugated steel roof. A cursory wire fence separated it from an exact replica several yards away, the paintwork on the twin building faded and peeling, the area around it covered in grass and weeds.

"I feel rather guilty letting the old girl go." Gibson spoke up to the large name board saying 'GIBSON'S GARMENTS'. "My first venture into the world of commerce and she hasn't failed me once." He strode away to the entrance. "And of course that would not prevent me from letting her go for a reasonable price John." Shouting over his shoulder as John followed him into the building, and the din. "Working to full capacity old man."

The noise of screaming sewing machines in the barn like interior bounced up and down from the steel roof. Full capacity meant no more than a dozen machines, all eyes on John as he followed Gibson to an office above the factory floor, and the man stood at the large window.

"This is the man." Gibson closed the door behind them and quietened most of the noise. He turned from one man to the other. "Tom Clark. John Mason."

Tom Clark in his mid fifties, medium build and height, his face neutral as he took John's hand.

Gibson smiled at him. "You used to work in the cutting room, didn't you Tom."

Tom Clark's slight grimace said he always carried the label of the cutting room worker who made it up to management.

"Tom knows everything there is to know about the business," said Gibson. "Any questions you have John, ask him." Lips pulled down to Tom so he'd look apologetic. "I have been rather neglectful about the old place lately haven't I Tom?"

A woman entered the office. "I should say you have George." She closed the door on the sound of the sewing machines.

"And this lady has tried to inveigle her way into my bed for many years," said Gibson to John. He shook his head. "But sadly Gloria absolutely forbids it."

The woman smiled. "And I absolutely forbid you to say that one more time George Gibson." She put a hand out to John. "Janet MacMartin, Tom's secretary."

"John Mason." He took her hand.

Janet MacMartin in her mid forties, brown wavy hair to her shoulders, dressed in a smart grey suit with a pencil skirt, black Cuban heel shoes. She looked attractive and very efficient.

She turned to Gibson. "You forget all about us, and when we do see you it's because you want rid of us."

"You know this is all Gloria's doing Janet," replied Gibson. "She insists I off load so I can spend more time with her in France. And you know me I do everything Glora commands."

"Of course you do George," replied Janet her face impassive.

Gibson gave a small smile and turned to John. "Well John, are you interested in taking a step into the rag trade?"

John nodded. "I will let you know in two weeks George."

Gibson took a key off his key ring and gave it to John. "You are welcome to the flat for the interim." A warning lift of his eyebrows. "I'm not trying to rush you John, but there are other interested parties."

John handed the key back to Gibson. "Then you had better contact the other interested parties George because I need at least two weeks to decide."

Gibson waved the key away. "Of course you do John. I will leave you with these capable people and I will call you in two weeks." He went to the door to leave. "If you would return John to the flat when he's finished here Tom." It was an order, no answer expected.

Janet smiled at Gibson's back. "I suppose you will have to use your City flat for your pied-à-Terre now George."

This stopped Gibson's intended quick exit. He turned, pointed a finger at Janet and smiled at her. "Watch this woman John; she's as clever as she looks."

# *Chapter Forty Four*

*John* turned down the ordered lift to the flat and for the following two weeks walked to and from the factory. It was a twenty minute walk, time to reflect and he needed the exercise after the hard physical work at the garage. Tom Clark, as Gibson said, knew every aspect of the business and Janet MacMartin, as John had gathered on their first meeting, was a very efficient secretary. They were a team of two, running the small business in a professional and competent manner. Tom and Janet pleasant and accommodating to John while they guided him through the day to day administration of the factory and answered his many questions. The three of them often huddled together at the end of the working day while John scrutinised every detail of the factory.

John also took the opportunity to take a good look around the area for other options that might be available and to follow up a few of his contacts. Some were vague, others not forthcoming on their promises. A couple looked hopeful, he held those in reserve.

John and Tom stood together at the end of the two weeks, the two men at the window looking down to the factory floor.

"Have you considered a buy out?" asked John.

Tom nodded. "Ten years ago and I would have jumped at the

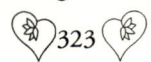

chance." He shrugged. "But a loan at my age…"

"The vacant building?" asked John.

"It used to be part of the same complex before George's uncle set up the factory," answered Tom. "He demolished the joining tunnel."

"It shouldn't be too difficult to rebuild," said John.

"It would treble our output if we took it on." said Tom. "But George was always unwilling to take on the financial investment it would take."

"I would look at quadruple, "said John. "It wouldn't be worth the trouble otherwise."

"That building has been empty for a few years now," said Tom. "It will need a considerable amount of work inside and out."

"That's why the price is so low," said John who'd made other enquiries apart from the building.

Tom turned to John. "So you are going to buy the factory?"

"It depends on two things," replied John. "George accepting my bid which is way below his asking price, and you taking on a ten per cent partnership with me."

Tom was an efficient manager but John needed an increased commitment to the business a partnership would bring.

John saw Tom struggle with this. He guessed Tom had the capital for a junior partnership but knew he was still asking a lot of the man. His savings would have taken him many years to accumulate and Tom wouldn't have the safety net of a regular salary coming in.

"Of course the wages bill will have to be slimmed down," said John not waiting for a response. "The sales manager…"

The sales manager was older than Tom, a loud man, inches from everyone's face when he spoke. To John he seemed to spend more time inside the factory than out of it searching for orders.

Tom continued to struggle with John's proposal. The step from factory floor to management an achievement itself, ownership a giant step he hardly dare view.

"He tends to be rather complacent," replied Tom who took the giant step by viewing how this man would impact on his own financial situation.

"Is he up to increased production levels?" asked John.

"No," answered Tom who'd initiated the order for the winceyette nightdresses the factory was churning out. The desperation for the order reflected in the very tiny profit margin.

"We could set on a younger man," said Tom. "I could train him. A smaller basic salary, more commision based." His son-in-law would be ideal; he would do as he was told and not waste time hanging around the factory. While ownership granted Tom the luxury of nepotism he allowed himself a pang of guilt at the unlikelihood of the sales manager obtaining another job at his age

"How would we do it?" asked John.

"The travel allowance is always considered the perk of a sales rep's job," replied Tom. Another pang at the thought of the man losing his company car.

John hoped the conversation would take that direction. The wages bill was far too high for such a small business. That was two good sized salaries down, Tom's hopefully and the sales manager's.

"It's going to cost, expansion," said Tom." Even if we bought reconditioned machines we would have to carry the cost of buying and refurbishing the twin building."

"I've looked at all of that," said John. It would work if everything moved along smoothly once he committed himself to the factory. If the twin building was completed and in production in the time frame he calculated, and if Tom delivered the orders, which he would to protect his investment.

"Anyway, who said anything about buying reconditioned machines?" asked John. "I've found a batch of old machines, we could update them ourselves."

Tom looked down to the machine mechanic who was hanging around one of the younger machinists. "I don't think he's up to that amount of work."

"I know," said John looking down to the same scene. "He'll be going anyway. I've taken a look at the machines, he's sabotaging them to look busy and chat with the girls."

"It won't be easy finding a skilled mechanic at short notice," said Tom.

"No need to," said John.

"Have you anyone in mind?" asked Tom.

"Me," laughed John who thought he'd seen the last of his overalls and dirty hands. "I'm sure I'm up to the intricacies of sewing machines. We can always find another machine mechanic when we are up and running."

He turned to Tom. "Well Tom. Are in you in for it? Do you want to take the chance?"

"Yes," replied Tom, who knew it was either that or regret it for the rest of his life.

The two men shook hands.

"Janet?" asked John. He needed her almost as much as he needed Tom. "Do you think she'll stay on?"

"She will if I ask her," replied Tom.

# Chapter Forty Five

*The* call duly came from Gibson who invited John to his club. It was one of the most exclusive in the City and it placed John at a disadvantage of negotiating in Gibson's territory.

John looked at ease in an overstuffed leather armchair with an after dinner drink and a cigar, the picture he intended to promote.

Gibson wasn't the self made man he made himself out to be. He inherited the garment factory from his uncle, and most probably the engineering works and the many businesses that had made him the wealthy man he was.

He acted astounded at John's offer for the garment factory. "I expected some haggling John but that is verging on the ridiculous."

"We could discuss it all night if you wanted George," responded John. "The fact is we could exchange contracts as soon as possible. You know I don't need to run around to raise the capital; it would be quick and clean. And if you insist on getting on the merry-go-round of finding another buyer, go ahead. I could easily buy up next door to you and set myself up there."

The haggling started and went on for several hours. They finally reached an agreed price and John to take on the lease of the flat. He left

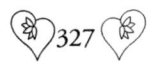

the club by taxi and told the driver to drop him off at the factory.

He stood in front of the two buildings in the early hours of the morning and visualised how they would look. It was purely cosmetic, but he allowed himself the time to enjoy his fanciful thoughts. The price agreed was just below the limit he set himself, but once the flood of money went from his bank account the time scale for recouping it was tight with no room for delays.

John decided to write to Flora that night despite her telling him not to. He'd tell her about the factory and the flat, and he was going to have to leave her at Clairgowan for a little longer than they anticipated.

John walked to the flat and decided to work out a schedule first. He sat at the table for hours setting himself a gruelling time table, not stopping until he looked up to see daylight. A shower to freshen himself up before he walked to the factory.

Later that morning a concerned Janet told him someone was viewing the twin building. Without it he would be left with a barely profitable small business with no room for expansion. John had to gamble that very day and buy the twin building before the factory contract had been finalised, and at more than the original price because of the other interested party.

John knew his mistake was mentioning it to Gibson who probably owned the building, the additional interest a ruse to sell it at an inflated price.

The sale of the factory went through without a problem and the money John worked so hard for started to evaporate at a frightening pace.

Tom fired the sales manager with aplomb on the evidence of his expense sheets, and John fired the mechanic following a check on his work on the sewing machines.

Chris Cardy, Tom's son-in-law brought in. Chris reminded John a little of Reg, dark hair, not very tall, but there the resemblance ended. Chris was bright and keen, he anticipated what was needed and did it without hesitation. He followed John and Tom's orders to the letter and his initial input into the factory had nothing to do with sales. To save money John, Tom and Chris built the tunnel and carried out the repairs to the twin building.

The two men from the cutting room turned up one night.

"You can pay us when you are both millionaires," one shouted.

John bought the extra sewing machines before they completed the building work and stored them in the twin building to await his input while Tom and Chris started the search for the much needed orders.

The years of everything being his responsibility hard to let go, John always at Janet's desk to check her work. Not that he needed to, Janet was the calm and efficient spot in the centre of the frantic activity taking place around her.

"You will have to learn to delegate John," she scolded. "You have enough to do without supervising me."

John smiled and remembered how Flora used to reassure him by checking everything with him. A cold wash of comprehension hit him with the force of a slap across his face. It was two months since he left Flora at Clairgowan, and he forgot to write.

# Chapter Forty Six

*His* time his most valuable resource, John's schedule for the day ahead of him to be a meticulous use of every minute. Birmingham first then the long drive to Scotland and Flora's wrath for leaving her for so long. John did think of writing to tell her to travel on the train but decided to collect her as a kind of apology. He was at the factory most of the night before finishing off the building work; he planned to drop Flora off at the flat and head straight for the factory to put a night in on the sewing machines. They needed to become productive as soon as possible so the money would start to flow the other way, to him. Tom's partnership paid for the sewing machines, but the extra expense for the twin building pulled John's bank balance down to a dangerously low level. The income from the working machines barely covered the wages bill; he tried not to think of what would happen if a large unexpected expense cropped up.

The money from the Hornet would help. He could have telephoned the dealer to tell him to send it on to him; the car was bound to be sold by then, but John had the need to go back to Birmingham and the garage for one last time.

The sales manager's car was a 10 year old Rover. It wasn't running

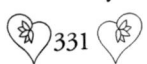

very well and John didn't have the time to put it right. So it was the old reliable Minx the Magnificent, which seemed appropriate for his last look at the garage.

He arrived at the car dealer as scheduled, at precisely 9 o'clock. Ten o'clock his deadline for leaving for Scotland which gave him an hour to get to the garage, give Reg his cut and have a look around for some tools for the sewing machines. John hoped his philanthropic act didn't mean Reg had stripped the garage bare.

The car dealer the first imposition into this well considered order, Reg hadn't delivered the Hornet. John raced off to the garage angrier at himself than Reg for being stupid enough to trust him and not seeing to it sooner. His mood not helped by a summer storm rumbling across the sky. Flashes of lightening sparked through the black clouds as he drove up the cobbled street, the windscreen wipers struggling to cope with the torrential rain. It was a week to the closure deadline, the derelict rubbish strewn street empty, even the strippers and fire raisers kept away by the foul weather. Most of the metal shutters had been ripped out leaving gaping holes at the entrances of the workshops, anything of value stripped away from the insides, a few of them burnt out shells.

Surprised and pleased to see the shutters at the garage still intact John dashed out to unlock and open the first one. He drove the car inside out of the rain so he could put any tools he found into the boot. The thunder and lightning started to recede leaving a torrent of water in its wake. No sign of Reg, the dark and quiet of the empty garage highlighted by the rain splashing up from the cobbles and rattling against the two closed shutters. Everything looked much the same except for gaps here and there where the larger machinery used to stand; Reg must have sold them on.

John tested the lights. They flickered on and revealed the Hornet at the far side of the garage. He thought Reg had done a runner with it, but soon saw it had a severe list, and a check at the other side revealed buckled wheels and a deep gouge down the body work. The damage made the car worth no more than scrap money.

He ran up the steps. Reg wasn't in the room, but the clothes strewn around said he was still living there. John picked them up, threw them down the steps and out to the street and the pouring rain. His overalls were on Flora's chair, where he left them; he pulled them on over his shirt and jeans to look for the tools for the sewing machines determined to salvage something from his wasted journey. The drawers and cupboards held the finer, smaller equipment.

An hour later stood looking down at the sink with the cold water tap full on. He heard the street door slam in the office and sprinted away from the splashing water in time to meet Reg as he walked into the garage.

Reg didn't see John, his head down as a hand pushed his wet quiff back into the place, the other holding the garage keys.

John pounced and grabbed the back of Reg's jacket collar, marched him over to the Hornet and clashed his face down to the bonnet. "The one time I trusted you."

Reg let out a yell; his face recoiled from the metal and left behind a smear of blood on the paintwork.

"The one time you had the chance to prove you could be trusted and you have to go and mess it all up," bellowed John. He clashed the face down to the bonnet again.

Another yell from Reg, more blood on the paintwork.

John turned Reg around and grabbed the front of his jacket, blood streaming down from Reg's nose. John gave the bloody face a hard backhand slap with his left hand, his signet ring adding to the bleeding by leaving a gash on Reg's cheek.

"You were so busy running around showing off in the Hornet

and wrecking it."

A forehand slap, Reg's head swung with the stinging blow.

"You couldn't put yourself out to use the garage."

Another backhand slap, another gash on the cheek.

"And do some work for a change."

Reg's head lolled back and his knees started to buckle.

John let go of the jacket.

Reg fell to his knees and flopped down with his face to the concrete floor.

John leant down to shout at him. "Did you think I'd forget about it?"

"It was an accident while I was driving it to the dealers," wailed Reg. He tried to push himself up but he couldn't make it, flopping back down to the floor again.

John put the toe of his shoe under Reg and turned him onto his back.

Reg had to swallow the blood from his nose so he could breathe. He saw John lean down to him and cowered away from him with his arms over his face.

John was after the garage keys. He grabbed them out Reg's hand and stepped back while pushing them into his pocket. "Get out," he ordered and took another step back so he wouldn't kick Reg from one end of the garage to the other.

"After what I've done for you," whined Reg.

"Done for me?" roared John down to him. "Anything you did was for yourself so you'd feel good. I've put up with you all these years because I knew you wouldn't have anything and I felt sorry for you. I even left you the garage to give you a chance." He pounced on Reg, yanked him up off the floor by his coat and bunched a fist ready to slam it into the bloody face.

"For God's sake John," pleaded Reg, he started to cry.

John suddenly had enough of Reg; he flung him away to the open shutter.

Reg wiped his face with his jacket sleeve and looked at the back of the garage. A deep breath to get his voice into its well practised reasonable tone. "Right, I'll go. I've got some gear stored in the back. I'll have to get something organised to get it picked up so I'll need the keys."

"You are not getting back inside this place," said John. "And you don't need the keys because it's all out there." He nodded to the wall of water outside the shutter.

Reg turned and saw the rain beating down on his clothes, smashed cameras, their leather cases and disintegrating cardboard boxes.

"Of course you could always take them back to the shop where you bought them," said John. "You can make up some excuse for the damage and ask for a refund."

The cameras were stolen of course, and a new enterprise. Dozens of them stacked up in boxes in the back of the garage. Definitely not around before he left, not enough room in the cupboards for them.

"And I've washed that junk you deal with down the sink."

John cursed his own stupidity for not keeping an eye on Reg after his first suspicions. It was the drugs that were the cause of his rage, not the stolen cameras or the Hornet. He had to stop himself from beating the life out of Reg because of the danger he put Flora in by bringing the drugs to the garage.

A wave of longing for her swept over John. His body ached to be near Flora, to see her, hear her voice, smell her presence, touch her, feel her arms around him. He went to close the boot of the car and saw his hands were covered with blood, walking over to the sink and rinsing it off under the running tap.

He shook the water off, a hand up to turn the tap off.

"You bastard."

The choking shriek in John's ear.

"It wasn't mine. They'll kill me."

John turned to Reg and pulled his face away from the narrow blade. A horrified demon with blood stained teeth looked at him. John jerked his head back as the knife jabbed at his face and put his hands behind him to grip the edge of the sink. He knew he'd probably lose a few fingers if he tried to fend off the razor sharp blade, or at least have them cut to pieces.

"I wonder how the lovely Flora would feel if her scar faced John had a matching one on the other side," sniggered Reg who was becoming quite elated with his game of knife jabs and head jerks. "Higher up so you can see it." Reg put the point of the blade at John's temple and moved it to his eye. "That's about right. So you can't cover it up." He stuck the tip of his tongue out, his bruised and bloody face a clown in a parody of concentration. "And…" The blade swept to the centre of John's cheek and down to his chin.

The hairs on John's face reacted to the tip of the blade. It was so close to his skin he wasn't sure if it cut him. The warm wet sensation of blood didn't happen and in his torment was the farcical realisation that Reg intended to cut the left side of his face, the side of the old scar. He pressed his lips together to stop a sound escaping from them, because if it had it would have been a scream at the injustice of it, for it all to happen again with everything he worked for so near. The running tap splashed water onto his overalls and soaked through to his shirt as he leant further away from the knife. Reg had to reach further over because of his smaller height and hesitated with the jabs while he glanced down to put a foot forward to balance himself. It gave John the impetus to make a desperate grab at Reg's arm. His right hand would have been more accurate, his left nearer. He connected to just above the elbow, just, and pushed the arm down. Reg's head went down with it and once he lost his chance with John's face jabbed the knife at his stomach and chest. John couldn't jump back because his back was to the sink; he turned sideways and lost his grip on the arm. All he could do was try to heave Reg away with his left arm. He felt his forearm push onto the point of the knife. The blade cut smoothly into the muscle, no pain, until it grated against a bone. A grunt came up from John's throat along with a fleeting weakness in his legs but he got a knee up and finally pushed Reg away with it. The blade withdrew from his arm, another grate against the bone, a sharp pain this time as it cut through more flesh.

Reg fell to the floor on his back with the knife in his hand.

John stamped hard on the hand with the heel of his shoe until Reg screamed and let go of the knife. The blade was covered with blood; John put a foot over it, took hold of the hilt with his right hand and pulled it up until with a crack it separated from the blade. He kicked the hilt and blade away; they skittered along the floor and clanked against something in the shadows.

His left arm numb and hanging loose at his side John stood bemused at the sight of Reg crawling away from him on his hands and knees. The sounds of the rain and splashing water from the tap mingled, receded and returned again.

Reg started to run with his hands still on the floor, almost falling onto his face as he ran out of the garage and disappeared into the pouring rain.

The numbness in John's arm suddenly changed to a searing pain, looking down to see blood drip down from his hand and fingers and splash into a greasy pool of red on the oil stained concrete floor. He stumbled over to the sink, pulled off the top of his overalls, stripped to the waist and put his injured arm under the ice cold water, the wound a gaping fleshy mouth an inch wide below the elbow. Using his teeth and good hand he ripped the clean sleeve off his shirt and tied it as tight as he dare above and over the wound. The bleeding abated a little, but blood soon started to ooze through the material. He wrapped the remainder of his shirt around the bleeding, pushed his good arm into his overall sleeve and shrugged the other side over his shoulder.

He pulled the top of the overalls together and stood at the open shutter looking out to the rain. Halfway to Sunny and Neelam's house before he remembered they moved out months ago.

Reg only ran as far as the corner at the top of the street. He stood with his back to the wall with his hair plastered down his bloody face. A quick check to see John hadn't followed him, his back to the wall again stomach churning.

He'd kept his head down since his room was trashed, even going as far as London to get his supply of drugs. The local gang soon forgot about him until Reg made the big mistake of selling on Freddie Thompson - Smythe's stash to them. They started to notice him again and soon heard he was bragging to everyone that he owned the garage. The gang paid him a visit one night and forced him to store the cameras and drugs for them. One of them decided to take the Hornet for a spin and returned it smashed up, which he seemed to think was very funny. The gang leader had been locked up and the rest of the gang didn't dare touch the drugs and cameras until he was out of prison. Reg ordered to stay at the garage to guard them, so he had to sit there and wait for John and the slapping he'd get over the Hornet. He'd gone that day to plead with the gang to take their stuff before the closure deadline, to be kicked out with a warning of what would happen to him if he didn't keep it safe. The beating from John nothing compared to what they would do to him.

Reg checked around the corner again and saw John stagger down the street, a smirk at him turning right at the cut to go to Sunny's old house. He saw John return a minute later and go along the cut to the shopping street. Reg knew where he was heading for, the bar.

He ran down the street to the garage. The shutter open, a snigger of satisfaction at the pool of blood on the floor.

Reg started the fire in the office. He pulled sheets of typing paper out of the desk, set fire to them with his lighter and scattered them around the room. The typewriter swiped off the desk before he ran into the garage with a torch of burning papers. The Hornet first, burning papers thrown into the cockpit. John's old banger with the boot conveniently open to receive the flames, the rest of the torch thrown into the room at the top of the steps. Cameras, their leather cases and sodden cardboard boxes, his clothes, all kicked and flung into the garage. They all had to go to make his story of another random fire look good.

A quick look up and down the street for John. The two cars well alight by the time Reg pulled down the shutter. He left a small gap at the bottom to help the fire along.

His stomach started to churn again, frightened his story wouldn't be believed.

He ran up the street, Reg Purvis ran for his life.

Patrick Malloy ran to the pounding at the back door of the bar and pulled in a white faced bedraggled John.

He cleansed the wound, pulled it together with sticking plasters and covered it with a thick wad of gauze and a tight bandage.

They were away from prying eyes in a back room, Patrick always discreet in that kind of situation.

"You should be at the hospital to get some stitches in that."

John flexed his hand and checked the bandage, it was dry. "I'll be fine Patrick. Thanks."

Patrick acknowledged this with a nod, left the room and returned with a jumper and a glass. He gave them to John. "You can't be running around bare to the waist, and get that good Irish whisky inside of you. It should put some colour back into your face."

John swallowed down the drink in one gulp. His overalls saved his jeans from the blood, they were damp from the rain but he looked quite presentable with the jumper on. He threw his overalls and shirt into a bin at the back of the bar on his way out.

The rain stopped, the clouds separating to reveal a clear blue sky.

His hand up to put the key into the lock of the office door when the small window above his head shattered. Smoke and long flaming tongues escaped into the air. He raced down the street to get to the back of the garage, running up to the shutter to see great clouds of black sooty smoke billowing out of the gap at the bottom. John stood looking at it, he knew the fire was down to Reg, willing him to be in the street laughing at him so he could get hold of him and kill him.

He kicked at the shutter with the heel of his shoe and walked away. An explosion came from inside the garage; the Hornet, another explosion a second later, much louder and nearer to him. Minx the Magnificent; he parked it just inside the garage. The force of the explosion blew the shutter off and forced John to duck away from the shards of metal and flames.

He walked away cradling his throbbing arm.

The garage roof fell in with a rumbling crash of sparks, smoke and shooting flames.

John caught a bus to the city and bought fresh dressings at a chemist's and the strongest pain relievers they had, he swallowed a few outside the shop.

He found a car hire firm, took the first car they offered and drove with his injured arm on his lap, eyes unblinking and staring straight ahead, the one thought in his head seeing Flora. It took him a while to realise his clenched teeth were the cause of the pain at his temples.

John flexed his jaw, stopped the car and took more tablets.

Patrick's first aid held well, but the aching throb in his arm wouldn't go away. More tablets, they stuck in his throat and made him feel nauseous. John wished he'd eaten before starting out that morning.

The journey a haze of flashing scenes, towns, countryside, and suddenly he was there. He couldn't remember driving through the glen or the village, but logic said he must have because he saw the trees racing up to him.

Irritated Flora wasn't waiting for him at the gates with her luggage all around her. Annoyed at the empty kitchen, no Flora or Mungo sat by the roaring fire. Angry at the empty bedroom, and he found himself clenching his teeth again as he imagined Flora walking amongst the trees, or in the village, or shopping in town. He ached to lie on the bed and relax on its soft surface until he slept so he could waken to order again with no pain in his arm and racing in his head, but he couldn't. So he decided to pack for Flora and store her luggage in the car so she could go with him as soon as she returned. Drawers pulled out so hard they crashed onto the floor, their contents emptied onto the bed. Every movement accompanied by a searing pain in his arm. Wardrobe doors slammed back, shoes, clothing and bags thrown onto the bed.

A voice penetrated into the chaos, he rushed to the door and looked down the dim passageway to the stairs.

The voice again, "Flora…Flora…Is that you?" It sounded weak and querulous and it came from Mungo's room, the door ajar.

It wasn't Flora's voice so he returned to her room to continue his packing while trying to remember if the door was open before, but there again he couldn't even remember going up the stairs.

He picked up a bag and pushed clothes into it and so engrossed with his work he jumped at the quiet voice behind him, Flora's voice.

"What are you doing?"

There she was at the door, her cotton dress tracing her wonderful shape, her question in her large brown eyes.

He laughed, he didn't know why, and left his packing to put his arms around Flora with a sudden need to take her to the bed.

She didn't resist his hold, or put her arms around him, no anger or furious words. Her placid body in his arms triggered a surge of fear. He put a check on it, kissed Flora on the brow and returned to his packing.

"I'll have to put it all back again."

He ignored her words, their meaning and closed the zip on the bag, picked it up off the bed to put it onto the floor, with his left hand. Something gave in the wound; he ignored it and busied himself filling another bag. "If you had a telephone in this God forsaken place I could have rang you." A reasonable excuse why he left Flora for all of that time, forgetting her pushed away.

"Flora…"

Flora's head turned to the voice, her body followed. Surprised at his speed he found himself pull Flora back by her arm and close the door.

"I have to go to him." Flora put a hand to the door handle.

He grabbed the wrist.

Flora pulled it away. "He needs me, he's ill."

He took hold of Flora's arms and swung her around to face him. "What's wrong with him?" The words forced up his throat, his real concern Flora not Mungo.

She looked down with a hand to her brow. "Old Mr Boyle must

have muddled everything up. The two hundred and fifty pounds didn't clear father's debts. He's definitely going to lose the house now."

Why didn't Flora put her arms around him? If she did he could put his face into her hair and breathe her in and take her to the bed.

"I'm not leaving him John. He needs me, I'm all he has. I can't leave him the way he is."

Another laugh, he couldn't stop it, hilarity pulled him along. Or was it panic at Flora's control?

"Can't Jeannie look after him?"

He heard the plea in his voice.

Flora didn't. "No." Her reply to the door, she opened it.

Why didn't she hold him and kiss him and pull him to the bed? He slammed the door shut out of Flora's hand and held her so tight her arms were pinned to her side. An imaginary knife probed the wound in his arm. They turned again and again in a shambolic dance until Flora was stood with her back to the bed. He followed her face down, his kiss so harsh the back of his pounding head told him he might bruise her lips.

Flora lay inert while he loosened his jeans. Leaning on his left elbow he put a hand down to her leg and moved it up her wonderful bareness.

He entered Flora with her legs dangling over the edge of the bed. Why didn't she stop him, fight with him and push him away? She juddered at his hard thrusts, her body moving over the bed and the shoes, clothes and bags. The plasters pulled at his skin, warmth oozed through the dressing. His last plunge into her very being with her completely on the bed. It was a loveless act, a need fulfilled by brute strength.

His breath on her white face, he saw her mouth open for the start of a question, his face cupped by her hands. This show of affection, this loving act forced him up and away from her. He readjusted himself with his back to her and turned his face to her.

"I haven't the time to stand and argue Flora."

Flora sat on the edge of the bed and pulled her dress down. "Have you ever John?"

Her calm voice and her look at the door, her interest in the person in the other room.

It triggered a rage unknown to him before. He grabbed hold of Flora's arm and pulled her to the door, he couldn't control it, stop it. The tussle a travesty of a fight, Flora pulled her arm away and fought him off by hitting him on the face and chest. John jumped back, shocked at his behaviour and Flora's determination to stay.

"Then stay," he roared.

"I will," screamed Flora. "And don't come back for me."

The finality of their words with faces almost touching.

John slammed the door back.

Flora followed him out of the room. "And take that with you," she screamed.

John ran down the stairs. He didn't see the wedding ring make an arc towards the back of his head.

"Flora…Flora…"

She turned to the voice.

# Chapter Forty Seven

*It* was the early hours of the morning, miles away from the dark and silent glen. A car stood at the side of a road, a man with wild eyes sat inside it looking at his shaking hands. John looked back to where Clairgowan might be. If he returned to the house and Flora rejected him again would he be the mad man again? Would he hurt again? The bandage saturated with blood.

He changed the dressing, put his head back and fell into a deep sleep.

John dropped off the car in Birmingham and caught a train to London. A shower as soon as he returned to the flat, a clean dressing, a rigid walk to the factory. An automaton flexing stiff hinges in its legs in order to place one foot in front of the other to move it along to its designated goal. He made do with the machine mechanic's tools and worked non stop on the sewing machines until he completed them, and he didn't need the money from the Hornet. Tom and Chris came through with the orders, the machines in production before the week was up, the money ready to start the flow to him.

Patrick was right about the wound needing stitches. It was slow to heal and working on the machines and hauling them around didn't help.

It took a month to the day for the gaping wound to change to a small clean hole. John sat down that night and wrote to Flora, he asked her to forgive him for hurting her and told her he loved her and he needed her. He addressed the envelope and left it on the table in the flat.

He hesitated in posting the letter because it would be far worse if he did.

He'd be busy, looking down. Certain something caught his eye, a flash of bright colour, lemon, white. A quick look up always resulted in a painful burning in the back of his eyes. The image of Flora the first day she arrived at the garage never there. Feet together, hands behind her, her wonderful smile.

# Chapter Forty Eight

*Flora* didn't return to the gates. She didn't stand for hours with her back against the cold steel flowers watching the road through the glen. Her daily vigils began a week after John drove away from her in his old car, her order to him not to write abandoned three weeks later. Running down to meet the post van as soon as she saw it leave the village for the house. The slow trudge back with letters for her father, and retrieving them before they were thrown on the fire. All of them bills of course, her purse more depleted as the weeks dragged by.

One of the letters missed the threat of the fire, the one her father secreted away from her.

Four weeks into her wait and the frustration of not knowing where John was and no way of contacting him.

Six weeks into her long wait and her father stopped eating and took to sitting up all night by the kitchen fire. He wouldn't leave the house and refused to see anyone, including Bob Brown.

Flora did as the doctor told her and gave her father lots of care and attention. She persuaded him to eat and to go to bed at night and for his afternoon nap. Caring for her father preferable than the humiliation of waiting for someone who was too engrossed with his new life to remember he had a wife waiting for him.

The afternoon she decided to tidy the study while her father lay on his bed. She hadn't been in the room since he became ill and saw her wedding photograph was missing from the desk, and the open letter beside Alasdair's photograph. His smiling face looked at her as she sat behind the desk and read the letter from Mr Boyle the solicitor, Mr Boyle the son.

The letter said Mr Boyle could do no more for her father because he failed to honour the agreement made in his office in June the year before. To pay 250 pounds in three monthly instalments until he cleared his debt of two thousand pounds for the land taxes. He pointed out that her father hadn't responded to his letters regarding the sale of the land around Clairgowan House and therefore he could only presume the 250 pounds paid in January was in fact an instalment towards the tax bill. He listed a previous instalment made in September and said while her father's other debt problems had been resolved it did not diminish the importance of clearing his tax bill. Mr Boyle expressed his regret regarding the lack of response from all of his previous letters and the inevitable consequences of failing to continue the payments, which would be court proceedings to take possession of Clairgowan House.

Mr Boyle ended the letter with a warning that his father's confusion over the matter would not be considered a valid enough excuse for failing to continue the payments.

Flora didn't own the trees after all. She'd presumed the documents for the sale were delivered to Clairgowan Houses and they went the way of everything else the postman delivered when she wasn't there, on the fire.

The money her father borrowed off Bob Brown must have paid for the first instalment and the 4 thousand pounds he mentioned on their return from Mr Boyle's office nearer to the true amount of his debts.

Flora remembered old Mr Boyle mentioning the land taxes must be from land her father owned years before. Two thousand pounds meant it must have been from many years before, maybe as far back as to when her mother left.

Flora dropped the letter onto the desk and put her hands to her face. Her father held it to himself for all of that time and his own daughter left him to carry the burden alone. The invincible man who carried on regardless of his losses didn't exist anymore, if ever her father needed her it was then.

She thought the noise from the stairs was her father up from his nap, until she heard him calling for her.

Her clothes strewn around the room, in front of her the moment she rehearsed for so many times in her head. She'd shout and scream at John, then she'd pack and leave with him, but that was before her father became ill and before she read the letter.

Flora's turmoil fixed her in its rigid hold. John, her anger because he forgot her and the need to lie on the bed with him, the need to kiss him and pull him to her. Her father, the need to see to him and stay with him and show him she cared. She could have stopped John when he pushed her down to the bed and punished him by not responding to him, Flora knew it would hurt him. Shocked at his fierceness, and it wasn't her loving disciplined John who looked into her face, but she left it too late to ask why. The return of the old John, his time more important than the man in the other room. Fighting with him and hearing words she didn't want to hear, screaming words she didn't want to say and doing things she didn't want to do.

Habit drew Flora to her father's room, not thought, to find he called for her to complain about the noise.

The realisation something was wrong, very wrong, John needed her far more than her father ever would. She ran down the stairs and through the kitchen, no John or car outside the house, the quiet frightening and absolute.

Flora didn't wait at the gates again because it meant she dare hope John would return for her, and the frightening part was she didn't know where to find him.

A week later the sound of the post van as it drew up outside the kitchen door. Flora rushed out and grabbed the letter out of the postman's hand certain it must be from John, to see Aunt Elizabeth's handwriting on the envelope, her flash of hope extinguished before it flared into life.

The letter to say her aunt would be arriving at Clairgowan House the following week.

Aunt Elizabeth's visit allowed Flora to do what she wanted to do since John ran away from her down the stairs. Go to her bedroom, lie on her bed and stay there.

"Have you and John argued?" Elizabeth sat on the bed and stroked Flora's brow. "Your father said he heard you both shouting."

Flora exposed her teeth to give an impersonation of a smile. "We're always arguing Aunt Elizabeth. I must be tired after nursing father. I told you, John has business to see to in London. He'll come for me as soon as father's well."

"Your father is well enough to eat three eggs with his bacon this morning and take himself off for a walk to the Brown's farmhouse," remarked Elizabeth. She took Flora's hand. "Come with me to London Flora. You should be with John. Your father has lived with losing Clairgowan House more years than I care to remember. It will not change a thing you being here with him."

Flora did think of going to London with her aunt, and she would have put up with the tea ladies, anything, if it meant she could walk every street and knock on every door until she found John. But the heavy folds of inertia pinned her to the bed and she didn't have the strength to push them away.

Jeannie appeared the day her aunt returned to London. Flora didn't mind, she sighed down to her soft comfortable bed happy she didn't have think of anything else but lying there.

The following weeks saw the start of a little daily ritual at Flora's bedroom door. Her father would knock and open the door. Flora would turn to him and say she was fine and she'd be up soon, and her father would close the door.

A change in the ritual one day, her father spoke as soon as he opened the door.

"I have sent for him. You have been lying on your bed for over a month now Flora. I cannot tolerate this kind of behaviour for any longer."

Flora sat up and tried to decide if she should brush her hair, wash her face, dress, have a bath or just run around in circles. "There's no need for him to come here father I'll go to him." Her father was closing the door. "Where is he?" she shouted.

The door opened.

"Somewhere over the water in an aeroplane I expect. Bob Brown will be collecting him tomorrow."

Robert!

Flora heaved and gulped at the closing door and finally allowed herself to cry. Her body wrenching every last tear out of her until she sank into the sleep of the exhausted.

# Chapter Forty Nine

*Flora* woke to a faint glimmer at the window. Uncertain if it was morning or evening she closed her eyes for a few moments and opened them again to long streaks in the dark. She lay watching the new day fill the sky, turning her head on the pillow to the sounds of her father's door and his footsteps to the stairs. The clear white light drew her to the window, to see the snow on the mountainsides reach as far as the glen. October's first snows of winter, spring to follow the long dark winter, summer to follow spring, autumn to follow summer.

A green sea of needles surrounded the house where the air from the mountains met the tops of the trees. A bird flew over them and swooped down to the dried up water fountain to peck at the grass and weeds growing from a bowl. It didn't stay long, flapping away through the gates and soaring up to the clear sky until she couldn't see it anymore.

Flora gazed out of the window until she started to shiver. She slipped out of the bedroom in her nightdress. Face down to her bare feet as she made a quiet descent to the bathroom, not wanting to be heard and seen, her usual practise over the past weeks. The cold room increased her shivers, freezing fingers turned the squeaking bath taps on.

The water was warm rather than hot, the fire in the kitchen mustn't have been lit for long, but Flora couldn't remember the last time she had a bath or washed her face. She lay back in the gentle warmth, the water welcoming and soothing. Her untidy mass of hair floating up around her head as she knitted her fingers over her front and contemplated the spots of the damp on the ceiling, half submerged, half floating in the water until it started to cool.

Flora jumped out of the bath so quick small waves splashed over the side. A cursory rub with a towel and nightdress pulled over her still wet body with feet paddling in the water.

She ran into the kitchen, bare feet leaving their damp imprints on the flagstones and wet hair dripping down her back. Her father sat drinking tea by the fire and Jeannie scrubbing at something in the sink. Two surprised faces at her entrance, which was no surprise to Flora seeing as she hadn't been in the kitchen since her aunt returned to London.

Jeannie first, the reason for her rush.

The girl jumped away from the sink with dripping hands, her thin face at Flora waiting to be sent away.

A start of giggle at the comical sight of Jeannie crouched and ready to run in her overlarge skirt and jumper and black laced up shoes.

Flora put her head down and lifted it with the sweetest of sweet smiles.

"I'd love a cup of tea Jeannie."

Jeannie scurried away from the sink drying her hands. "And I'll make ye some toast if ye can manage it Flora."

"Yes, toast would be lovely Jeannie. Thank you," replied Flora grateful for the girl's thought. She hadn't eaten a proper meal for weeks. A mouthful here and there off the tray Jeannie left at her door, if she

thought to pick it up and take it into her room.

"You should be taking yourself off to your room," retorted Mungo. "Not sitting in the kitchen eating toast in your nightdress and bare feet."

"Ach father," laughed Flora. "I've been stuck in my room for weeks and you want me back in it the moment I come out." She sat at the table with her back to the fire, and her father while Jeannie made the toast and a fresh pot of tea. A smile up to Jeannie while she poured the tea. "Are you going to sit at the table and drink a cup of tea with me Jeannie?"

Jeannie couldn't stop the pleasure on her face as she refilled Mungo's cup and stirred in the milk and sugar. "Ach I have a lot to do Flora. I heard the water running for the bath so I lit the fire and tidied your room for ye and changed your bed. I still have the sheets to finish and put on the line."

Flora grimaced at the state of her bedclothes after lying on them for weeks, a quick sniff at her nightdress. She ate her toast and drank her tea to the sounds of Jeannie washing the sheets and clattering out of the door with them.

The girl scurried into the kitchen and over to the table. "Your hair's nearly dry from the fire Flora. Shall I brush it for ye?" Fingers put to her lips at daring to suggest such a thing.

Flora gave Jeannie another sweet smile. "Why thank you Jeannie that would be lovely."

"I'll be away for the brush Flora."

Jeannie dashed out of the room and returned seconds later with the brush.

Flora put her head back. "See if you can put some order into that lot Jeannie." She knew her hair would be a mad tangle but Jeannie didn't pull at it once. "I haven't paid you for ages Jeannie. I must owe you a fortune." Her words up to a dark cloud over the cream wash on the ceiling. The residue of smoke blowing down the chimney and cooking on the range must have taken years to accumulate above her head. She hadn't noticed it before, the same as the marks on the bathroom ceiling.

"Ach, there's no worry over the money Flora," said Jeannie.

The brush stroked through Flora's hair until the bristles gently massaged her scalp. She knew Jeannie would be the easiest. Her simplicity required no more than a smile and a thank you for her efforts, and she tidied the bedroom, lit the fire and washed the sheets without expecting either. Flora remembered her spite towards the girl, squeezing her eyes shut against the tears, a hand to her neck to hide a hard swallow.

"Your hair's finished now Flora."

"Thank you Jeannie." Flora stood, took the brush from Jeannie and turned to her father. "I suppose I'd better go to my room now and prepare myself for Robert."

Her reply the smile she knew so well, the smile her father used to put people at ease and to encourage them to bring profit his way. Flora had the overwhelming need to slap her hands to her knees and scream with laughter. She didn't, but she did do something she couldn't remember doing before and to her shame hadn't thought of doing before, she kissed her father on the brow.

She turned her back to him without waiting to see his reaction and walked out of the kitchen, head down as she went up the stairs to her room.

A search through her wardrobe for a dark grey woollen skirt she bought from the little clothing shop at its closing down sale. Flora hadn't worn her rash buy before, she always thought of it as a 'laird's daughter's' skirt with its old fashioned large box pleats. It looked perfect with a white blouse, black cardigan and her low heeled black shoes.

A serious face with white cheeks looked at her from the dressing table mirror. Three weeks. No! She was putting it off by stretching it out that far. Two weeks, the last day of October, it gave her the time to be sure she made amends for all the hurts and slights. Enough time to be sure she put everything right, or as right as she could. No more running away, no chasing away, shouting and screaming, no more of that.

Caitlin next, a letter to ask Caitlin to forgive her for not saying a proper goodbye and to tell her she loved her, and to pass on her love and goodbyes to Danny and Patrick at the bar and Paddy. A special kiss for baby Patrick of course. Flora smiled and shook her head at herself in the mirror at her antics with Patrick. Neelam, a letter with the same request for forgiveness and to tell her she loved her, and to pass on her love to Sunny and Madhar.

Jeannie must have arranged her pearls in a straight line on a piece of linen full of Aunt Elizabeth's embroidery. Miniature white moons of the night lay over colourful blossoms of the day.

Flora fastened her pearls around her neck, eyes on her fingers in the mirror.

A pensive look to her feet as she walked down the stairs to meet Robert. She knew he'd be waiting for her, and alone. Jeannie sent running to the farmhouse to tell Robert to come calling on the laird's daughter at Clairgowan House, the laird following at a more sedate pace. Or her father might have decided to go himself, or with Jeannie. Flora stood giggling at the kitchen door at the sight of her tall father and little Jeannie running through the gates hand in hand.

Robert didn't hear her open the door. He was walking away from her, the heels of his shoes clicking on the flagstones. A scraping noise as he stopped and swung around, he was pacing the room. In a thick shop bought jumper and plain dark slacks, hair a little thinner than at

Christmas and shoulders a little broader. He'd turn into an exact replica of his father one day.

"Flora!"

She stood with her back to the door and looked at Robert over the long wooden expanse of the table. "We have to stop this Robert. We have to stop the laird and your father from doing this to us."

Robert nodded. "Yes, but I'm not here because of Clairgowan House, or dad, or the laird Flora. I'm here because you've had a pretty rough time of it lately."

The soft lips she knew so well pulled down in a sympathetic smile.

"You sure don't have much luck do you Flora? I run out on you and then this guy runs out on you."

Flora shook her head. "I appreciate you coming Robert, but I'm going to spend the day with the laird."

Robert looked down to his feet, a nod. "Right. It must be a shock me being here." He opened the door to go outside and smiled back at her. "There's no hurry, I fly back in fourteen days. Remember Flora I'm an old friend here to help. I still care for you whatever you think of me."

Flora watched the door close and put her head back. Robert surprised her with his acquiescence, once he would have ignored her words and insisted he stay.

She waited until she was sure Robert had returned to the farmhouse and walked to the gates to look down to the village. Grey blue columns of smoke rose from the chimneys to form a soft fragile haze over the houses. The villagers, how she used to snort and giggle at them. All they asked of her was to give them the respect they were due and for her to stand at the laird's side while he opened the gathering. Always carrying with her the anger at her father's assumption she would smoothly step in as a convenient replacement for her mother.

A slow return to the house looking down to the gravel with folded arms, and a wait by the fire for her father's return

No smile as he entered the kitchen. "I would think after Robert coming all the way from America you could give him more than a few minutes of your time." The pale eyes noted Flora's clothes, and her bare legs. "Though I see you have at last made some small effort to dress more appropriately."

"Why thank you father."

Flora rose from her chair and kissed his brow, and her friendly approach to Jeannie resulted in something most unexpected.

The girl rushed into the kitchen later that afternoon. "I'm going to cook all of your favourite meals Flora."

Flora ushered to the table and her plate set in front of her.

"Now eat all of that up Flora. You've hardly had a bite between your lips for weeks."

Flora smiled, shook her head and did as Jeannie told her.

She slept well that night, for an hour. To wake bright and alert to a quiet blackness and the long hours ahead of her until the morning. Head down to her bare feet as the oil lamp lit her way down the stairs. The grate filled with logs  before she sat on her chair and pulled her legs up under her nightdress, gazing at the sparks and flames with chin resting on her knees. A slow creep up the stairs hours later, a slow creep down minutes later, falling into bed hours later desperate for sleep.

# Chapter Fifty

*A* knock on her door woke Flora, opening her eyes to bright daylight.

"It's Jeannie Flora. I have your breakfast."

"Thank you Jeannie, but I would have eaten it in the kitchen."

"Ach, I don't mind bringing it up for ye Flora. I've boiled an egg to go with your toast." Jeannie's worried voice through the door. "Promise to eat it all up Flora."

Flora smiled. "Yes, I promise I'll eat it all up." She lifted her head from the pillow. "Has the laird left for the kirk?"

"He has another hour yet Flora."

Flora left her bed, opened the door and took the tray from Jeannie. "Tell the laird I will be going the kirk with him Jeannie."

Flora watched Jeannie rush off to the stairs and looked at the tray. She would have preferred to return to her bed and sleep not eat or go to the kirk, but she arrived in the kitchen an hour later dressed the same as the day before in her grey skirt. This time with her brown wool wrap over her shoulders and a headscarf she borrowed from her aunt's room. The headscarf covered with the imprints of horses' heads, some with manes flying, others with ears pricked and soft eyes. A few with lips drawn back exposing tombstone teeth in a snicker of a smile, or ready to bite.

"Good morning Father."

He was stood in front of the fire with hands behind his back and feet apart, head down to receive her kiss. The damp bathroom told of his preparation for the kirk. Face pink and smooth, hair oiled back, dressed in his best tweed suit and beige moleskin waistcoat, white starched shirt, dark green tie in a perfect knot, brown leather shoes reflecting the light. Mungo Ballardine the laird ready to present himself to his small world.

"The day you condescend to attend the kirk with me and you will have me late," he retorted. "Jeannie has already taken herself off down there."

Flora smiled at him. "Then we'd better go now father."

She looked at the grey stone walls of the house as she walked with her father over the gravel. Bob Brown was the true laird of Clairgowan because of the lands he owned around the village. Her father retained the title because of the long held loyalty of the villagers and Bob Brown, and the fact that he still owned the land on which the house and the trees stood. The day Mungo Ballardine lost Clairgowan House would be the day he'd become nothing more than another villager attending the kirk with his daughter.

Flora slipped her hand through her father's arm and squeezed it. The smile to her face edged with creases in the soft skin above the pale eyes; she didn't know how soft until she kissed it.

They arrived at the kirk, and Flora coped with the surprised faces and eyes following her to the front and the laird's pew. It was the building, the 7 year old girl sat with her mother and father at the service for her dead brother. The wood, dust, polish and damp, breathing them in with the sudden comprehension of never seeing Alasdair again.

Kicking and screaming at the gates each time her mother and father tried to take her to the kirk again, until they gave up and left her there. Two years later a 9 year old girl starched and ironed the laird's shirt for the kirk. Then she ran outside and hid behind a tree to watch him stride through the gates alone in his best tweed suit.

They were all waiting for her as soon as she stepped out of the kirk, the minister and the villagers. Their faces blurred around her, a cold hand and stiff smile no recompense for their warmth and care. If Robert was there she didn't see him, Flora pulled her wrap around her and hurried away to the safety of Clairgowan House.

She wrote her letters that night, in between her weary back breaking trudges up and down the stairs.

# Chapter Fifty One

$\mathcal{A}$ knock at her door. "Your breakfast Flora. I'll leave the tray by the door."

"Thank you Jeannie."

Jeannie's worried voice. "The fire was well away again this morning. Are ye not sleeping well Flora?"

"No. Not very well Jeannie."

"Ach, it can take ye that way. Robert Brown's sitting in the kitchen, but don't rush yourself down for him Flora. Take your time with your breakfast."

Flora listened to Jeannie rush away with a bustle of noise and lay looking at the bed quilt wishing she had a fraction of the girl's energy. A bright shaft of sunlight slanted through the window and cut across the gold satin. It created a moving wand of sparkling hues across the bed, streaks of fiery orange merged with metallic strands of ambers, reds and browns.

She threw the bedclothes back determined to try again with the villagers, and did as Jeannie told her, took her time with her breakfast. Arriving in the kitchen over an hour later dressed in her grey skirt with her wrap over her shoulders and headscarf in her hand. Robert sat opposite her father by the fire.

"Good morning Robert."

She saw his mother's bread and scones on the table.

He jumped up to her. "I've brought dad's car Flora. I thought we could take a run into town."

"Sorry Robert. I have things to do in the village." Her letters in her hand, the post office first and Morag Fraser.

"You could spare a few minutes with Robert for bringing the bread and scones," grumbled Mungo.

"And a good morning to you father." Flora kissed the soft brow. "So that's why Robert came all the way from America, to deliver the bread and scones." She put the headscarf over her head, fastened it under her chin, turned her back on the men and walked out of the kitchen.

She heard Robert's footsteps on the gravel behind her and turned to him. "I'm sorry Robert."

He shrugged. "It's OK Flora."

"No. It isn't OK Robert. It wasn't fair of the laird to bring you all this way."

"I'm here because I want to be here," replied Robert. He laughed. "You sure have changed." A nod at Flora's headscarf and skirt. "It suits you."

Flora walked around the corner of the house with Robert behind her. He'd parked his father's car between the fountain and the large main door. She hadn't noticed the colour at Christmas, a two tone green. It looked striking with the Egyptian head above the large radiator, a fitting mode of transport to be stood outside the laird's residence.

Flora stopped and turned to Robert. The villagers, Robert's parents, she had to start somewhere. "Did you know your mother and father blames me for you going to America Robert?"

Robert shook his head. "It was because of them I left Flora." He shrugged. "I suppose a part of it was because of dad dropping heavy hints over us setting a wedding date. But it was mostly because of mom. She was always going on about dad being a crofter's son who made good. I saw it as my last chance to try to make her as proud of me. If it's really important to you I'll put them straight Flora."

Flora smiled. "Yes it is, and thank you Robert." As easy as Jeannie, she hoped it would be the same down in the village.

"I know I should have told you sooner Flora." Robert grimaced and lifted his shoulders. "But I knew how you'd react."

Flora nodded. "Yes. The usual Flora, shouting and screaming." She laughed. "I didn't know you could run so fast."

Robert grinned and shook his head. "Yes, I sure broke all records that day." He looked into Flora's face. "Mom always said it should be up to me and you if we married Flora. And do you know the first time I heard her say it?"

Flora held her breath.

"I was eleven years old and it was the same week the laird's wife left, your mother. Mom was going on to dad and saying the laird's wife took her money with her when in walked the laird. They chased me out of course, so I hung around until the great man left. And as soon as I went back inside it was the first thing I heard mom say."

A gust of cold wind nipped at Flora's legs.

Robert dug his hands into his pockets. "And do you know the funny thing about it all Flora? Dad didn't need bribing. You know how he's always loved the laird and how he'd do anything for him. Dad might have been a hard nosed business man in America but all of that must have all changed the moment he returned to Clairgowan. The laird knew dad was obsessed with Clairgowan House and he took advantage of that. Dad paid well over the odds for all of the lands he bought off the laird; he paid a fortune for that field in front of the farmhouse. Mom stopped him subsidising the laird as soon as I left, but knowing dad he'll still have slipped him something."

Flora pulled her wrap around her. "Thank you for telling me Robert."

Robert smiled and looked at the car. "I'll drive you down to the village in the hearse if you want Flora."

She shook her head. "No. I'll walk down Robert. And then I'm going to spend the rest of the day with…"

"The laird," broke in Robert nodding. He laughed. "Dad's bought a new tractor so I'll go and play with that."

Flora waited at the gates. Her hand up in reply to Robert's salute with a finger to his brow as he past her in the car. 'The laird's wife took her money with her.' Bartered the same as a piece of land at 9 years old. Flora knew of course, but she didn't know it was so blatant or as soon as within a week of her mother leaving her. Robert was right, it was funny. She had to laugh out loud it was so funny and it was even funnier when the wind pushed at her back while she walked down to the village. Laughing at the wind blowing her hair over her face when she pulled off her headscarf, laughing and grabbing at her wrap before the wind lifted it off her back.

It started as she intended, at the post office. A bedraggled figure pushing her hair from her face while she bought the stamps for her letters. Surprising Morag Fraser by taking her hand while she enquired after her three girls. Posting her letters and seeing Andy McManus, hurrying up to him and taking the bemused man's hand to enquire after his son Alex. Dashing down to the shop and taking Mrs Stewart's hand to enquire after Mr Stewart's arthritis. The wind pulling at Flora's skirt and hair as she stood outside the shop. A slow walk up to Clairgowan House, head down, headscarf and wrap in her hand.

Another night creeping up and down the stairs with the oil lamp, Jeannie's knock on the door waking her in the morning. Mrs Brown's bread and scones on the table, a kiss on her father's brow, sending poor Robert away and hurrying down to the village.

It pulled Flora along. Taking the hands of everyone she saw until people started to dart away, but she didn't care. With each solicitous touch came the exhilarating boost of setting her life in order, and it didn't stop there. She knocked on Mrs Drummond's door one day to say thank you for Jeannie. A hug this time, the scrawny woman held to Flora's breast while she apologised for being so nasty to her daughter. Panting up the steep walk to the farmhouse to tell the stout Mrs Brown how wonderful her bread and scones were, another hug and apology from Flora for not saying so before. The promise of the black, black nights waiting for her at end of her joyful days.

Sunday and Flora walked down to the kirk with her father. Her week of reparation over she knew then the peace she craved for waited for her at the end of her allotted time. A soothing composure descending around her as she sat on the pew.

The minister and villagers at the end of the service, they must have seen the calm on her face, gathering around her, their love and care bringing a lump to her throat and tears to her eyes. Robert stood with his parents, a gentle smile to her.

# Chapter Fifty Two

"*I* knew I'd get you inside the car with me." Robert leant down to the paintwork "I'd better check the hearse. Dad takes a magnifying glass to it every time I use it." He laughed. "I don't know why he bought an Armstrong - Siddeley, it's massive."

Flora watched him rub a line of dust off with his finger. It was a new patient Robert, uncritical, gentle and kind. Her love for him flooded through her. Or it might have been guilt for using him. It was difficult to tell the emotions so close.

Robert gave Flora a sidelong look. "You should see the new Jag they've brought out. Now that's my kind of car, neat and snazzy."

"Thank you for taking me into town Robert," said Flora. She grimaced. "Or should I say thank you for taking the laird's mad daughter into town."

Robert straightened up from the car. "You're not mad Flora. It's your way of coping with a difficult situation." He smiled. "You sure made a quick disappearing act as soon as we arrived."

The Seed Merchant's office first and disappointed to find all the people she used to work with had left. Her friends from school, she found one, Fiona MacDonald who worked in another office, and she was too busy to talk. It was the start of Flora's finishing off, the tidy ending. No more need to touch, more a need to talk of old times with old friends. She hadn't succeeded, but she did try, the real point of her visit into town. Sitting back in the comfortable car while Robert drove her along the road through the glen to Clairgowan. Looking out to the mountains and feeling as though she was suspended in the air, a motionless pendant resting from its drastic up and down swings. Each day a steady progress to the ultimate calm waiting for her, but the problem was her grim nights hadn't changed, and they were exhausting her. The reason why Flora allowed Robert to take her into town.

Robert jumped into the car. "I'd better get going. Dad's squeezing as much work out of me as he can." He laughed. "You wouldn't believe it Flora, but I'm actually enjoying it. You know how I used to hate farm work. Now I understand why dad plays at being a farmer."

A hand up to Robert's salute as he drove through the gates and a slow walk around the corner to find no Jeannie in the kitchen and the high backed chair empty. Sitting with her father consisted of gazing into the fire for hours and listening to his complaints over her ignoring Robert. Flora sank onto her chair, Thursday; she hoped she had the strength to see her through to Saturday.

It happened that night, stood at the bottom of the stairs with the oil lamp, her third try. A glint opposite the bathroom door, Flora put the lamp onto the floor, knelt down and forced a finger between the carpet and the wall, working away at it until it popped up into view, her wedding ring. It must have bounced off the wall at the bottom of the stairs and slipped into the gap, Jeannie's ferocious brushing pushing it even further down. Flora kissed the ring and slipped it back onto her finger, where it belonged. Shivering while she searched the study, forcing open a locked drawer in the desk with a sword shaped letter opener to see her face looking up to her on the top of a bundle of envelopes and papers. Flora kissed the glass over John's face and put their wedding photograph next to Alasdair.

She returned to her bed, wrapped herself in the bedcovers and slept the deep sleep of the contented.

# Chapter Fifty Three

*The* trees moved with Flora's little rhyme. "Snow, snow, stay away. One more day, one more day." Grey edged clouds scudded across the sky; she turned from the window satisfied they'd do no more than put a shine on the road through the glen. A check in the mirror, she looked smart and severe in her black jumper and trousers.

She took her purse out of her cotton duffle bag to check its contents. Notes put into an envelope, another check to see if she had sufficient money left over, she did, just. The grey skirt hung in the wardrobe and headscarf returned to Aunt Elizabeth's room. Entering the kitchen to see her father sat at the table eating his breakfast and Jeannie at his side stirring his tea.

"I see you have decided to rise at a more appropriate hour." Mungo's words to a forkful of bacon before he put it into his mouth.

Flora leant over the table and kissed his brow. "And a good morning to you father."

Jeannie smiled at her. "Ye must be sleeping better Flora. I had the fire to light this morning. I'll put your egg on to boil."

"No." Flora took hold of Jeannie's arm to stop her rushing away. "I'll boil my egg later." She pressed the envelope into Jeannie's hand.

"This is the money I owe you Jeannie. I've put a little extra in and you have to promise me that you'll go into town and spend it on new clothes for yourself."

Jeannie's eyes filled up with tears. "Can I treat my mammy with some of it Flora?"

Flora put her arm around the bony shoulders. "Of course you can Jeannie. It is your money." She led the girl to the door, took the shabby brown coat off the peg and gave it to her. "You take yourself off now and come back tomorrow. I'll see to everything for the rest of the day."

Jeannie's pigtail was fastened with the ribbon Flora gave her at Christmas. Most of the silver threads were missing and the blue almost faded to a grey.

Flora touched it and smiled at Jeannie. "And treat yourself to a new ribbon Jeannie."

Jeannie nodded. "I'll go into town today and take my mammy with me." A slow shake of her head. "No one's ever taken my mammy for a treat before." She opened the door, stepped outside and turned to Flora. Head down, a small smile on her thin face. "Will ye promise to be here for me tomorrow morning Flora?"

Jeannie knew, she knew as soon as Flora ran into the kitchen that morning in her nightdress and bare feet. The girls simplicity stopped all introspections and contrivances from occupying her mind, and it gave her facility to see what other people might miss.

"Yes." Flora returned her smile. "I promise I'll be here in the morning Jeannie. But you'll have to be early." She stood at the doorway and watched Jeannie scurry away.

Mungo clattered his knife and fork onto his plate and scraped his chair back on the flagstones, a snort. "The Drummonds going into town to treat themselves." He sat himself on the high backed chair with his cup. "And I see you have discarded your skirt."

Flora stood at the doorway and smiled. A breeze lifted her hair and created a rustle through the trees. "It's cold for a skirt father. Would you prefer I wear jeans?"

"Stockings covering your legs would suffice," retorted Mungo. He emptied his cup and held it up. "And I will be requiring another cup of tea when you have closed the door and stopped the draught."

"I'm waiting for Robert." Flora looked down the side of the house. "He's late."

Mungo smiled at the fire. "Robert Brown might have other things to occupy himself with this morning."

Tyres crunched over the gravel at the front of the house.

"He's here!" Flora closed the door and walked to the corner. Expecting to see Bob Brown's large car she stopped at the sight of Robert grinning over to her at the side of a bright red car which looked very new and very fast.

"Do you like it?" asked Robert.

He walked over to Flora and saw she wasn't wearing her pearls. Another good sign along with the missing wedding ring, he made a point of looking for it on the first day.

Flora's first thought was the price of the car would have probably paid off her father's debt, but she shrugged rather than say it. "It's very nice Robert but I can't imagine your father driving around in it."

Robert laughed. "The Jag's mine, not dad's." He lifted his eyebrows. "Dad couldn't handle it on that road through the glen Flora."

"Yours!" exclaimed Flora. "But you said you were flying to America tomorrow."

"I'm not Flora." Robert put his hands out, the magician waiting for a response to his latest surprise. "I'm staying." The rag tag girl he left behind not the beautiful woman he saw at Christmas. She wouldn't leave his head, racing around like a mad man to catch the first possible flight the moment his father called him to say this guy had left her. Finding his fortune turned out to being sat behind a desk all day. Watching the rising sun cast a rosy hue over the mountains while his father drove him through the glen that first morning and wondering at the fool who ran off and left it all behind him.

Robert leant down to Flora and smiled. "Now I needn't ask dad to borrow the car whenever you need a lift."

Flora shook her head. "Robert I'm here to say goodbye."

Robert, a parting of old friends, no chasing away, no shouts and screams.

"I'm leaving early in the morning on the first bus into town. I'm going to London to stay with Aunt Elizabeth."

Aunt Elizabeth, she'd be so happy to have her to stay, and Flora would sit with the tea ladies as often as her aunt wished, a small recompense for all of her love and thought over the years.

"Robert, the laird."

Her father, her kisses and companionship to show she loved him whatever her actions were in the future.

"He's going to lose Clairgowan House Robert. It's a wonder it hasn't happened before now. I don't know how he'll cope with losing the house but I do know it would kill him if he has to leave Clairgowan. Do you think your mother and father would take him in? "

Flora waited for Robert to respond but he was staring at her face.

Robert looked at large brown eyes so bright and clear they asked to be gazed at every second of everyday life gave him. Lips full and red and waiting to be kissed, wonderful cheeks with their bloom of pink, black hair a gleaming weave of raw silk. Amazed at the fool who longed to scrub the cheeks white and hack at the hair with scissors. Flora was becoming more beautiful by the day, and in front of her the idiot who went off and left her.

John, the love of her life, her wonderful, glorious, handsome John.

"I've mislaid my husband." Flora laughed, head back, a hand to her jumper.

Robert saw the wedding ring on her finger, and there they were, her pearls. As near as they could be to her, lying against Flora's skin where her hand pulled the jumper away from her neck. He'd travel, he had the car, France, Spain, go where the mood took him, he knew his mother would be proud of him whatever he did.

"You know me Robert. So busy shouting and screaming I didn't give John the chance to tell me where to find him. He's in London somewhere so I'm going to look for him while I stay with Aunt Elizabeth." Her search to start on Monday with a telephone call to George Gibson, grateful she'd taken a quick look at his card before she put it into the cabinet. Flora refused to consider the possibilities that he might be out of the country or didn't know John's whereabouts.

Robert stood behind Flora, put his hands onto her shoulders and walked her to the gates until they both looked down to the village.

"Do you see that red telephone box?" Robert put his face down to the black mass of hair.

"Yes." Flora's head moved as she laughed. "It has been there a long time Robert."

He might find someone, but it would be difficult. Because Robert Brown knew he'd always compare every single woman he met with Flora, the laird's daughter.

"Go down to that telephone box Flora and ring Mr Boyle's office." Robert's mouth to Flora's ear so he could be close to her skin. "He'll have an address. Dad couldn't resist it; he contacted Mr Boyle to say he'd pay off the laird's debts. He thought you and I…" Robert shrugged.

"Anyway, he found out they'd already been cleared by this John of yours a couple of weeks ago. I thought you knew Flora, I honestly thought you knew. I thought it was some kind of settlement and it was truly over with this guy." Another sign Robert chose to misread.

Flora turned to face Robert, her eyes glittering with tears. John's silence had been the most difficult part for her to bear. He'd put his hand out to her to say, 'I'm here, find me, I still love you.'

"This John," said Robert. "He's not the average kind a guy we all thought he was."

Flora laughed, tears splashing down her cheeks. "No. John Mason's anything but average Robert."

"So I guess this is goodbye Flora."

"Yes." Flora put her arms around Robert and kissed his cheek. "Goodbye, and thank you Robert."

She hurried to the corner with a hand to her pearls. Flora wore them to give her strength and they had, and she had something more to do before she telephoned Mr Boyle. Behind her the roar of the car, tyres screeching through the gates, a clatter of gravel over the fountain.

Her father, it would always be that way.

Flora's acceptance stopped her fight. It gave her freedom to be the laird's daughter if she wished, or John's wife, or Aunt Elizabeth's niece, or herself, the part belonging to her and no one else.

She closed the kitchen door behind her, sat on her chair, crossed her ankles, put her hands between her knees and looked at the smile.

"I'm leaving tomorrow father."

No running away, no notes left behind.

Mungo snorted at the fire, a hand up dismissing her, the smile gone.

"Please don't be like that father."

"What would you have me do celebrate?" The pale eyes accused

380

Flora. "You all leave me. Elizabeth, Alasdair, your mother."

"But I should be with my husband."

The eyes turned to the fire. "And he will take you away from me again."

"No. I took myself away father, not John."

A sharp turn of the head, a keen look of flinty grey. "Are you sure you are married?"

Flora smiled down to her knees. "Yes. We are married father." She left her chair to kneel in front of the high back chair. "Aunt Elizabeth visits and I'll do the same. I'll visit so often you'll be sick of me." She'd accompany her aunt on the train, the years of her solitary journeys to Clairgowan over, and each visit with the anticipation of returning to John, her wonderful John. "And I'll go the kirk with you whenever I'm here. And I'll see to it that I'm here for the gathering so I can stand by your side."

"And in between these visits you leave me with the village simpleton," snorted Mungo.

"Jeannie takes better care of you and the house than I ever did. You are very lucky to have her." Flora looked up at her father; he looked so old hunched up in his chair. She put her arms around him and pressed a cheek to his chest. His shirt and old waistcoat redolent of Clairgowan House and the man, smoke from the fire, tea, whisky, wood, pine.

"You have me worried at times Flora."

The low voice vibrated against her ear.

"Why father?"

"All of this touching and kissing. It is not natural Flora."

"I think it's the most natural thing in the world to show I love you father. But I should be with John my husband. My place is with him."

"He left you for all of this time without a word," muttered

Mungo.

"Not quite father." Flora looked up to her father and tightened her arms around his body. "Have you anything to tell me?"

Mungo looked at the fire. "I expect Robert has told you."

Flora gave a slow nod. "Yes. Robert told me John paid off your debts."

"And now he will be in debt."

Flora smiled. "John Mason makes money father, he doesn't borrow it." She sat back on her heels. "I'm going down to the telephone box now to ring Mr Boyle for John's address."

"There is no need."

The hands left the leather armrests. Flora thought they were going to go around her body to hold her, but they took hold of her arms to lift her away.

They stood together.

"I have a letter." Mungo left the room and returned with an envelope. He gave it to Flora. "I see you have interfered with the drawer."

Flora took the letter out of the envelope. "You will insist on keeping secrets away from me father." The letter from Mr Boyle informing her father of John's payment and listing two contact addresses and telephone numbers. She knew which address to try first and decided not to telephone John to say she loved him. Her face would tell him that the moment he saw her.

Mungo cleared his throat. "If this husband of yours is so clever at making money he can afford to pay for the electricity."

Flora looked up from the letter. "Do you really want bright lights all over Clairgowan House father?"

"As a matter of fact I do," retorted Mungo. "And if Clairgowan House had its own telephone you could talk to me every day."

Flora raised her eyebrows. "Anything else you'd like John to pay for father?"

Mungo rubbed the side of his nose. "There is the consideration of Andy McManus and the money I owe for the whisky."

# Chapter Fifty Four

John stood looking down to a desk in the office above the factory floor, bright lights above his head, dark and quiet below the large window. Tom, Janet, Chris, the machinists and everyone else hurrying off hours before to the promise of a Saturday night out enjoying themselves or at home with their families sat in front of the television.

John and Tom decided to continue trading under the 'GIBSON'S GARMENTS' brand name until they became more established. On the desk amongst large white cards and coloured pencils the end result of several tries. 'M & C GARMENTS' in large black letters to go onto the new name board outside the two buildings.

John earned more in the last few weeks than he did in a year of toil and grind at the garage, and it would get better. The order book was so full they had to bring in more machines and start an extra Saturday shift, and they were so successful another garment manufacturer expressed an interest in buying them out. It was a much larger organisation with its own design department, but John had a better idea, buy them out. Tom admitted to feeling the stress of the last few months and said he was happy to remain with his share of the factory. John would have to go it alone, and if he did succeed with the buyout he'd have to think of his own brand name.

So why was he hanging around the factory fiddling around with cards? Why wasn't he out there running around with his fists in the air and kicking his heels? Why wasn't he shouting 'I'm here, I've made it'?

Because without Flora it was all dry sand trickling through his fingers, it had no substance, it was nothing.

John put his hands onto the desk to study another card with 'MASON'S GARMENT' in large black letters, but it reminded him of the garage, and that day. He closed his eyes, took a deep breath and decided to go to Clairgowan.

Chris, Tom's son-in-law, had taken over the elderly Rover and it still needed some attention, but he didn't live far from the factory and it was the quickest way John could get to a car. He didn't care if he had to stutter and putter all that way because every mile he covered would take him nearer to Flora. He'd park himself outside those gates until she took pity on in, and he'd sit there for months if necessary. If he lost everything he worked for he could always start all over again, and this time he'd see to it that Flora remained right by his side, where she should have been all along.

A sensation deep within his ear alerted his brain to a noise. Logic said it had to be clicks and creaks from the steel roof, but he had to look up; John always did, in the hope...

Flora's disembodied face looked up at him at the other side of the window, and it wasn't an apparition created by desperation because there he was beside her, with no recollection of how he arrived there. No bright dress, mass of black hair blending into the dark around her, black jumper and trousers, cotton duffle bag hanging down by her side.

"I knew you'd be here."

Mr Boyle's letter listed the factory and a flat.

"Did you? You're lucky to have caught me."

"Am I?" Flora looked around her. "It's big."

"This is half of it. There's another building next door." John took Flora's hand. "I'll show you something." He led her to the office and the cards on the desk. "What do you think?"

"M and C Garments?" asked Flora.

"Mason and Clark. I'll introduce you to Tom my partner on Monday."

Flora nodded and looked at the 'MASON'S GARMENTS' card.

John shrugged. "I'm thinking of expanding on my own."

Flora smiled, put her hand to John's beard and gave him a soft kiss on his lips. "A partner and expansion so soon. You have been busy."

John's arms remained down at his side, frightened to spoil the moment by snatching Flora to him.

She put her bag onto the desk and found a blank card. "I think you should have something less conservative and with a bright colour in it." Writing 'JayMas FASHIONS' in black she picked up another pencil and highlighted the capital letters in red.

John looked over Flora's shoulder, his hand caressing her hair.

"What do you think?" asked Flora.

"That looks fine," nodded John.

Flora turned to him with a smile, that wonderful smile.

"Or would you like your other initial included?"

"No." John frowned and shook his head. "I think I'll leave the Jacob out thank you."

They laughed, happiness spilling out of their mouths.

John couldn't wait any longer. He took hold of Flora and put his face to her hair. "I don't know what happened that day, but you have my promise it won't happen…"

Flora shushed him with fingers to his lips. "You needed me and all I did was shout and scream at you and chase you away."

They walked out of the office hand in hand, past the lumpy covered machines with their cables like disjointed snakes hanging down from the black.

John closed the large double door at the front of the building and locked it. "I wrote…" He did post the letter, willing to put up with anything in the hope of seeing Flora again. "I thought I'd lost you when I didn't hear from you…"

Flora laughed and shook her head. "You know auld Mungo. Anything he's unhappy with and it goes straight on the fire."

They walked away hand in hand.

Flora looked around her. "No Minx the Magnificent?"

"It went with the garage. I'll explain later."

"Where are we going?"

"To the flat."

"Is it nice?"

"Yes, you'll like it."

Flora grimaced. "I suppose it will have a kitchen and a cooker. And you'll expect me to be waiting for you at the end of the day with a proper cooked meal and mushy potatoes."

"No." John squeezed her hand. "Because you'll be with me all day. We'll cook the meal together and I'll do the potatoes."

Flora's large eyes looked up to him. "It's a large place John. I don't think I'm up to that amount of work, especially the typing."

"Janet the secretary deals with all of that. She does all of the hard work, Tom and I just stand around looking good. I'm sure she'll enjoy a helping hand but you are going to be with me so I can see you whenever I raise my head."

Silent as they walked together in the dark. John knew Flora's

temper would always storm though his life and Flora knew John's single minded approach would always drive her to distraction. It drew them closer together because they both understood it was an essential part of the person they loved.

"Do you usually walk to the flat?"

"Yes. I haven't a car at the moment. I took a look at the new Jags they've just brought out but I had a better use for the money."

Flora squeezed John's hand. "Such as paying off auld Mungo's debts."

"I knew it was important to you," replied John. "But it was more for me. To get a response from you." He squeezed Flora's hand. "It worked."

"No it didn't," replied Flora. "I was on my way before I knew."

"The payment for the latest consignment from the factory should be coming in soon. We'll take a look at the Jags together."

"Did you like the red?"

"The Fire Engine Red?" asked John with a puzzled look. "No, I thought the Midnight Blue or Racing Green."

"There's a surprise," smiled Flora. "And I'll be missing some afternoons."

"Why?"

"Because I'll be visiting Aunt Elizabeth for tea."

"I should hope so. She's a nice lady. You'll have to learn how to drive. There's another new car coming out. It's quite small, they're calling it a Mini-Minor."

"That's nice. You can have the Mini and I'll have the Jag."

Silence from John.

"And I'll be visiting auld Mungo every now and again."

"I can take you in the Jag."

"No. You'll be busy earning the money to pay for the cars and other things."

John looked down to her bag, it looked empty. "I suppose I'll have to buy you new clothes."

"Yes, but I didn't mean clothes."

"What did you mean?"

"Auld Mungo did mention having the electricity put into the house."

"Right."

"And a telephone so I can speak to him every day."

"Right."

Flora put her fingers to her mouth to stop a giggle. "And there is the consideration of the money he owes for the whisky."

John stopped and turned to Flora. "Anything else?"

"Yes."

The very last line on her list, Flora took a deep breath. "The first time my cool and calm husband loses it and now I'm pregnant." Her bag wasn't empty, inside it a tiny white matinee coat as delicate as a spider's web. Jeannie must have bought the new wool in town and sat up all night knitting it for her. "I know...You said we had to wait and you might not want this baby. But..." She put a hand to her stomach. "I do."

John shook his head.

Something took Flora's breath away.

John shook his head because he couldn't speak. He pulled Flora into his arms and kissed her.

A car caught them in its headlights...

# About The Author

*JJ* Andrews was born in Co Durham in the Northeast of England. She is a retired Psychiatric Nurse and has always enjoyed writing, both in fiction and in relation to her profession. Following her travels around England to work in various hospitals she decided to return to her roots and now looks out to the North Sea everyday watching the ferries hurry in and out of Tynemouth. She has enjoyed writing her first novel and is now making steady progress with a follow up to Rhythm of Echoes.

Printed in the United Kingdom
by Lightning Source UK Ltd.
133324UK00002B/43-117/P